FRIENDS FOR LIFE.

KN

BETH. The caterer. A

GEORGY. The photo ...st chance.

VIVIENNE. The socialite. Her first choice was her worst choice.

CATHERINE. The receptionist. Danger makes no appointments.

SALLY. The free spirit. Seeking what no man can give.

LOVE THEM.
THE CRITICS DID!

"Superb . . . highly entertaining . . . deftly interweaves the lives of five intriguing women . . . breezy and as smooth as fine champagne."

—*Cleveland Plain Dealer*

"Adroitly plotted . . . keenly observed . . . Smith generates suspense and maintains the tension. . . . Every character has come so vividly to life that the reader is hooked, ready to be reeled in."

—*Publishers Weekly*

"Highly enjoyable."

—*The Times* (London)

more . . .

"A fine job . . . worthwhile entertainment for a summer day, rain or shine." —*Flint Journal*

"Brilliant . . . spellbinding. . . . A taut, fast-paced story with an absorbing plot, well-defined characters, and dozens of strings that Smith successfully controls . . . races to a page-turning end."

—*Rocky Mountain News*

"Riveting reading." —*Romantic Times*

"An engrossing plot, cleverly crafted, and deftly executed."
—**Susan Sloan, author of** *Guilt by Association*

"Fast-paced, fascinating . . . richly written and dramatically paced. . . . The characters are all vividly brought to life . . . a lively book and fun to read, a perfect accompaniment for a summer trip to the beach or mountains."

—*Bookscapes*

"This writer is very good. Every character comes brilliantly to life, and the suspense and tension is almost unbearable. I highly recommend it." —*Ellenville Press*

"Deliciously suspenseful . . . unfolds at a nearly perfect pace . . . building unfalteringly to its startling conclusion."
—*Booklist*

"I was delighted to pick up a book that blends women's fiction and mystery. . . . An entertaining read and something different." —*The Poisoned Pen*

FRIENDS FOR
LIFE

CAROL SMITH

FRIENDS FOR LIFE

WARNER BOOKS

A Time Warner Company

First published in Great Britain in 1995 as *Darkening Echoes* by Little, Brown and Company

WARNER BOOKS EDITION

Cover designed, conceived and created by Elaine Groh
Cover photos by Alexa Garbarino, Robert Geogee Young/ Masterfile and Damir Frkovic/Masterfile

Warner Books, Inc.
1271 Avenue of the Americas
New York, NY 10020

W A Time Warner Company

Visit our Web site at
http://pathfinder.com/twep

Printed in the United States of America

Originally published in hardcover by Warner Books.

First Printed in Paperback: August, 1997
10 9 8 7 6 5 4 3 2 1

For my parents
Winifred Emily Mapleston
and
Cecil Daniel Smith

Prologue

Death came stealthily on a tranquil summer's afternoon with a step so light and a smile so familiar she failed to recognize the danger even when she saw it face-to-face. She was making peach jam in the low, cool kitchen, with the door open to allow the breeze to circulate and the radio murmuring fifties dance music from the center of the scrubbed pine table. Soft music, sweet and evocative, to which she tapped along with her bare foot, all the time stirring the thickening syrup with a wooden spoon, in tune with the hot, still afternoon and the heavy aroma from the huge black cauldron on the stove.

"Hi, sweetie!" she called when she heard the first soft footfall. "Back so soon? How was the game? Aren't you sweltering? Shall I open you a beer?"

Then: "Oh, it's you. I thought it was your dad. If you want to make yourself useful, start topping and tailing those beans. And fetch me a soda from the cooler, will you, hon?"

She smiled contentedly and went on stirring. Life in this lazy backwater was not so bad after all, not at moments of pure pleasure such as this. Quality food, fresh air, the basic comforts of home and family she had once so much despised. All she could ever want, in fact, contained between these four stone walls amid scenery so dramatic it could knock the breath right out of you.

The brick found its mark with a force that did just that, and as she staggered and reached for the rail of the stove, she gazed up through a bewildering haze of streaming blood and watched it fall again. Watched in disbelief as it swung toward her, wrapped innocuously, she now saw, in one of her own expensive stockings, culled in stealth from her drawer.

She lay on the cool stone floor and gazed up at the stove, at the black iron cauldron, so heavy she could scarcely lift it, bubbling above her head. When she saw it topple toward her she knew she was going to die, but by then it was too late.

Part
One

Part
One

Chapter One

Mornings like this, thought Beth, made living in Central London totally justifiable. Church bells ringing from across the road, the pervasive aroma of spring lamb spiked with rosemary wafting from the Aga stove, the kitchen door propped open on this fine May morning to let in the scent of honeysuckle and the occasional buzz of a lazy bee. She spread tiny new potatoes in a single layer across a cast-iron pan and deftly drizzled them with olive oil. From here you could scarcely hear the dull thunder of traffic and if you looked out of the window, as she did now on her way to the stove, all you could see through a trellis of green willow was the sloping lawn, a white wicket gate, and the curve of gravel which fronted the church. Just like living in a cathedral close, she was fond of saying, and had had her good friend Richard Brooke immortalize the view in one of his stylish watercolors, now hanging on the paneled wall in the hall. Visitors to the house never failed to comment on it.

"Surely that can't be an original," they would say, peering at the minute signature. But it was and Beth was proud of it, proud too of the gamble she had taken all those years ago when Richard was still a starving student and she had risked a month's rent money in order to help him out of a jam by backing her conviction that he had real talent, talent that would last. Creative people, she was fond of saying, should back each other, and what was the point of money if you couldn't use it to help a friend? Beth thought for a moment of her own circumstances and how Pop had come up trumps just when she had needed it most. What goes around comes around. Certainly she could not have been more right about Richard, and she hadn't heard many complaints from Pop either in these last few hectic years.

She opened the fridge and poured herself a glass of chilled Chardonnay. There were moments when life seemed pretty near perfect, and this was one of them.

"Mum," said Imogen from the sofa, sprawled like a young gazelle in a welter of Sunday papers, "it says here Dad may be coming home."

She looked up through the straggly fringe that badly needed trimming and pointed to a paragraph in the *Mail on Sunday*. At twelve, Imogen was growing fast and was already almost as tall as her mother (though Beth had never been so slender), with long, coltish legs. Beth wiped her hands on her bleached cotton apron and crossed the room to take a look at the paper. After three years of being a smash hit, it seemed the American musical *Autumn Crocus* was transferring to London in the autumn with its distinguished choreographer/director, Gus Hardy, and full Broadway cast.

"Brilliant!" said Imogen, cheeks flushed, dark eyes alight with happiness. "Will he come and live here? There's tons of room. Shall I call him now and ask him?"

She was on her feet and heading toward the phone before her mother could stop her.

"Hang on a sec! Leave it for a while," Beth said, rolling the tiny potatoes expertly around in the oil and dusting them with pepper and fresh coriander. "We'll talk about it later. You never know with Dad, he may well have made other arrangements. After all, there's the whole company to think of and it isn't as if it's just for a week or two. Besides," she added as an afterthought, "it's early in the morning in New York, and you know your dad. He won't thank you if you wake him this early, not after one of his legendary Saturday nights."

She topped up her glass and sliced zucchini briskly into a colander. Beth ran a catering business and had three weddings and a charity ball to cook for. Life was complicated enough as it was without Gus Hardy reappearing on the scene.

"Just what I need," she said to Jane later, spread out on the sofa in a postprandial slump after Imogen had disappeared on her rollerblades to join up with friends down the road. "They say it never rains but it pours. Oliver gets back from Johannesburg on Thursday, and now this, the return of the prodigal for God knows how long."

Jane laughed. As Beth's best friend, she was used to her hectic personal life.

"You can cope, you've done it before. Besides, you thrive on friction. And it won't do Oliver any harm either to have a bit of competition." She disapproved of Oliver. Most of Beth's friends did.

"Yes, but what am I going to do if Imogen insists on having him stay here? You know what she's like once she sets her heart on something. And the truth is, we do have the space."

"I wouldn't worry. Gus will have his own ideas, and can you really see him wanting to play Happy Families again? But it will be nice for Imogen to be able to see a bit more of him. Kids need their dads. And it ought to give you a bit more breathing space, too."

"For Oliver?"

"For you. There's more to life than wasting it all on a selfish man."

Beth laughed. She had heard this tune many times before but, as she never stopped reminding her, Jane had Alastair, as well as a demanding career.

"Well, we'll see. Now I suppose I'd better do those damned dishes. I've got a dinner for twelve tomorrow night and the smoked salmon mousse still to prepare."

When the pain came, it caught Beth unawares, as she was

lifting a heavy tray of delicate chou pastry cases from the oven. She gasped and managed to set them down without dropping them all over the floor. She clasped her stomach and cold sweat broke out on her forehead. Damn it to hell! Why did it always happen on occasions like this, when she was already up to her ears with no time even to sit down? Deirdre, chopping parsley, looked up and frowned.

"You really ought to see someone about that. Doesn't do to ignore health warnings, and how would the rest of us cope if you were really ill?"

Selfish cow, there she went again. Dear though she was, Deirdre could be a right pain. But after seven years of her relentless pessimism, Beth was well used to it and even found herself missing it on the rare occasions Deirdre wasn't around. She was like some sort of wretched albatross, hung around Beth's neck to ensure she didn't have too good a time. Beth stood upright and smiled bravely.

"Don't worry, probably just wind."

"Sounds like your innards to me. You most likely need a hysterectomy." Deirdre, with her four raucous children and scream-makingly monotonous existence, could always be counted on to put in a hefty boot.

"Thanks a bunch," Beth shot back. "I'm not that old!"

"Look what happened to my sister," said Deirdre dourly, shuffling the neatly chopped parsley into a tidy pile and reaching for another bunch.

"With respect, your sister was at least ten years older than me, and there's a history of it in your family. I'm not about to pop off yet."

Beth was already feeling better. It was nothing more than her ovaries giving her an early warning. Her period must be due around now. It was all totally unfair; when God created woman he might have given her a more effective reproductive system. She poured a glass of mineral water and downed two aspirin. No need to worry, she was ridiculously healthy and always had been. Luckily Imogen seemed to have inherited her genes, too. She was not going to let an old misery-guts like Deirdre scare her.

She slammed another tray of pastry cases into the Aga and forgot all about it.

Beth was right about Gus. He called later in the week and confirmed that the newspaper report was true. Things were going so well he was taking a gamble and putting in a subsidiary cast for the show while he brought the original stars to London.

"Jesus, but I hope it works. Marla's already having the vapors because she hates to travel, and Vic's agent's been on the blower, muttering about a revised contract and the extra emotional strain of having to modify his accent for British audiences."

He sounded buoyant and breathless with excitement. Gus was nearly always on a high. That was one of the attractive things about him. Some people found it exhausting but Beth had always been invigorated by his energy. Just talking to him made her feel better; she hung up the phone in a happier mood. A little of Gus went a very long way but having him around recharged her batteries like nothing else could. And he wasn't planning to invade her privacy, she had been almost sure of that. Although they remained good friends all these years after the divorce, they had always respected each other's space. Gus had arranged to move back into his own house in Islington because, fortuitously, his tenant had an operatic tour of Australia planned for the same time as his visit.

It would be great for Imogen, who idolized her father. One of Beth's main areas of guilt, in fact, was the absence of Gus from her daughter's young life. She needed her talented, exuberant dad with whom she always had so much fun. Gus had his faults but he was an excellent father. In a fair world he would have had loads of children. But they had both made new lives for themselves and were happy. Moreover, they shared Imogen, a spirited and delightful child who seemed to have suffered little harm from the early separation. Still, a son would have been nice for Gus; a son he could take sailing and tutor in the rudiments of football and cricket—or, more likely, the way things had turned out, baseball.

Oliver edged the dark blue Mercedes into a space outside the white wicket gate and Beth, still damp from the bath, stood at the upstairs window and watched him. Some girlish instinct, a relic perhaps of her Nottinghamshire past, still gave her a thrill when in the presence of serious money. Although her socialist principles would have made her hotly deny it to most of her acquaintances, sneakily, deep down inside, she had to admit she found style and class a definite turn-on. She watched now as Oliver slid from the driver's seat, glanced each way to check that his beloved car was suitably parked, then ran a manicured hand over his immaculate hair. That was another thing about Oliver. No matter what he might be doing, he was always well turned out, with never a hair out of place or a torn cuticle, or even a razor cut on his stern, handsome face. Beth watched him reach into the back for the arrangement of pewter roses that had become a tradition between them. He locked the car, and only then did he look up, directly at where she was standing. Beth backed away guiltily behind the gauzy curtain, still embarrassed, after all these months, to be caught peeping.

She wrapped the apple-green silk kimono more tightly around her generous figure—there was not a lot of point in getting dressed—ran a brush through her short, curly hair, and raced down the wooden staircase to fling open the door and hurl herself into his arms. This was always the best part, the coming together again after yet another of their frequent separations. She laid her head against his lavender shirt front and breathed in the exotic mix of Trumpers lime aftershave and expensive starched cotton. Oliver brushed the hair back from her forehead as he kicked the door shut

with one foot and tossed the roses onto the shabby sofa. He
planted a kiss on her nose then another, more seriously, on
her unpainted mouth. His eyes roved around the room.

"Imogen?"

"Alice's. For the night."

She snuggled her head into his neck and let him guide
her to the sofa to scrunch down next to the roses.

Two years ago, when Beth first set eyes on Oliver, it was
love at first sight—or at least lust, which was usually the
case and more or less the same thing with Beth. She was
forever making fresh resolutions to put her head before her
heart and try to assess a man's character, solid worth, and
kindness to defenseless beings before noticing the slant of
his cheekbones or the neatness of his bum, but all to no
avail. She was not at all sure how she managed to achieve it,
she who had never been as slim as she would have liked and
was far from happy with her nose, but Beth had managed
from a very early age to surround herself with very handsome men. Gus Hardy was one of the most beautiful beings
in God's creation, very nearly the whole world was agreed
upon that, but Oliver Nugent, with his stronger jaw and
slightly satanic good looks, ran him a pretty close second.

It was in the private dining room of the Hong Kong and
Shanghai Bank, how would she ever forget, and Beth was
fussing over the table arrangement—straightening the pure
linen napkins, arranging dark mints in perfect arcs, and
worrying in case her inspired menu of *raviolis de ris de
veau aux truffes* followed by a ragout of scallops and oys-
ters, instead of the more cautious melon and parma ham
followed by lamb cutlets, might prove too revolutionary for
the suits and end her career in the City just as it was getting
under way—when in he walked. He stood in the doorway
looking for his host and crossed the room to shake the outstretched hand without a further glance, just as if she really
were the housekeeper instead of London's latest rage in

chic nouvelle cuisine, hired for the morning at exorbitant cost.

That was one aspect of the job that still rankled slightly, however hard Beth tried to control it. The actress in her hated not being in the limelight, particularly when she had labored so hard and so long to achieve the perfection she was about to set before them.

Oliver stood talking by the panoramic window and, by moving round the table, then round again, Beth was able to keep him in her sights without making it obvious. One of the pluses of her job was that she seemed to cater for a lot of men-only lunches, the idea being that the boys could concentrate better on the business under discussion without any of the tiresome interruptions that mixed company imposed. Oliver was talking to three other City gentlemen and looking very grave indeed. When Beth got to know him better she discovered this was one of his two basic expressions.

She ran her eye over him as lingeringly as if he were a prime cut of Aberdeen Angus beef, and liked increasingly what she saw. Tall enough—at five ten and a half, height could be a problem for Beth—fit without being jocklike, and, best of all, unself-consciously well groomed as if it happened accidentally and did not involve one iota of vanity. Vanity was something she could not abide in a man; with her theatrical background, she had had enough of it to last a lifetime or two.

His voice too, she discovered, was cultured and modulated, as finely tuned as everything else about him. This, in short, was one class act. Beth wanted to know more and was frustrated when the course was served and she had to withdraw, silently and with metaphorically downcast eyes, behind the green baize door.

Just when she had given up hope Oliver redeemed himself; extraordinarily and so out of character, she was sure, that her heart leaped into her mouth and she sensed, against all the odds, that she had him on her line, however tentatively. She saw him leave, hurriedly, with his eyes on his gold Rolex, while the others were still cradling their brandy snifters and the perfume of Havana was sweet on the air, and returned silently cursing to her borrowed kitchen, sick that she hadn't even found out his name or managed to engage him in direct eye contact.

And then, miracle of miracles, the door from the corridor had swung inward and there he was again, this time looking for her. To shake her briefly by the hand, again with that slightly distracted expression she had since learned to love, congratulate her (genuinely, she was sure) on the meal and ask if she carried a card in case he could throw some business her way. This might have been construed as patronizing but Beth didn't see it that way. She saw only the slate-gray eyes and chiseled lips and the level stare that turned her stomach to blancmange and gave her heart palpitations she had not experienced since she first saw Springsteen performing live. She wandered home in a lust-ridden trance and spent the rest of the afternoon on the bed, listening to Streisand and thinking it must surely by now be her turn again to have a break.

It took him two weeks but he did eventually ring, and when the call came through she was up to her armpits in lamb Marrakesh and hadn't a clue who he was. She was very nearly quite rude to him—the chef's prerogative—but caught on just in time, smiled sweetly (over the phone), and agreed to meet him for a drink the following night at seven.

And that was where it really all began. Chemistry did the rest. Oliver was already waiting when Beth swanned in, a sophisticated twelve and a half minutes late, in a corner booth with chilled Krug in a silver cooler, his inscrutable eyes watching the door as if it really mattered whether or not she showed. She didn't actually like champagne, preferred a single malt or even Scotch, but now was not the time to tell him. The thought was charming and positively seductive. Beth hadn't wanted to appear too eager so had settled for a black suede wraparound skirt with a plain silk shirt and, in her ears, the gold hoops Gus had bought her once for an anniversary present.

She had forgotten the firmness of his handshake and the way his black hair swung down from his widow's peak over one eye. Forgotten, too, the maleness of the man and his smell: macho, expensive, almost feral. Ninety-three minutes later, the drink was over, and Beth rose from the table as Oliver politely held back her chair. Her knees had turned to putty and she was suffering a severe attack of love. She had also agreed to spend the weekend with him in Strasbourg.

So here they were now, two and a half years later, wrapped in each other's arms and each other's souls, two halves of one being, ecstatically happy, replete, content just to lie silently among the welter of Beth's Victorian lace pillows, hips touching, hands entwined, one of Oliver's legs thrown possessively over one of hers, a gentle breeze fluttering through the Bruges lace curtains and cooling the satisfying film of sweat on both their bodies.

Soon, all too soon, he would stir, glance at his watch, mumble an expletive, leap from the bed and into the shower, calling out his regrets through the power of the water. For the moment, he was serene and hers completely. Sometimes there was the phone call, elegantly done, downstairs in the living room so that she could not overhear, the door partially closed to protect her sensibility. Then the rapid departure, the thrown kiss in the doorway, the promise to call as soon as the meetings in Geneva were concluded, followed by the quickening crunch of tires as the sleek Mercedes streaked away, back to The Boltons, back to his real life. All in all, not too bad an existence, especially when compared with other women's lives, and rather on a par with her profession of paid cook. Once again, it was not left to her to clean up the mess. And at least he didn't carry one of those vulgar portable phones.

Of course there was a wife, one he rarely mentioned and

then only in the most indirect of terms, but, as Beth often pointed out to Jane, when was there not? Considering the other things Beth had endured in her thirty-something years, married was not too bad at all, certainly livable with. At least it meant Oliver had a healthy appetite for the finer things, which, as far as Beth was concerned, were headed by an enthusiastic sex life.

"Give me a three-times-a-nighter," she would often say to Jane, "and I'll show you a contented woman."

As the downstairs clock chimed eleven and Beth lay in a state of pure tranquilized pleasure, Oliver stirred and ran through the familiar routine, only without the phone call.

"Must go, sweetheart."

"Mmm."

"Things to do. Early start." Already he was off the bed and pulling on his socks. Silk, she noticed, monogrammed. Bought by Her.

"Off so soon?" She stretched luxuriantly, reveling in the cool breeze on her skin, voluptuous and, for once, confident of her own considerable pulling power. She reached out a strong brown arm and drew him close.

"Stay, can't you?" she murmured. "Just this once? Imogen's not here. And boy, have I got things I want to do to you."

He smiled and backed away, knotting his tie (matching, she noticed), and smoothed the perfect hair into place. As he shrugged into the Savile Row jacket, his mind had already left her. He slipped the pigskin wallet into his inside pocket and palmed the keys. And then, unforgivably, he glanced at his watch.

"Don't get up. I'll see myself out. I'll call you."

And was gone, running lightly down the wooden stairs and closing the front door with a discreet click. Seconds later she heard the powerful engine surge but could not, this time, be bothered to leave the bed to take up her usual standpoint.

"Fuck," said Beth, switching off the lamp.

Chapter Two

Dorabella had almost finished in the bedroom by the time Vivienne finally emerged, still bleary-eyed, from her morning bath. The heavy silk coverlet was back in place and last night's clothes had been gathered up and put neatly away. The vast room, with its heavy brocade drapes and Regency furniture, was as immaculate as a hotel suite. And as impersonal, thought Vivienne bitterly as she wandered over to her dressing table. Dorabella ducked into the bathroom, then tactfully withdrew, her arms full of linen for the laundry. Vivienne might have time on her hands but Dorabella's days were simply never long enough.

Vivienne perched on her ornate stool and leafed listlessly through the gilt-edged pages of her appointments book. Lunch with Betty, a 4:30 fitting with her dressmaker, then six o'clock drinks at the Austrian Embassy, followed, if he was home in time, by dinner *à deux* at the Connaught with her husband. If he were not, which these days was more than likely, then Dorabella would bring her something light on a tray to consume alone in front of the box.

Not what you might call a life for someone who had started out with such high hopes and so much promise. All around her in the ornate bedroom, on every conceivable surface, were photographs of Vivienne; on her pony looking like

Elizabeth Taylor in *National Velvet,* at Queen Charlotte's Ball the year she came out, haughty in the Prince of Wales' feathers, the portrait photograph by Snowdon taken for *Tatler* when she got engaged. Vivienne Appleby, Débutante of the Year, on her wedding day, standing triumphantly smiling on the steps of St. Margaret's, Westminster, while policemen held back the crowds.

She leaned forward wearily and scowled at the perfect image in the glass. Alabaster skin, or so the society columns were fond of saying, night-black hair, violet eyes, this morning underwritten by shadows of a paler hue. A perfect beauty or the wreck of a woman in her prime. It all depended on where you were standing.

Dorabella had left her tray on the footstool but as usual Vivienne had no appetite. She sipped at the freshly squeezed grapefruit juice, served in a crystal glass on a dinky silver coaster, grimacing at its sharpness, then opened one of the drawers of her dressing table and delicately spiked it from a miniature bottle concealed in a beaded evening bag. *Well, whatever turns you on,* she told her reflection defiantly and this just happened to be the best, the only way Vivienne knew these days of jump-starting herself in the mornings.

Ferdinand landed with a graceful thump on her silk-covered knee and she bent her head slightly to receive his whiskery kiss. From the bed, Isabella watched her with eyes of pure topaz. Like all great beauties, she rarely rose before noon and, were it not for Betty and her damned Thursday lunches, Vivienne would still be in there with her, safely huddled under the silk sheets, out of harm's way.

On her way to San Lorenzo, Vivienne made a slight detour into Harrods' Perfumery Hall and steeped herself in twenty minutes or so of pure indulgence, wandering among the makeup counters, sniffing, testing, occasionally buying, so that when she finally emerged, ten minutes late for lunch, she was carrying several glossy packages looped with waxed string over her suede-gloved wrist. She would save the fashion floors for the afternoon. Betty nearly always had some

committee or other to rush off to and Vivienne preferred to
shop alone so that she could give this most consuming of
passions her undivided attention.

The restaurant was buzzing and Betty was waiting at their
regular table, clawlike hands hooked together under her chin,
a cigarette in an onyx holder gripped between perfect teeth.
She waved one finger while continuing to work the room
with darting eyes under lizardlike lids, today painted
turquoise to match her Hartnell silk suit. If she were honest,
Vivienne didn't much care for Betty but, as they said in New
York, she gave good gossip and it was easier to give in to her
imperious summonses to lunch than to have to devise yet another weary excuse.

"Hi," she said, sliding into the proffered chair and letting
the waiter shake out her napkin and flick it expertly into
place. "The traffic was truly awful."

Betty eyed the pile of glossy packages but did not bother
to comment. She raised one jeweled finger and indicated to
the waiter at the bar that they required *instanter* another
round of martinis, straight up—one with a twist, the other
with an olive. He nodded and smiled and within seconds the
drinks were on the table. Betty and Vivienne were regulars at
San Lorenzo. He knew not to keep them waiting.

Conversation was sparse as it usually was unless there was
a particular scandal to pick over. The two women toyed with
their salads and discussed today's more pressing concerns,
Betty's facelift, her latest divorce, and whether or not
Vivienne should think about having her eyelids done. At ten
to three Betty fished her platinum card out of her Gucci bag
and signaled for the bill. She had to be in Wimbledon to
chair a committee on autistic children. Vivienne, with a lifting heart, was free to head back to Harrods for another glorious wallow before she moved on to Madame Hortense for a
final fitting of her Ascot suit.

Sometime after five o'clock, with throbbing feet and a
slight martini-induced headache, Vivienne let herself into the
silent house and dropped her packages onto the sofa in the

hall. It was Dorabella's afternoon off and the only sound in the vast silence was the distant ticking of the ormolu clock in the first-floor drawing room. She kicked off her tight shoes, wandered into the kitchen for a glass of mineral water, then slowly mounted the stairs, leaving the strewn purchases for her maid to bring up when she returned from visiting her sister in Balham. For Vivienne it was the chase that was the thing. Once the prey had been alighted upon and the purchase made, she often lost interest in the actual goods.

The walk-in closets that lined her spacious bedroom were packed with clothes bought in fits of frustrated idleness but never subsequently worn. One entire wall was devoted to furs alone. Whenever her husband was away for an unusually long time, or after a particularly spirited disagreement, often something to do with an unexplained stain on the collar of one of his hand-sewn shirts, she succeeded in conning another furry little something off him.

"Come the holocaust," she was fond of saying, "I'll be the warmest bag lady in the park."

Every now and then, in order to create fresh hanging space, she had a blitz and then, as she liked to joke to her friends, there were a whole lot of well-dressed Third World immigrants walking the streets of southwest London.

The door to the drawing room stood ajar. Vivienne wandered in and perched on the piano stool, running her fingers over the keys and inhaling the heavy scent of flowers. The pure white linen covers were replaced daily on the chairs and sofas, even though the room was rarely used, and today Dorabella had prepared a stunning arrangement of dark blue delphiniums and white jasmine in an alabaster vase for the table fronting the bay window, dramatically set off by the elaborately swathed damask curtains. Vivienne's house was a real showplace and featured often in the glossy magazines. But in truth, these days it gave her little pleasure. More and more she felt trapped in all this splendor, stifling to death in a cage of her own devising.

She closed the lid of the Steinway—another useless extravagance since neither she nor her husband played—and trailed slowly up another flight to begin her preparations for the Ambassador's party.

On the dressing table was a note in Dorabella's childish hand: *"Mister he ring to say he no get back in time from Brussels."* Vivienne smiled and dropped her gloves and bag on the bed. *So tell me what else is new?* She slid out of her suit jacket and tossed it onto a chair for Dorabella to deal with, then lay down on the immaculate coverlet and closed her weary eyes. On cue, Ferdinand appeared from nowhere and stalked on silent feet across the bed to crouch companionably on her stomach. She scratched his velvet head with her finger and relaxed to the comforting vibration of his purr. Without her cats God knows where she would be. Her world seemed to get smaller daily, and more confining. She felt about as exciting as a bowl of cold porridge and longed for something new, something different, to come along to ruffle the stagnant surface of her life before it was too late. These days her skies seemed to be set in a permanent shade of middle-aged gray.

Yet it hadn't always been this way. When Vivienne was a child, growing up in an idyllic country setting, the sun seemed to shine all the time and her memories, stretching back as far as she could remember, were uniformly golden. Eugene Appleby, her father, who was not of British descent but covered it up with a veneer of upper-crust poshness so that only the occasional vowel sound gave him away, doted on his only child and did everything within his powers to bring magic into her life. They lived on a large, sprawling estate in a village outside Cirencester, with dogs and ponies and hens, as well as servants to take care of life's essentials, something Vivienne grew up accepting simply as a fact of life. If she lacked anything at all in those blissful early years it was her father's company, for he seemed to be constantly absent. Rumor had it that her mother, Irene Appleby, had once been a beauty, but now it was not easy to see it in her tight-lipped, rarely smiling face. She only ever kissed her daughter in public or last thing at night, as she tucked her in and turned off the light to stop her reading and ruining her eyes.

Eugene, however, more than made up for his absences when he was there, giving his adored child anything she set her heart on. He had the highest possible ambitions for his daughter so that after the exclusive boarding school in Bristol, there was Switzerland (to be finished) and a trip to Kenya to stay with distant relatives before returning to London for the Season. For Vivienne, seventeen and the prettiest girl in London, life was one great adventure with promises of better things to follow.

She had shared a flat in Lennox Gardens, taken a day course at the Cordon Bleu—less in order to know how to cook herself than to be able to oversee future servants effectively—played tennis at the Hurlingham, rode to hounds with the Berkshire, and danced the nights away at Annabel's. There was no time for a job and, in any case, what could she do? Finishing school hadn't prepared her for anything other than how to act like a lady and conduct herself properly at all times. As long as she was wined and dined and featured in the society columns, it was all right with her father.

Regardless of the fact that she only ever achieved two O levels, and one of those was art, on the social front Vivienne was always a straight-A student. Like the girl in the song, she not only danced with the Prince of Wales but was his guest more than once at Balmoral. She was also admired by a viscount and a Spanish marquis and, for a short while, was close to being engaged to a relative of the Duke of Westminster. Eugene was pleased; his investment had not been wasted. By the time his daughter reached twenty she was the toast of the town and might have had any man she chose. That had always been her problem. The one thing Eugene never gave her was an awareness of life's limitations. No one ever taught Vivienne Appleby the meaning of the word no.

It had been June, the night of the Rose Ball, and Vivienne

was part of Sukey Portillo's party at Grosvenor House. She wore a stunning gown of ice-blue satin by a new designer called Zandra Rhodes, a striking change from the slightly frumpy dresses worn by most of the other debs, who were all decked out to look like junior versions of their mothers. With her smooth dark hair and dramatic eyes, Vivienne stood out as she always did, and by two in the morning, when even the band was growing tired and the air was thick with cigarette smoke and the smell of flat champagne, she was more than ready to move on to something a little more adult. When one of the men in their party, an officer in the Grenadier Guards, fresh back from Germany, suggested a foray to the Clermont for a spot of late-night gambling, Vivienne, ever the sport, jumped at it.

They drifted through the imposing entrance of the exclusive club in Berkeley Square and, as the others headed for the main room and the roulette tables, Vivienne was drawn to a smaller side room containing only a few people, all of them clustered round a green baize table watching two men play vingt-et-un. One was Lord Lucan, whom she already knew slightly; the other, the handsomest man Vivienne had ever seen. That was the first time she ever set eyes on Oliver Nugent. She knew at once she had to have him. It hadn't been easy and later Vivienne tried to block out some of the details of the period leading to her marriage to Oliver.

Well, the girl had been silly, there was no denying that, as well as almost certainly unstable too if you listened to just a fraction of the mutterings at the time. (William Hickey had hinted at it in the *Express* and it must have cost old man Hartley a pretty packet just to hush it up. Or so they said.) Face it, if she had really loved him the way Vivienne did right from the start, how could she possibly have just stood aside like a piece of wet lettuce and watched him being snared by another woman? It simply made no sense and to this day Vivienne felt she should not have been made to shoulder so much of the blame. She had endured an uncomfortable few weeks, during which she had popped home to

Gloucestershire to look after her ailing mother, or so she said, and just lain low until the ugly rumors that were circulating had run their course and died down. Which, of course, they did eventually, leaving room for true love to win the day.

Right from the start it was plain to Vivienne, and later also to her parents and their set, that this was indeed a marriage made in heaven. On that triumphant day in early March, when she stood on the steps of St. Margaret's, listening to the roar of the crowd as she leaned on her husband's arm, she had known for certain her fairy-tale romance was meant to be. She had conquered a great deal of adversity to get this far and intended to live happily ever after. Now, years later, she was still working at it.

The Ambassador's party turned out to be more amusing than Vivienne had hoped, despite, once more, spending an evening without Oliver. Quite a number of her more fun friends were there, including the divinely decadent-looking painter Richard Brooke. Vivienne ended up joining them for supper at a stylish new bistro one of them knew in Battersea. It was farther afield than she was accustomed to go and she felt slightly wicked as she arrived home at The Boltons by taxi, slightly the worse for drink. The car was parked outside so Oliver must be home, but no light shone from the drawing room and even the bedroom was empty, with only the side lamps on and her nightdress neatly folded on the pillow. Vivienne kicked off her shoes, shrugged out of her fur, and stumbled back down the stairs for one more shot before she turned in. She made it a double, couldn't be bothered to add ice, then scooped up Isabella, who was weaving and mewling around her ankles, and carried her up to bed.

From the floor above she could see a dim light and hear the sound of distant talking. He was obviously incarcerated in his study, making late-night phone calls, and that could mean he'd be entrenched for hours. She considered interrupting him—it was her house too—then remembered the vodka she had drunk and thought better of it. He really hated it when she had too much to drink and although she knew she was totally in control, she could not face another ugly confrontation so late at night. With luck, she'd be safely asleep by the time he deigned to join her in the bedroom. She undressed swiftly, slid inside the peach satin nightgown, and dived into bed, leaving her makeup on. Isabella followed her and one of her claws snagged the expensive satin as Vivienne snuggled comfortably into her pillows.

"Tomorrow morning, my duck," she said, kissing the moist nose, "we'll pop in to see Uncle Duncan and have your lovely paws properly manicured."

That cheered her up. A visit to the vet, no matter how light the pretext, always acted as a tonic, not least because she fancied him mightily. Not only did it get her adrenaline pumping but it gave her the illusion of doing something worthwhile, caring about her cats. She knew the sexual attraction was entirely reciprocated even if Duncan Ross was far too much of a gentleman to act upon it. That, after all, was part of the allure. Vivienne was used to being admired and there was no denying that the hunky Australian, with his relaxed manner and attractive drawl, did wonders for any girl's morale. *The Noble Savage,* that was how she thought of him, and she had to admit to herself that she found it fairly thrilling simply to be in his presence. She had a recurring fantasy of him throwing her to the surgery floor and having his way with her while his other patients and that constipated receptionist sat quietly waiting in the crowded room outside.

That was what she'd do tomorrow, and afterward she'd go and look at Saint Laurent. The new collection must be in by now. If she wasn't quick off the mark she'd miss the best. Then, hearing a slight movement from above, she swallowed the contents of her glass in one gulp, dived beneath the covers, and feigned sleep, just like a guilty child.

Chapter Three

What Catherine liked best about her job was its contrast to the rest of her fairly tedious life. Just walking down the friendly little Kensington mews, with its uneven cobbles and picturesque hanging baskets, and inserting her own key into the pretty, blue-painted door, made her feel she belonged at last to the real world. It seemed like paradise after the stifling confinement of Albert Hall Mansions. She would have liked it well enough had she just been a cleaner or there to do the filing, but she was actually a receptionist in a much-respected Kensington veterinary practice, which gave her day a focus and a sense that she was doing something she enjoyed which was also useful and rewarding. At first she had only worked two afternoons a week, all the time her mother would allow and then only grudgingly, but as she grew more confident, she also gained in usefulness so that when the other receptionist took time off for maternity leave—a late baby and totally unexpected—the vet asked Catherine, as a personal favor, if she could possibly cover for her until things got back to normal. Catherine, overwhelmed after all these years at being actually needed, let alone noticed, overcame her fear of her mother's petulance and agreed.

It hadn't been easy, of course. There had been monumental scenes at home, with slammed doors and heavy sulks and the usual song and dance, but for once Catherine had stood firm, surprising herself, and her mother even more. The new arrangement had become a fixture, even though the baby was now born and weaned and Vanessa back in the fold. Catherine worked for part of every weekday and was also available to do extra hours when necessary which, because the practice was thriving, meant more and more time clocked up each week. It made her feel really great. It was not the money, which could not have been further from the top of her list of priorities, but the fact that something very basic had altered in Catherine's life. To her own surprise, she found she was actually happy—happier than she had thought it possible ever to be again.

The vet, Duncan Ross, was a strong, calm and charismatic Australian, vital and full of energy. Catherine liked him a lot, largely because she felt at ease with him and he made her feel safe. She also liked the informality of the practice which, despite its smart address, had a door constantly open to all comers, while providing a service that was both efficient and humane. Duncan's reputation was widespread and Catherine felt a warm glow at belonging to his small team, in a way part of his extended family. Walking home at night along the busy Gloucester Road, worn out from another stressful day spent answering the telephone, updating the records, and doing her level best to stay calm when other people were panicking and sometimes being difficult and occasionally rude, she had the satisfying feeling of a good day's work well done, something she had not experienced for years. Occasionally they had a drama, even a tragedy, and it was a rare day she didn't feel she was really contributing. For that reason alone, life had taken on a whole new meaning.

Duncan was quite wonderful to work for. Despite his size—he was six-foot-four and muscular with it—he had the gentlest of touches with his small, nervous patients and a natural affinity with anything four-footed, which meant that even the most panic-stricken animal rapidly grew calm under the soothing probing of his skillful fingers. Animals trusted him, and so did their owners. The quivering acceptance in the eyes of the creature on the examination table Catherine saw reflected in the owner; if anyone could make things better, Duncan could. Quite a number of his regular customers were openly and longingly in love with him and, even after all these months, Catherine's own heart beat that much faster whenever he was near, a feeling she found pleasurable but also a little scary.

Animals were Duncan's passion and he was lucky enough to have found his vocation at an early age. The kindness in his bearded face as he examined a sick pet was truly inspirational, yet in many ways he remained something of a man of mystery. He was always alert to other people's problems, prepared to listen to the most trivial of worries and hand out advice when it was asked for, yet, Catherine had learned, he very rarely said anything about himself. He came from Western Australia, by way of the Chicago stockyards, was fortyish, single, and extremely attractive, but beyond that his life was a closed book. Which, of course, only served to make him that much more alluring. Catherine was constantly having to fend off inquisitions from fascinated pet owners curious about his private life and availability, and, as a result, had grown fiercely protective of him.

Just the prospect of seeing him made her leap out of bed in the mornings, while the very nature of the work brought its own catharsis. For the first time in years, at least while she was in the surgery, she knew a sort of peace. At last her life had found some meaning again. These days she walked with a sprightlier step and her pale eyes were that much brighter so that even Duncan Ross, preoccupied though he so often was with his work, became aware of the subtle change. *Amazing,* he thought to himself with compassion, *at times she can be almost pretty.*

It was late afternoon on this particular Friday and the last few patients were in the waiting room, pressed up together like passengers on a Calcutta bus. Duncan had it about right; he had no time for what he called fripperies so that, no matter how much money came rolling into the lucrative practice, most of it was plowed straight back into improved conditions for the animals and the latest and most advanced scientific equipment. Pandering to the comfort of the owners who actually paid his bills came bottom of his list but Catherine rarely heard anyone complain; far from it. For some odd reason, being with animals seemed to tame even the most difficult and cantankerous of the regulars, and women who would not normally be able to sit still for more than five minutes at the hairdresser's without calling for attention or demanding coffee or to use the phone would wait indefinitely without so much as a murmur until Duncan was free to cast his eye over their own beloved pet. That was the thing about animals, they were tremendous levelers. And it certainly didn't hurt that most of the owners fancied the vet rotten.

Perched behind the computer, being in charge, was the part Catherine liked best. It gave her a feeling of belonging, something she really wasn't used to. The phone rang constantly, which in other circumstances might have rattled her, particularly when Mother was going through one of her more trying phases and Catherine's head was heavy from a night without much sleep, but here, surprisingly, she found she could cope. The animals were adorable and not all of them sick, and she even enjoyed chatting to their owners, many of whom seemed keen to linger and unload some of their anxieties onto her. It was, she realized, like nursing all over again, a bit like being a priest or a shrink, somewhere to take the weight off your feet and a load off your mind. Mainly she felt proud to be doing something so worthwhile. She had, if she were honest, taken up nursing in the first place in order to escape from the hell of home but also because she did basically take life seriously and wanted to feel she could do some good in the world as a contrast to the hollow environment in which she had been raised.

Growing up in embassies, with all the pomp and ceremony that involved, had not really constituted a proper childhood, in addition to which she had also had to endure the nerve-wracking experience of being constantly on the edge of the limelight with a mother who was feted as an international star. Catherine had inherited her father's reserve and still cringed with distaste at the memory of all that glitter and glory which had, fortunately, come to an abrupt end with her father's tragically early death. Then, they had been obliged to clear out of the embassy in Vienna and return, somewhat ignominiously, to London where they had both lived in semi-seclusion ever since. Lady Palmer still chafed at the loss of the diplomatic life but Catherine, much though she had loved her father, felt a quiet relief. Life with Mama was by no means easy at the best of times but at least it meant she could return to some semblance of a normal life. And, after all those sterile years, here she was, at last, doing her bit to help make some other wretched creature's day a little brighter. It was more than she might have hoped for; she knew she was lucky to have been given a second chance.

The patients in the waiting room were a fairly representative selection of the mixture of types who floated in to see Duncan on a regular basis. A depressed-looking woman in head scarf and mackintosh sat close to the door, hugging against her knees an elderly Alsatian with rheumy eyes and a pronounced limp, while next to her—engaged in lively and slightly overloud conversation—were the Plunkett-Smiths, an aging baronet with a facial tic that Duncan said denoted generations of inbreeding, with his brittle, arriviste third wife, whose face grew sourer yet more blandly unlined on each successive visit.

Perched on the shoulder of the baronet's overcoat was a splendid scarlet macaw, watching the activity in the room with an alert eye and muttering to himself in a low tone.

Catherine really liked Hercules, the bird, who came in every few months to have his claws and beak trimmed, but she was altogether less sure about Sir Lionel and his lady, in reality a long-forgotten Rank starlet who had been clawing her way up the lower echelons of the aristocracy ever since. Mama, in her snobbish way, would certainly not approve of them, but then those who did pass the acid test of Eleanor Palmer's approval were very rare creatures indeed.

There was the crunch of tires in the mews, the muted slam of an expensive door, and in came the beautiful and stylish Mrs. Nugent, clutching one of her exotic Burmese cats. Now Catherine could relax and smile. She genuinely liked Vivienne Nugent, who was a regular dropper-in. Despite what Vanessa, her colleague, said about her having it in her to be a right bitch-on-wheels at times, Catherine had never found her anything but charming. She also liked the beautiful cats, who resembled their owner with their grace and beauty and large luminous eyes.

Vivienne returned her smile distractedly, placed Isabella on the bench beside her, and slowly unwound the silk scarf from around her neck. She nodded slightly to the Plunkett-Smiths and scratched the bird's extended neck with one manicured nail. Lady Plunkett-Smith, ingratiating as always, flashed two rows of perfectly capped teeth and graciously moved up a little so that Vivienne could squeeze into the space beside her, like rush-hour travelers on the tube.

"It's hot in here," she announced, ignoring Catherine's presence. "You'd think he'd have air-conditioning at the very least."

Take your fur coat off, then, you stupid woman, responded Catherine silently, and saw her feelings reflected in the brilliant eyes of Mrs. Nugent, who looked as if she might even slip her a wink. Right on cue, the buzzer went to summon the next patient, and as the Plunkett-Smiths rose to take their turn, the rest of the waiting room could see that Hercules had done a number right down the back of the baronet's expensive coat. *At least,* thought Catherine, *the bird has taste.*

"It *is* a little warm," confessed Vivienne, once the door had closed behind them, fanning herself with a cat AIDS leaflet as she crossed one elegant knee over the other. "For the time of year, that is." And gave an apologetic smile.

Isabella stretched and yawned, then stepped daintily back onto her mistress's lap. There was nothing wrong with her, Catherine could see from the shine on her coat that she was in tiptop condition, but Vivienne was always fretting about her cats and it was, Catherine supposed, better to be safe than sorry, particularly when you had the wherewithal to pay the exorbitant bills. Although any thought on the subject of pregnancy brought Catherine out in a cold sweat, she couldn't help being curious about Vivienne. It seemed odd that she had never had children. Then she shook her head in irritation at the pettiness of the thought. *None of your business,* she told herself sharply, as she did so often. *Keep your nose out of other people's lives if you want them to do the same by you.* Yet she couldn't stop thinking about Vivienne, draped so elegantly in front of her as if the uncomfortable bench were a quilted sofa in the Palm Court at the Ritz. *Poor soul,* she reflected. *Probably some health problem she's far too brave to mention.*

She looked at her and politely inquired about the racing calendar and whether Vivienne was going to be at Ascot again this year. Vivienne smiled wanly. It was, she confided, the most awful bore but yes, dear friends always organized a party and she could not let them down.

"Though I doubt my husband will make it," she said. "Something always seems to come up on the other side of the world and I end up having to drag out there on my own. Usually in pouring rain."

Duncan appeared, ushering out the Plunkett-Smiths, who stopped for a further word with Vivienne and promised her an invitation to dinner, very soon.

Duncan grinned broadly at the sight of Vivienne, and

Catherine watched her light up inside. How well she understood that feeling; a woman like Vivienne, with so many
other things going for her, deserved only the best and
Duncan was so wonderful he could probably have any
woman he wanted, if only he could be bothered. Despite her
midnight longings for him, Catherine knew she was
nowhere in his league, but Vivienne Nugent was something
else entirely. In a way it was a pity she was already married.
By anyone's standards, Duncan Ross would be a most
colossal catch and Catherine had always favored happy end-
ings.

The woman with the Alsatian followed Duncan into the
surgery and Catherine nipped out from behind her desk and
slipped the bolt on the door. That was it for the weekend,
thank God. All emergencies were automatically rerouted to
the other surgery.

"How's your mother?" Vivienne asked. Catherine was
touched she remembered.

She shrugged. "Much as ever."

That said it all, though Vivienne was not to know since
Catherine was rarely expansive. She had learned long ago
that this sort of question was nearly always rhetorical, that
most people were too immersed in their own problems to
care about yours. Still, it was nice of her to ask.

Vivienne flicked open a thin gold compact and quickly
checked herself in the mirror. Even here, in the shabby waiting room, she acted as if she were playing center stage,
something Catherine was more than a little accustomed to
with her own mama. Well, good luck to her. Catherine had
often seen Vivienne's photograph in one or other of the
glossy magazines littering the surgery, and envied her dazzling self-assurance as well as the opulent lifestyle that apparently protected her from the starker realities of life. Hers
was obviously a real fairy-tale marriage, for her husband
was equally prominent (she saw him too, in the City pages)
and gorgeous as well. So what if her pampered cats did have
imaginary ailments and rarely needed anything more serious

than the occasional nail clip? At least she took proper care of them.

Today, Vivienne wore beige suede, with a casually draped Hermès scarf and slim, well-fitted lace-up shoes which subtly displayed her shapely calves and the elegance of her feet. The discreet gold pin on her lapel had the distinctive mark of Cartier, and three interlocking bands of different-colored gold encircled her delicate wrist to match the Russian wedding ring. Small wonder Duncan was such a fan. This one was the genuine article. Even an Aussie could tell.

Eleanor was practicing her scales when Catherine let herself into the flat later and hung her maroon raincoat on the antlered hall stand in the lobby. She could hear the full, fruity voice, still excellent for its time of life, warbling up and down with gusto from the room that these days was designated the music room. She carried her library books into the kitchen, switched on the kettle and the old black-and-white television to catch the seven o'clock news, then went on through to greet her mother.

Eleanor stood in front of the grand piano, dressed dramatically in purple from head to foot. Today, because they were expecting no company, her hair was tied up in a garish chiffon scarf but she was wearing her full war paint, including eyelashes, plus the famous pearls she was hardly ever without. She ran through a few phrases from *Aida,* then leaned forward and extended one puffy cheek for her daughter's kiss. She smelled of eau-de-Cologne and sickly sweet talcum powder, as if fresh air never touched her, which, in fact, it rarely did. She didn't ask how Catherine's day had been— the subject of Catherine's newfound independence was still very much a war zone between them—just peered at the faded sheet music on the piano and launched into *Lucia di Lammermoor*'s dying aria.

Eleanor Palmer had always been supremely selfish. It was one of her most distinctive traits and something her downtrodden daughter secretly envied. Her primary reaction to her husband's early death had been irritation, for it caused them to quit the Embassy at the height of the season and leave Vienna, which was, so she insisted, her spiritual home. Now that Eleanor was comfortably ensconced next to the Albert Hall, her London social life was at its height, and her musical soirées as firmly a part of drawing-room society as they had been when she was still the wife of an ambassador. Eleanor was coping with widowhood with her usual aplomb. As the years went by she grew statelier and more impressive and her voice, that glorious gift, still rang forth across the rooftops of Kensington Gore until Catherine had visions of poor Prince Albert on his lonely throne across the road clapping bronze hands over anguished ears to shut out the racket. But that, she knew, was ungenerous. If she only had one iota of her mother's spunk, she'd never have let her own life get into such an unholy mess.

It was ten to seven now, and soon the old girl would be wanting her supper, so Catherine slipped back to the kitchen to start preparing the poached haddock with spinach and an egg that was frequently their Friday fare. First she poured a couple of glasses of amontillado sherry and put them on a tray with a dish of salted peanuts, ready for the imperious summons once the music practice was at an end. Soon the Proms would be starting again and then all would be crazy activity for six weeks or so. A stream of overseas visitors would pour into London and Eleanor would have the supreme pleasure of once more playing the famous diva and inviting the cream of them to her personal box in the Royal Albert Hall, from where she could mince and scrape like an eighteenth-century Florentine noblewoman acknowledging her courtiers. It was perfectly sickening but something which had to be endured. And at least it provided a blessed diversion for Mama.

Catherine had brought home the evening paper and perched herself on a kitchen stool to skim its pages while she waited for the news headlines on Channel 4. It went against Eleanor's grand ideas to have a television in the kitchen, or indeed anywhere else in the flat, but this one remained from the days when they kept a Filipino girl and since now it was Catherine who did most of the cooking, Eleanor's snobbish remarks went unheeded. Another dreary Friday night with storm clouds gathering and a sadistic weatherman promising squally showers in the south with nothing to break the tedium of the weekend, unless Eleanor demanded her presence at church.

As Catherine read, she lit a cigarette, then, without thinking, lit another before the first was even finished. She glanced through the television programs for the next two days but there was nothing on that really caught her fancy except her favorite medical soap on Saturday. Her mother would not permit her to watch it, and though it sounded cowardly, she really couldn't face the constant battle. There was a time when Catherine had possessed a certain amount of spirit but the fight had left her long ago and she had resigned herself to the knowledge that the line of least resistance was the only way to live harmoniously with Mama.

The sounds from the music room had faded so she tossed the paper aside and unwrapped the fish from its greaseproof paper. She laid both pieces in a white enameled casserole that had seen better days—oh, how mind-blowingly tedious this whole rigmarole had become—then poured on a little milk and dotted it with bits of butter and a sprinkling of black pepper. She glanced round the kitchen with its serviceable white walls that had not seen a fresh coat of paint in the years they had lived there and its high, ornate ceiling which vanished into the shadows along with the cobwebs. When she became aware of the cigarette smoke, Catherine pried open the window a fraction, wedging it with the handle of the dishmop to let in some air before her mother noticed and caused one of her routine scenes.

Then she picked up the silver tray and carried the sherry through to the drawing room where her mother was arranging herself in her accustomed chair. Next on the agenda would be ten minutes or so of stilted cocktail chat before they moved back into the kitchen for supper and, if Catherine was lucky and Eleanor was feeling gracious, the last fifteen minutes or so of *Coronation Street*. It was pathetic. Even Eleanor agreed these days that it was a shame to dirty their best linen when only the two of them were home, and a sneaky glance at the despised television did help to get them through the meal.

The weatherman had been right and outside the rain was already sluicing down, effectively obliterating the hideous canvas canopy that shrouded the ornate structure of the Albert Memorial and would for the rest of Catherine's natural life, if the latest newspaper reports were to be believed. Why did they have to do this sort of thing, the powers that be, and deprive the ordinary people of another little everyday pleasure at a time when unemployment was high and the future of the world seemed bleak? Life was sometimes so meaninglessly sad. Catherine sipped her sherry and let her mind wander back to the time long ago when she had once, fleetingly, been happy.

Chapter Four

There was a note on the door when she got back from the laundry, telling her to join them at the pub. She dumped the two full pillowcases on the kitchen table, ran her fingers through her tumble of tawny hair, and long-legged it back down the steps and around the corner to the Earls Court Road. It was a glorious holiday lunchtime at the end of August. A clear blue sky but the nip of something serious in the air—time, her juices told her, to be thinking of moving on.

"Hi, Sal!"

Dave and Sam were settled at a wooden table on the pavement, full tankards before them, legs stretched out along the benches, making the whole table their territory. She grinned as they made room for her and took a swig from Dave's full pintpot as Sam went off to fetch her one of her own. Living with a group of guys certainly had its pluses. It was a good time, a golden time, and she was glad she had made it to London.

A fine spiral of wood smoke rose from the tennis courts opposite, behind the garden center where they were already burning leaves.

"Well, old muckers," said Dave, their leader, stretching out full length to make the most of the retreating sun. "So what are our plans?"

"Plans?" For a second she was startled. Had he read her thoughts?

"Plans. What are we going to do? The last bank holiday until Christmas, remember."

"Oh." Sally relaxed and tucked her knees, in their tight jeans, childlike under her chin.

"Do we have to do anything? Can't we just sit?"

It was a comfortable group and for the time being she was content. She had met them in Amsterdam, at a bar in the Joordaan on one of the lesser canals, got on with them, and followed them to London where they shared two floors of a house in Lexham Gardens, right on the edge of the Earls Court Road. "Kangaroo Valley" it used to be called because of the preponderance of Aussie and Kiwi visitors, but that was a term you didn't hear so much these days.

"Carnival?" suggested Sam, the broker, from his bench on the other side of the table. He loved watching Sally, found it hard to keep his eyes off her, for which he was constantly being ragged by the others. He gloried in her beauty and absolute lack of inhibition. She was a child of nature, free as a feral kitten with her mane of tawny hair, her freckled skin, and those strange translucent eyes that were as clear and as shallow as a rock pool yet at the same time oddly unfathomable.

Jeremy came strolling round the corner from the direction of the flat, hands stuck into blazer pockets, head down, thinking. Sam waved and Sally immediately straightened, arching her back and running languid fingers through her hair, displaying her delectable breasts under the skimpy T-shirt and the wide smile that welcomed the world indiscriminately. Sam gritted his teeth. He wished she would not be so blatant, that the attraction of the Englishman were not so apparent, but that was Sally all over, heart forever on her sleeve, incapable of dissembling. Jeremy crossed the road to join them, flipping his fingers to the barman inside to indicate that they all needed a drink. He sat astride the bench next to Sally and grinned at them.

"This round's on me. I won a hundred and sixty pounds on a nag at Cheltenham on Saturday. Not bad going on an outsider."

Sally pulled a floppy cotton sunhat down onto her unruly hair and fixed her catlike eyes on him from under its brim. Whenever Jeremy was around she seemed quite mesmerized, though why was not at all clear, at least to Sam. Dave was taller, broader, far more fit, while he himself was no mean looker, or so the girls back home had always allowed him to believe. Jeremy was nothing special, your average condescending middle-class Englishman, slightly on the weedy side if he was going to be dead honest, but with an edge to his wit and an aura of being in charge which dated back, Sam supposed, to the days of the Raj. Whereas his own ancestors had arrived in Botany Bay aboard a convict ship, so legend had it.

He hated to see Sal mooning over Jeremy like this. She was worth ten tight-arsed Englishmen any day, only she didn't appear to realize it. It was all part of her charm. The truth was he had adored her ever since that moment four months ago by the canal, when she had first come loping along with the sun on her hair and a light in her eye that they had all found instantly challenging. They had liked her looks right then but before any of them had had a chance to make a move on her she had dumped her knapsack on the ground and perched on the wall of the lock in front of them, long legs swinging.

"Hi, guys. What's cooking?"

And that was it, more or less. She had been with them ever since, attaching herself quite naturally to the group without any need for explanation. Sally Brown was a free spirit and now seemed always to have been part of their lives. Like them, she was a New Zealander, cruising the world on her own and, as it happened, vaguely headed to London. She had simply tagged along. There was room in the flat for another small one since one of their fellow Kiwis had just moved on, and Sally filled the slot, fitting in as naturally as any of the boys. She couldn't cook, which might have been a minus, but then neither could Rod, as Sam was quick to point out. And she was better looking than Rod, and her socks smelled better.

She was also terribly good-tempered and didn't mind doing her share, though she needed someone to give her a gentle prod. Today she had done the laundry but really only because it was her turn. She never seemed to have much cash to spare yet nonetheless managed to get by. She worked sporadically at whatever came her way but never seemed fazed when she drew a blank and never, ever complained. If she hadn't any money, then she went without. It didn't seem to worry her that her clothes were shabby and her scuffed cowboy boots rapidly nearing the end of their life. She was a good sport, was old Sal. She had brought a light into all their lives and they were the better for it. Except, Sam thought, for this awful ache in his heart and his groin which was going to have to remain a secret until he could think of a way of resolving things.

"We were just discussing what to do today," said Dave, opening his eyes and levering himself into a sitting position as the barman set down foaming pintpots and collected the empties. "It is, after all, August Bank Holiday and we're already halfway through it."

"We were talking about the Carnival," said Sam, but Jeremy shook his head.

"Naagh. Too crowded and not all it's cracked up to be. Once you've seen a couple of floats and burst your eardrums on all those ghetto-blasters you're lucky to get out without being knifed."

"But it's also the biggest street carnival outside Rio," argued Dave, irritated as he was so often by the opinionated Englishman. "They're expecting three million punters this year. We should at least take a peek while we're here. We might not get another chance."

Sam agreed. "I'm game. How about the rest of you? Coming, Sal?"

He tried not to see the glance she shot at Jeremy, then breathed more freely when she nodded. That was another thing about Sally, she was always in there, ready for any challenge. She was brave and fearless and unstoppable. In the time they'd known her, they had taken her rollerblading in the park, hang-gliding near Dunstable where Jeremy's family had a country cottage, sailing off the Norfolk coast, even pony-trekking in the New Forest, at which she had excelled. She'd grown up in the country, she told them, though she revealed little else. The boys accepted her just as she was but Sam noticed, as he noticed everything, that she seemed not to like to hark back to old times, to her life in New Zealand before she hit the road. For one who gave so much of herself to so many, Sally Brown was a surprisingly difficult nut to crack.

Jeremy glanced at his watch, then up at the sky, and shook his head. The sun still shone but there were dark clouds gathering ominously on the horizon, typical bank holiday weather.

"Count me out. I promised Simon I'd meet him at The Windsor Castle for a few jars, then we're going to Radlett to watch the Old Boys play."

Unhurriedly he rose to his feet, dusted himself down, then, almost as an afterthought, glanced at Sally.

"Coming?" he said, without much conviction.

"Oh, okay."

She hesitated for only a second, then, cramming her silly hat down on her glorious hair and grinning at the others, she leapt off the bench and followed him up the Earls Court Road.

"Just like a little dog," murmured Dave lazily.

But Sam was not in the mood.

"Cut it out," he said savagely.

And right on cue, typical of the British climate he had grown to respect, the first drop of rain splashed on his hand.

As it turned out, the Carnival was a riot and they stayed till the bitter end, despite the sporadic rain. When the crowds began to disperse, Sam and Dave split to an Indian restaurant in the Old Brompton Road and mopped up the copious amounts of beer they had consumed with chicken vindaloo and masses of pilau rice and naan bread. Dave wanted to go on drinking but Sam knew when he had had enough, so they drifted back to Lexham Gardens and were inside and slumped in front of the telly by ten, more cans of Foster's in their hands.

The flat was silent. No sign of Jeremy or Sally. Sam tried not to care as he passed the open door of her room and saw the usual mess—unmade bed and clothes all over the place as if she had been burgled. Jeremy's door was ominously closed, but then it usually was, and since there was no sound from within, and the lights in the hall and passageway had not been turned on, it was obvious they had not yet returned from their cricket match. The evening was oppressively warm with occasional muted mutterings of thunder on the air.

At eleven-thirty Sam called it a day and went upstairs to his own room, nestling under the eaves with a friendly view over the Kensington rooftops toward the Cromwell Hospital, which people said was like a miniature Bahrain. He tried to read but the beer finally got him so he rolled over, switched off the light, and drifted away.

Sometime during the night he awoke abruptly with a raging thirst and a bursting bladder. He was running with perspiration in the clammy night air. He rolled over on damp sheets and groped blindly across the room to the bathroom on the landing. When he returned, still half-asleep, to his bed, he saw for the first time that the reason for the excessive heat was that he was not alone. In the dim light from the open window he could make out the form of another body lying where he had been, white dawn light gleaming on a naked thigh. He reached the edge of the bed and fumbled around. Sure enough, smooth skin, an uncovered shoulder, a riot of honey-smelling hair.

He found his way back between the crumpled sheets and continued moving his hand until he found her breast.

"Sal?" he whispered tentatively, unable to believe his luck.

She didn't speak but rolled over into his arms as if she'd

been waiting for him, burrowing her head into his neck like a child, opening herself to him as his body jerked awake. For a moment he lay there stunned, electrified out of his senses, then allowed his instincts to follow their natural course.

After a while the storm subsided and they lay there passively, limbs interlocking, her long legs around his waist, her hair in his mouth and across his eyes. She was wide awake but motionless and he lay there in a state of consummate bliss, feeling her regular breathing, inhaling her delicate scent of fresh air and lemon soap. Then slowly, gently, he disengaged himself and propped himself up on one elbow to look at her face.

"Sal?" he tried again but she simply raised one hand and stroked her hair away from his face.

Later, Sam woke again to find her gone and the sunlight streaming through the uncurtained window. Downstairs he could hear the sound of voices and the clink of china. His watch told him it was almost noon. He slid into his jeans and T-shirt, splashed cold water on his face, and went down to join them, apprehensive yet hopeful as he had never been before.

"And about time too!"

Dave was leaning back with his boots on the table, rolling a joint, while Jeremy was hunched over the weekend papers, a Bloody Mary in his hand. The kitchen was full of smoke and Sally, bright as a new-minted penny in a man's white shirt, her hair wet, stood at the stove, turning sausages and bacon in a greasy pan, smiling a radiant cat's smile.

"Hi, Sam," she said softly as he entered the room. "How do you like your eggs?"

And that was that. No mention of last night, no meaningful look or special sign or any indication at all that things had changed. Nothing except a general feeling of bonhomie as the others argued amiably about the day ahead.

Sally plonked plates of burned sausages and underdone eggs in front of each of them, then went back to sit alongside

Jeremy, who continued to ignore her. When the meal was over and Jeremy finally bestirred himself, setting off to meet some fellows from the rowing club, she tagged along too, even though she had not been asked.

"Odd pair," remarked Dave as he piled greasy plates in the sink and swirled detergent onto them.

The following morning, Sally emerged at around eleven, which was her usual time while she was working on bar shift, and slopped down to the kitchen for a cup of instant tea. It was a working day and the boys were all gone, leaving the kitchen neat as a pin. She pulled out the loaf and hacked herself a thick slice of bread which she covered with orange marmalade, then settled down to the local paper which someone had left on the table. A small ad was circled—"*Part-time waitress required for private caterer in Ladbroke Grove*" it read—and she smiled and pushed it aside. Good old Sam, always looking out for her. She might follow it up if she felt like it later, but it was a fair way from here, so then again she might not. That was the glorious thing about Sally's life, she was free—free to do whatever she damn well liked as and how the mood took her.

And that, she reminded herself, was how it was going to remain. It was convenient here, living with the boys, and she was fond of them all, particularly Jeremy, but Sally Brown was far too worldly-wise to allow anything like emotion to cloud her vision of who she was and where she was going. She hadn't done the things she had done and traveled all these miles to be caught in the old familiar sex trap. No, indeed. There were plenty more where these guys came from and Sally had never had any trouble finding them. Shaking them off was the hard part, but she was pretty expert at that too. She got up and slopped back upstairs, leaving the loaf and her marmaladey knife for the boys to clear up.

Yes, her earlier instinct had been on target. Time to be thinking about moving on, but first there were one or two things she had to do.

Chapter Five

The ride in from the airport was uninspiring and Georgy was disappointed. She had visited London years ago as a child with her parents and the other kids, but then they had traveled first class and a limo had magicked them from Heathrow to Claridge's, which was where her father habitually stayed. Riding in on the Underground like today, along with a mass of chattering, sweaty tourists with their cumbersome baggage and plastic carriers from the duty-free shop, was pathetic, though she was forced to acknowledge that this time she was, in essence, a tourist too.

It was October and London was already well on its way to winter, with a leaden sky and skeletal trees in the tedious little suburban gardens they passed on the way into the center. Sure, the ride from Kennedy was nothing much to shout about either, but there you did at least get the adrenaline fix, once you were past Shea Stadium, of that truly amazing skyline. Native New Yorker though she was, that was one sight that never failed to catch at Georgy's throat. Whereas this ride was tacky in the extreme. Apart from the amazing greenness of everything, something visiting Americans always marveled at, apparently, this might be any drab ride to nowhere special. Even Frankfurt, with its fir trees and open fields, had more to offer.

Georgy unzipped her canvas holdall and dragged out the *A to Z* street guide she had had the foresight to pick up at the airport. Friends from New York were lending her their house in Fulham so she had to get off at Earls Court and then drag her baggage down to the Fulham Road, which shouldn't be too much of a hassle since she had got these nifty little wheels attached to her suitcase. Georgy Kirsch was nothing if not organized. Very few details escaped her meticulous mind.

The train gathered speed out of Barons Court and she started to assemble her things. Suitcase in the doorway, ready to be towed; bulging camera bag which weighed a ton but which she would simply have to heft; hand luggage from the plane containing passport, traveler's checks, credit cards—all the vital props without which she would be stranded in this foreign land. No return ticket, for, as of now, Georgy had no firm plans for ever returning home. These last few months in New York had been almost more emotionally draining than her fragile spirit could sustain. Besides, in London she had more important aims to conquer. She would wait and see how things panned out here. With luck and a little Machiavellian cunning she would find a way to stay on and make herself a new life in the UK.

She swung her pristine Burberry over one shoulder along with the camera bag, toted the hand luggage, and grabbed hold of the suitcase, which trundled along behind her like a little dog. The platform at Earls Court was dark but luckily the automatic elevator was working. That was one blessing; from what she knew of London it might well have been out of order and she would not relish having to wrestle this lot up an escalator without help. A taxi was waiting at the lights when she emerged into the Earls Court Road and she hailed it with relief. She piled herself and her baggage into the back and rode the last few blocks in style.

The sun was almost gone and the temperature was dropping fast. The Earls Court Road reminded her bleakly of

Forty-second Street with its crowds, its litter, its row of tacky little eateries of varied nationalities, all crammed together. Even its drunks and beggars, something she had not expected over here, not in this part of town. Suddenly a great cloud of despondency descended on her. She felt lonely and disorientated and not a little depressed. She had come a long way on what was really just a silly whim and knew scarcely anyone in this huge and dismal city.

Her driving motivation, if she were honest, had been to get away from her loving, suffocating family whose glorious summer had driven her mad with envy and a dark sense of personal failure. London had seemed as good a refuge as any. This assignment had come up out of the blue, just when she badly needed it, and, for many reasons, she was determined to make it work. They might have their happiness, her sisters, with their solitaire diamonds and happy-ever-afters, and she shared their joy, of course she did, as any elder sister would. But she had her career stretching out ahead of her and to Georgy that was far more challenging. This was the breakthrough she had been waiting for and she was determined not to fudge it. Then maybe she could at last turn to her parents and tell them: *See, there is more to life than catching yourself a husband.* Ballet might have let her down; let them see what she could achieve with her camera.

The streets were grimy and not getting any better. Georgy realized with a sinking heart that she had based this dream on little more than a childhood memory. Traveling with her father was not the world as it really was, she had learned that lesson long ago. It was foolish to imagine that all London would be like Mayfair, with its elegant houses and ornate doorways and liveried doormen to protect you.

They were on the Fulham Road now, going west toward the football stadium, and Georgy's anxiety grew as she saw a council estate, a college building, and a high stone wall with huge iron gates that turned out to be Brompton Cemetery. Oh, great! Just the thing to come home to at night, especially in the winter. Then they swung off to the right and pulled up outside a friendly-looking pub called the Fox and Pheasant and all of a sudden Georgy's anxieties evaporated in a wonderful release of tension. For facing her was a quiet cul-de-sac of two-story artisans' cottages, painted in subtle pastel colors and reminding her vividly of San Francisco, one of her favorite cities. As always, the Hunters had come up trumps; how could she ever have doubted them? He was a *Time-Life* photographer, recently seconded to the Paris office, and his wife had always had impeccable taste, witness their pretty apartment on East Sixty-third Street.

"All right, love?" inquired the driver as he hefted her cases to the doorstep and waited while she located her keys. She nodded, once more in control. This was more like it; this actually looked like home. The Hunters' house was painted white, with a plain varnished pine front door and window boxes of hardy green perennials, flourishing as if they had just been watered. Georgy sorted through the keys and managed to undo all three brass mortise locks, ranged in a row down the woodwork.

Once inside, she was not disappointed. It was small but furnished with taste and care to take full advantage of the open-plan interior. Clean rush matting covered the floor and French windows led to a tiny patio at the rear. Being the last house in the row, it shared a wall with the grave-yard, so her neighbors on that side at least should give her no trouble. Then she wandered to the windows at the front and saw the looming outline of the stadium against the darkening sky. What was it Betsy Hunter had warned her, something about Saturday afternoons and Wednesday evenings? Well, adapting to your surroundings was the name of the game, especially when you were living in someone else's space.

The kitchen was in the basement, down a dark flight of stairs with a strong rope in place of a rail and lit at both top and bottom by attractive art nouveau lamps made of opalescent glass. The large fridge-freezer was packed with good-ies—milk, orange juice, eggs, a French baguette—and a bottle of champagne waited in the cold compartment with a note round its neck saying *"Happy Landings!"* How sweet. Upstairs there were bronze chrysanthemums on the coffee table, plus *Time Out* and another copy of the *A to Z*. Georgy was thrilled. This place was really neat and welcoming and she planned to stay here for at least six months.

Up a narrow staircase, with another rope handrail, she found two bedrooms—a large one overlooking the street with clean sheets, towels, and duvet cover piled on the dou-ble bed, and a smaller one at the rear that she saw immedi-ately would easily adapt into a darkroom. The bathroom was compact but charming, fitted out in pine, with a pol-ished cork floor and large wall mirrors that were properly lit. An old pub sign, advertising Worthingtons Bitter, hung over the lavatory, complemented by a row of wood-mounted paintings of game birds lined up above the rim of the tub.

She dumped her bags in the larger room, then unearthed a coffeemaker in the kitchen and set about making a restorative pot of coffee with her own Colombian beans. And then, in an action as reflex as brushing her teeth, she reached for the phone on the kitchen wall and dialed home.

The highspot of the Kirsch family summer had been the wedding of Risa, daughter number two, while Baby Lois, just nineteen, gave signs of following right behind her. The aunts and uncles had gathered in force to crow and congrat-ulate and Myra Kirsch had rinsed her hair a bolder shade of bronze and held her head that much higher in temple. Georgy had joined in with the celebrating but deep in her soul she was weeping. It was no use trying to ignore the truth, even to herself. She was single, alone, and almost twenty-seven, and the way she felt these days, twenty-seven was pushing thirty. No matter what she might have achieved on her own account, in the eyes of the world—

that is, the world according to Myra Kirsch—she had
failed.

Risa had known David nine months, a suitable length of
time, and his father was a dentist in Queens, which was entirely acceptable, assuming you couldn't catch a doctor.
David was five years older than Risa and therefore the
same age as Georgy, and Myra had been tasteless enough to
remark that it was a shame he had seen Risa first and not
had the decency to hang around for her eldest daughter.
Still, it felt good to be marrying off one daughter with the
other practically stepping on her train, particularly since
Emmanuel Kirsch, who was already two partners and an
extra child ahead of her in the marital dance, was the one
who had to foot the hefty bill. Myra was enjoying a temporary renaissance with all these arrangements to make so
that Georgy, to her infinite relief, found the heat for once
diverted from her while all attention focused on The
Wedding.

There was no denying they made a handsome couple and
seemed ideally suited. Risa worked in the travel business,
which meant they got a discount on their honeymoon trip to
Palm Springs, while David was a tax lawyer, doing very
well on Wall Street with infinite prospects, or so his mother
said. They met at a family bar mitzvah, introduced by
cousins, and now Myra saw his parents on a regular basis
and joined them for bridge when they needed a fourth. It
was all very cozy and correct. Just thinking about it gave
Georgy claustrophobia at the same time as she was bleeding inside.

The ceremony took place at Tavern-on-the-Green and the
bride arrived in a flower-festooned hansom cab with rosebuds plaited into the horse's mane. With her tiny waist and
delicate features, Risa was breathtaking in her grandmother's lace and the press were there in force with their
cameras as her handsome, famous father helped her to dis-
mount. Lois, as maid of honor, had made her own dress and
those of the tiny flower girls while Georgy, the eldest, man-

aged to escape attention by appointing herself official photographer, thus having to weave in and out of the guests
and not being forced to appear in most of the family shots.
They were very talented, the Kirsch girls, she could imagine them saying. Pity the two youngest had won the race to
the altar.

Myra was at her most resplendent in russet silk, which
set off her complexion, and a tiny mink hat with a coquet-
tish eye-veil which had sounded the essence of petit bour-
geoisie when described but was actually rather effective.
And the presence of Emmanuel, flown in specially from
southern California where he was involved in a much-head-
lined wife-murdering trial, put the seal on the occasion and
brought them fleetingly together again as one family.

Georgy's heart swelled with love and pride as she stood
among the guests and watched her father escort the bride to
stand beneath the silk canopy next to her groom. In his expensive suit, with the black silk yarmulka setting off his silver hair, he looked more like an actor than a criminal
psychologist and she knew the eyes of the congregation
were focused upon him as the rabbi began to speak.

As a child, Georgy had always been the closest to her father, his firstborn and therefore his confidante while the babies came toddling far behind. They had shared a special
relationship until she was thirteen, when he left them
abruptly to live with another woman, and the bitterness of
the divorce had meant he was rarely around anymore, especially since he had changed partners once again and moved
permanently to the West Coast.

Sylvia, his fourth wife, was actually rather nice and had
provided him with the much-longed-for son, but at least
she'd had the good grace to stay away today. The pain of
the original betrayal had faded in the light of Emmanuel's
later misdemeanor, so that these days Myra was able to
meet him in public without wanting to gouge out his eyes
or dissolve into the hysterical weeping Georgy had always
found so distasteful.

The vows had been exchanged and the wineglass ceremoniously crushed, and now the rabbi was pronouncing the couple man and wife. Violins began to play and as David swept his bride proudly into the dance, Emmanuel turned courteously to her mother and led her onto the floor. They still made a fine couple as they whirled away in a waltz, their bodies fitting quite naturally together in the ease of longtime familiarity. Again, Georgy felt her throat swell. She missed her daddy dreadfully and grieved for the loss of proper family life.

She danced listlessly with a couple of cousins, then slipped away before Risa threw her bouquet and they all expected her to catch it. She made a lame excuse about having to be back at the studio to finish an urgent job, and she knew she was being ungracious on her sister's big day. Bitter tears burned at the back of her eyes as she ran outside and hailed a yellow cab and, once safely inside and on her way, she could not prevent them from bursting forth.

It wasn't fair. The one thing in the world she had ever really wanted and Risa had got there first.

Myra answered on the first ring, sounding querulous and anxious but relieved to know she was safe.

"Is it raining? Was the flight on time? Did you remember to take your raincoat?" *(Did you meet anyone?)*

Yes, yes. Georgy knew her mother well and smiled at her predictability. They chatted awhile, then Myra told her not to waste her money and rang off. Georgy dialed the number in Newport Beach but the machine was on and Sylvia's pleasant voice instructed her to leave a message and they'd be sure to call back. She swallowed her disappointment and went upstairs to unpack.

Once everything was out of the case and in its place—her wash things in the bathroom, her nightdress on the pillow, the photograph of her father on the bedside table—Georgy went downstairs again and poured herself a large Scotch. It was ten to seven London time but she still felt wide awake and half inclined to go into town if only there were someone to go with. Instead she would scramble some eggs, wash her hair, and try to get some sleep in order to adjust to the time difference. Tomorrow she had work to do and wanted to be at her best the first time she walked into the theater and up onto that stage.

She sat on the cream-colored sofa and flicked through the evening's television programs to see if anything took her fancy. One of the things about London was its marvelous television. That was something they were always saying back home and they were right. She was in time to catch the early news and it made her feel good to sit there in her own space, drinking her whiskey and feeling in charge of her fate, slowly becoming part of this city that so much attracted her. After the news came a wildlife program, so she watched that too, kicking off her shoes and beginning to unwind as the alcohol hit the spot. She pulled the barrette from her long curly hair and let it cascade down over her shoulders. Daddy called it her crowning glory and she knew it was her one striking feature, which was why she had never given in to convenience or fashion and allowed it to be cut.

She switched off the television and went down to the kitchen, neat and impersonal as an operating theater with every possible cooking aid known to man. She beat up a couple of brown eggs, broke off a chunk of the fresh baguette, and spread it thickly with homemade duck pâté, courtesy of her hosts. The door of the fridge was lined with bottles of white wine, so she pulled the cork out of an Australian Chardonnay and settled down for her meal with some muted Bach on Radio 3 as background music. This was exactly how she had always imagined living in London to be: quiet, cultured, and eminently civilized. Light-years from the noise and raucous energy she had left behind her in New York.

She rinsed the dishes, took another glass of Scotch upstairs, and changed into the fine wool robe she had treated herself to in Bergdorfs. If no one else was going to spoil her, then she would do it herself. The water was hot so she'd have a nice long soak, then wash her hair. She laid out her things, methodical as always, and moved the radio to the bathroom so she could go on listening.

Only then did Georgy Kirsch let go of her iron control and allow compulsion to get the upper hand. She picked up the telephone one more time and asked Directory Enquiries for the London number of Gus Hardy.

Chapter Six

The barn was a good place to hide, dark and cool and full of exciting corners where a small person could secrete himself without fear of detection. He often went there to escape his mother but today he was searching for his brother. The great timbered door stood partly ajar and the men were long gone, driven over in the truck to the Long Meadow for the seeding.

Normally the place smelled of shadows, musty and comforting like the pages of the old family Bible, but today there was a sharp metallic edge to it which halted him in the doorway and made him want to turn back.

"Alec?"

Sunlight slanted across the stone floor in a hard bright triangle from the partially opened door and he glimpsed dark shadows strung across it like a row of paper dolls. Huge dolls and bulky, swaying slightly as if dancing. Curiosity overcame his faint distaste and he ventured farther into the cavernous interior, so suddenly cool after the fierce heat of the afternoon sun.

"Alec?"

The thing about big brothers was they did like to creep and terrorize. He faltered on the threshold, balancing nervously on one sneakered foot while he scratched the back of *his ankle with the other, wondering if he dared risk losing face by calling it a day and going back home for tea where Ma was making jam. He clutched at the door for support but it gave under his touch and swung wide, throwing the monotone scene into sharp relief and explaining the acrid smell.*

The pigs. They hung like half-deflated blimps, snouts pointing downward in an orderly row so that the blood could flow freely into the aluminum trough placed beneath them for just that purpose. "Good black pudding." He could imagine his mother's approval. You did not grow up on a farm without knowing such things but the spectacle was nonetheless shocking. The pigs, his friends: Daisy and Thelma and Santa and Sam, whom he had known since birth and played with until they grew too cumbersome and, Ma said, unpredictable.

He reeled back, stunned, clutching his throat in horror, lungs filling with the hideous stench, wanting only his mother's arms about him and the reassurance of her comforting touch. Then he saw his brother.

"Alec?"

Lying across the butcher's block, unmoving, his throat slit from ear to ear in the parody of a grin. And only then did the shadow across the sun-streaked floor move so that he realized he was not alone.

Chapter Seven

You've got a lump in there the size of a grapefruit," said the doctor grimly, pressing cold thumbs into Beth's abdomen. She walked to her desk and started to write, nodding curtly to indicate it was all right for Beth to put her clothes on.

"What exactly does that mean?" asked Beth carefully from behind the screen, slipping into her panties, hooking up her bra.

"Fibroids," said the doctor with a brisk sort of satisfaction, as if she were enjoying it. "It means, of course, a hysterectomy."

"But . . ."

Beth was silenced. She had no plans for any more children, had put all that sort of thing behind her years ago, was totally happy with just Imogen, couldn't envisage the thought of more dirty nappies, more potty training, but still. *Jesus Christ!* She was young yet, and wanted to keep her options open. Zipping up her tracksuit she emerged from behind the screen and stood, dumbfounded, facing the grim-faced stranger who was so casually delivering sentence.

"Why would you mind?" It was a statement, really, not a question, as the older woman flicked a soulless eye over Beth's medical history. "It's not as if you're still married."

And that, apparently, was that. Beth was speechless, her killer repartee deserting her for once. This cold bitch had made her pronouncement and no further discussion was called for. She gave Beth a tepid smile to indicate her time was up and glanced toward the door.

Beth tottered home meekly bearing a letter to the hospital, to find Deirdre and Imogen huddled as usual in the kitchen by the Aga, watching *Neighbours* on the television.

"I've got to have an operation," she wailed, opening a bottle of New Zealand Cabernet and fishing three clean glasses out of the dishwasher. Imogen was allowed the occasional snifter on special occasions or at moments of crisis, just as long as she didn't tell her dad.

"She says I need a hysterectomy—at my age—but it doesn't matter because I don't need any more babies because I'm not married."

Deirdre sniffed and resumed peeling carrots.

"Knowing you," said Imogen, "you'll probably want one now. Yuk, an awful squalling brat! Can you imagine? I'm off to live in Islington the minute it arrives."

"Shut up," said Beth, aiming a swipe at her. "This isn't funny. It's serious stuff." She turned to Deirdre with a tragic face.

"What am I going to do?"

"These days," said Deirdre dourly, "it's all plain sailing. They have you in and out and don't even have to open you up it's so easy, just hoover it out and send you home. Sounds good to me. What do you want with periods and all that stuff? I'd count my blessings if I were you."

"But I'm still young," wailed Beth. "I've still got my future ahead of me. Supposing I meet Person Wonderful tomorrow. Supposing he wants to settle down and have some kids. Supposing no one fancies me anymore when my juices are all dried up."

"You're not thinking of having Oliver's baby?" asked Imogen suspiciously.

"Heaven forfend, the very idea!"

But it had crossed her mind, she was a liar if she didn't admit it. Poor man, he had lived all these years in that sham of a marriage, with no little baby of his own to cuddle and no one to carry on the family name or inherit the family wealth. Of course she'd thought of it. How could you love a man so fiercely and not have dreams of one day carrying his child? But she said nothing to her daughter or the disapproving bird of doom still scraping carrots across the table.

"It's the principle that counts," was all she said. "I'm going to talk to Jane."

Jane put her right.

"Don't listen to the doctor, what does she know about childbearing and being a real woman? That's the trouble with the medical profession these days, they always want to take the easy way out. You don't have to have a hysterectomy, not if it's only fibroids and they're not malignant. Talk to the consultant and see what he has to say. Fight for your womb if you must. Don't let them castrate you unless it's really necessary. Remember, it's a man's world and we women have to stick together."

"Dad," said Imogen, biting deeply into her cheeseburger, "can fibroids kill?"

"What?" Gus leaned forward to hear what she was saying. They were having a late lunch in the Hard Rock Café, having spent the morning looking at the dinosaurs.

"Fibroids!" shrieked Imogen, through a mouthful of crumbs. "Are they fatal?"

Gus, thinking she was still back in the Neolithic age, shook his head vaguely and went on studying the framed poster for a Rolling Stones concert on the wall beside him. They were great, these Sundays spent together, father and daughter, but he did find them tiring, particularly after the sort of week he had just had, putting those cretins in the chorus through their paces.

"She says she can't have another baby."

The background noise was deafening; what was it about kids these days, they seemed to have eardrums made of steel. Or was he just getting old? Gus smiled vaguely and successfully blocked out the sound of the sixties while his fingers drummed on the table the more familiar rhythms of *Autumn Crocus*. Seven weeks till opening. The way he felt today he doubted they would get there, not intact.

Imogen sucked her Coke through a double straw and studied her father's face. She was really proud of him and it was great to have him back in London, even if he didn't live with them. She loved it on the rare occasions he turned up at school and the other kids noticed him; some even asked him for his autograph. Compared with the other fathers, hers was fairly sensational, with his athletic body and silver hair even though he was still quite young. Her best friend, Sylvie, said he looked like Richard Gere. She watched the way women looked at him and was proud to be the one hanging on his arm, his only girl, so he always told her.

There was that girl at the theater, the American. She certainly had the hots for him the way she carried on. With her bossy manner and fancy cameras and the affected way she flicked back her hair whenever she wanted to be the center of attention. She was always around when he was rehearsing, running up to him backstage with silly queries, trying to grab his attention in a really gross way. And she wasn't even pretty. Imogen could not understand why he gave her so much of his valuable time.

"Is she your girlfriend?" she asked, snapping Gus out of his inner dialogue. There had to be a reason.

"What?" Gus was miles away, back in the theater.

"That girl. The thin one, the photographer. Is she your girlfriend?"

"Who, Georgy? No. She's here on an assignment for one of the New York magazines, doing a photo story on the opening of a musical. She's very talented. Don't you like her?"

"Not much. She looks like a stick insect."

"She's a bit intense."

Gus laughed and Imogen curled her toes with pleasure.

"Or a weasel, with that rodent nose and those fussy little paws always on the fidget."

"Now you're being beastly, sweetie. She's a perfectly nice person, you just don't know her very well."

That was Dad all over. Always sticking up for people, taking the underdog's side.

"Actually, you could do a lot worse than turn her into a friend. She started off as a dancer before she switched to being a professional photographer. You have more in common than you might think."

Gus was looking at Imogen and thinking how well she had turned out. She was great, this kid of his, with her glossy brown hair and huge dark eyes and persistent chatter that showed how bright she was. She had grown enormously since he was last in town and looked like reaching Beth's height, though she was far more slender than Beth had ever been. With luck, he'd make a dancer out of her yet, though he knew it must never be mentioned in her mother's hearing.

Pity, really, because that was what had finally finished the marriage, though he wondered now how long it could have limped on if Beth, with her usual impetuousness, had not made a snap decision and walked out. All he had ever wanted was to work in the theater and she had backed him fully until the child came along. And then, overnight it seemed, all that northern middle-class caution had surfaced and it was mortgages and settling down and permanence that occupied her mind, instead of the excitement and uncertainty and magic of their life together.

Yet here, eleven years on, was this beautiful child all set to be a dancer, if only her mother would let her. If only she would allow her duckling to fly where she herself had not dared. Gus was glad to be back in London for a while, close enough to take a look if not to interfere. This was his child too and a father had his rights, even if they were benign ones. He was fully aware of the burden Beth had had to bear these past eleven years and he would never forget or cease to be grateful. For her grounding had enabled his own star to shoot. And for that, if for nothing else, he would love her forever.

Which reminded him. What was it the child had just said about a baby?

Imogen's lemon meringue pie arrived and she dug into it while Gus lit a cigarette and wondered how to broach the subject. She had grown up so quickly he found it hard to get her right. Sometimes she was a child, sometimes a woman. There was not much that passed her critical eye.

"This bloke, the one your mother's seeing, what's he like?"

"Oliver? Oh, he's all right. Quite nice really. Super car. Not much sense of humor."

Gus laughed.

"Doesn't sound much like Beth."

Imogen gazed at him seriously and licked the cream from her silver brace. Once she got through the ugly duckling phase, she was going to be a cracker.

"She was lonely, Dad. What else was she to do?"

Ouch. The accusation was so direct he was startled and mentally backed off. Imogen softened.

"We don't see a lot of him because he travels."

"Do you think it will last? That she'll marry him?" Beth had always sworn she'd never marry again, but you never could tell, things changed. And besides, he no longer had the right even to comment.

Imogen laughed.

"No way. Besides, he's already got a wife!"

That was news. Certainly not like Beth.

"But the baby. What were you saying about a baby?"

The laugh vanished and the brown eyes grew stern.

"Dad," said Imogen in exasperation, "you never do listen to a word I say."

The consultant was better-looking and male, as well as far

more diplomatic, but delivered much the same message as the doctor in the clinic, only more expensively.

"I'm afraid," he said cutely to Beth, steepling his fingers in an attempt to look older than his rather junior age, "ladies get very attached to their wombs. But you see, my dear . . ."

(*"Don't 'my dear' me,"* snarled the voice in Beth's head.)

". . . what we don't need anymore is often better out of the way."

He smiled at her winsomely; he had ridiculously long eyelashes for a man.

"Do you still have your tonsils?" he asked politely. Or your appendix, your adenoids, your wisdom teeth. Beth suspected she knew what was coming.

"That's not the point. Just because the operation's more difficult doesn't mean I can't have it. What's mine's mine and I'm hanging on to it. I've paid my contributions just like everyone else and I'm entitled to a say in my own future, thank you very much."

Beth was quite surprised at her own vehemence but for once she really meant what she was saying. For someone who rarely had a cause, here was one worth fighting for. She was damned if they were going to take away her sexuality just because of some lump. She glowered at the cute consultant and waited for him to demolish her argument in his smooth, patronizing way.

But he was reaching meekly for the phone.

"What about the first week in January, right after Christmas?" he inquired. "I think we can fit you in then."

Chapter Eight

Have you seen my cuff links?"

Oliver was going out. He was late.

Vivienne sat at her dressing table, staring into the glass, not much liking what she saw. Today had not been a good one, best forgotten as fast as possible. The second he was gone she would pour herself a very large glass of something soothing to help speed up the curative process.

He stood in the doorway, flapping his cuffs like a petulant child but still as handsome as the day she first clapped eyes on him at the Clermont. She wanted to beg him to stay, to throw herself at his knees and beseech him not to leave her, to love her again, to turn their sterile marriage back into a living one. Instead she frowned gravely at her own reflection and asked where he had seen them last.

The light fell full on the lines round her eyes, delicately etched but nonetheless there. She smoothed her upper lip with tapered fingers and gave a tentative smile. At least she had so far avoided that dreadful telltale pleating which hit so many women around this age. The second there was a hint of it, make no mistake, it was collagen treatment for her, and if that didn't work, it would have to be a yashmak. Or a closed order in a convent, maybe, which, the way she felt these days, might be the best solution all round.

He was still fretting around her, poking through her jewel box.

"They're not in there. Try your hankie drawer, that's where Dorabella usually puts them when she sorts the laundry."

Really, men were such babies, and this one couldn't do a thing for himself. Oh, but he was lovely when he took the trouble. It was just such ages since he had looked at her with anything resembling the old passion. With his pinstriped suit he was wearing a Prussian blue percale shirt, made specially for him in Hong Kong, and just looking at him made her ache inside. What had happened to their fairy-tale marriage? When had it all gone wrong? And was it too late to resurrect what they had once had, to get back some of the long-lost magic?

He had found the links and was leaving, checking his pockets for his wallet and car keys.

"Don't wait up," was all he said as he disappeared down the stairs and she heard the final clunk as the front door closed. He was out a lot these days, more and more, and Vivienne sometimes wondered if he could be seeing someone else. Well, why on earth should he not? If she was honest, she had to admit she was only a shadow of her former fascinating self and somewhere along these last lonely years even her wit had evaporated. Whereas Oliver worked hard and was still in peak condition. Maybe he deserved younger flesh in his bed; that was another truth she was beginning to learn to accept as the years ticked by.

Once, she would have cared a great deal more, would have fought like a wild thing to hold on to him while she still possessed the wherewithal. Lately, nothing seemed to be that important. Probably all part and parcel of the incipient condition she had learned about only this afternoon in Harley Street.

She slid open her dressing table drawer and took a mouthful of Stolichnaya straight from the bottle. Nothing could beat the good old-fashioned remedies when it came to crisis time, and if this was the beginning of the slippery slope, she really couldn't seem to care. For some strange reason, for the first time in months, she caught herself thinking of poor Celia Hartley.

The other men she knew that season were really little more than boys but Oliver Nugent was a man, no doubt about it. He was dark and suave and at least ten years older, which was, of course, part of the initial attraction. But despite her sophisticated air and beautiful gown, he gave Vivienne scarcely a glance. The card game was more absorbing. She stood in fascinated silence and watched him win, over and over again until he had quite a pile of chips on the baize in front of him. Then he glanced at his watch, swept them up into a pile and into his pockets, made his apologies to Lucan, and was out of there without a backward look. Then and there, in her spoiled little girl's heart, Vivienne vowed that no matter what, this was the man she meant to marry.

Cold reality struck almost instantly when she rejoined her party and Sukey, seeing her glow and the light of battle in her eye, took great pleasure in deflating her. Oliver Nugent, she said, was strictly out of bounds.

"Your daddy would never approve," she sneered. "He's got a Past and is definitely not Safe in Taxis. Besides, he's not available."

Sukey's triumph was complete. She pushed back the mousy hair from her flushed face and positively gloated.

Vivienne was caught temporarily off balance.

"He's married?" Surely not.

"As good as. He's practically engaged to Celia Hartley, has been taking her out for ages and I gather it's heavy."

And you don't mess with money that serious was the underlying message.

Well, engaged is not married, thought Vivienne fiercely, her spirits rising again. *And there's many a slip . . .*

"Celia Hartley? That funny little thing?" said one of the

boys with amusement. "She was at school with my sister and was forever fainting."

"Nevertheless," persisted Sukey, chewing the hereditary pearls her grandmother had lent her for the night, "he's as good as hooked. Why do you think he left so abruptly? He doesn't mess around with silly girls. He's far too intelligent for that."

She underestimated Vivienne, who simply laughed and strolled away. Vivienne would not let her see she was in any way concerned, but under the ice-blue satin her heart was banging like a hammer. *I want, I want, I want,* she was screaming inside, and for Vivienne Appleby that meant the same as *I will have.* Daddy could do nothing to help her now. He was off in Europe somewhere, doing one of his dubious deals. This time she was on her own but was not going to let that stand in her way.

It took a certain amount of maneuvering, though eventually she managed it. As a slightly older man, Oliver had long since lost his interest in being a deb's delight and didn't, therefore, frequent the places Vivienne was used to going. If all they said about Celia Hartley was true, she seemed to have him pretty firmly under her thumb, though why that should be it was not at all easy to see, apart of course from the money. The Hartleys were far posher than the Applebys—their money was old enough to have become respectable over the years—so that the two families simply did not connect.

But Vivienne did her homework and tracked Oliver down as assiduously as a professional private detective until she knew every relevant detail—his clubs, his hobbies, even the locations of the flat in Duke Street and the *pied-à-terre* in Cannes. He swam at the RAC Club and played tennis at Queen's but sport was not really her thing, despite having the most famous legs in London. So she had been forced to swallow her pride and make nicey-nice to Sukey Portillo, who was fairly ingenuous for all her bold talk and had always been slightly in awe of Vivienne, who was one year older but eons ahead of her in sophistication and low cunning.

Without much effort on Vivienne's part, Sukey became her intimate, flattered by the attention Vivienne showered upon her and secretly pleased to have such a glamorous friend. They lunched at Drones, did the Chelsea Flower Show together, even shared a room at a ski chalet in Klosters. And when at last Vivienne got around to mentioning Oliver, all Sukey did was giggle and punch her arm and then came through with a weekend invitation to her uncle's place in Dorset, close to where Oliver had grown up.

Thus they met again. They were ten for dinner that night in Sherborne when Vivienne looked up from her vichyssoise to find the slate-gray eyes fixed at last on hers. And after that it was pretty plain sailing, as she had always known it would be. Celia was not with him that weekend—something to do with a septic throat and a mother who fussed. It made little difference: there was no way she could have stopped the inevitable. Quite simply, Oliver looked at Vivienne then never looked away again. And she, with a singing heart and the certainty that he was hers for the taking, had a wonderful time ignoring him all weekend, then driving home alone.

After that it was telephone calls and flowers and invitations to Wimbledon and the opera and, within a matter of weeks, Oliver had asked her to marry him. The Celia business was unfortunate, and afterward, Oliver blamed it all on her, but Vivienne was not going to spend the rest of her life feeling guilty. A person didn't own another person, not even after they were married (as she was just beginning to realize), and they did say Celia had a history of instability.

She hadn't given it a thought for months; she remembered her now.

There was nothing really wrong with her, apart from an occasional jerking ache down below, but the truth was her hairdresser was away and most of her girlfriends were beginning to be caught up with the start of the pre-Christmas exodus to sunnier climes which Oliver was always too preoccupied to do, so she began to feel lonely and insecure. Selfish bastard. He always said she could go if she wanted and he'd join her later for a few days when things weren't so hectic, but what fun was Barbados or St. Moritz if you were a woman unaccompanied? Particularly when you were part of a fabled marriage and still had a public facade to protect. So she took herself off to Harley Street instead for a general going-over before the start of the new season.

Mr. Armenian had been her mother's gynecologist before her and had that sleek, well-manicured look of the high achiever and the clean, pink skin that comes from pampered living and a careful diet. He purred and oiled his way around Vivienne, complimenting her on her beauty, marveling at how little she had aged since their first encounter when she was still a girl. He was in pretty good shape himself but she was in no mood to tell him so and, besides, it was her tab so he could do the smarming.

She explained her problem—nothing really except a slightly bloated feeling, a sensation that something might be wrong down there, plus an unaccountable lowness of spirits. At first she had wondered if she were pregnant but, well . . . In truth, she had hesitated before making the appointment, deterred by the recurring terror that it might be her liver, that she might really be drinking too much and that he would detect it and tell Oliver or, even more dire, insist she stop. But fear of something worse had driven her on so that now she was here and it was too late to turn back. But she certainly wasn't about to tell him that.

He called in his nurse before he examined her, delicately, with cold, clinical fingers, then over a cup of Earl Grey tea let her know the worst. Nothing terribly serious that a hysterectomy wouldn't fix. Just a bit of tidying up that became necessary to ladies of her age and the good news was—he flipped through the pages of his diary—he could get her a bed at the Princess Grace within the next five days.

Vivienne was silent, stunned with horror. This was far worse than she had imagined; even cancer might have been preferable. Then at least she stood the chance of a beautiful and poetic early death, to be immortalized in everyone's hearts for her goodness and her bravery. But a hysterectomy was another thing entirely and she absolutely wasn't ready to confront the horrible truth of her own aging. It might mean nothing to Mr. Armenian, in his affluent sixties with the graduation photographs of his children all around the room, but she was childless, still in her prime, and the thought of losing her womb was the worst conceivable catastrophe.

She remembered a pressing appointment on the other side of town, swept up her sable coat, and told him brusquely she would call him later but was far too busy just now to make such a commitment. He sensed he had offended her but it was a situation he was quite accustomed to. It was one of the ways he earned his fat fees; ladies could be very touchy about these matters. She had to be allowed to absorb it in her own good time. He pressed her hand intimately as he saw her to the door, and asked to be remembered to her mother. Then he smiled and penciled her into his diary. She'd be back.

With her head in a whirl and her mind teeming with all kinds of doom-filled possibilities, Vivienne went the following night to a charity ball at Grosvenor House, in aid of Cancer Research. Oliver was off on one of his jaunts to Strasbourg but Vivienne had bought the tickets before she knew his plans and was sick of constantly having to rearrange her life to accommodate his. She hated being without a partner but tonight that was not her main concern. She knew nearly everyone there so it was more like a private function than a ball.

That morning at breakfast Oliver had told her that the bank was sending him off on a six-week tour of the Middle East, leaving right after Christmas, first stop Singapore.

"You'd hate it, darling," he said. "Meetings all the time with dreary businessmen and wives who'd bore the pants off you."

"That's all right."

Oliver was suspicious of her compliancy, which usually alerted him to trouble brewing, but today there was no backlash. Vivienne sat contemplating her grapefruit as a wild plan began forming in her mind, and later that night, she had one of her rare pieces of luck.

The ball was organized by Phoebe Harvey, the rich American wife of a Harley Street consultant, whom Vivienne knew slightly from other charitable occasions. Phoebe was one of the nicest women she knew, slim and pretty with a cloud of dark curls and the sweetest smile imaginable, truly one of nature's angels, from all accounts. Vivienne strolled over to join her as she organized the tombola, snatching a couple of glasses of champagne from a passing waiter to keep her going.

"Hi!" Phoebe's great charm was her undimmed enthusiasm; she always gave the impression that you were the one person she most wanted to see, an irresistible trait. She kissed Vivienne warmly on both cheeks, taking in the two glasses of bubbly but making no comment.

"Here, let me help," said Vivienne, putting down one of the glasses and grabbing hold of a book of tickets. These events bored her within minutes; she could hardly wait for it to be time to decently slip away.

She explained Oliver's absence with a rueful shrug then asked politely if Phoebe's own husband was present. She'd heard a lot about him but never actually met him. Like Oliver, he was a busy man. She was curious.

"Over there," said Phoebe, arranging hampers in order of value, and indicating a heavyset man with graying hair and an expensive suit. Addison Harvey looked every inch what he was—affluent, successful, the darling of the chattering classes, strongly tipped to be next in line as the Queen's Gynecologist yet still with one foot in the National Health

Service. A man of principle and discretion, indeed. Vivienne looked him over with approval. Maybe it was time to ditch Mr. Armenian and move on to someone she found a touch more sympathetic. At least she liked his wife.

"Phoebe," she said, finishing the first glass and starting on the second. "Have you time for a word?" And she confided her plight.

Later, on the journey home, Phoebe outlined Vivienne's request.

"Actually, I already know her old man," commented Addison, purring down the motorway in the Corniche, Phoebe at his side. "Play squash with him at the RAC on Wednesdays. Nice bloke, bloody clever."

Phoebe had one soft hand resting lightly on her husband's thigh. She was concerned about Vivienne and wanted to do something to help. The drinking was definitely getting worse and more flamboyant, and there was a new haunted look in the beautiful eyes that she found distinctly alarming. Poor soul, it was no wonder, with her husband away on business so much of the time.

"I know it sounds crazy," Phoebe said, "considering how well off they are, but she is terrified of letting him know and can't think of a way of getting a bill as hefty as that past him without comment."

Women. Addison Harvey had made a lifelong study of them and they were, indeed, his bread and butter.

"So, what?" There was a favor hovering, waiting to be asked. He glanced fondly at his wife, and squeezed her knee in return. "Spit it out. Don't keep me in suspense."

"Sweetie," she said beguilingly, nestling her dark curls against his shoulder and playing the ingenue, a role she only brought out *in extremis,* "it's not a huge favor but I know how much it would mean to her."

Vivienne needed the operation, she explained, but was scared to death of telling Oliver in case it put him off her sexually. It sounded foolish but Phoebe could well understand. It was a normal, feminine fear which, however ill-founded, could prey on a mind as fragile as Vivienne's and cause who knows what damage. Just look at the quantities of champagne she had been putting away this evening. Oliver would be abroad at the beginning of the year when, as a rule, things at the hospital were inclined to be slack. So . . .

"Okay, okay." Addison was there ahead of her. What a peach she was, to be sure, his wife. Never failed to dazzle him, even after all these years. And anything for a quiet life.

"I really don't know how to thank you," said Vivienne in relief some days later. She had taken Phoebe to lunch at the Connaught as a small gesture of gratitude. "You cannot imagine what a load this takes off my mind."

She was already into her third martini, Phoebe observed as she sipped her Perrier. Poor lamb, perhaps this small kindness would sort out her inner worries once and for all.

"I'll tell you what you can do," she said, inspired, opening her bag. "You can take some of these tickets for the opening of a new musical just before Christmas. I don't know a lot about it, except that it was a huge hit on Broadway and is supposed to be brilliant. And it's all in a good cause."

"*Autumn Crocus,*" Vivienne read, as she scrawled her check to Cancer Research. Oliver would almost certainly not be able to make it but, if necessary, she'd round up a party without him. It was the least she could do for Phoebe, who had just saved her sanity if not her life. And it would be something to look forward to before she embarked on her big adventure as a guest of the NHS.

Chapter Nine

It suited her pale complexion, the lavender and white striped cotton of the uniform they wore as probationers, and Catherine was pleased when she pinned on the neat little Nightingale cap and viewed herself in the full-length glass. The wide white belt accentuated her tiny waist, and fine black stockings flattered her graceful legs. She missed being pretty by a whisker but this crisp uniform showed her off to her best advantage. Training at St. Thomas's Hospital, Lambeth, was turning out to be exhilarating and even the long hours and grueling hard work failed to dampen her enthusiasm.

Nor did the crowded conditions of shared digs, for this was her first big adventure and Catherine was determined nothing was going to stop her relishing every moment of it. Throughout her life she had suffered the loneliness of the only child whose parents were constantly on the move, so that the sheer enjoyment of being part of a ready-made gang of girls, mucking in together, was all the more accentuated after the opulence of home. She loved the rickety old house in Vauxhall, with its creaking stairs and exploding Ascot in the bathroom, and grew to look forward to hurrying home after a long, hard shift, knowing that no matter what time of the day or night it might be, she would always find someone to talk to in the shared kitchen. Catherine was shy by nature and cautious by inclination but at last, for the first time ever, she felt she was making real friends among the other nurses.

They didn't have much money but that didn't stop them having fun. Most weekends there was a party they could crash, or else she'd tag along with the crowd to the pub for a beer or two. Then there was the Old Vic nearby, Catherine's heaven, where as often as possible she queued for tickets—Standing Room Only, which was all she could afford. Father had offered her an allowance, of course, but this was the beginning of adulthood and freedom, and Catherine's fierce spirit of independence made her determined to go it alone.

Those were heady days and full of fun; she looked back on them now with a warm nostalgia. She had never before lived in the heart of London and, with her parents safely abroad, was finally free to explore and experiment at will. She had a lot of innocent fun, learning to cope on her own and soaking up the sights and sounds of this marvelous city, but she worked hard too. She was determined to pass her finals, if only to shake off the tyranny of her mother, and the thought of one day being in a position to announce she was never coming home again was sufficient incentive to keep her slogging away.

Until she met Tom.

The outside door was pushed open with a clang of the bell and Catherine was brought back to the present. A young woman in a quilted flak jacket over baggy corduroys strode into the waiting room. Her hair was streaked with blond and tied back in a ponytail, she wore huge dark glasses pushed up on top of her head. It was late morning but already the light was beginning to fail in the acceleration of days toward Christmas.

"Is he in?" The voice was confident and over-loud, so different from Catherine's at about the same age, all those years ago.

"Do you have an appointment?" Automatically, Catherine scanned the book.

"No, it's social. Tell him I'm here, would you."

Catherine felt her hackles beginning to stir. The sheer nerve of some people, especially these Sloaney types whom she particularly disliked. Who did they think they were?

"He's in surgery, I'm afraid. I can't disturb him."

The girl snorted with derision and leaned on the counter so that she was at Catherine's eye level and could make her point more succinctly. Speaking slowly, as if to a child, she repeated: "Just tell him I'm here."

Catherine held her ground, her fingers, hidden beneath the keyboard, curling in fury.

"You'll have to wait until he's free. Surgery ends at one."

Then, as another woman backed slowly into the room, carrying a huge wicker cat-basket: "Perhaps you'd be good enough to wait outside in the mews. There's not a lot of room in here."

It was a small victory but Catherine's wan cheeks flushed with triumph. Duncan's working life was full of this sort of interruption from young women—pushy, determined, often ravishingly pretty—and she considered it part of her duties to hold them at bay as much as possible. She knew he was grateful to her for it, even if it was never discussed.

When, finally, he did emerge for a breather, white coat unbuttoned to reveal his faded denim shirt and a good slice of his tanned and muscular chest, it was clear to anyone just what all this fuss was about. His huge bulk filled the tiny waiting room and he stepped outside for a breath of air. Concentrating on his patients always made him stiff. He needed the occasional break like this to stretch and unwind.

"Hey, Serena!" Catherine heard him exclaim. "What brings you here? What a nice surprise."

"Lunch," said the cut-glass voice. "At Drones at one. I'm meeting some chums and thought I'd pick you up on the way." Her Land Rover was parked on the cobbles and a couple of Labradors were standing inside, tails wagging with pleased recognition.

She followed Duncan back inside and Catherine saw the look on her face, transformed now from one of sulky hauteur to sheer, desperate adoration and longing. Duncan reached one long arm over the counter for the appointment book and ran his eye quickly over the pages.

"No can do," he said, with what looked like genuine regret. "I've got a full surgery till then and a couple of emergencies in Putney directly after. Sorry. I'll have to take a rain check."

He stooped to kiss her cheek.

"Got to get back," he said with his devastating grin, and was gone behind the closed surgery door before she could reply.

Poor kid, thought Catherine, softening, observing her stricken gaze. *I know just how she feels.* For that was the way she used to run after Tom; just remembering hurt more than she was able to handle, even after all these years. She tested a smile on the now disconsolate Serena, but it went unacknowledged.

Tom was a surgical registrar when Catherine first encountered him, a clever, opinionated scholarship boy from County Durham, with a gold medal in surgery and a soft, seductive regional burr that was part of the initial attraction. There were no fireworks or anything like that to begin with; they met in the course of their normal hospital duties and simply rubbed along. Tom had his heart and mind set on the top of the surgical ladder, while Catherine was usually too tired to think about anything other than her routine work. She liked his confidence and his energy inspired her.

Then, as their paths continued to cross, Tom started to notice Catherine, with her trim waist and fragile prettiness, and enjoyed bringing a faint flush to her cheeks with his slightly risqué remarks. As a rule, women found Tom attractive and he was used to them coming on to him, but this pale creature presented something of a challenge. He started to look out for her, and when eventually he bumped into her in the pub, surprised her hugely by asking for a date.

He arrived to collect her in a spectacularly decrepit car, an ancient Morris Minor held together with string and a prayer. He wore shabby cords and an old tweed jacket, with a long, long scarf wound, Bob Cratchit-style, round his neck. And he never, ever stopped talking. He was nothing special in the looks department but his eyes were mischievous and his tongue wicked and before she realized what was happening, he had Catherine under his spell.

"He's totally brilliant!" she told her roommate, Nancy, and Nancy—who had been around a bit—merely smiled.

"So when are you seeing him again?"

They were in their room, the size of a shoebox, squeezing past each other as they undressed and got ready for bed.

"Thursday. He's studying for his fellowship and wants me to hear him go through his notes. I said I'd cook him a meal at his digs. Spaghetti bolognese, I thought, if you'll show me how to make it."

"How romantic!" mocked Nancy. "The last of the big spenders."

But secretly she was impressed. At one time or another they had all had an eye on Tom and she was slightly jealous that her insipid friend seemed to have stolen a march on them all. With his brains and charisma, Tom was quite a catch and known to be going places fast. Maybe there was more to Catherine than met the eye.

Catherine's cooking was basic but she obviously passed the test, because more invitations followed and soon she and Tom were something of a couple. He was a miner's son from Consett with very little money and had to work in the vacations in order to keep himself while he studied. That meant nothing to Catherine; just being with him was enough. He was bright and forceful and utterly captivating. Soon, she became a creature obsessed.

To subsidize his scholarship and help pay for books and

things, Tom played the clarinet in a doctors' jazz band that was so popular for student hops and other occasions that they were thinking of turning professional. He was impressed when he discovered who Catherine's mother was; he had always been an opera fan, he said, and hoped one day to hear Eleanor Palmer sing in person, maybe even meet her if she ever came back to London. Catherine was thrilled at the implication but also a little scared. She had never taken a boyfriend home to meet her parents, mainly because she'd never really had one. She tried not to think about the cross-examination she knew he would be bound to face but her heart fluttered at the very idea of one day presenting Tom to her parents. Was that how things went in Consett? she wondered. Was it still the fashion in Tom's circles to ask a father for his daughter's hand?

Meanwhile, whenever she wasn't on duty, Catherine followed Tom to most of his gigs and her happiest memories were of sitting in the smoky depths of some dive in Brixton or Enfield, sipping a half of lager and lime that would last her most of the evening, watching her boy perform. The energy he put into a single night's session was amazing. He seemed to hold the whole audience in the palm of his hand, just the way he had her. There was no doubt about it, Tom was a star and, on this one subject, Catherine was an expert. He could have turned professional, she felt, if it weren't for his burning ambition to be a great surgeon and save lives.

His group, the Sawbones Seven, was getting fancier and fancier bookings, had performed on the radio a number of times, and even cut a record which was heading up the charts. Catherine felt so proud standing shyly at his side, watching other women press close to him and try to chat him up.

"Hey, Tom! You were fabulous, let me buy you a drink."

"Hey, Tom! Will you autograph the back of my hand?"

"Hey, Tom! Where's the next gig? I'll be there, bet your life on it!"

"Hey, Tom! What about a date sometime? I'll give you a ring."

He had charm, he had talent, and he was going a long, long way. They were all after him but she was the one he had chosen. Catherine still couldn't believe her luck. It made her feel quite humble. It all seemed a long time ago now.

In the early afternoon, Vivienne Nugent stopped by at the surgery, also without an appointment.

"I'm sorry to interrupt," she said with genuine contrition, "but I thought you might like to have some theater tickets to this new musical. You and your mother, perhaps. It's short notice but I hear it's terrific and it's going to be quite a glittering occasion."

Catherine was surprised and pleased. It was less than two weeks to Christmas but she had been feeling fairly ropy, with a nagging pain in her lower abdomen, and had scarcely given the festive season a thought. *Autumn Crocus—The Musical.* She had vaguely heard about it, the latest smash hit newly transferred from Broadway. Mama might enjoy the outing and it would make a good start to the holiday season. It was a kind, kind thought.

Vivienne glanced hopefully at the surgery door but it remained closed.

"He's not there," said Catherine helpfully. "Had to go over to Putney for an emergency. Won't be back till after five."

"Well, never mind," said Vivienne. "Perhaps you'd just mention I called. I'll try to catch up with him later."

Poor lady, thought Catherine, watching her walk away. *Even she's not impervious—though why, with that glamorous husband, I'll never know.* Life certainly was rum. She'd never be able to figure it out.

Catherine had been a virgin when she first met Tom, but he quickly took care of that.

"You must be joking!" he laughed, the first time they lay

together on his lumpy bed and he slipped his hand inside her panties and inched them down toward her knees. "Come on, baby, don't be a spoilsport. This is the twentieth century, you know. Who do you think you're saving it for—Prince Charles?"

Catherine had made a vague attempt to push him off but without any real conviction. Tom was on top and he was stronger. His hand was firmly between her thighs and his kisses robbed her of all willpower. Besides, she was enjoying it.

"I'll take care of you," he said softly in her ear, stroking her fine fair hair and closing her eyes with his kisses. "Trust me, I'm a doctor."

Then later, after they were dressed and were eating fish and chips in his shabby room in front of the television:

"Don't get uptight. It's the most natural thing in the world, didn't your mother tell you? As natural as breathing or brushing your teeth. And don't say you didn't enjoy it because you'd be lying. And this is only the beginning. Wait till you've had a bit of practice."

Then he took her in his arms and started all over again.

"That's the stuff, I knew you'd come round. With a bit of coaching you'll soon be a ten. Just you wait and see."

Tom had been a thoughtful and skillful lover and soon had Catherine addicted.

"What do you do about contraception?" Nancy asked casually, the first time Catherine stayed out all night.

The question had startled and confused Catherine.

"Oh, Tom takes care of all that," she said. "We've never discussed it."

"You mean he uses a sheath?"

Catherine was unaccustomed to such personal questioning and didn't want to spoil her romance with matters so sordid. The truth was she had never talked about it, not now with Tom, nor in the past with her school friends. Not ever with her mother, heaven forbid, though she must surely have seen a thing or two in her time.

"I trust Tom," she said simply. "He loves me."

True, he'd never actually said the words, but his actions spoke out loud and clear, and for Catherine that was enough. Nancy snorted with disbelief. She was a plain-talking girl from Birmingham who had been round the block a time or two, and she hated to see a sucker.

"And I suppose you believe him, you ninny!" she said, though not unkindly. "Well, it takes all sorts."

"He *is* a doctor," protested Catherine. "And a brilliant one too. He knows what he's doing and is far too responsible to let me get pregnant, at least not yet. He has his finals to pass first and his fellowship to get."

Nancy looked at her with amusement in her eyes but the coarse quip died on her lips when she saw how serious Catherine really was.

Poor girl, she thought, *she believes it too.* But she was fond of her roommate and nice enough to button her lip and leave Catherine to her dreams. Maybe she'd have been a better friend if she had spoken up, but that didn't occur to her till later.

It was almost five in the afternoon now, the surgery quiet, when the pain returned. Just thinking about Tom and her shattered dreams was enough to bring it on again. Catherine remembered her mother's cruel words—"Chalk it up to experience and look for someone with a little more backbone"—resounding down the years, an epitaph for the ruined love that might have been. Twenty years it had been but it still hurt unbearably.

Duncan stepped in from the cold, wet street just in time to see her crumple and had his arms around her before she even hit the ground. *Dear God,* he thought as he lifted her tenderly and laid her on the bench with his white coat cushioning her head, *how thin she is, nothing but skin and bones.* How had he let her get to this state without even noticing? He cursed himself for his lack of interest and vowed to be more alert in the future. He smoothed her hair as she sobbed her heart out and waited for the storm to pass. Her eyes were closed and her skin was clammy; she was obviously very sick indeed.

"Tomorrow, my dear," he said firmly but kindly, "you are going to the doctor. Can't have you fading away like this, it's more than my reputation is worth."

And at that moment Vivienne Nugent rang to ask if he would take her husband's place at the opening of a fancy new musical the following week.

Chapter Ten

The barman was West Indian with a cute bum and a diamond in his ear. Sally liked him immediately. She also liked the hours he was suggesting—two shifts daily, since she didn't want to be residential, of three hours at lunchtime—eleven till two—and five or even six hours at night, to start at six.

"At least that way you'll miss the first shift. Clearing up and cleaning out the loos," said the barman, and Sally concurred. That would give her the freedom she insisted on, to potter around, sleep late when she felt like it, and generally get on with the business of living her life in her own space at her own speed. Sally was entirely tolerant but could not understand people who allowed themselves to become enslaved by a rigid timetable. Quite simply, life was too short.

It was barely past eleven but Joe insisted they celebrate and set about mixing an exotic cocktail which he shook expertly in a chrome shaker, moving his hips seductively as he did so.

Sally spluttered as she took the first sip.

"Jesus, man, what in hell's name's in it?"

She clutched her throat theatrically and made as if to fall off her stool. Joe smiled, showing excellent teeth.

"That will put hair on your chest, sister, I guarantee. As

well as clean out your sinuses. Back home we drink it on the beach for breakfast."

Sally sipped again.

"Guess I'll stick to beer," she laughed, tipping back her head and emptying the glass in a single swallow.

Joe watched appreciatively, polishing a glass. This one would do, no doubt about it. Not only was she one cool chick but she had the attitude for a popular pub like this. No need to check references or tedious things like that, she would be a definite asset behind the bar and the punters would love her. They were all the same, these Kiwis, hard drinkers, good mates, easy come, easy go. Plus they all knew each other and spent their lives crisscrossing the world, sleeping on each other's floors and swapping connections, which in this trade was definitely an asset. He made a mental note to order in more Foster's and Four X. Joe knew women, and he also knew the local lads. On Wednesday nights, when Chelsea was playing at home, they'd be lined up out the door and round the corner once they got an eyeful of this babe.

"Here, I'll help you with that," said Sally. She reached for a cloth and started polishing with an efficiency that surprised him. She looked a mess with all that hair and those patched jeans and broken-down boots, but the hair was squeaky clean and the smile . . . well, the smile just took his breath away.

"You've done this before," he said, unlocking the till and emptying rolls of coins into the drawer.

She smiled. "Guess you could say that. In Singapore, Bangkok, Cairo—you name it. And that's just the ones I remember."

She finished the last glass, then gave the bar a rubdown and folded the cloth neatly on the edge of the sink. Joe was impressed. She looked too young and strangely unsullied to have traveled so far and seen so much. But that was Kiwis all over. They hit the ground running as soon as they fell out of the womb.

"How long you been traveling?"

"Long enough."

She grinned, and Joe wanted to grab hold of her and do something he oughtn't. *Back off, boy,* he told himself. *At least let her settle in.*

"So now you're ready to slow down and put down a few roots, I hope?"

"For a while, I guess. I kinda like it here."

Sally liked it all: the sunny day outside, the pleasant aftertaste of that zinging cocktail, and the general ambience of this friendly well-kept pub right in the heart of Chelsea where the action reputedly was. Joe seemed nice enough, with his neat bum and persistent smile, though the gleam in his eye and the bulge in his skin-tight jeans foretold trouble. Ah well, she could handle that if and when. God knows, she had had plenty of practice.

Sally wandered home through Brompton Cemetery, stopping at the garden center to buy a pot of geraniums for the kitchen table. It wasn't really her style to pretty up the places she passed through, but the boys had made her so welcome they were beginning to feel like family. Now she had this new job, she might as well linger on awhile. She liked the look of Joe, thought they might have fun together, and winter was nearly here. Once she had the cash for a new pair of boots, London was as good a place as any to hang out in, so she'd leave moving on until the spring. The great thing about these days was that nowhere was more than a plane ride away. A thought Sally found comforting.

Family. Even the unspoken word tensed her up and brought her out in a clammy sweat. Sally lay in the bath, her hair pinned up on top of her head and a cooling beer within easy reach. She stopped the memories coming. Being alone was a way of life; she traveled fast and she traveled light. Bar work suited her because of its very transience. It was straightforward labor, requiring very little specialist knowledge and easy to catch on to, and no one was likely to ask uncomfortable questions or expect you to fill in forms. Because she was paid direct from the till, she did not have to bother with tax or National Insurance, though lately Sam had suggested she ought really to be buying her own stamps, just in case she were ever sick and needed to go to a doctor. One of the great things about Britain, he explained, was its marvelous health care, second in the world to none. Sally had scarcely had a day's illness in her life but you could never be entirely sure, accidents did happen. Sam was inclined to talk good sense; just occasionally she even listened.

Sally had never had any trouble going places alone or making friends, and she moved on as and when the whim overtook her. She had quit the last job because the landlord had shown signs of becoming heavy and she really couldn't be doing with that. And this job had fallen into her lap the way things had a habit of doing. She stopped by to use the lav in the pub on her way back from Chelsea Harbor one day and saw the card propped up on the corner of the bar. That was the way life happened to Sally. It suited her capricious nature.

Downstairs a door banged and footsteps approached up the stairs.

"Sal? Is that you?" called Sam's voice from the landing. Sally smiled and slipped down into the scented water.

"I'm in the bath. Bring us another cold one from the fridge, there's a fellow."

"Would you like me to scrub your back?"

He stood in the doorway in his City suit, beer in hand, tie loosened, eyes alight—scarcely able to believe his luck. Sally stretched her arms above her head and rose like Venus from the foam.

"That," she said softly, with her catlike smile, "is the best offer I've had all day."

"You've got to be out of your mind," said Joe, stretching back on the grubby pillows and inhaling slowly with closed eyes. It was midafternoon and the windows were closed, reducing the traffic and street sounds of All Saints Road to a distant roar. He passed the joint to Sally and she took a long pull. An ancient bedspread with a faded terra-cotta design was pinned across the window and the light that shafted through it was laden with dust. The room was untidy and practically unfurnished. Piles of newspapers and cardboard boxes littered the floor and Sally and Joe lay on a mattress in the middle. The only other item in the room, apart from a broken-legged chair, was a brand-new drum kit in the corner. Joe, it turned out, was only an occasional barman. He had aspirations.

"No one signs up, are you crazy? What's the point of hanging loose, man, if you go and toe the line like any wet honky?"

"The thing is," said Sally, rolling on to her tummy and pushing the heavy hair away from her face, "Sam says it works out in the long run if you get sick and want free medical care."

"But you're not sick," said Joe, drawing in the heavenly smoke.

"Are you?" he asked after a long pause, opening one jet eye to give her a wary sideways look.

"No, of course not." She punched his well-muscled arm affectionately and sank her teeth playfully into his bicep. "But just in case I ever am, I thought I should make sure. What's the point of being here if you don't take advantage of the facilities? I thought you'd tell me what I have to do."

Joe responded by stubbing out his toke and rolling over on top of her. His hairless chest was slick with sweat and he gave off a powerful animal smell that kept her permanently aroused. It was just after four and soon they would have to get going.

"All you need to do," he said lazily into her hair as his fingers probed her most intimate regions, "is go to the nearest doctor and sign on so that you get a number, then never bother to buy your stamps. It's simple. Every illegal immigrant can tell you that. It's one of the great rip-offs that make this country so spectacularly badly run. You don't pay tax, don't have a permanent address or even a steady job. It'll be years before they catch up with you, even if they bother, which I doubt."

Sally gave him a slow smile of satisfaction, flexing her spine and raising her pelvis.

She chose a man because she liked them better and kept remembering those nuns with their icy fingers and cold, searching eyes. A woman might have been more sympathetic to her particular requirements but she wasn't ready to risk that yet. After a bit of asking around, she chose the youngest member of a local practice—Chinese, newly qualified and fairly devastatingly beautiful, though this was hardly the time or place to be thinking along such lines.

He asked a few questions and wrote inscrutable notes, then got her to hop up on to the bed for an internal examination. It was unusual, he said, though not impossible and when she was ready he would give her the appropriate reference. Sally reappeared from behind the screen, buttoning her shirt, appeared to give it some thought and came to a sudden decision.

"Let's go for it," she said. "Why not? Do it now and get it over with. God knows when I'll need it but I might as well be prepared, doncha think?"

"Oh, it's not nearly as easy as that," the doctor said, alarmed. "There's a waiting list for anything non-urgent of up to two years."

"You're kidding! I thought this was the country of opportunity and free medical treatment?"

"That's the reason. Everybody comes here." He went on writing. "To jump the queue and be admitted out of turn you'd have to have some sort of emergency. It's the only way. Either that, or go private."

"Oh, I reckon I can arrange that," she said, winking.

Then she slid into her battered boots, slung her canvas

bag over her shoulder, looked him up and down with a cool appraising eye, and went off whistling into the late afternoon.

"What in hell's name were you doing?" gasped Joe in horror when he heard her faint cry and ran to see what was going on. Sally stood in the small, cramped kitchen, blood pouring all over the Scotch eggs as she clutched ineffectually at her streaming left hand. It was a really nasty gash, right across her palm. The bloodied bread knife lay in front of her on the table.

"My Lord, you'd better do something about that," said Joe, grabbing a towel and wrapping it tightly round the wound. "Reckon you'll need stitches. Best get you to the hospital." Then, recollecting himself: "How do you feel?"

"All right."

She was a little pale but entirely composed. She was some cool chick, this babe. He still couldn't quite get the measure of her. He thought quickly and made a decision.

"I'll call a cab to take you over to St. Anthony's. I can't leave the bar so will you be all right alone? I can ask the driver to help you, if you like."

"No sweat." Sally smiled bravely and clutched her bulky hand under one armpit as if to ease the pain.

"Funny," she said cockily, as he helped her into the cab and gave her a tenner to cover the fare, "I'm usually quite good with knives."

When Jeremy got home, Sally was sitting at the table, pale but valiant, one hand heavily bandaged and fairly useless.

"Do me a favor, mate," she said, "and rub some marmalade on that bread for me."

Her color was returning a little but he could see she was more upset than she was letting on. He made her a sandwich and a mug of tea, examined the dressing, then made her go and sit quietly in the other room.

"You're probably suffering from shock," he said, remembering his Boy Scout days. "Better take things quietly for an hour or so, just to be on the safe side."

It was probably that, her wan little waiflike face glimpsed unawares over the edge of the *TV Times,* that caused him to make his big mistake.

"Say," he said, slumping down beside her, with the paper and a can of beer, "my mater's just sent me tickets for a show next week. Some charity do she's sponsoring in Drury Lane. Care to come with me?"

Sally brightened. She still had a bit of a thing about Jeremy, found his aloofness hard to fathom and refused to give up on a challenge.

"Great!" she said. "I'd love to. Haven't been to a show since I got here."

Jeremy looked at her carefully, cautious about his next words, anxious not to offend.

"Just one thing," he said, eyeing her general disarray, with the fat white bandage that would soon be as grubby as the rest of her. "It's black tie."

She stared at him uncomprehending, then laughed.

"No sweat, cobber," she said. "I'll borrow one from one of the others!"

Chapter Eleven

Wafts of stale sweat and dust and the all-pervading smell of greasepaint swept over Georgy whenever she went backstage, rocketing her back to her childhood days at Juilliard, when she was still the apple of her father's eye and determinedly set on a career in ballet. Camera in hand, she threaded her way behind the flats, careful not to trip over the ropes, and took up a new position directly left of center stage, from where she had an uninterrupted view of the leading lady still trying to perfect her main solo dance number.

Marla Henderson—all curves, curls, and baby-blue eyes—was trouble in the Monroe tradition and a bitch on wheels to boot. *Autumn Crocus* was due to open in just six days, yet Marla's performance still left a lot to be desired, certainly in the eyes of the perfectionist director.

"Again, Marla," shouted Gus from the third row of the stalls, "and this time try to put some feeling into it. She is, after all, awakening to the one great love of her life, not facing a visit to the orthodontist. Get some zip into it and try to smile. Make the audience fall in love with you the way it's happening to Vic. What's the matter with you? You were never this wooden on Broadway."

Marla flounced across the stage, a dark pout on her face, wiping her neck with a towel.

"It's this goddamn theater, that's what," she complained. "The stage is all splintery and there's nowhere in my dressing room that I can unwind. I feel like a hamster in a cage with no air-conditioning. It's an insult."

"Okay. Take five."

Gus vaulted lightly onto the stage and put a consoling arm around his star. Marla Henderson was a monumental pain in the butt but he had known that from the start. It had been a gamble bringing her to London but she had that extra magic which made the constant sparring worthwhile.

Georgy clipped the lens cap back onto her Leica and slung the camera resignedly round her neck. She hated it when Marla played up, stupid cow; even more so when Gus fell for her histrionics and went to such lengths to pacify her. She simply wasn't worth it, no actress was, but even though Georgy had tried to insinuate this fact into Gus's ear, he never seemed to listen. Now he was pacing the boards slowly with Marla, his arm still slung protectively around her fleshy shoulders, while Georgy gritted her teeth and turned away, furious with a mixture of envy and frustration to see her idol so obviously in thrall to the older woman.

One good thing, though, it made time for a smoke break. Georgy fished through her camera bag for her Marlboros and stepped outside into the alley for a quick hit of nicotine. On the whole, she was enjoying her time in London, even though, in almost five weeks, she had made no real friends, just nodding acquaintances among the company. Her mother, Myra, sensing her loneliness, had made threatening noises about coming over for a while but Georgy had managed to hold her off. London at this time of year was cold and dank, she explained, and besides, all her time was taken up at the theater. This assignment was the most challenging of her career so far and she was determined to make it work for her. Having failed once, as a dancer, she felt time was running out. At twenty-six, another change of direction was out of the question, and even though photography was by no means a cushy number, it was a challenge that suited Georgy's fiercely competitive nature. More to the point, it enabled her to stay close to Gus Hardy, though she wasn't telling Myra that. No, the last thing she needed at this particular time was a fussy mother in tow. Her father might have been a different matter but, needless to say, he hadn't offered.

Even without a busy social life, Georgy's days were kept pretty full. Each morning she was up early, as rigorously punctual as if she were punching a time clock, to wash her long hair, get in groceries and things like that, and be in Covent Garden by midmorning to watch the cast go through their paces. She took this assignment very seriously. *New York Life* was a notoriously hard market to crack, prestigious and overly choosy about who they used, and if she got it right, this could be her break into the big time. Georgy's contract was open-ended but once *Autumn Crocus* had premiered and her pictures had been dispatched all over the world, there was little else she could do with the company or, indeed, in London unless she was lucky enough to get more work while she was still on the spot.

So, just in case, she was using every second of her time as profitably as she could. Nights that Gus told her he didn't want her hanging around backstage, she took herself off to other West End theaters and managed to cram in, over the weeks, practically every show that was running in London, even the hard-to-get-into ones like *Les Misérables* and *Phantom.* Her coffee table was strewn with programs and she played the soundtracks incessantly on her personal stereo as she worked on her portfolio or whiled away cramped hours in the chilly space behind the stage while the cast was warming up and photography was banned.

On weekends she rose even earlier, sometimes at five or six, in order to visit the famous street markets and indulge in her second passion, shopping. She scoured Brick Lane and Bermondsey as well as the more expensive Portobello Road and Camden Passage, and her money just leaked away as she amassed china and porcelain and hallmarked silver, all of which she carried lovingly back to Fulham to stash in boxes in the room she used as a darkroom, ready for transportation back to New York, if and when that time ever came. Georgy's family was well heeled and from somewhere she had inherited an unerring eye for quality. Compared with Myra's opulent clutter on Long Island and Emmanuel's more gracious but starkly modern style in Newport Beach, Georgy's own studio apartment on East Seventy-eighth Street was a model of enduring taste, one in which both her grandmothers, rest their souls, might well have felt in harmony and at home.

Every now and again, on a Sunday, when the church bells rang and the world stayed home and read the papers, Georgy would unpack her booty and spread it carefully about the Hunters' tidy living room, reveling in her purchases and wishing this were her permanent home so that she could display her own things all the time and build a proper nest. She would make some basic alterations, of course. She would change the wall color from pristine white to apricot, buy Oriental rugs for the rush-matted floors, and insert some Victorian stained-glass panels, from a shop she had discovered in the Portobello Road, into the fanlight over the front door and the bedroom windows.

Since her early teens, Georgy had been a nest-builder and her china alone, back home in Manhattan, was filling all her storage space and threatening to burst out into the rest of her rooms. One of Myra's favorite jokes about her oldest daughter, not meant unkindly, was that when she did at last manage to snare herself a husband, she would be able to feed him on different dishes every night for a week and still have whole services over for special occasions.

The rest of Sunday Georgy spent rooting through the antique shops at the far end of the King's Road and the auction rooms in Lots Road where she often saw bargains that made her want to weep—things she would swoop on and carry off without a thought if only she had a permanent place to put them. All of which led straight back to her basic loneliness and the real hunger that was all the time gnawing at her guts. Gus Hardy. And how in the world she was ever going to get to know him better.

He was just so beautiful. The first time Georgy ever saw him, at Juilliard where he was teaching part-time, she had flipped over his lithe, sensual body and silver-haired good looks, and her obsession had grown over the years so that she lived, breathed, dreamed Gus Hardy to the exclusion of practically everything else. Friends in New York had laughed and warned her off. Men that neat usually traveled solo, they said, and if at forty-something he was still unmarried, there must be a secret life she didn't need to know about but which was unlikely ever to include her. But Georgy was tenacious, something she had inherited from her father, and what she set her heart on she meant to have. She followed Gus's career as assiduously as any biographer and it was not entirely a coincidence that, when dancing let her down, she reinvented herself as a photographer specializing in theater and dance.

Gus treated her with a lazy tolerance, touched and amused by the intense, nervy girl with the Botticelli hair and the prominent nose that just stopped her from being pretty. He allowed her into his final rehearsals because he could see she had talent and could be relied on to behave like a pro. Other than that, he seldom gave her a thought and was only mildly surprised when she turned up in London, on a special assignment from *New York Life,* to cover the British production of his vast Broadway hit. Surprised and pleased because he knew she would do an excellent job which would help to promote the show. He was aware that she always arrived on time and lingered longer than she needed to at night, but his own life was so complex that he hadn't the time or inclination to spare for hers. In Gus Hardy's eyes, Georgy Kirsch was a little like a mascot—hardworking and pleasant to have around but in no way central to his life. She would have been devastated had she known how it was.

Autumn gave way to winter and still Georgy lingered on in London. Due to various problems with the cast, the opening of *Autumn Crocus* had had to be delayed but Georgy was lucky enough to have found other work and was still on a retainer from *New York Life,* which paid well and gave her an authenticity which led to other things. She managed to get in on an ambitious outdoor production of *Aida* at Earls Court and filled the gaps with one or two advertising jobs, courtesy of a New York acquaintance who worked at J. Walter Thompson.

Thanksgiving was looming and Georgy felt homesick. She still had no real friends in London. She had teamed up, to an extent, with a dancer from Gus's company called Lindy. They started to hang around together and go to art galleries and concerts on weekends. Lindy lived in Paddington, in one cramped room in a down-at-heel lodging house, so Georgy invited her for Thanksgiving dinner.

"Who else shall I invite? Gus, do you think?"

Georgy could just about squeeze eight round her table and she loved to cook. Lindy seemed doubtful. She suggested a couple of other dancers but thought Gus would most likely be otherwise engaged. He was, after all, English and did have family here. Besides, Thanksgiving was not a British festival.

Nonetheless, Georgy phoned him. Gus was pleasant but regretful.

"Sorry, sweetie. With things running so late, we have to rehearse. And I rather think I have to go on to the Ambassador's house with Vic and Marla and a bunch of the cast for late-night fireworks and dancing and all that jazz—boring, I know, but that's show biz and we have to fly the flag. It was darling of you to ask me. Have a wonderful evening and be sure to raise a glass to me!"

In the end, five of them shared a turkey and a Harrods-bought pumpkin pie and Georgy found sparklers in a local shop and tiny American flags which she stuck in the pie. It was all quite jolly but her heart wasn't in it. When they had left, in the small hours, leaving the table to be cleared and a stack of dishes to deal with, she rang Gus's number again but no one answered. So she called her family instead, on Long Island, and found them all together and right in the middle of their dinner. They were thrilled to hear her voice, of course, and had planned to call her later when they'd finished eating, forgetting all about the time difference.

When she hung up Georgy cried. They had each other while she was here alone. For the first time she felt like throwing in the towel and heading home.

For the night of the opening of *Autumn Crocus* at Drury Lane, two weeks before Christmas, Imogen had a new velvet dress and Beth dug out her old Jean Muir and sent it to be dry-cleaned.

"Got to put on a show for the old man," she told Jane. "Actually, I'm rather looking forward to it. He's talked so much about it and it's ages since I last had a glam night out. He's putting us in the royal box. Très posh."

Secretly she wished that Oliver could be there too but, of course, that was out of the question. He was off in Zurich on bank business so wouldn't have been able to make it in any case. Ah, well. Beth was used to doing things on her own; it went with being Oliver's bit on the side. And tonight, in any case, she'd be there to support her ex, which was as it should be.

Phoebe and Addison were in the third row of the stalls when Vivienne swanned in with Duncan, who was surprisingly suave and well groomed in a well-cut dinner jacket and ruffled shirt. Vivienne looked radiant and Phoebe was pleased; Addison's little favor was obviously doing the trick and, once the operation was over, maybe she'd be able to rebuild her life. Though, from the look of the man at her side, Phoebe was surprised it was necessary.

"You didn't tell me Oliver looked like Kris Kristofferson," she hissed to her husband, and Addison turned his head in surprise, then grinned.

"That's not Oliver," he said. "Oliver's a stiff in a suit. Goodness knows where she picked up that. Probably a gigolo."

Phoebe giggled and squeezed his hand. She was really enjoying herself; evenings together like this were all too rare. Like Vivienne, she suffered from being married to a workaholic, though she felt that time devoted to the hospital was a lot more worthy than merely making money.

Serena, sitting beside Sally and trying to ignore her, saw Duncan too and let out a yelp of outrage.

"That's Duncan Ross," she said. "My bloke. I was going to ask him to come this evening but he said he wasn't free."

"He's stunning," said Sally sympathetically, taking a look. "But then, so's she."

Serena glared at Sally with hostile eyes and deliberately turned her back. She looked a right little slut, whoever she was, in her tawdry, semi-transparent nylon dress which looked like a slip and showed everything she'd got. Serena certainly didn't want to be seen talking to the likes of her. To add insult to injury, she had one paw wrapped bulkily in a great white bandage which was none too clean. Really, Jeremy's standards were slipping. If she'd known his party was going to be this raffish, she certainly wouldn't have come. And who the hell was that devastating woman on Duncan's arm? She wanted to storm across and make a scene but managed to restrain herself.

Eleanor Palmer, on the right of the fifth row and all done up like a dog's dinner, was looking around the theater with an air of hauteur, waiting for recognition. She would have preferred to be in the royal box, where everyone could see her, but that was already occupied by just two people, one of them a child, which seemed a terrible waste. She checked in case the woman was Diana or Anne, then lost interest. Her attention was caught instead by something far more riveting; she sat up straighter in her seat and trained her opera glasses on Addison Harvey, two rows in front and slightly to her left.

Even after all these years, there was no mistaking him. The hair was graying, the eyes were pouchy, and he had put on a lot of weight but Eleanor had an eye like a hawk and a memory as sharp.

Good heavens, she thought incredulously, *there's that frightful little upstart who practically ruined my daughter's life!* She glanced swiftly at Catherine, slumped despondently beside her, but she appeared not to have noticed him. Thank God. Eleanor prayed for the house lights to dim and her daughter to remain in oblivion. Secretly, she still had faint qualms about what had happened twenty years ago, but was damned if she'd ever admit it, even under oath. He'd been bad news, that was all there was to it. Eleanor was glad she had got rid of him before he could do more harm.

Gus found Georgy lurking backstage, though for once without her camera.

"What are you doing back here?" he said. "Your place is out there in the house tonight. You deserve it after all your hard work and I want you to see how it looks."

Georgy confessed she hadn't got a ticket; had forgotten all about it in the rush of the last few days. Gus grinned and took her gently by the elbow.

"Come with me," he said mysteriously, propelling her through the door and up the stairs.

The orchestra was already tuning up when Gus opened the door and ushered in a stranger. Beth looked up from her program and smiled as Gus made the introductions.

"Georgy Kirsch," he said, "ace photographer from New York. Meet my daughter and my former wife."

Then he shot off out and left them together, sprinting down the corridor in order to get backstage before the action started. He had worked for months for this one night; his whole career and creative future depended on its success.

The overture came to an end, the plush curtains parted, and the magic of Gus's musical began to unfold onstage. The audience was appreciative and in festive mood and the entire house, top and bottom, was packed with ladies and gentlemen in evening dress, like a gala performance at the opera house. Gus, hovering in the wings, began to relax; despite the setbacks, the grinding months of work and the last terrible panic when they'd been forced to put off the opening until this close to Christmas, he could see it was going to be all right. His toe began to tap as he lost himself in the music.

Serena sat glowering in the dark, miserable at seeing Duncan with another woman, while beside her Sally was making plans for putting the make on Jeremy once she got him alone. Her hand was still stiff and unusable but that shouldn't deter her, and he must be more interested than she'd thought, to have asked her to this fancy do.

Vivienne was happier than she had been for months, safe with Duncan at her side and secure in the knowledge that soon her little health problem would be sorted out, and all without her husband's knowledge. Georgy sat bolt upright in her box, impervious to the spectacle on the stage, unable to believe what she had just heard, all the while shooting little darting glances at Beth, to check that she was real.

Eleanor focused on the music, critical of the leading lady, who needed to shed a stone or two and whose voice she found excruciating; while beside her Catherine remained sunk in a stupor, feeling like death and dreaming, as ever, of Tom.

Now it was New Year's Eve, and once more Georgy was

alone. All the excitement of *Autumn Crocus* was over, at least for her. The show had been brilliantly reviewed and was playing to packed houses. Georgy's photographs had appeared in magazines all over the world and received their own share of praise. Yet she'd spent Christmas Day alone, slumped in front of the telly with a tray of Marks & Spencer boned turkey and one mince pie, trying to get interested in the James Bond movie and longing to be with someone she really cared for.

She had booked a call to her father and Sylvia, on vacation in the Caribbean, but the lines were all busy and she never did get through. When she spoke to Myra and her sisters, she found them still celebrating—even more so now since Lois too had announced her engagement. This was undoubtedly Myra's year, with two daughters down and only one to go, but Georgy couldn't seem to care. She brushed aside her mother's clumsy questioning and rang off. She hated to be mean-spirited but could see her life ticking away with the years and nothing at all to show for it.

Lindy and her friends were off to Trafalgar Square tonight, to see in the New Year in traditional London style, but Georgy had refused their invitation to join them. She was feeling a little off-color, with a dull pain in her stomach, and could not face the crowds and the noise, nor the prospect of the end of another year, so far away from her family and friends. She felt incredibly homesick and when her father called to say they were back and to wish her a happy new year, she was inches away from bursting into tears.

She spent the afternoon in the darkroom, finishing an assignment, but by nine could bear it no longer. She was only twenty-six years old; it was criminal to be sitting here alone, feeling sorry for herself as she listened to the distant laughter of New Year revelers. Time to get out there and grab life by the throat; she brushed her hair, slipped into the sable jacket her father had sent her for Christmas, and set off down the Fulham Road before she could change her mind.

Inevitably, of course, she ended up in Islington. It was almost midnight when Georgy stepped out of her cab outside the elegant town house that was ablaze with light and buzzing with the sounds of a party in progress. She had been there once before, but only on an errand; now she stood unseen in the cold street, gazing, through undraped windows, into a huge room packed with people. Lamplight picked up the silver sheen of Gus's elegant head as he passed among his guests, a bottle of Bollinger held high in either hand, welcoming them into his home. He was giving a party for what looked like half of London but he hadn't included Georgy. Even though they had worked together all these weeks and she was a stranger in this city on the one night of the year that really mattered. Among the crowd she glimpsed the fluffy curls and famous profile of Marla Henderson, and a cold hand clutched at Georgy's heart. It was true, then, what she had long suspected yet tried so hard to suppress. That bitch of an actress was in there where Georgy longed to be.

All she ever wanted in the world was in that room, yet the door stood firmly closed and the sounds from within were muffled by expensive double glazing. Yet there was a holly wreath on the door and an immense welcoming Christmas tree in the window. Surely they must stand for something? New hope had filled her when she met the wife and daughter; if he had done it once, surely he could do it again? All her friends' cynicism was suddenly devalued and Georgy was more determined than ever to conquer Gus and win his heart. If only she could work out how.

It was five minutes to midnight, almost the hour for first-footing, and who, on a night like this, would turn away a stranger? On an impulse, Georgy gathered the sable jacket close up against her chin and banged on the door with the huge brass knocker.

She waited for a while, but nothing happened, so she knocked again.

"Door!" shouted someone from inside, and "Get it!" in the authoritative tones of Gus. Georgy had her smile all ready and a suitable excuse on her lips—"*Just passing, saw the lights, felt I must stop by to wish you a happy new year*"—when the door opened and she found herself confronting a stranger.

The young man who stood in Gus's lit doorway was graceful, ash blond, no more than twenty-two at the most and not smiling at all. He raised one eyebrow in silent inquiry and the greeting died on Georgy's lips.

"Who is it?"

Gus, still wielding a bottle, appeared behind the young man and draped one arm casually round his shoulders.

"Georgy Kirsch, what a surprise! Come on in out of the cold and join the merry throng. Karl, do your stuff, old boy, and get her a glass—chop, chop."

Radiating that amazing smile, Gus swung back into the party, leaving Georgy still hovering in the doorway, facing the scowling stranger. Karl held out one stiff hand for the sable jacket but Georgy had turned away, sick to her stomach.

She made it to King's Cross station, where the crowd was almost impenetrable. As she waited miserably for a tube train, the pain in her stomach grew worse and she was violently sick. Then she blacked out.

Hours later, feeling like death, she awoke to find herself in the hospital.

Part
Two

Chapter Twelve

Addison Harvey sat at the wheel of his silver Corniche and wished himself back in Gstaad, where he had left the family skiing. The traffic along the King's Road was unusually light for a Friday morning but then it was early January and most of the world was still slacking off, enjoying the last few days of the extended holiday. Lazy sods. The older he became, the more reactionary he seemed, so that these days he occasionally heard himself sounding exactly like the older consultants whose blimpish attitudes he had, for decades, so much despised. As it was, he voted Conservative—something he kept to himself whenever he returned to Consett—and the fact that his boys were at Harrow only went to demonstrate how far he had strayed from those solid, old-fashioned, working-class roots.

But who the hell cared? He had worked damned hard for what he had achieved and was not about to apologize for it now. The house in Sunningdale, the lucrative private practice, the rich society wife who was the envy of all his associates—these were things he had labored for, and if the extra graft of two days a week in a miserable NHS hospital was the price he had to pay for the ultimate accolade, appointment as Queen's Gynecologist, then so be it. It was almost within his grasp and he wasn't going to risk ruining things now. He swung into the forecourt of St. Anthony's Hospital and prepared for his ward round. At least there would be no bloody students present today, which was one small blessing for which he was devoutly thankful.

Beth wanted to go on her own.

"No trouble," she said. "It's no worse than checking into a hotel or health farm, which is the way I intend to treat it. Time for a nice long rest and to catch up on my reading. Time to lose a few pounds, if I'm lucky."

But Imogen, for once, was unusually clingy and teary and followed her around like a much younger child.

"Don't worry, lovie," said Beth kindly, giving her a hug. "It really isn't any big deal, just one of those routine things. I wouldn't know anything about it if it weren't for that dratted smear test."

"Just as well you had it," sniffed Deirdre dourly from across the kitchen where she was scouring saucepans. "It doesn't do to let these things drag on. You never know where they may lead."

That made Imogen laugh, and she and her mother swapped secret grins. Trust old Deirdre always to take the gloomiest view.

"Besides," said Beth, "you've got your dad. It's an excellent opportunity for you to spend more time with him away from your clucking mother. Think about that lovely house and all those things he showered you with at Christmas. I'm almost jealous. If I had the choice of St. Anthony's or Ripplevale Grove, I know which one I'd choose. He'll spoil you rotten while I'm in there suffering, and you'll be unlivable-with by the time I come home."

"You said it wasn't serious."

"Nor is it. I lied."

"Dad says I can help him backstage," said Imogen, brightening. "That girl we met, the photographer who's always hanging around, she trained as a dancer before she took pictures. Dad says I can get some career tips from her."

Oh Lord. But Beth had the sense not to interfere. Now was not the time to be arguing about her twelve-year-old daughter's future. She had years to go yet before it was necessary to make a decision and she would undoubtedly change her mind several times before then.

"Actually," said Imogen, lowering her voice confidentially, "I think she's sweet on Dad but he denies it. She's certainly there a lot and never takes her eyes off him."

Beth snorted with laughter.

"And much good may it do her."

But she did feel a fleeting pang, remembering. Thank God all that was over, long ago. She did miss Oliver, who was on an extended tour of the Far East for the bank, but the Oliver pain had nothing to do with the Gus pain— softer, less cutting, altogether more sophisticated. Miss Oliver she might, but she was also grateful he would not be around to see her at her direst, in a hospital ward without the benefit of makeup, with her stomach all cut to shreds. With luck, by the time he returned she should be up and about again, all stitched up and as good as new, ready to leap back into his arms. And at least, through fighting for her cause, she'd still have all her working bits.

In the end they put the answering machine on and all three went to the hospital. The first week of January was never that busy and there wasn't a lot Deirdre couldn't handle on her own. She was big on drudgery, less hot on responsibility. That was the secret of their successful team, what made it work. Deirdre insisted on carrying the overnight bag and Imogen lent Beth her teddy bear, in case she got lonely at night.

They arrived at Florence Ward, as directed, and found a cheery, glass-walled room with one patient already tucked up in bed and a second bed clearly in use, though currently unoccupied. A pretty nurse with a friendly smile checked Beth in, then led her to a bed next to the one by the window where a beautiful black-haired woman sat listlessly leafing through a magazine.

Beth stowed her few possessions in the bedside cupboard. She didn't need much here, just socks and a T-shirt borrowed from Gus (she normally slept naked), a few pairs of pants, and her washing kit. And a thin toweling dressing gown for going to the bathroom. Plus a pile of new paperbacks, a box of tissues, a great big pot of Clinique moisturizer—her single indulgence—and a pad and pencil for making lists, one of her pet neuroses.

"Well, you never know," she said. "I might be struck by inspiration while I'm lying here and come up with a revolutionary new menu or something."

From the next bed, Vivienne watched with lackluster eyes as this vibrant, energetic woman organized her space, all the while chattering gaily to the dumpy older woman and the slim, coltish teenager who was arranging a teddy bear on the pillow. Beth wore denim leggings and a man's white shirt, long enough to cover her middle which was not as flat as it might have been. Her sleeves were rolled up to reveal capable arms and her short brown hair curled naturally above frank gray eyes and the friendliest of smiles. Clearly a nice woman, with the sort of life Vivienne had grown to envy. Overweight but relaxed about it, overflowing with laughter and incident and friendship, which was evidenced by this send-off committee.

"Better get going," said Beth once she was sorted. "I'm supposed to hop into bed like a good girl and wait for the doctor to visit."

She hugged Imogen hard, then pecked Deirdre on the cheek and waved them both away.

"Don't bother coming tomorrow," she said. "If the op's in the morning, I'll be out of it for hours. And don't worry about a thing, Deirdre. I'll be home again fighting fit before you can say marzipan."

Then she smiled ruefully at Vivienne and slipped out of

her clothes and into her T-shirt without even bothering to draw the curtains.

Vivienne was still feeling miffed. She had arrived two hours ago and they had made a fuss when she asked for somewhere to hang her fur coat. The single bedside cupboard was not nearly spacious enough for her things, so she'd had to leave most of them in her suitcase and stick it out of the way under the bed. The nurse had had the impertinence to suggest that she send the coat home with one of her visitors but when Vivienne had explained she was expecting none, they had made arrangements to have it stored in the hospital safe. But she could tell they weren't pleased. Nor did they approve of the diamond bracelet she had forgotten to remove, or the quantity of makeup she'd brought which would not fit into her drawer.

Now she was marooned in bed waiting for a visit from the anesthetist and regretting already that she hadn't availed herself of Mr. Armenian's offer and gone into the Princess Grace, where at least she would have been properly treated. But then she remembered the bill and her anxiety that Oliver should never find out the truth. Better to stick it out, now that she was here. At least it was only for ten days or so; she would just have to chalk it up to experience.

She was luckily having a bath by the time Duncan Ross appeared, supporting Catherine, otherwise she would have died of shock and that would have been that. The nurse ran forward to draw the curtains round the cubicle and he swung Catherine onto the bed as easily as if she were a rag doll. As she knelt to help slide off her shoes, she noticed the care with which he lifted the sticklike ankles and laid her feet tenderly on a pillow at the foot of the bed. He treated Catherine as delicately as if she were a frightened bird, smoothing the hair from her forehead and talking to her softly as she cowered against his shoulder.

"She's pretty sick," Duncan explained. "She's collapsed a couple of times in the surgery before, so this time I thought I'd bring her straight here."

He stood looking down at her with incredible gentleness, his blue eyes troubled. It was typical of that ghastly mother that she'd let him take all responsibility, hadn't even wanted to come to the hospital. *Not well enough,* she'd said but he knew she was bluffing. He recognized a hypochondriac when he saw one—and also the cause of all poor Catherine's problems.

"Are you a doctor?"

"No, a vet," Duncan explained. "But when it's a question of basics, like life and death, there's not a lot of difference."

He had a few more muted words with Catherine, who was clearly very distressed, then handed her over to the care of the nurses and prepared to leave.

"Look after her," he said, "and I'll be back tomorrow."

Lucky woman, thought Polly, the nurse, watching him stride away.

The next patient was brought up from Casualty, where she'd been having the stitches removed from a serious cut. Since things were relatively slack at this time of year and she'd already been admitted as a patient, the doctor had checked her into the gynecological department as an in-patient. She was the healthiest-looking sick person Polly had ever encountered and she beamed a happy smile at everyone in the ward as she dumped her shabby knapsack on the allocated bed as if she were in a youth hostel and helped herself to tea from the trolley.

"G'day," she said, strolling over to talk to Beth. "Sally Brown. This looks like fun. How're you doing, mate?"

Actually, it did look all right to Sally, better than she had expected. Clean white walls with big, bright windows, only six beds, and a bustle of busy nurses always on the trot, fetching and carrying and generally making things hum. All right for a few days' break and all with the compliments of the wonderful NHS. Sally wasn't complaining. She intended to make the best of it and it certainly beat having to work.

The empty bed in the corner was obviously in use and

at six o'clock two porters wheeled the incumbent back from theater and the nurses closed the curtains while they rolled her off the trolley and back into the bed. She looked a sad little thing when they opened the curtains again, lying there on the starched white sheet, as thin as a ferret with a chalk-white face. She had beautiful hair, even though it was scraped back off her face beneath a hospital cap, for hygiene's sake. But her face was thin and under-nourished, with a beaky nose. She was American, apparently, and had collapsed on a railway station with a burst appendix.

Good God, thought Beth, watching her from across the room. *It's that funny little photographer friend of Gus's. The one that's got the hots for him. How amazing! Wait till Imogen comes in, she'll bust a gut. Better warn Gus to duck.*

Then Beth realized it couldn't have been fun, and on New Year's Eve, too. When she'd revived a bit, she'd go across and talk to her. They were all in this together, after all, and Georgy could probably use a friendly face. When Georgy did finally come round, though, Sally got there first.

"Hi, there," she said, plonking herself amiably on the foot of the bed. "How's it going? You look real crook. Anything I can do?"

Her voice was warm and friendly, as honeyed as the hair that cascaded over her shoulders, and Beth felt all the better just for watching her. The American stared at Sally for a moment, as if trying to gather her wits, and the saucer in her hand shook so much she had to put it down.

"I feel ghastly," she complained. "Like I want to throw up all the time. And the nightmare I had while I was under—real spooky, real bad."

All of a sudden her pinched white face puckered up and she began to cry. She hadn't noticed Beth watching from across the room. Sally moved impulsively closer and cradled her head on her denimed shoulder. Despite urgings from the nurses, she had not yet changed out of her street clothes.

"Hush now, it can't be that bad. You've been through the worst, it'll all be better now."

Georgy fumbled for a tissue and blew her nose loudly. Crying had not improved her looks, but her eyes, now they were open, were truly beautiful.

"It's not the operation. You don't understand."

She began to bawl, her mouth open like a child's showing her tonsils, tears dribbling down her chin.

"What, then?"

Sally bent to listen, full of compassion, drawing her close. What a nice person, thought Beth, totally absorbed in the touching little scene. The nurse, Polly, at the other end of the ward, paused in what she was doing, afraid she was going to lose control completely. But the other girl seemed more than able to cope.

"Tell me, what is it?"

"He's . . . it's . . ." She almost choked in her grief. "It's just too awful. I can't tell you. I just don't want to go on living."

"Come on now, it can't be that bad."

"It is. It's worse."

Oh Lord, thought Beth, vanishing into her book.

Chapter Thirteen

They took the sad woman down to surgery at five-thirty, and the whole ward watched her go. Two porters came and gently rolled her onto a trolley, fragile in her white hospital gown, her hair scraped back beneath a gauze cap.

"Poor thing, she looked dead scared," said Beth, comfortable now in her narrow bed, propped up against the pillows with Imogen's teddy bear and making the best of it. One finger marked her place in Noel Coward's *Diaries* and her reading glasses were sliding down her nose.

"I hope it's nothing serious. She looked awful when she first came in."

"I rather think I know her," contributed the dark-haired beauty in the next bed, worriedly working at her nails with an emery board.

Beth turned to her; this was her chance. They had not really spoken till now and she was dying to find out more about this mysterious woman who looked as if she'd got off at the wrong floor.

"She's the receptionist at the vet's," the woman went on. "At least, I think she is. Quite honestly, she looks so sick I can't be sure."

Beth took a good long look at her while her head was bent over her nails. She was stylish and elegant and obviously not happy here, though she didn't look as though she were particularly ill. She was a year or two older than Beth but in splendid shape. Her negligee was definitely Paris while the hair and nails shrieked Bond Street. How interesting, Beth thought, a first-class passenger traveling steerage. Probably down on her luck, poor thing, and finding it hard to adjust. At least Beth had never had that problem. What you saw was what you got; she was only glad she had bothered to keep up buying her stamps.

Sally Brown was still up and about and dressed, though the nurse had asked her more than once to settle down and get into bed. She came over now and plonked herself at the foot of Beth's bed.

"Hi there, how's it going?" She was Australian or something. She was brown and glowing and looked the picture of health and the smile was infectious. Beth closed her book and settled down for a good old gossip. This was more like it. She'd come here for a rest-cure herself and intended to enjoy every minute of it. She thought of poor, doleful Deirdre, valiantly holding the fort back home, and her feeling of well-being increased. Now she came to think of it, it was ages since she'd last had a break. The punters would just have to manage without her for a while. She meant to make the most of it here, at least while she still felt well enough. Sally was a welcome diversion.

"We were just discussing old Flossy over there, going off to surgery looking like death. This lady," indicating Vivienne, "says she knows her."

"Well, I'm not quite sure," said Vivienne nervously, working on her cuticles now and clearly getting rattled. She wished they'd leave her alone and not try to include her in their mindless conversation. The whole point of being here at all was to keep it private. She wanted to stay anonymous and not get involved with these two busybodies, no matter how nice they seemed.

"Last week when I saw her she seemed quite well, but now she looks as though she's falling apart," Vivienne explained. With luck they'd grow tired of the topic and she'd be left in peace.

Sally agreed. "Looked pretty crook to me. Maybe that's why she's in here."

Beth laughed. "So what are you doing here, may I ask? You look as fit as a flea to me. Skiving off work, I bet."

Beth liked this young woman instinctively. She was warm and cheerful and lacking in malice. That was the thing with these Antipodeans, they were certainly full of get-up-and-go.

"Oh, no reason, really," Sally laughed. "I came in for an emergency"—she showed Beth her hand, now covered with a layer of sticking plaster—"and thought I'd get myself sorted out while I was passing through because they say your health service is so good."

"And so inexpensive?"

"That too." Sally grinned beguilingly, not at all fazed. Beth laughed. Sally might be freeloading but at least she was straight about it. Not like the buttoned-up creature next door who had now drawn the sheet up to her chin and was hiding behind the latest issue of *Tatler*. Beth leaned across the narrow gap between their beds and patted her arm.

"Come on, now," she said softly, "we're all in the same boat. Tell us about yourself. What's your problem and why are you here?"

Sally leaned closer too, keen to hear every detail, but Vivienne was not in the mood. She wished they'd go away and leave her alone. Suddenly she longed for the privacy of the London Clinic or the Princess Grace. If she wasn't very careful, her business would soon be all over the hospital and her secrecy blown.

"It's nothing serious," she said stiffly. "Just a little tidying up and I'll be out of here."

And at that moment the anesthetist arrived for a consultation and drew the curtains around her bed.

"Saved by the bell," said Sally, helping herself to Beth's grapes.

They came to fetch Vivienne at seven. She looked terrified, poor thing, so Beth pushed back the covers and moved over to sit on her bed.

"Please don't worry," she urged her. "I'm told there's really nothing to it and I know you'll feel heaps better once it's over."

Vivienne stared back with baleful eyes. They had changed her out of her expensive finery and into a hospital gown and the nurse was hovering ready with her premed injection. Even wearing a hospital cap she looked remarkable. Her bone structure was flawless and her unmade-up skin like that of a twenty-year-old. Beth was impressed.

"You look absolutely stunning," she said impetuously. "Are you an actress or something? Should I be asking for your autograph?"

Vivienne smiled wanly. She was attracted to this warm and genuine stranger, and in other circumstances would have liked her as a friend. She was the sort you could rely on, definitely not one to stab you in the back.

"Just a woman of little importance," she said softly. "A woman without a name."

Polly drove Beth back to her own bed—they were an unruly lot, these patients—and closed the curtains to allow Vivienne a bit of privacy. Beth returned to her book but she was thinking. She felt real sympathy for the lonely beauty in the next bed. Entering an operating theater could not be fun, though up till this moment, she had not allowed herself to dwell upon it. Now she did. Like going to the Tower of London to have your head chopped off, without a friend beside you to hold your hand and let you know you were loved. This beautiful woman must have a husband or lover. Where was he? What sort of man let his wife go through an ordeal like this all alone? She didn't even have flowers beside her bed.

"Are you all right over there?" called Beth, cuddling her daughter's teddy bear. After a short pause a soft voice replied:

"Yes, thank you. I'm feeling fine."

"Who is she, anyhow?" asked Beth as they watched the porters wheel Vivienne away. "She looks and acts like something out of Hollywood yet she's quite shy and retiring."

"Greta Garbo maybe?"

Sally was still up and about although the nurses had now bullied her out of her jeans and cowboy boots and into a voluminous dress shirt, filched from Jeremy's wardrobe while he was out of town. Only Sam knew where she was and she had let him into the secret solely to stop them from going ape if she went missing without an alibi. On the strictest instructions, mind, that he was not to tell the others, and that no one—that meant NO ONE—was even to think about visiting, upon pain of death. They were like that, her boys, and although at times she found their protectiveness sweet, on the whole it irritated her. Why couldn't they leave her alone? The last thing she needed was an audience when there was nothing really wrong and it was her business anyhow. She imagined all the questions if they ever found out, and shuddered.

She was now at the foot of Vivienne's empty bed, studying her chart.

"Mrs. Vivienne Nugent," she read out. "Age, forty-three. Weight . . ."

"Sally!" shrieked Georgy, who was much recovered, from the other end of the room. "That's AWFUL. You should never, ever do that. Nurse, turn my chart over immediately. I can't have her snooping on me too."

Everyone laughed, except Beth.

Vivienne Nugent—whoever would have thought it? Oliver's wife. What a small world, to be sure. First Georgy, now her. The one positive thing in a potentially explosive situation was that Oliver was away and not likely to visit. And how come she was in here while he was whooping it up in

Singapore? What, come to think of it, was she doing here at all? With money like that, she should have been in the London Clinic at the very least, even in a private nursing home in Lausanne.

Beth was aroused from her reverie by whoops of laughter from Georgy's cubicle where Sally was making herself very much at home, helping herself to Georgy's chocolates and examining the few possessions she had ranged along the top of her bedside cabinet. She was holding a silver-framed photograph and staring at it intently.

"Speaking of film stars, who's this guy? He looks dead familiar. Where have I seen him before?"

"Nowhere. That's my father. He lives in southern California."

Sally wrinkled her pretty nose.

"Where I've not yet been. But I could swear I've seen him before. You're certain he's not in the movies? Or television, perhaps?"

Georgy was sure. But she was flattered.

"Positive, not a chance. He's a psychologist. Nothing particularly glamorous about that."

"Oh," said Sally, "how interesting. Mine was a lawyer."

Beth strolled over to join them. Georgy had recognized her immediately, of course, but up till now had been in no state for socializing.

"Hi," she said, and took the photograph out of Sally's hands. "Mmm, he's certainly gorgeous. Will he be visiting you while you're here . . . I hope."

" 'Fraid not. He's tied up in court on a major murder case and hardly even has time to see his wife."

"Shame. Just my luck. For one glorious moment I thought I'd hit the jackpot." Beth gave her a brilliant smile and carefully replaced the photograph. If Georgy was going to be embarrassed at seeing her so soon at such close quarters, she was anxious to clear the air. What went on in Gus's life was no longer her business, but she hoped the younger woman would take care.

Sally was still puzzling, trying to get a fix on the stern, handsome face.

"So he's not married to your mother?"

"Not anymore."

"What happened?"

"Oh, the usual thing." Georgy was growing tense, unwilling to go on with the interrogation. Sally seemed unstoppable, though it was clear to Beth that she was simply bored and meant no harm. "He traded us all in for a younger model. And then a younger model still. You know how it is these days."

She made light of it but was clearly hurting. Beth leaned over and took her hand.

"That must have been tough," she said. "It's hard to lose a father, particularly when you are a child. How old were you?"

"Twelve."

"That's the age my daughter is now, only her dad left us when she was just a baby so she's sort of grown up accepting it. And so many kids these days are from one-parent families that it's becoming the norm. My kid's got the best of it, or so she says. Two doting parents who vie with each other to spoil her rotten."

Sally, unusually for her, had sunk into a brooding silence.

"What about you, Sal?" asked Beth. "Do you have family?"

There was a pause.

"No," she said. "Not now. Not a one, thank Christ, and that's the way I like it!" The words were lighthearted but there was real emphasis in the tone. "Travel light and travel fast, that's my motto."

Beth laughed and wandered back to her own bed. She very much liked the wild colonial who went through life with a laugh and a song and looked remarkably chirpy for someone on the eve of surgery. Whatever her problem was, she was clearly not going to discuss it, and that, so far as Beth was concerned, was her own business. Good for her. She admired that sort of spirit.

Once they were out of this hellhole she hoped they'd all keep in touch. Vivienne might prove to be a problem but she liked the other two. Especially Sally.

Catherine was slowly coming round though she did look unnaturally pale. She lay silently in her corner bed, as still and straight as a corpse, and responded only faintly to the sympathetic inquiries from the other inmates. In the afternoon, Duncan Ross was due to visit her and Polly helped Catherine sit up against a pile of fluffed-up pillows. She combed Catherine's fine, straight hair and tied it back with a ribbon, then searched through her possessions to see if she could find a lipstick and some blusher. Catherine gave a watery smile and waved her away.

"Don't bother. It doesn't matter."

"Don't you want to look your best? A bit of color might help to brighten you up."

"Don't worry. He's not that sort of a friend."

When Duncan arrived every eye in the ward was on him. No one else had had visitors yet. Vivienne was still down in the theater so was spared the embarrassment of his discovering her guilty secret. Duncan wore jeans and a big white sweater and carried a great armful of lilies, which he dropped onto the foot of Catherine's bed.

Now that's *pretty tasty,* thought Beth, seeing him for the first time and gazing approvingly over the edge of her book.

Sitting up, with her hair brushed, Catherine was looking altogether healthier, and Duncan gave her a bear hug and a kiss on the forehead.

"How's it going today, old love? Feeling any better?"

He picked up a chair from the other side of the ward and swung himself astride it as he spoke. He'd tried to get the old lady to come but she said she could never abide hospitals. *Germ-ridden places,* she said. Dangerous for her voice.

Catherine's own voice was so faint the others couldn't

hear what she was saying, but Sally pulled off her earphones for a closer inspection. There was something about this woman, returning Lazarus-like to life after all these days, like a piece of frozen veal straight out of the freezer, that was vaguely familiar, though she could swear she had never seen her before.

Only when Duncan was leaving did the wires begin to connect. His powerful Australian voice filled the room with his cheery good-byes and one of the little locked doors in Sally's brain flew open.

Jesus Christ, she said to herself, diving for safety under the covers. *It's that anemic Pommy nurse from Sydney.*

Who ever would have thought it? After all these years.

Addison was just finishing his ward round and this time he did have students in tow. He'd sort them out, finish here, and then, if he was quick, could still make it down to Bucks for a late lunch and perhaps a game of backgammon. Then he'd join Phoebe and the boys for the rest of the week before they went back to school. He gathered together his medical notes and led the way out of the gyn ward and along the corridor to his private consulting room, the students following in his wake like baby ducks.

Once there, he wasted no time. He was weary of the inside of hospitals and often wished he need never see one again. All those sick people, many without hope, each awaiting his pronouncement and sometimes a miracle to make them recover. But miracles were not that commonplace. Occasionally even Addison Harvey—senior consultant in gynecology—had to let them down. He'd learned that a long time ago, when he was not much older than this bunch of pimply young hopefuls. Looking at their eager faces, with the dark circles under their eyes caused by too little sleep, he remembered as clearly as if it were yesterday. But barren remembering did no one any good; they were here for a purpose, and that was to learn. He would give them what he could and very soon they would be out there on their own. Facing up to life, finding out about the real world, watching their dreams, their ideals, crumble into chalk before their eyes.

He couldn't warn them, and anyway why would they listen? Once he too had been an idealist with the arrogant belief that he could change the world. Now he saw only too clearly that in the eyes of this new generation of bright young doctors he was nothing more than just another overpaid old fart gone soft with age.

He switched on the overhead light box and slotted a couple of X-rays onto it for easy viewing by the whole group. The students gathered round. Diagnosis, they had been taught, was vital to this profession they were hoping to enter, and Addison Harvey was legendary for his intuition and accuracy, one of the best doctors in the country. Tuition of this caliber was not easily come by and each one of them fervently hoped one day to follow in the consultant's revered footsteps.

The X-rays were clear to see but Harvey was still absorbed in the case notes. A distant memory was nagging at the back of his mind, and had been for some days now, but he shoved it away impatiently, keen to get on with the business in hand. Five new patients, most of them straightforward, a useful sampling for this group of students. But one case stood out, something he had never encountered before, not outside a textbook.

"Well, I'll be blowed," he muttered, looking up from the notes in his hand to peer more closely at the X-ray on the right.

"She's not going to make it, is she, sir?" asked one of the students, close beside him.

Harvey glanced at the left-hand X-ray without a lot of interest.

"Probably not. But it's this other one that is particularly intriguing. Gather around all of you and take a look at that."

Part
Three

Part
Three

Chapter Fourteen

The figure on the doorstep was little more than an outline, silhouetted against the brilliance of the afternoon sun.

"You don't remember me, do you?"

She squinted into the glare but her eyes were not as good as they had been; how embarrassing. She fumbled round her neck for her glasses but had left them in the other room.

"I'm afraid I can't quite see you. Come a little closer, will you, so that I can take a proper look."

For a moment the stranger paused, then stepped into the porch and stood beside her on the mat.

"Come inside. It's hot out here and I'm sure you'd like to get into the shade."

She led the way along the passage into the comfortable room at the rear, overflowing with newspapers and books and a pile of legal textbooks she was in the process of using, all the time trying to gather her scattered wits. After a long, hard day in court, following an exhausting weekend with the grandchildren, all she longed to do was take off her shoes and settle down with a nice cup of tea and the evening paper before she started again and had to change for dinner at the club.

Now who on earth could this be? Perhaps the voice would provide a clue.

"There's no real reason why you should remember."

It was a soft voice, well modulated, and rather pleasant.

"It was, after all, a long time ago, and I'm sure more important things have happened in your life since then—even if they haven't in mine."

"Would you like a cup of tea?" The all-time panacea. "Sit down over there and take the weight off your feet."

She bustled into the tiny kitchen, still wondering, but her mind remained a blank. Oh dear. They'd warned her about this, her daughters, when they joked and told her she was overworking and detailed the early symptoms of Alzheimer's; maybe there was more truth in it than she had realized. She made the tea, then opened the cake tin on the side and levered her daughter's fresh walnut cake onto a silver platter. No harm in being hospitable even if her memory was no great shakes. She piled cups and saucers onto a tray, stuck a knife on the side of the platter, and carried the whole lot back into the room where the stranger was standing, examining the photographs of the boys.

The smile was bright. "We're talking sixteen years here. Long before these little fellows were even thought of. Almost a generation ago."

In the shady room, without the light in her eyes, an image was definitely beginning to form, the echo of a face long-forgotten, once part of every moment of her waking and nighttime consciousness.

"You said I was beyond redemption."

Now she remembered. The laugh had not changed. Transfixed with shock, she poured the tea and handed her visitor a cup.

"Cake?" She indicated the platter but the visitor was already holding the knife.

"I knew you'd remember, once you'd had a few minutes to think about it. Sixteen years is a long time, especially when there's nothing else going on in your life. You've had it all"—indicating the pleasant room, the framed pho-

tographs on the mantelpiece of her daughters and their sons—"and now it's my turn.

"My plan is to make up for all the life I have missed," said the stranger pleasantly, still playing with the knife. "But first I'm here to make sure you never, ever forget me again. That's only fair, don't you think?"

That smile. However could she have forgotten the smile?

Chapter Fifteen

Beth awoke slowly to the sound of howling wind and the rattle of hailstones against the windowpanes. One of the cozy things about this house, she thought as she snuggled deeper into the duvet, was the illusion it gave her of living in a lighthouse. The scream as the gust forced itself round the eaves and down the chimneys was positively banshee-like. Or, Beth thought, like a witch on a broomstick circling the house, trying to get in. *Nice,* she thought, snuggling deeper, then, *Christ, whatever time is it?* as she jerked awake in a reflex of panic. She reached across and switched on the bedside radio, in time to catch the end of the weather report. Blustery showers and snow flurries, with gale warnings and reports of canceled ferries and airports in chaos.

Then she remembered. It was Good Friday and the start of a four-day holiday weekend with customary British Easter weather. The rattle of hailstones stirred her again so she shuffled out of bed and across the room to the bathroom, where she splashed cold water on her face and brushed her hair, before pulling on a wrap and descending to the kitchen, warm and welcoming from the quietly slumbering Aga.

"Gone to live with Dad. Don't wait up" read a note on the table, propped up against a jam jar of freesias. Beth

scratched her head and filled the kettle, then set about putting together the rough rudiments of breakfast.

"April Fool!" screeched a human banshee, dodging out from behind the pantry door to give her a mammoth hug. "Were you scared? Did you think I'd really gone?"

Imogen, a crumpled fawn in blue and white striped boy's pajamas, looked enchanting, even with her long hair unbrushed and that awful steel brace which detracted not at all from her prettiness.

"Some chance," Beth grunted as she filled a pan with water then set it on the stove to boil eggs. Good Friday, and for once she did not have to race around getting her act in order, as for the next four days, the world—or at any rate London—would be closed.

"What do you want to do today, hon?" she asked, smoothing the silky head as she placed the eggs on the table. Then she slid open the knife drawer and extracted a chocolate bunny holding a foil-wrapped basket in one paw.

"Correctly you shouldn't really have this till Sunday," she said. "But what the hell. Who's to know?"

And at least I'm one ahead of the Old Man, she thought with satisfaction, as she settled down with a cup of black coffee to read the paper, knowing only too well how profligate Gus was inclined to be, especially where his only child was concerned. Love and guilt, those were his motivations. Imogen, crunching a piece of toast and marmalade, was scanning the columns of the *Radio Times*.

"*The Sound of Music*'s on at ten to three. Can we watch it?"

"What, again? You must have seen it thirteen times already."

"Oh, go on, Mum, you know you love it. Christopher Plummer with those eyes and the moment they get together in the garden . . ."

Beth smiled and returned to her paper. It certainly beat video nasties, that was for sure, and those interminable cartoons. And Imogen was right, she did fancy those stern, high-principled types rather than the sexually ambivalent morons so popular these days, with their earrings and shoulder-length hair and no hint of real *cojones* between the lot of them.

I may be old-fashioned, she reflected, *but give me Clark Gable or Gary Cooper any day.*

The main thing was, it was a holiday and they should spend it together.

The doorbell rang as Beth was upstairs, dressing.

"Get it," she shouted. "It'll be Sally."

But it was Georgy, back unexpectedly early from New York, wearing a new suede jacket and clutching an armful of presents.

"What a surprise," said Beth, kissing her and whisking the honey suede to safety beyond the hazards of the kitchen. Georgy placed a camellia in full flower, a bottle of Moët & Chandon, and a mammoth box of Belgian chocolates on the kitchen table and sank into a chair. That was typical of her New York largesse; she always overdid it, but Beth couldn't stop her. She gave a sideways glance at the three place settings which Beth caught as she came back into the room.

"He's not coming today," she volunteered, pouring Marks & Spencer plonk into two glasses. "He's gone to some antiques do in the West Country and won't be back till Sunday. Why don't you join us? It's just us and Sally. The more the merrier."

A truly wonderful aroma was issuing from the Aga; Georgy needed no further encouragement.

"What is it, Mum?" asked Imogen idly, chair tilted back against the stove, still flicking through the listings magazine.

"*Lapin à la moutarde,*" said Beth after a pause, knowing her daughter's sensibility. "Rabbit to you."

"Yuk!" said Imogen on cue, pulling a face, but Beth just laughed and plonked herself down next to Georgy.

"You can't expect to live in the adult world," she said,

"without getting over your childish squeamishness. Rabbit is every bit as nice as chicken and you wouldn't know the difference if I didn't tell you. Now let's hear about New York. How was the wedding?"

Georgy looked even thinner and her hair had been properly trimmed, which suited her. On one slender wrist she wore a new watch, gold with a chain bracelet lightly dusted with diamonds. She caught Beth looking at it.

"My father gave me this," she said defensively, "as a sort of consolation prize, I suppose."

She tried to make a joke of it but it didn't work. Beth saw the pain etched into her eyes and longed to give her a hug, but all she did was simply refill their glasses. No point in treating Georgy like a child; she was twenty-six and deep down as tough as old boots.

"The wedding," said Georgy as if she had forgotten. "Ah yes, The Wedding."

An image arose before her of Myra, looking not a day over thirty-nine in a short, puff-skirted dress in primrose silk with pearls and an eye-length veil, and most nauseating of all, that awful old lech, Aaron Gottlieb from the temple, supporting her elbow with his liver-spotted hand and dancing attendance like a star-struck suitor. And Risa, sleek and serene now with her husband, her Henri Bendel suit, and the telltale thickening about her waist that kept her one up on her baby sister.

And Lois, the bride, still not much more than a kid, translucent in loose cream shantung with color-coordinated rosebuds woven into her long, dark hair. They were off to live in Israel once the groom had completed his internship. The cup of the Kirsch family was certainly running over in the happiness stakes.

Dad was there too, shadowed by Sylvia, snatching time from his endless jetting between capitals to give away another daughter; playing the genial host and father of the bride with a word and a shoulder squeeze for everyone, yet finding time for scarcely more than a few private words with his firstborn. The one he'd always called his Little Princess, who needed him most but could not find the words to tell him.

"It was okay. What can I tell you? I came back early because there wasn't a lot to do once it was over and I'm really getting to hate that city. Yes, I am. It's noisy and dirty and you can't walk on the street anymore for fear of being knifed. This is where I belong now. This is my spiritual home."

Her glance embraced the warm, untidy kitchen with its battered sofa and patchwork cushions and a ridiculous old stuffed rabbit of Imogen's propped defiantly in the wickerwork log basket next to the stove. Beth watched her and understood. It was not this house specifically, it was London. From this kitchen there was a clear view through the rain-battered willows of the church across the road, from which worshipers were now pouring. The white wicket gate, immortalized by Richard Brooke, hung skewwhiff, a victim of the storm, but it was real and somehow solid and comforting. *I'll have to get that fixed,* thought Beth idly, *next time Gus or one of the others comes by.*

It was odd how fate had seen fit to throw them randomly together—Georgy and Beth, Beth and Vivienne—apparent strangers yet with lives that already touched. Spooky, as Imogen would say, a case of synchronicity if ever there was one. Arthur Koestler would have been fascinated. She hadn't particularly warmed to Georgy at first but she did recognize pain and need when she saw them and had enough love in her own life to be able to spread it around. Friends told her she was a soft touch, but where was the harm in that? All she had she'd achieved herself—home and career and her marvelous friendships—and what went around came around. That surely was what life was about.

"Also," continued Georgy, lighting another fag, "I have this yoga spread to do for *Living* and I really need to get down to it."

Yeah, yeah, thought Beth as the doorbell rang again. This time it really was Sally.

The last gust of hail had caught her, and her hair was bedraggled and her nose bright red, but she looked, as always, quite delicious, a ray of sunshine in a wet and windy world. She beamed as she unwound her long woolen scarf and unloaded into Beth's arms a mass of daffodils and tulips, beaded with damp and looking slightly the worse for wear.

"I walked across the park," she explained, removing her soggy felt beret and lobbing it into the log basket. "This was all I could get you. Happy Easter!"

There was a moment of stunned silence.

"You mean . . . ?"

"I would have got you cherry blossom," she went on serenely, "only I couldn't quite reach it. The Household Cavalry were exercising there and I asked one of them if I could climb up on his horse but the sergeant was watching so he couldn't oblige."

Sally pulled off her dreadful boots, revealing mismatched socks with holes in them, and settled down comfortably to warm her toes at the stove. She chuckled and accepted a glass of wine from Beth.

"You stole them!" Georgy didn't approve of Sally. A workaholic herself, she couldn't abide skivers, and the irritating thing about Sally was that she appeared to waltz through life with the minimum of effort yet always landed on her feet. But Sally had Georgy's number, had right from the first encounter.

"No," she said. "I picked them for Beth. As an Easter present, to make her happy. Do you have a problem with that?"

"They're there for everyone to enjoy. Not to be vandalized."

"Well, no one's in the park today apart from the Household Cavalry, and we're enjoying them now, so where's the harm? And by tomorrow they'll probably be dead."

"Won't we all!"

Beth grinned. Sally was priceless and she loved her for it. After all these weeks Georgy still hadn't learned not to tangle with her. It was a pity really. Georgy was too much up her own arse ever to appreciate Sally's warmth and generosity of spirit. Sometimes she caught Georgy watching her with bitterness and envy, yet Georgy had been given so much right from the start while Sally had nothing.

Beth topped up their glasses, then lifted the lid of the steaming casserole. "Imogen wants to watch that dreadful Julie Andrews film," she said.

They lazed around all afternoon, drinking wine, swapping stories, generally hanging out together. The film was over, the dishes stacked, and Imogen had withdrawn upstairs to play with her Gameboy. They ought really to go for a walk but outside it was still pelting down, so they talked about the hospital which had brought them together, and enjoyed renewing the camaraderie of their shared ten days' incarceration. *One of the great things about any sort of institutionalization,* thought Beth, *is that it brings people down to the same level.*

Which brought them naturally to Vivienne, but not in any detail since none of them really knew her and Beth was not about to spill the beans about her own extraordinary secret connection with the uptight woman. Sally found her posh and Georgy thought her snobbish. That just about summed her up, thought Beth.

"Do you ever see old Whojamaflip?" asked Sally.

"Who dat?" asked Beth.

"You know, the pale one, the one who works for the vet. She looked a bit like death warmed up even when she left. I wonder what happened to her."

"Don't know," said Beth. "She's not really my type but I

agree she looked fairly grim. What was she in for, anyway?"

Sally thought.

"Something gynecological," she ventured. "Something Down There."

They all laughed, even Georgy.

"Twit, that was true of all of us."

"Yeah, but we seem to have come out of it better than her. That's all I meant. She looked pretty sick."

"She lives with her mother," announced Georgy meaningfully, "and, believe me, that's often all it takes."

"Maybe we should have a reunion."

"You mean of the old lags?"

"Would we recognize each other with our clothes on?"

"And without our urine bags?"

"Should we include Polly?"

"And Mr. Harvey maybe? He of the grim mouth and come-to-bed eyes."

"Sally!" they chorused. "You mean you fancied him?"

"Yeah, well, why not? He's only human, isn't he? And the things he must have seen in his job . . ."

They all screeched with laughter.

"Talk about coals to Newcastle!"

"Did you hear the one about the gynecologist looking in the pet-shop window . . ."

The telephone rang somewhere offstage. Beth took it in the bedroom. It was Oliver.

"Sweetie! What are you doing home? On Good Friday too?"

"I got back early, managed to get a cancellation. Any chance of dinner? Why don't I pick you up at six-thirty and we'll grab an early meal at Bibendum."

Beth hesitated, hearing the laughter from below.

"Better not, I've got people here. Why don't I meet you there at seven. But what are you going to say to your wife?"

"No problem. She thinks I'm still in Strasbourg. And what the heart doesn't know . . ."

Later, lying in a steaming bath, Beth thought about Oliver and tried not to linger on the sad-eyed wife as she got herself ready for an evening of sin. Vivienne Nugent was not her problem; any cracks in the marriage had been there long before Oliver's path crossed Beth's. Beth was a stalwart believer in sisterhood and fiercely opposed to hurting another woman if it could be avoided, but this case was different and absolutely none of her business. She felt she was doing her bit for mankind by bringing some happiness into Oliver's sterile life.

She giggled to herself and sank under the suds. Well, that was her story and she was sticking to it.

Chapter Sixteen

At least there was no visible scar, for that much she could be thankful. Vivienne lay on her back on the pine slats of the sauna and squinted along her flat stomach toward her neat, pedicured feet with their vermilion-tipped toes. Not that Oliver ever looked at her these days, certainly not without clothes on. They were like two strangers sharing a hotel suite, obliged to acknowledge the other's presence only when they happened to pass in a doorway. So much for Happy Ever Afters and the fairy-tale marriage. Even today, Good Friday, he was off somewhere in Europe, mindless of the long weekend and the fact that this was supposed to be a family occasion. Perhaps if they'd had a family, things would be different, but somehow she doubted it, and that was a train of thought she no longer cared to follow.

The sweat was running down her well-toned body, so Vivienne gave it another couple of minutes then ducked under a freezing shower and rubbed herself down. Considering all she had been through in the past few months, she did look good, she had to admit it. Small, neat breasts, narrow hips, trim legs, and smooth ivory skin—Vivienne did not believe in fake tans, found them aging. She toweled off her hair in front of the full-length mirror and took careful stock of herself. As good now, in some ways, as she had been the day she married. Greater poise, better carriage, a flatter stomach, and sleeker thighs. She had Mr. Armenian's friend with the magic scalpel to thank for that. Yet where had it all gotten her? she might well ask.

Home alone at Easter, with only the cats for company and a frozen dinner waiting in the fridge ready to be popped into the microwave. Even Dorabella had more social life than she did, plus a noisy, overpowering set of relatives who ran through Vivienne's kitchen quarters like a creeping weed, threatening her composure with their life and laughter.

She slipped into leggings and a T-shirt and did her daily stint on the exercise bike, grunting with exertion yet determined to complete the full fifteen minutes before she quit. Andy, her trainer, would be back on Tuesday, and she'd hate him to think she had been slacking and was not following to the letter the rigorous exercise program he had created for her. Vivienne was not a quitter, it was simply not part of her nature.

Though where on earth it was all leading, she really didn't know. Andy had firm brown skin and thighs like a footballer's under the sleek Lycra of his exercise suit. Lying in the sauna thinking about him always made her randy, though she knew it was ridiculous. He must be all of twenty-four yet Vivienne was ashamed to admit she lusted after him, even found his image invading her dreams. What wouldn't she give at this moment to have him here, to smell his sweat and feel those firm thighs clamped about her own, pounding and hurting, giving her what she so much missed? A shiver of anticipation ran right through her and she felt the familiar ache in the pit of her stomach. Well, that proved one thing, blessing or not; she had certainly not lost her libido. All she needed, to be back on the tracks again, was the love of a good man. The sad irony was that she had married the only man she had ever really wanted, and where had it gotten her?

Back in the bedroom Vivienne wandered around disconsolately, fiddling with things on her dressing table, watching the unseasonal hail drive past the casement windows. The master bedroom of this opulent house came equipped with twin dressing rooms and separate bathrooms, so Vivienne had plenty of room to play. Her own dressing room was fitted with wall-to-wall walk-in closets packed with clothes and fashion accessories, while the bathroom cabinets held enough cosmetics to last her a lifetime and make redundant her basic compulsion to shop. The bedroom held a television, a video, and a Bang & Olufsen sound system, as well as a small fridge next to the bed stocked with chocolate pecan ice cream, one of Vivienne's occasional cravings, and Evian in case either of them felt thirsty in the night. Vivienne and Oliver had every conceivable luxury in this fun palace they had created. It lacked only the one thing she most craved: intimacy.

She wandered into Oliver's dressing room and riffled through his ranks of Savile Row suits. Oliver was tidy by nature and this private domain would have made any army batman proud. Color-coordinated shirts and ties were neatly filed alongside the suits, and his handmade shoes were lined up beneath them, each on a pair of shoe trees to keep them in shape. What a dandy he was, this husband of hers, as fastidious and vain in his private way as she was in hers. They had so much in common, so much they could have shared, yet these days she felt she hardly knew him at all.

What was he doing, for instance, in Strasbourg on bank business when he should have been home with his wife on a day both Church and State had long decreed a holiday? Were his colleagues as conscientious? she wondered. What about the ones with children, surely they were not expected to put bank business first? Why was it always Oliver who volunteered to carry the company flag as if he had nothing of his own worth staying home for? Well, maybe that was it.

They hadn't planned not to have children, it had simply happened that way. When they first got married they were so much in love that all they wanted was to be together—alone. Their first home was a sweet little mews house in Chelsea, all bottle-glass windows and hanging flower baskets and scarcely room for anything but the two of them. Which suited them just fine since they were tired of the social scene and wanted to play at house without having to include the world as spectators. They ate in restaurants, they partied a little, they did the social things like Ascot and Glyndebourne, but mainly they stayed at home in bed and made love as though it were going out of fashion.

Oliver was ten years older than Vivienne and had been around quite a bit, but he had never loved anyone as much as he loved her, and he couldn't get enough of her. Each morning he tore himself from her side to drive to his office in the City, then raced back as soon as he could to leap back into her bed. He was totally besotted and a baby would have been an intruder. Besides, there was heaps of time. Starting a family meant settling down, and the Nugents were still far too frivolous for that.

Time went by and, with a little help from his father-in-law, Oliver grew more successful as a fashionable stockbroker in the fast lane, notching up success after success. Then he received an offer he could not ignore from the Hong Kong and Shanghai Bank and reluctantly traded in market mobility for the greater rewards of solidity, respectability, and wealth. They moved from Chelsea to this Victorian villa in The Boltons, which had rooms enough for any number of nannies or whatever and a whole floor that would convert very nicely into nursery and playroom.

Vivienne had always had a flair for design and now she threw herself into creating the home of her dreams. The house was vast, with so many rooms whole armies of nannies and their support teams could have been lost in it. When she had finished the drawing room, the dining room, and the spectacular conservatory, Vivienne and her squad of decorators moved upward to the bedroom floors. She had set aside the largest suite on the second floor as a future nursery for their baby, whenever it came along.

Then fun had beckoned and they were off to Argentina for the polo season, and somehow they simply never got round to it. It was always something they could talk about tomorrow. Money had never been a problem and Vivienne was in tip-top health. These days it was marvelous what modern medicine could achieve and people were having babies well into their forties and beyond. The truth, which she hated to admit even to herself, was that Vivienne had been scared of ruining her figure. And now it was too late. Her selfishness had deprived her of her child, a companion who could have been here now, helping to fill these lonely hours when the whole of London except her was out enjoying itself.

Time for a drink, not that Vivienne waited anymore for the sun to be over the yardarm. She wandered down to the kitchen for ice and poured herself a massive Bloody Mary, then took it and the cats back upstairs to the bedroom. This was where she spent most of her time these days, more welcoming than the sterility of the reception rooms below. Before her stretched an entire day with nothing at all to do. There was nothing on the television, just some slushy musical she'd seen a million times before, full of nuns and things, and she simply hadn't the energy to go through her extensive video collection.

What she craved for more than anything was human company, but where did you find it on a holiday weekend when your husband was away? There was always church, but she couldn't be bothered and besides, by now the service would already be under way. What did single people do at times like this? With a sudden nostalgia, Vivienne thought back to her stay in the hospital—at the time such a nightmare—and realized she was missing the easy to-and-fro of shared conversations and jokes. She missed the other women; it was an eye-opener that stunned her.

She looked at Ferdinand and Isabella, lying together under the radiator, content in each other's company. Even they had each other, while she had no one. But that gave her an idea. Catherine Palmer was not the brightest of company but she was reliable, and since their shared experience at St. Anthony's they had struck up a sort of friendship.

I bet she's not doing anything, thought Vivienne, as she leafed through her address book. Then, just as she was working up the courage to phone, she remembered her mother. Eleanor Palmer was a legend and they had all been fascinated to discover that Catherine was her daughter. Even in her depleted state, Catherine had raised the energy, once she was through with surgery, to tell them tales of her mother's horrendous doings that had kept them all amused. Oddly enough, they brought out the best in Catherine. When recounting yet another dreadful story, a sparkle would come into her flat eyes and a faint flush to her cheeks that gave life to her passive face and a hint of the prettiness she must once have had. Maybe one day, if they kept in touch, Vivienne would get a chance to meet the old girl and judge for herself. But now was not the time. Not in her current bleak mood.

Thinking of Catherine reminded her of Beth, and there she did feel a slight pang of regret. Beth had seemed so lively and outgoing, so overflowing with life and zest, that Vivienne had instinctively warmed to her and made a secret resolve to turn her into a friend. She admired women who had made their own way in life and built up a successful career without the apparent support, emotional or financial, of any particular man. Yet, Beth had that attentive ex-husband and the rather charming daughter but, from what she had been able to fathom, he was only a part-time parent and didn't even normally live in this country. Beth was all the things Vivienne might once have wanted to be, had life dealt her a different hand. She was gutsy, optimistic, and fun, with a charm so powerful it acted like a magnet to practically everyone around her.

She was not particularly glamorous, though her skin was good, and could do with losing quite a lot of weight. Yet things like that didn't appear to faze Beth in any way. She laughed and joked and told risqué stories that kept the nurses, and the patients too, in fits of laughter. She was also extremely kind. Vivienne still remembered the soft voice from the other side of the cubicle curtain just when, consumed with terror, she thought she was facing her ordeal alone. And the thoughtfulness toward everyone on the ward, and the generosity too, passing around boxes of homemade biscuits whenever her rather dowdy sidekick came to visit. Yes, she was a professional caterer, but that was no reason to be quite so open-handed toward strangers. If she acted like that in the general course of things, she would rapidly go out of business.

No, in Vivienne's book Beth was all right, which was why she still felt hurt and slightly puzzled by the casual way the other woman had appeared to shrug off any suggestion of an ongoing friendship. It was rather odd and Vivienne was still trying to work it out. They had all got on well enough, apart from that spiky American who was always whining, and Beth had definitely given her phone number to both the younger women and probably Catherine too. Yet when it came to saying good-bye to Vivienne she had simply shaken her hand, wished her luck, and looked, if anything, a little embarrassed.

For a fleeting moment, Vivienne wondered if it might be a class thing but then dismissed it. Despite her northern background and the slight trace of Nottingham still in her voice, Beth was far too sensible—and successful—to take any notice of possible class divisions, not in this day and age. She might be a full-time worker, entirely responsible for herself and her kid, but she was not the type to be intimidated by someone just because they had a posher accent and lived at a fancy address. If anything, Beth ought really to have been encouraging Vivienne, as she could have been a source of business with all her rich and influential friends, not to mention a husband in the City with a stratospheric career. In fact, the thought had already occurred to Vivienne as she lay in her hospital bed, and she had derived a quiet satisfaction from all the good connections she could give to Beth, starting with Betty, who was constantly organizing fund-raising lunches for all sorts of charities.

In the end, though, she hadn't had the chance. Amid a

bluster of cheery good-byes, her handsome ex-husband there to carry her case and some of the potted plants that had smothered her part of the ward, Beth had simply waved and vanished from her life. Vivienne did know how to locate her—she was well signposted in the phone book—but felt reluctant to make the connection for fear of being snubbed. Now there was an admission; Vivienne felt quite startled. Never in her life, and certainly not since her marriage to Oliver, had such a thought popped into her mind. As a child, Vivienne had always been the popular one, the one whose birthday parties the whole class wanted to attend. And later, in her dating days, the hordes of suitors that had constantly besieged her flat had ensured a continuing popularity with the girls as well. Even Sukey Portillo had come around in the end and they still occasionally lunched when Sukey, poor thing, could slip away from her drab husband and brood of tedious children and make it into town for the dentist or a timid shopping spree.

No, Beth Hardy was a mystery but one Vivienne felt too despondent to try to crack. She returned to the kitchen and helped herself to another drink and a slice of Stilton from the fridge, then went back upstairs to lie on the bed for yet another run-through of *Terms of Endearment*. Oliver hated these sentimental movies so this was the perfect time to indulge herself. She didn't know where he was exactly or when he would show up, and right now she really didn't care. Let him come home when he was good and ready and they would doubtless have a row or, more likely, an icy impasse and spend the rest of the weekend not communicating, eating out at Oliver's club or the Connaught because Vivienne had made no preparations for the weekend and couldn't be bothered to cook.

Thinking about Beth had soured her mood. Vivienne immersed herself in the movie and tried to obviate the nagging hurt by ignoring it.

Chapter Seventeen

Catherine was surprised when Sally called. She hadn't felt they had made any real connection but then she had to admit she had hardly been at her best in the hospital.

"Just thought I'd check and see how you were," said the friendly colonial voice, and Catherine felt a foolish blush of pleasure sweep up her neck.

"I'm much better, thank you," she faltered, slightly tongue-tied, which was silly, yet unable to help herself. "Still in a bit of pain but that's only to be expected. And I'm sleeping better at night. How about you?"

"Me? Can't complain. I'm fit as a fiddle—but then I always was."

There was a pause while Catherine sought wildly for something else to say, but Sally was in there, burbling away as if they were old friends well used to chatting about nothing in particular and not merely passing acquaintances with not a thing in the world in common.

"Are you back at work?"

"Not really. Not full-time. I don't seem to have the strength somehow. I just do the odd day to fill in when the other receptionist can't make it."

And even that knocks me out for the rest of the week, thought Catherine grimly.

"Only I thought perhaps I'd drop by and see you. You work for a vet, don't you, and I really love animals."

How kind, thought Catherine, alarmed at the idea of this wild unpredictable girl invading the surgery yet moved nonetheless by the unexpected thoughtfulness.

"Who is it?" shouted Eleanor petulantly from the other room. It was getting near suppertime and she wanted her sherry.

"Just someone," said Catherine with her hand over the mouthpiece. "A friend. I've got to go now," she said nervously to Sally. If her mother came to investigate there was no telling what might happen. Catherine could not risk it; she had far too few friends as it was.

"It was good of you to call."

"Hang on a sec," said Sally. "I'm not through yet."

What now? thought Catherine wearily, feeling a familiar wave of exhaustion sweep over her as she heard the ominous sound of Eleanor's chair scraping back.

"Don't hang up. What do you say to me coming over sometime for a glass of something or a cup of tea? A few laughs, talk about old times—nothing fancy."

Catherine paused. The girl sounded genuinely concerned, as if she really cared and wanted to make sure for herself that all was well. She was moved by the gesture and felt her resolution weaken.

"I'd like that," she said in a lower voice, searching for escape yet reluctant to end the connection. "We could meet at Barkers, perhaps, or somewhere else in the High Street and have a cup of tea."

"No sweat," said Sally cheerfully. "I got your address from the hospital. Why don't I just drop round sometime when I'm not too busy and take potluck? I'd really like to meet your ma after all those stories you told us, she sounds a game old buzzard. Now you take care and don't go overdoing things. You still sound a bit crook to me."

She had gone before Catherine could protest, and in any case Eleanor was descending, pulling her Spanish shawl around her ample shoulders and demanding to know who could possibly be bothering them at Easter.

"What do you mean—a friend? What sort of friend telephones on Easter Sunday? Don't they know that this is a sacred time and that I have to rest my voice for next week's recital?"

She retreated, muttering, leaving Catherine to cope with the sherry. She was the one who was officially sick but her mother seemed impervious to that, or to the fact that the hospital had expressly told her to take things easy for a week or so. After a lifetime of being waited on hand and foot, her daughter's illness was merely another irritation to Eleanor, a personal inconvenience which she took in her stride in her usual way, by ignoring it. The child had always been on the sickly side. That was their fault, she supposed, for being too indulgent. There was that time, twenty years ago, when she'd nearly cracked up altogether; very inconvenient and also very thoughtless. Eleanor's memory was good for her age but it was also selective. She was a master at editing her own scripts and remembering only that which was personally palatable.

Catherine lay in bed and thought of Tom Harvey. At no time during the past twenty years had he been very far from her mind but just lately something seemed to have happened to intensify his image and make him more vivid, as though he had just stepped out of the room for a moment and was likely to return.

She had only to close her eyes to see his image in sharp relief and could still hear his voice—that light, musical, vibrant voice—just beyond the borders of her consciousness. She found it strangely reassuring, as though he had never really left her.

These days, instead of dreading the night, Catherine longed for it to be bedtime and was thankful for the excuse of doctor's orders to leave her mother to her own devices at an increasingly early hour and slip away to the blessed privacy of her own room, to indulge in her secret store of memories and dreams. Wrapped in her flannel nightgown, fresh from the bath and smelling of Vaseline and Johnson's baby lotion, she would climb into the high wooden bed that had been hers since childhood, with her hot-water bottle in its faded woolen cover and a glass of water, and curl up like a child waiting for sleep. She no longer read in bed, she hadn't the strength, but sank into a blissful cave of memory the moment she turned off the light. On the old-fashioned dressing table her china dogs and glass animals were still ranged and she also had all her childhood books— E. Nesbit, *Alice*, and *The Wind in the Willows*—lined up in their ancient bindings on the bedside table.

Time had barely touched this room; its contents had followed her parents around the world, like a time capsule. This was Catherine's private territory; the only place she felt really safe. Here she was free to dream her private dreams and reinvent the past, safe from the mocking laughter of her erstwhile friends and her mother's withering scorn. For, as it turned out, Nancy's cynicism had not been misplaced. Tom hadn't loved her at all.

So many references were made by Tom to Catherine's background, and the possibility of one day going to Vienna to visit her folks, that when her father rang in July to say they would be over for Glyndebourne, her heart leaped at the chance of making the introductions as painlessly as possible. Brown's Hotel would be neutral ground and, with so many other commitments to cram into her short visit, there was little chance of Mama wanting to meet Tom more than once, which was a relief. So a date was duly fixed and Tom and Catherine presented themselves at the Palmers' suite for predinner cocktails.

In a panic of nerves, Catherine rooted through her wardrobe and chose a demure Laura Ashley dress, boat-necked and tied with bows at the elbows, in pale lilac sprigged with white. Mama, of course, would be done up to the nines but Catherine had learned from an early age never to try to compete. Not that her mother could ever consider her daughter any sort of competition, despite her youth. She was, Catherine was all too aware, in her mother's eyes beneath contempt, having inherited her milksop meekness from her father. Tom, for once, was surprisingly presentable in his one good suit and a shirt that was not too frayed. Catherine sensed he was quite keyed up about this meeting; maybe he really did have something dramatic up his sleeve.

Sir Nicholas greeted them in the drawing room, looking shockingly older since Christmas, thinner and altogether more frail. He kissed his daughter and shook Tom's hand, then set about mixing the drinks. There was no sign of Mama other than a distant warble from the bathroom which kept Tom's eyes glued to the door, waiting for her entrance.

Which indeed she made, only twenty minutes late, dressed as if for an audience at the Palace in violet satin with a triple choker of pearls and a neckline down to her knees. She proffered a cheek for Catherine to kiss, then swept straight past her to hold out her hand to Tom, palm down in queenly fashion, as if inviting him to kiss it. Really, she was such an inordinate ham; Catherine felt her cheeks beginning to burn, but Tom was quite clearly bewitched. He placed himself next to her, gazing into the compelling eyes, dramatically outlined in kohl, and gave himself up to blatant adoration.

To Catherine's surprise, he revealed quite a depth of knowledge of opera. Either he'd boned up on the subject specially, which was entirely possible, or else he really knew his stuff; whatever, he was able to talk quite fluently about some of her greatest performances, which was exactly the way to handle Eleanor Palmer. Catherine watched in admiration as her mother purred and smiled at him benevolently. But she would have been shaken had she known what was going on inside the well-coiffed head.

Sexy, Eleanor was thinking, *but an utter little toady*. And she was concerned to observe, as the evening progressed, that her daughter was already clearly quite horribly smitten.

The thing about Eleanor Palmer was that she was not entirely what she appeared. She had learned to play the grande dame early on, during years spent suppressing her humble Hastings origins while scrabbling up the incredibly slippery pole which leads to glory and success in international opera, a world as ruthless and dirty as any other where great reputations and vast sums of money are involved. But for all her superficial toughness and a history of broken hearts and scattered favors, deep down she was as frightened as the next person, which was why, when she thought her magnificent voice might be losing its power, she had opted for marriage to a decent but slightly dull diplomat. Catherine had been born when Eleanor was thirty-nine; she had been working out her frustrations on her ever since. But that didn't mean Eleanor didn't care. She despaired of her daughter ever developing any guts, but when she saw the hopeless way she was mooning over this brash and patently insincere young man, her mother-tiger instincts leaped to the fore.

"I'll tell you what, young man," she said, the fourth time Tom mentioned his desire to hear her sing. "If you're not doing anything tomorrow, why not motor down to the country with me? I'm having tea at The Maltings with Britten and dear Peter, to discuss a new production of *Gloriana*. Nicholas will be tied up all day with matters of diplomacy. I'd be glad of someone to do the driving."

Tom was bowled over but secretly confident. He had always had a knack with women, particularly older ones. It was one of the assets that led him inevitably into gynecology.

"May I come too?" Catherine's voice was almost plaintive as she watched herself, not for the first time, being upstaged.

"No, darling," said Eleanor smoothly. "If you're so hard-pressed you can't find time to visit home, I wouldn't dream of taking you away from your important work."

Then she turned back to Tom with a radiant smile and coquettishly tapped the back of his hand.

"They'll love it if you come. Poor Ben is in such bad shape these days, this could be the last chance you'll get to meet him. You can give him the benefit of your medical wisdom. That ought to cheer him up."

So off they went the next morning at the crack of dawn, Tom driving the rented Rover, Eleanor resplendent in what she considered a concession to country visiting, an Italian two-piece in pale beige linen with a huge straw hat to protect her from the sun. And, of course, the obligatory dark glasses. Just outside Aldeburgh, she signaled a stop.

"Pull off there," she ordered. "I booked a table at the White Lion for lunch. I think we deserve a little treat, don't you?" She placed one manicured hand on his knee and Tom felt his heart turn a tiny somersault of excitement. This was what he'd heard about these show-biz types; couldn't get enough of it. Well, Tom Harvey was certainly the man for her. Once, in his first year at medical school, he'd indulged in a fucking competition, which he'd won. Thirteen strikes to his opponent's mere eleven, as he recalled. A gleam came into his eye and a smile to his lips as he maneuvered into the car park and helped her alight.

Lunch was a riot and Tom enjoyed it thoroughly; whoever would have imagined staid little Catherine's mother to be such fun. They laughed and flirted and he reveled in her company, made all the more enticing by the amount of homage she was attracting from hotel staff and other lunchers alike. She treated him just like an equal, deferring to his opinion and hanging on his every word with her great luminous eyes as if she could not get enough of him. When coffee arrived she made an excuse to slip away, returning ten minutes later with a satisfied smile as she slid back into her seat and ordered them each an Armagnac.

"Slip this into your pocket," she whispered, offering him a closed fist, and Tom's heart missed a beat as he felt the cold metal and realized she was giving him a key. "It's a pity to rush things, don't you think, so I've booked a room upstairs for the rest of the afternoon."

He was thunderstruck. "But Mr. Britten . . . ?" he stuttered, his cool quite gone.

Eleanor waved airily. "Oh, Ben and Peter won't mind, they're men of the world. There'll be plenty of time for *Gloriana* once we've finished our own private party." She gave him a blistering smile.

"Trust me," she said.

For the sake of discretion, Eleanor suggested that Tom go on up while she settled the bill and she'd join him a little later. Hardly able to believe his luck, or the great honor she was bestowing upon him, he hurried away up the carpeted stairs and unlocked the door of Room 14, catching his breath when he saw the size of the bed and the lavishness of the fittings. If only the folks back home in Consett could see him now. Humming a jaunty tune, he ripped off his clothes and took a quick shower, then lay down nonchalantly on the bed, admiring himself in the mirror while he waited for her to join him.

An hour later, when she still had not appeared, Tom dared to phone down to the desk. Cautiously, as if he really were the chauffeur, he inquired about the whereabouts of Lady Palmer—only to be told that she had departed, immediately after settling the bill, but had left a note for him.

"If you really believed, you insignificant little squirt, that you could pull me," the note read, *"then you're even vainer and more stupid than I thought. You, with your vulgar manners and pit village accent. Come near my daughter again and I'll blow your cover. The Ambassador will not like his daughter being trifled with."*

Ignoring the grin on the face of the desk clerk, Tom shot out into the car park, but he was an hour too late. She had taken the car.

He hitched his way back to London, arriving—tired and bad-tempered—at his digs in the early evening. He was so angry he wanted to kill, but the object of his venom was so far out of his reach, he would have to make do with the daughter. Right on cue, she rang. She had something to tell him, she said. Her face was strained and her eyes puffy when she let him into the house but there was hope in her eyes as, with a slight half-smile, she opened her arms and begged him not to be angry.

Duncan watched Catherine with concern. She had been back at work for only a few days, still on a part-time basis by doctor's orders, yet it was clear to him that she was a long way from being right. She had always been on the thin side physically but now was near transparent, and her hands shook with a perpetual tremor whatever she was doing— sorting papers, dialing telephone numbers, carrying in cups of coffee. He had tried to discuss it but she brushed the subject aside. She was, she told him firmly, on the mend and it was only a matter of time before she'd be back working full-time. She was sorry for the inconvenience.

Duncan laughed and gave her thin shoulders a light hug. What was he going to do with her? He had suggested a holiday, somewhere restful in the sun, perhaps, but she had brushed the idea aside. And it wasn't his style to intrude too much; everyone was entitled to their privacy. Yet he did care. He was a kind man with a full life of his own, and his caring for damaged creatures, which he had made his life's work, extended also to his staff. He would have liked to see her happier but didn't know how to fix that, and he feared she might be iller than she realized. Today, for instance, she was sorting out appointment cards with a slight smile on her face and a flush of pink on her cheeks which was not normal. Furthermore, she was humming.

Catherine floated home that night on a wave of silent song. She had the strangest feeling about Tom, as if at any minute, around the next corner, she might bump into him. It was almost as though they had recently met, but it could only be in her dreams, perhaps induced by the strong medication the hospital was making her take. Just thinking about him brought a tightening to her throat and a flutter in her stomach, and twenty years dissolved as if they had never happened. She would get her hair done stylishly, perhaps with a few discreet streaks, and sort out her lighter clothes in readiness for the warmer weather. Having lived her life in Eleanor Palmer's shadow, Catherine abhorred makeup that showed, but a little light mascara could do no harm, with perhaps a touch of blue shadow to accentuate her eyes and some pastel lip gloss. Tom had always commented on her smile, and at least her waist was as small as ever and her legs, though thin, had retained their shape.

The driving wind had dropped for a while and the sun had come out so that, despite the biting cold, it was not impossible to see that spring was finally on its way. Any minute now the temperature would improve and people would shed their coats and their winter blues.

Catherine positively bowled into Albert Hall Mansions and up the first flight of stairs to her own front door. It was twenty past six and Mama would be waiting for her sherry, but tonight, for no particular reason, Catherine was determined to make a fuss of her. She stopped in her tracks as she heard distant voices, and there was no imperious shout from the drawing room to signal her arrival home. She took off her mac and hung it in its accustomed place, then smoothed her hair and went into the music room to investigate.

Sally was lolling across an armchair, as much at home as if she lived there, while Eleanor sat at the piano, laughing and picking out phrases from arias as she talked. Both looked up in surprise at Catherine's entry and Eleanor even glanced at the clock as if she were intruding.

"Hi," said Sally brightly. "I've met your ma and she's a real hoot. The stories she's been telling."

Eleanor extended one floury cheek for her daughter to kiss, then beamed in welcome.

"This young lady," she said with approval, "has been

brightening up my afternoon. The life she's led! All around the world on a shoestring, and entirely on her own initiative too."

There was a veiled criticism in the words that Catherine chose to ignore.

"So she's going to join us for supper."

Catherine was about to protest that there were only two pork chops and some sprouts in the fridge but Eleanor waved her aside with a queenly gesture.

"We'll go to the Brasserie St. Quentin," she said. "Call and book a table for seven-thirty. And then let's have a sherry. I'm positively parched."

And she laughed like a giddy young girl.

Chapter Eighteen

It was extraordinary how Eleanor took to Sally, and so quickly too. Catherine had never known anything like it and, in her usual spirit of self-deprecation, took it as a mark against herself. What a dull stick she had become in these past few years. No wonder her mother, exiled from the world of glamour and high society that was her lifeblood, took so readily to the breezy, uninhibited New Zealander, for she was certainly fun. Dinner at the St. Quentin was a riot, and both mother and daughter cracked up at some of Sally's stories about her travels around the world.

But she was a good listener, too. She sensed instinctively exactly when the moment had come for her to cease the ice-breaking tales of her own crazy escapades in order to defer to the older woman, and once Eleanor had regained the limelight, she held them both in the palm of her hand for the rest of the evening. Eleanor Palmer might be a private nightmare but her public persona was entirely different, and tonight Sally saw it at its very best. She was known and revered at the St. Quentin and the waiters could not do enough for her, giving her party the table in the window and hovering throughout the meal just within earshot so that they could attend to her slightest whim.

Eleanor was in her element. Once they had settled what

they were going to eat—the goat's cheese salad, she recommended to Sally, and then perhaps a little grilled fish—she settled back to enjoy herself and match Sally's storytelling with anecdotes of her own, of Vienna, of the world of opera, of the days when she was the celebrated diva, constantly traveling, ever in the public eye. And Sally could see, as the years fell away, the handsome woman she must once have been, with her fiery eyes and the lustrous indigo hair, dyed now a flat theatrical black.

She was entranced. She had no knowledge at all of opera, and the only music she enjoyed was pop, but that didn't deter Eleanor from spilling out the stories of the good old days when she sang Madame Butterfly in Rome and the real-life Pinkerton fell in love with her and pursued her across three continents with his wife in hot pursuit; when she took New York by storm as Lucrezia Borgia; when she first sang Salome in Milan and had a standing ovation which lasted twenty minutes. She talked and laughed and flashed those dramatic eyes and occasionally put one hand to her fine bosom and warbled a phrase to stress a point, until soon the rest of the restaurant fell quiet and when Sally turned she found herself part of the cabaret, the rest of the diners recognizing and transfixed by the star at her side.

It was heady stuff and Sally would not have missed it for the world. How Catherine could have been raised by this woman, spent most of her life in her presence, even inherited her genes and yet remained so mousy and inhibited was a mystery that defeated her. What an opportunity! She scarcely remembered her own mother, but what a gas to have had one like this. When Eleanor finally paused for breath, Sally leaned across and told her so and was rewarded by a kiss on either cheek and a demand that she consider Albert Hall Mansions her home from now on, with an open invitation to drop in at any time.

Catherine smiled and shook her head ruefully as Eleanor, in imperious tones, called for the bill. When she finally rose to leave, with the maître d' helping her out of her chair and walking her to the door like royalty, the rest of the restaurant broke into spontaneous applause. To which Eleanor responded with a gracious bow before stepping out into the Brompton Road and allowing Catherine to hail a cab.

"They really love you," said Sally, taking her arm and giving her a kiss on the cheek.

"One has one's admirers," said Eleanor modestly. "One has been around for a very long time, y'know."

Sally got out of the cab with them but, recognizing the exhaustion on Catherine's face, declined Eleanor's invitation to come up for a glass of white port.

"Some other time, maybe," she said, helping the old lady with her wrap as the night was growing chilly. "I'd really love to hear you sing."

"The voice is not what it was," said Eleanor, pleased. "But certainly come again and we'll see what can be arranged."

Poor Catherine looked as though she were dying on her feet and Sally was quite alarmed. Eleanor ignored her daughter completely and swept ahead of her through the door and into the lift.

"Now, remember," she called, before the doors closed behind her, "I shall expect to see you again soon. Sunday, at noon. Before lunch. Why don't you?"

Why not indeed? Sally walked home to the Earls Court Road, zigzagging along the plusher streets of Kensington, with Eleanor's laughter ringing in her ears, feeling she had made a real friend and found, perhaps, another bit of surrogate family. She thought of Catherine and the stories she had told in hospital about her mother's tyranny, and reflected that all either woman really needed was to be loved, only they came at it from such conflicting angles it was a foregone conclusion they would clash.

If only she would learn to stand up to her, she thought, *they might become real buddies.* Ah well, it was probably too late for that, but Sally counted herself lucky to have bumped into Catherine. Life contained these little richnesses if you kept your eyes open and had the tenacity to follow things up.

"I met this really great old lady," she told Joe next morning as she stood in the bar, polishing glasses. "She was an opera star in the thirties and forties until she married this upper-crusty ambassador and went to live in Vienna and became a great social hostess."

Joe gazed at her bleakly. It was five past eleven and he had had a hard night.

"What are you on about?" He had to check the bar stock before they opened and there was still the cellar work to do.

"She's like something out of an old black and white movie. Really great. She must be a hundred and four but she looks like a duchess, a cross between Carmen Miranda and Edith Evans."

Joe laughed in spite of himself.

"You're daft, that's what," he said fondly, swatting her backside with the end of a dishcloth. "Get a move on with those glasses, will you, and start the oil cooking for the chips."

Sally looked into the fryer and made exaggerated retching noises.

"This looks and smells really gross. When did you last change the oil?"

"Never you mind, get cooking. And if you're so fussy, eat at home."

"You have to be joking."

He laughed again, showing a melon slice of perfect teeth.

"Listen, doll, we're here to sell booze. Nothing more or less. And what the punter doesn't see won't hurt him."

"Yeah, but the salmonella will."

"Shut it. And get cracking, will you. Otherwise I'll dock your pay."

Still chuckling, Joe put a CD of the Pogues on the sound system and carted a couple of cases of tonic water from the hallway into the bar. She was a right case, this Sally, but life was a lot more fun with her around.

"So when's she coming in, then?" he shouted after a while.

"Who?" Sally, armed with a long wooden spoon, was poking disconsolately at the inside of the fryer, which was belching out black fumes like a juggernaut.

"Your old lady. The opera star."

Sally laughed. He didn't believe her.

"Any day now, just you wait."

"I will."

And he would. And she'd come. Sally had no doubt of it.

She did too, the following Sunday evening. Joe couldn't believe it and neither could Catherine. She was worried about allowing her mother out on the town with only a crazy kindred spirit like Sally to keep her in check, but what could she do? Eleanor made her own decisions and these days Catherine felt so wrung out she could hardly cope with just getting through the day.

"You look knackered, love," said Sally with concern, after they'd all had sherry and a lamb chop lunch and Eleanor had sung them a few arias from *Norma* and *La Bohème*. "Why don't you go and have a lie-down and I'll take care of your ma. Go on, you need it. We're getting along fine."

They were, too, closeted together in the drawing room with Eleanor's press cuttings and some faded sheet music and a bottle of Harrods white port "just to wet her whistle." She really shouldn't allow it, she knew that, but she felt so tired and wretched and the pain in her side had returned, though not as acutely as before. Sally was an angel, a regular saint, and Mama simply doted on her, so where was the harm? Maybe just forty minutes on the bed, if they didn't mind.

As if they would, she thought, as she slipped off her shoes and cardigan and lay down under the eiderdown.

They were like a couple of kids with their laughter and their stories, each vying to outdo the other, and she fell into a doze secure in the knowledge that her mother was safely incarcerated in the other room and that Sally had her eye on her.

She awoke hours later to Sally's gentle tap.

"We're just going down to the pub," she said into the twilit room. "I hope that's all right. Eleanor's longing for a pint of Guinness and I have to get back to my evening shift. I promise I won't keep her out too late and I'll see she gets home safely."

Catherine sank back into her pillows with scarcely a grunt. Her neck, when she tried to raise her head, felt like overcooked spaghetti and her brain wasn't functioning at all. She'd have another five minutes and think about it later.

Joe fell in love with her, and so did the punters. With a little encouragement and a bottle of champagne to spice up the Guinness—"Black Velvet, my boy, keep them coming"—Eleanor was prevailed upon to hitch herself up on the edge of the bar, showing legs still surprisingly shapely for a woman of her years, and belt out a few arias from *Carmen* followed by some bawdy music-hall numbers that had them all in stitches.

"She's amazing, your friend," gasped Joe, wiping his eyes. "Do you think I could sign her for a regular spot? She's dynamite!"

"Ask her," said Sally. "There's lots more life in the old girl yet. Far more than her daughter's ever had, poor thing."

Eventually Eleanor started to fumble her words and appeared a little short of breath, so Sally took her home. It was inconvenient because she was still on bar duty but it was the least Joe could do in the circumstances. The saloon bar was packed and the customers were staying, instead of drinking up and moving on. He hadn't seen anything like it in years. It was as good as an East End knees-up and livened up the King's Road no end.

"All right, Gran?" he asked, as Sally helped Eleanor into her wrap and tidied her hair, a little like a kindergarten teacher with a small charge.

"Less of your lip," shrieked the Ambassador's widow, then turned in the doorway and executed a perfect curtsey to the delight of the audience.

"Let's not tell poor Catherine," said Eleanor snugly, as she sat with Sally in the cab, her hand tucked safely into Sally's arm like a trusting child.

"Don't you worry," said Sally soothingly. "Your secret's safe with me."

"And can we do it again, maybe?"

"You bet!" said Sally, rapping on the window to tell the driver they had arrived. "The sooner the better as far as I'm concerned."

So Sally Brown became a regular visitor to Albert Hall Mansions and the Palmers were all the better for it. No longer did Catherine drag herself home from the practice, exhausted and tensed up at the prospect of another battle with the bored old lady. Sally got into the habit of dropping around before her evening shift and was therefore happily ensconced long before Catherine got home. She brought small gifts—a handful of flowers, a bag of apples, anything that caught her magpie eye—and these days Eleanor was ready for her, done up in her formal clothes with the full slap on her face, glasses and sherry bottle set out on top of the piano and old sheet music on the stand.

Catherine came in one evening to find the piano silent and Sally and Eleanor sitting close together on the sofa, deep in the pages of a photograph album. Oh, Lord. They had been through the ones of Eleanor onstage and as a young girl, all teeth and flashing eyes, and were now into the more formal ones of Sir Nicholas and Lady Palmer at home. Sir Nicholas looked a decent enough old boy, with white hair and a pleasant smile and now Sally could see where Catherine had inherited her gentleness.

"He looks great, your dad," said Sally, looking up to acknowledge Catherine's presence, flashing her radiant smile. Eleanor took no notice; as far as she was concerned they were still alone.

"He was a fine man," she said with a sigh. "And gave his life for his country."

Sally was startled. She thought he had been a diplomat.

"Died in the saddle, so to speak, worn out with all those diplomatic functions. And they made him travel about too much. Mind you, I wanted Milan but the best we ever got was Vienna."

Sally caught Catherine smiling and winked at her. What a case she was, entertaining in the short run but probably horrendous to live with day in, day out. Catherine went off to dump her things and put on the kettle and when she returned they had moved on.

"That's never Catherine?" Sally was saying, her finger on a faded black and white portrait. "You looked really wonderful," glancing up.

"She's in her nurse's uniform," said Eleanor approvingly, "the day she received her diploma as a State Registered Nurse."

I'd never have recognized her, thought Sally, *not from the faded, uptight shadow of herself I knew in Sydney. I wonder what happened?*

Catherine came to peer over their shoulders at the pretty, fair-haired English rose she had been all those years ago. Before the lights went out in her life. Like Sally, she'd never have recognized herself. What a waste.

"It was just before she took that job in Australia," said Eleanor, still behaving as if Catherine wasn't there. "She's never been the same since, have you, darling?" And suddenly, she looked her daughter straight in the eye, with such venom that both the other women felt the fallout.

Chapter Nineteen

The way Georgy figured things was this: if Gus Hardy had once had the hots for Beth (and Imogen was there as the living proof of it) then he was not, no matter what they might say, a dyed-in-the-wool *faygeleh* like so many of his ilk but simply a red-blooded male with a taste for adventure who had not yet found his proper focus in life. And since the Hardys had been divorced for years and Beth was, in any case, almost a generation older than Georgy and inclined to let herself go a little, it was up to Georgy to get in there and snatch him before anyone else did it first.

She knew he liked her, that was clear from the way he talked to her backstage, and on closer acquaintance with the beautiful, pouting Karl, she realized he was not the threat he had originally appeared but nothing more serious than a chorus boy from *Autumn Crocus*. He was young, foreign, and probably homesick, and Gus, in his role as director of the show, had given him temporary house room. The company needed accommodation, and living in rented digs must be no fun at all, while Gus maintained that great empty house in Islington all for himself. Sharing with girls would put him in danger of casual gossip; far better to have a fella as a house guest, and he had naturally used his discretion and chosen Karl. Or so reasoned Georgy.

To begin with she had been jealous of Beth and seen her as a rival. Once she established that the tie between the Hardys was founded on a kind of sibling affection rather than passionate love, Georgy began to relax. Beth had other men in her life and, besides, Georgy gathered from what she had overheard in hospital and since, it had been she not he who had elected to end the marriage. Quite simply, Beth was central to Georgy's master plan, so she cultivated the friendship.

Georgy had never been particularly strong on female friendship. New York was a veritable forest of feral females, all out for what they could get and each one jealously guarding her back, her job, and, if she had one, her man. Georgy firmly believed that all is fair in love and war and she was not about to let any female friend get in the way of that. Besides, it wasn't as if suitable men were exactly thick on the ground; certainly not in New York, nor even here in London where the going was fractionally less tough.

Georgy preferred male company and flattered herself she got on better with men. She was sparky and ambitious, thrusting and efficient and the equality battle held no worries for her. She had chosen a profession in which she could be equal and, through sheer hard slog, had risen quickly and made quite a name for herself without pulling any special favors along the way. She watched other more pliable females scoring points by simply scoring but tried not to let that make her bitter. She was essentially feminist and scrupulously fair. She was tough on other people but no tougher than she was on herself. She fired from the hip and took no hostages. You knew where you were with Georgy Kirsch.

But she did, badly, long for a boyfriend of her own and that was her Achilles' heel. Deep down, beneath the toughness and bluster, Georgy was simply a nice, old-fashioned Jewish girl looking for a partner.

She was nervy and taut in her manner, which was not an

advantage, but positive in her likes and dislikes, and, once a target was sighted, ruthless in pursuit. There simply wasn't time to mess around; she was more than halfway through her twenties already and thirty was looming on the horizon like the man with the scythe. Despite what the ladies of *Cosmopolitan* might preach, there was no room in this game for finesse. If she saw a man she even half-liked—married or single, it made little difference—then Georgy would go after him. After all, women had sacrificed their lives to achieve equality.

Back home she had a small apartment on the Upper East Side, immaculate like her, and this was the web into which she enticed her prey by giving regular small dinner parties for which she loved to cook. Out would come one of her eight complete dinner services and the Villeroy & Bosch stemware, together with the sterling silver, registered at Tiffany's for her thirteenth birthday and added to, piece by piece, ever since. Her meals were plain but perfect and her preferred number of guests was six or eight. She never hesitated to risk rejection by calling an interesting stranger after the most cursory of meetings, and it was surprising how, on the whole, this strategy worked.

Men had to eat and were also often flattered to find themselves the sudden target of Georgy's unswerving attention. She was lively and intense with a keen intelligence that masked her lack of humor and, although not classically pretty, her thinness, her cloud of Botticelli hair, and her style made her better than that—chic. In the arty circles of Manhattan, that mattered.

For a while these transitory relationships would flourish, with Georgy doing most of the running and the man being simply sucked into her orbit by the force of the effort she put into it. But later, as the net began to close, the poor chap would usually see what was happening and begin to struggle before he went down for the third time. The second phase of Georgy's courtships was inclined to get messy, punctuated by late-night phone calls and urgent scribbled notes, endless monologues (on her side) about commitment and expectations followed by tears and recriminations and then weeks of solitary lamenting as she failed, once again, to understand where it had all gone wrong. And, since she had always put such little value on the friendship of other women, the lamentation had usually to be done in private, with the result that the mistake was compounded countless times.

But if all that had been the rehearsal, Gus Hardy represented the real thing. He was all she had ever dreamed of— attractive, cultured, older, successful, and fashionable. That above all else. Like many fiercely ambitious young women, Georgy was mainly turned on by obvious success and Gus, currently the rage of Broadway, represented the pinnacle of her aspirations. He was cool, he was trendy, he would look good on her arm and on her résumé. Most of all, he was likely to impress her father, who might have reservations about the theater but always respected another high-flier. A star himself, he wanted nothing less for his three little girls.

So Beth was the target, but the problem was Sally, who seemed to have got in there first.

Beth and Sally had become friends at first sight since they were both warm, open, and outgoing and shared a similar sense of humor. When Georgy began to accept Beth's invitations to drop round for a drink or a meal, she usually found Sally there ahead of her, sitting at the table shelling peas or helping Imogen with her homework, or else draped over the sofa just gossiping, her boots on the edge of the stove, a glass of something in her hand. It should have made Georgy feel loved and appreciated to be included in this amiable quartet, but it didn't. What she felt was jealousy and resentment at not having mother and daughter all to herself. She wasn't going to compete with Sally so she usually sat there in silence, which was a drag for everyone.

Beth was aware of this faint antagonism but chose not to intervene, and if Sally saw it she ignored it totally, just continued to prattle on, drawing Georgy into the circle as if they were best buddies, which they could be if only Georgy would let up a little. Sally was five years older but certainly didn't seem it and since they were both transient visitors to London it made sense for them to pal up. As Beth pointed out.

"I would if she wasn't so spiky," Sally demurred. "But she's altogether too edgy and up her own arse. Life's too short."

Occasionally Gus would walk in while they were there—at times Beth's house resembled Paddington station at rush hour—and then Beth and Sally would watch with fascination as Georgy went into instant overdrive. She had a strange sort of theory, considering she proclaimed herself a dedicated feminist, that certain subjects were out of bounds in mixed company and was in the habit of changing tack abruptly when a member of the male species came within earshot. It was really rather ludicrous, and it was not a matter of prudishness; Georgy was starkly outspoken and normally didn't care what she said or to whom. It was more a question of selectivity. Her traditional upbringing clashed in some weird way with her avant-garde posturing, resulting in a certain coyness where subjects she considered too girly were concerned. Love, human relationships, things like that. Beth and Sally agreed she was a scream.

"If you fancy him that much," remarked Sally, as they were walking home one Sunday after lunch with the whole of the Hardy family, "then go for it. Men like that don't grow on trees. Beth doesn't want him so why not grab him while the going's good?"

"Don't you fancy him?" asked Georgy suspiciously, still unsure how far she could trust Sally.

"Be my guest." Sally liked Gus but he wasn't her type. She preferred them more rugged and to smell of good honest sweat rather than Paco Rabanne.

"So what do I do?"

"Aw, come on! You didn't come down in the last shower of rain. Let him know how you feel. If necessary, pounce. What have you got to lose except your dignity?" Which, in Sally's mind, Georgy had done already since she behaved like a silly kid whenever he was about.

So Georgy started to follow Sally's advice, albeit cautiously, because she still didn't entirely trust her.

Gus was at Orso's having a late supper when Georgy tracked him down. He was with Marla Henderson, her leading man, and a handful of chorus members including Karl. They were all ravenously hungry after three hours treading the boards. Georgy appeared like a wraith just as they were digging into their main-course pastas. She hovered at the edge of the group, uncertain.

"Hi there," said Gus, seeing her first. "Grab a chair and come join us. Have you eaten?"

Georgy waved aside the offer of food but accepted a glass of red wine. For one split second Marla's face was a mask of fury, then the consummate actress took control and she continued holding center stage and ignored Georgy completely. That was all right. Georgy only wanted to be near Gus, and this she had achieved. She stacked her expensive camera equipment on the floor beside his feet and settled down to bask. Karl, as mutinous as Marla but allowing it to show, jostled her slightly from time to time and made it clear he thought the table far too crowded for an extra person, but Georgy hung in there. You could always rely on her for that.

She was rewarded by an occasional smile from Gus, a pat on the hand, and an alertness to her every need, even though his attention was elsewhere. At the end of the evening he even bothered to check that she had the taxi fare home. He was a nice man, Gus, with excellent manners. And he felt sorry for her. Besides, she was a friend of Beth's and good to his kid. She'd do. One of the most compelling things about Gus Hardy was his innocence: he was totally impervious to the effect he had on men and women alike.

Some days later, Georgy was buying gloves in Harrods when she sensed a presence beside her, the strong scent of expensive perfume and a fur jacket to put her own sable to shame. It was Vivienne Nugent, pale and preoccupied as she pondered the relative merits of pale gray suede over serviceable black kid.

"Vivienne?" Georgy spoke spontaneously, before she had time to think. She was obviously learning more than she realized from Sally.

Vivienne turned wintry eyes on her, hesitated as if trying to recall who she could possibly be, then smiled tautly with her mouth but not her eyes.

"How nice to see you." Georgy could see her mind running frantically through an invisible Filofax.

"Georgy Kirsch," said Georgy, extending a hand. "St. Anthony's, remember?"

How could she possibly not, the cold cow? Vivienne obviously did and turned a shade paler. *Oh, Lord.*

"Of course," she said graciously, as the assistant fussed with her charge card. "How are you getting along?"

"Not bad. The scar still itches but seems to have healed okay. How about you?"

Vivienne's smile could have nuked a rain forest. For a moment, Georgy thought someone more important must be standing right behind her but it was merely English upper-class good manners telling her to get lost.

"I'm fine," said Vivienne softly, sliding her card back into her pigskin wallet. "And now I really must be going; I'm late as it is."

Chapter Twenty

The girl in the straw hat and the canary-yellow dress stood out like a beacon among all the suits in the crowded foyer of the concert hall. It was the hottest night of the year and, even despite the air-conditioning, men were removing their jackets and women fanning themselves with programs.

He stood slightly elevated, at the top of a short flight of steps, and looked across the monotone crowd—gray suits and gray faces—toward this one bright splash of color. Nice. As if feeling his eyes upon her, she turned slightly and smiled at him; even across all those heads he could tell she was singling him out and he started to move on automatic pilot toward her, like a moth to a flame. It had been a tough, hard, harrowing day and he felt in need of a little light relief, something to release all that tension. His own suit was gray (but the shirt hand-stitched) and he felt anonymous in the middle of the sweating, querulous city crowd.

Barbara Cook, the American torch-singer, was in town for just a couple of concerts and it was amazing how many people had turned out to hear her, particularly in all this heat. That was some sort of pulling power, he thought, as he wove his way among the crowd, like the enticement he could feel from this unknown young woman, with her luminous lips and dazzling tan.

He stood looking down at her with a lazy smile and watched her melt.

"Here for the music?"

"You bet."

"Like Barbara Cook, do you?"

"Of course."

"What do you do?"

"I'm a lawyer. And you?"

"Not a lot. Here, let's get out of here. This heat's really getting to me."

"But the second half . . ."

"Don't worry. I'll buy you the disc if you're nice to me."

They threaded their way through the crowd and out into the blessed relief of the cool night air. That was more like it. Two swift knife-blows to the solar plexus and the mission was achieved. What people remembered later—apart from the blood and the screaming, and the general confusion— was a crushed straw hat, trodden underfoot.

Oh, and the smile. That smile.

Chapter Twenty-one

Oh-oh-oh-Yes, I'm the Great Pretender ..." warbled Beth as she banged about in the kitchen, opening cupboards, picking over the vegetable rack, making a list. It was Saturday morning and she was singing along with Brian Matthew's *Sounds of the Sixties*. It was a muggy spring morning so she had all the windows open. Outside a fine drizzle fell.

The phone rang. It was Georgy with murder in her heart, keen to unload her venom at having been snubbed by Vivienne in Harrods. Beth grinned as she listened. Attacks on Oliver's wife always made her warm inside, although she knew that wasn't quite fair.

"And that's all she said," screeched Georgy, once she had spat out the whole sorry tale in one long gabble of rage. "Dismissed me like royalty meeting the housemaid on her afternoon off. After all we've been through together!"

"Indeed," said Beth solemnly. "Shared bedpans, urine bags, the lot."

Georgy didn't know about Beth and Oliver, and Beth intended to keep it that way. Sally had long ago wormed out of her the basic details but only on the strictest injunction to absolute silence and the threat of certain death if she ever slipped. She wondered what Georgy would say if she did find out, whether she'd be sympathetic. Envious, yes; supportive, maybe—but only in the most extreme fashion. One word about illicit love and she'd be nagging Beth to have it out with him, to confront Vivienne on her own doorstep and tell her she was snatching her husband, so there. Beth shuddered. She loved Oliver to distraction but had no wish to break up his marriage. One husband had been enough for her; these days she was very content as she was. And besides, she recognized she was the one in the wrong, something Georgy would never be able to comprehend. Georgy who, by her own admission, had been known to phone her best friend's boyfriend while the friend was away for the summer and entice him into bed. Just as good friends, you understand; nothing serious.

"Can't stand here gossiping all day, hon," she said. "It's Saturday. Time for the Big Shop."

She was cooking lamb couscous for eight for Sunday lunch and had a row of directors' lunches the following week.

"Anyone coming?" she trilled over the racket Imogen was making from her bedroom. Imogen despised sixties' music and was playing Meat Loaf at full volume in opposition.

"Where are you going?" Imogen's head, still uncombed, hung over the bannister rail.

"Sainsbury's, eventually. Come and help."

"Yuk, major yawn," said her charming child, and disappeared back into the chaos of her bedroom.

Beth backed the Volvo out of the driveway and drove up to Bleinheim Crescent to the cheery beat of "Pretty Flamingo." She loved Saturday mornings, even though they were the busiest in the week, and she enjoyed the casual, ethnic area in which she lived when the whole population seemed to be out on the streets, shopping or simply hanging out. She popped into Books for Cooks for a word with Clarissa Dickson-Wright, then continued on to the Portobello Road for her vegetables and meat.

Turnips, butternut squash, fresh coriander—at this time of year there were vegetables in abundance and Beth simply wandered, her wicker basket over her arm, touching but not squeezing, having a friendly word with each of the familiar stall-holders, torn by the dreadful dilemma of having to decide which of their sumptuous offerings to add to her growing load. Aubergines, Jersey new potatoes, Jerusalem artichokes. One thing: with her busy work schedule, it would all get used. With her northern shrewdness and business brain, there was very little waste in Beth's shipshape kitchen. She hadn't forgotten that she'd been hungry enough in the past, and now it all added to the fun of making things work economically.

When her arms were starting to ache in their sockets she called it a day and headed back to the car. She packed all her produce into the boot, then drove on up to Sainsbury's. She loved this place with a passion; just wandering along its air-cooled aisles with her trolley was Beth's idea of absolute happiness. In the way that others might seek solace in a church, Beth visited Sainsbury's when she needed a break, to get a little peace, absorb the atmosphere, study the other shoppers, see what the world was eating these days. And just occasionally, like now, she ran into a friend.

"Beth, my darling," hooted Richard Brooke, crashing his trolley into hers to prevent her moving on and giving her a smacking kiss. "How *are* you?"

It was months since she'd seen him but he hadn't changed. He still wore the same paint-spattered chinos and disreputable striped shirt, still looked as dashing and piratical as ever.

"I'm fine, what about you?" She was thrilled to see him, one of her oldest and most cherished friends, who had known her since her early days as an actress, back in the childhood of Methuselah.

"Not so bad."

"Selling?"

"Occasionally."

Richard was fashionable these days and his prices had rocketed alarmingly, but he still retained the diffidence which was his principal charm.

"Drop into the studio for a beer when you're finished, why don't you? I'm heading back there right now and a couple of my mates will be over."

"I'll try." She still had a mass of shopping to get through but she was fond of Richard and liked to keep up with him. Creative people, among whom Beth loosely numbered herself, had to stick together. Likewise old friends. Life these days was altogether too tense and uncertain and old friendships, like good wines, were the best and improved with the keeping. They kissed again and she wandered on, aisle after aisle—admiring, pondering, plucking. Apricots, sun-dried tomatoes, goat's cheese. Tinned tomatoes for her quickie pasta sauce, crushed dried chilis for tomorrow's Bloody Marys. More Clamato juice. Fresh basil. It was not yet the basil season but Sainsbury's, miraculously, now seemed to stock it all year round. It was expensive but who cared. There were certain little luxuries a person could not, for the benefit of their soul, afford to do without and basil was one of them. As was saffron.

With her cart piled a mile high, Beth at last propelled it through the checkout and outside to the car park to unload. It was a major undertaking, the Saturday shop, and she preferred to have Imogen along to help, which cut down the time considerably. But shopping, at least for food, was not one of life's excitements when you were twelve so Beth was perfectly happy to do it alone. And it gave her space to think.

Poor Georgy, she couldn't help smiling as she remembered her outburst. Georgy's problem was she was so intense. It was hard to believe Vivienne Nugent would be quite so rude, but you never knew, and what, in the long run, did it matter? She was unlikely ever to become more than a passing acquaintance—she had made that abundantly clear in hospital—and it was also against the odds that Georgy's path would cross hers again, other than by accident. If Georgy were more aware, she would learn to make more use of Sally. Sally was young and on the loose and, more to the point, she was fun. Georgy could do a great deal worse than turn Sally into a friend; she might also learn a lot about life from her.

Richard's studio was at the top of a converted warehouse backing onto the canal. It had huge, arch-shaped windows with wide, low windowsills and a clear northern light that was the envy of his artist friends. It was spacious and rather cluttered and smelled comfortingly of charcoal and turpentine. Beth loved it. Just walking up the rickety outside staircase brought back so many memories.

"Anyone home?"

Richard emerged from the room at the rear, beer can in hand, and hailed her with joy.

"You're here! Splendid. Come on in and warm your bum."

In the center of the room a wood-burning stove was smoldering. The day was mild but the warmth offset the damp and made the studio more homey and enticing. A couple of sagging sofas, covered in filthy afghans and smelling strongly of mildew, lined the walls; the rest of the space was taken up with wooden plan chests, canvases, and, by the window, Richard's work area, a battered pine table that had seen better days, covered with brushes, sticks of charcoal, and tubes of paint.

Two more men were lounging by the window, drinking beer and watching a coal barge crawl by along the canal. Beth knew them both already—Ben the builder, Adrian a part-time poet—and they all embraced as Richard flipped open a can of Worthington's for her. Outside it was definitely grayer and the rain was growing more serious.

"Typical Saturday," said Ben. "There goes this afternoon's match."

Beth flicked through a pile of Richard's rough sketches,

mainly local views skillfully understated in pencil with a watercolor wash. He hadn't lost his eye; she was impressed.

"When do you become a tax exile?" she asked and Richard's eyes, the color of treacle, met hers for a moment and held them thoughtfully.

"Would you come with me?"

"Like a shot."

He laughed. "If I thought you meant that, I might consider it." He'd always had a soft spot for Beth and she knew it. "But lotus-eating on your own can't be a lot of fun."

"Go to Andorra," said Ben, "then you can ski."

"Are you kidding? Have you seen it? It's nothing but a long ugly strip of camera shops and liquor stores, like an airport duty-free shop writ large. No, if I did it at all I'd go to Cannes. Or to Malibu, maybe, alongside David."

"And paint swimming pools?"

"And make a fortune?"

"Something like that."

Beth drank up. It was ten to two.

"I've got to go. My infant will be squalling for her food and I've still got the car to unload."

"When will I see you again?"

"Tomorrow? I'm doing lamb couscous and you're welcome to join us. The same applies to you two if you're doing nothing better," she said. "I've already got eight, another three won't hurt." She picked up her car keys and her bag and headed down the stairs. "Twelve thirty onward," she shouted. "Bye now. Hope to see you."

"Now that really is one classy lady," said Adrian, as they all three watched her go, hurrying through the rain in her jeans and cheesecloth shirt, oblivious of the rain soaking her hair and sticking it to her head in rat's tails.

"Yes," said Richard dreamily, leaning against the glass but looking back into the past. "She always has been, a genuine life-enhancer."

"Odd she's never married again," said Ben. "If I were free I'd be after her like a shot."

"She wouldn't have you," said Richard. "That's the original cat that prefers to walk by itself. And she's better off that way. She's a nest-builder, a nurturer, and she likes to spread it around, but don't be fooled. I knew her when she was married and she wasn't a shadow of what she's become. No, Beth Hardy is unique. Let's keep it that way."

"Mum, I'm starving," Imogen whined, hovering in the kitchen doorway as Beth humped Sainsbury's bags onto the kitchen table.

"Then give me a hand and you'll get fed all the quicker."

She passed Imogen a basket of aubergines and squash, misted with rain and looking too perfect to destroy, and reached farther into the boot for the lamb. It was a good thing she was strong because catering certainly took it out of you. All this lifting, heaving, and stowing was a fitness program in itself. If it weren't for the downside that went with it—tasting, assessing, adjusting—it would be a perfect health cure. Ah, well.

"Dad rang. He wanted to come over for lunch tomorrow but I told him he couldn't because we had company." There was just a hint of accusation in her voice.

"Then ring him right back and tell him it's okay. We're up to eleven, he'll make it a round dozen. Unless he insists on bringing Karl. Did he mention him?"

"He didn't. He wants to fix the shelves in my bedroom and then go see the orangutans, if there's time."

Beth smiled as she hung the garlic rope on a nail on the side of the dresser and put the coriander and parsley into cold water to keep fresh. He was a love, her ex. Imogen was lucky to have such a consistent man in her life and so, indeed, was she.

"Tell him they're both welcome," she said.

Thirteen, hmmm. Judas Iscariot.

But she'd cope, she always did, and at least if she had

both Gus and Richard Brooke around her table, chances were she'd finally get that gate fixed. There was nothing like a little healthy competition among men to get them hopping. She laughed, threw a couple of handfuls of elbow pasta into a pan, and set about chopping shallots and parma ham to make a fast lunch for her starving child.

Chapter Twenty-two

Harrods Food Hall was crowded, but then it always was. Vivienne pushed her way through the throng in the charcuterie department and headed on into Wines and Spirits in order to be able to breathe. And to look for a bottle of framboises in case the weather picked up at the weekend and Oliver was home and wanted kirs in the garden. Fat chance.

This shop was becoming more and more of a showplace, with its Egyptian Hall and the band of marching pipers that patrolled each floor, but she loved it as much as ever and came here whenever she was feeling insecure. It didn't matter that she often had nothing she particularly wanted to buy. She could always find something; that was never an issue. Harrods was not about shopping, it was a way of life, an attitude of mind. Vivienne had been coming here since childhood and although it had seen great changes, in essence it remained the same. Solid, secure, and comfortingly affluent. Some people turned to food when they were feeling unhappy or out of control. Vivienne always headed for Harrods.

She took the number 10 escalator to the first floor and trawled through the designer department as a matter of course. The thing about Harrods was knowing your way about it, and Vivienne was essentially a Knightsbridge

child. Nothing here especially to make her want to linger
but she enjoyed looking and touching and occasionally trying on. Service was not what it once had been but they did
still treat you with an element of courtesy, and they also
had changing rooms that were not communal, with full-
length mirrors and flattering lighting, enough space to turn
around, and thick fitted carpets to stand on when you'd
kicked off your shoes. And, most important, they didn't
hustle. If you wanted to spend the morning debating the
merits of just two outfits, Harrods was the place to go.
They would even bring you accessories to try from other
departments and when you left, your packages could be
sent separately and would often get home first.

It was a pity about the fur department, once Vivienne's
mecca, but alas no more. Furs were no longer politically
correct.

She flicked through Lingerie and bought herself a couple
of satin bras, then went on up to Cook's Way where she
slowed her pace. Although she rarely cooked these days,
Vivienne did appreciate copper pans. They looked so nice
in the kitchen, even if they were hard work, and she did
have Dorabella to care for them and scour them with lemon
juice before use to avoid poisoning the guests. She studied
the Le Creuset range and saw they now had a wok with a
draining rack. She didn't know if Dorabella would ever use
it. She had terrible arthritis, and would constantly complain. Since they usually went out for Chinese, Vivienne
decided to leave it, at least for the time being. No point in
upsetting the hired help unnecessarily.

She wandered into Informal China and bought an Italian
ceramic soup tureen just because it was so pretty, pale
green with embossed butterflies, grapes, and vine leaves, so
delicately wrought that she wondered if she would even get
it home in one piece. So she asked for it to be sent and then
added the platter and soup bowls so that they would have a
matching set. And the jug too, which would be useful for
lemonade in the summer if they ever had an outside party.

Which they rarely did because the weather was so unreliable and Oliver away so often. That thought brought her back to the coming weekend and her basic anger with life in general and her husband in particular.

Vivienne wandered on into Linens and bought matching sets of table and cocktail napkins in apple green to go with the china, then on into the pet department in case they had Burmese kittens. There were no cats today—probably just as well, the way she was feeling—but there was a scarlet macaw. She was reminded of the veterinary surgery, then thought of Duncan Ross and poor Catherine. Her mind flicked over Catherine, who had looked so weak and frail the last time she had seen her, and settled—as it usually did—on Duncan, the Delectable Vet.

Big, broad, male, capable Duncan, with those strong, serviceable wrists and sensuous hands. There was something so basically physical about him, it made Vivienne quite weak just remembering. Since the night he escorted her to *Autumn Crocus* he had been scarcely out of her thoughts, and the dreams she had about him, both waking and sleeping, were dirty in the extreme. After the show he had taken her out for a late supper, to a small trattoria she had not before encountered, informal and intimate with just the right level of lighting, where he was greeted like one of the family. They had ordered a simple meal, just salad and grilled fish, and Vivienne had had the heady experience of sitting close to a man she revered and pouring into his sympathetic ear all the things that were currently vexing her, those, at least, that bore repeating.

And he listened without interruption as if he were fascinated, occasionally touching her hand, once stretching out a finger to flick a lock of her hair from her eye, all the time holding her gaze with his wise, all-seeing blue gaze. By the time he signaled for the bill, she felt almost too weak to rise. All the way home by taxi, she was intensely aware of his strong male presence beside her, and her heart beat faster as she wondered if she dared invite him inside for one more drink. He kept the taxi waiting while he walked her to her door and when she finally summonẽd the courage to issue the invitation, took her silently in his arms, held her against his chest for a moment, then kissed her on the hair and let her go.

"Better not," he said softly, with what she sensed was genuine regret. Then he smiled, squeezed her hand, and let her go. She had been dreaming of him ever since.

Vivienne felt an attack of the vapors coming on and dodged on down one floor to the Dress Circle bar for a cup of cappucino and a wicked slice of Black Forest gâteau while she indulged this particular fantasy. Duncan Ross was a man of mystery, to be sure, but he was also a man of principle. In her more rational moments, she knew there was no way she was ever going to get closer to him, so after she had sipped at her coffee and eaten a couple of mouthfuls of the sinful cake, she ruthlessly pushed aside her plate, paid her bill, and then wandered on along the street for a rapid trawl of Harvey Nichols and a glass of chilled wine at the Fifth Floor bar before hitting Bond Street, her true spiritual home.

She didn't bother with an appointment but Jean Paul was ready for her. A girl took her packages and helped her into a gown while the man himself ran practiced fingers through her hair and gazed at her through half-closed eyes, like the seer he was, before directing her to a washbasin and summoning the manicurist to deal with the silk-wrapping of Vivienne's nails. The rain still sluiced down, heavier now, and outside in Bond Street shoppers hurried by under umbrellas while Vivienne relaxed into the womblike comfort of Jean Paul's salon and gave herself up to his care.

Vivienne shopped for one basic reason: a need for love. She was not aware of it but once she realized the magical effect her platinum credit card had wherever she went, she was hooked on the gratifying attention it brought and could not now get enough of it. It was potty training all over again. The more she bought, the more they oohed and aahed and the better she felt as a result. She found a pair of Charles Jourdan boots that really suited her, so she bought them. Then returned next day for five more pairs in all the available colors, in case she needed them when they were out of stock. She saw a silk shirt in classic black that went well with her Chanel suit, so she took it in beige and cerise as well, as basics for her spring wardrobe. And so it went on. Shopping made her feel good, that was all that mattered, and each new purchase was a reason to celebrate— and step up the spending.

Much the same was true of Jean Paul's salon. The moment she set foot within the perfumed inner sanctum, with its hushed music and thick-piled carpets, she felt cosseted, cherished, and, most of all, important. The staff ministered to her in every possible way and time spent there meant a temporary immunity from the harshness of the real world. Today was a gray, wet Saturday and ahead of her loomed another uncharted weekend which Vivienne preferred not to think about. Jean Paul was there as he always was—smiling, sympathetic, with his artist's hands—to assess her mood and subtly massage her ego by making her remember just how beautiful and fascinating she really was. He did not come cheap but that was all right. In his own area of expertise, he was the master.

At five forty-five Vivienne left with new nails, hair that had been trimmed and restyled, and a makeup job from the Japanese stylist that might have turned heads as she paid her bill but would be lost on the empty house in The Boltons. On an impulse, she crossed Piccadilly and dropped into the Ritz for a martini in the Palm Court. It was a pity to look so good and have it go to waste. A girl in a long black skirt was playing the harp and a couple of tables of Japanese tourists were finishing smoked salmon and cucumber sandwiches as Vivienne sat in solitary splendor in one mirrored corner and waited for her drink. This was the hour when the city was at a lull, the shoppers were heading home on their Underground trains, clutching their chain-store packages and thinking about supper, while visitors and Londoners alike were preparing for a night on the town. The tourists at the nearby tables, just settling their bills, doubtless had plans for a nap and a shower and a change of clothes, followed by the theater or dinner in a Soho restaurant.

Only Vivienne seemed to be alone; on occasions like this she felt it more acutely. Stopping off here had been a mistake. All she had to look forward to was an empty house and the television remote control to help her while away another empty evening. She ordered another drink and tried to look as if she were waiting for someone. She knew she was looking good and, although she did not show it, was gratifyingly aware of the deference of the waiter and maître d' as well as the occasional admiring glance from men passing by. But it wasn't enough, not nearly. Vivienne Appleby, debutante, had thrived on admiration. Vivienne Nugent was more mature and altogether too bright for such a wanton waste of her best years. Sitting alone in a lit showcase like this simply made her feel sad and futile, like a creature from the red-light district of Amsterdam.

She studied her glossy new fingernails, long and immaculate and totally useless, and glanced at her face in the ornate mirror, a mask of perfection. And for what? No one really cared for her. What was it all about and where was it going to end? She was still paying for what she'd done to Celia Hartley but surely by now she had served her sentence many times over. Vivienne drained her second martini and called for her bill.

The rain was clearing but the early Saturday rush hour had begun and the chance of a taxi was virtually nil unless she was prepared to wait in line on a breezy, mud-spattered street, which she was not. She thought about going back inside but resisted the impulse. Vivienne was reserved and nicely brought up, and sitting alone in bars, even one as exclusive as the Ritz, was not really her scene. In the end she impulsively leapt onto a number 14 bus, ran upstairs to escape the crush of shoppers, and, by a stroke of good fortune, found herself alone in the front seat on top, with a panoramic view across Green Park. The sun came out, bathing the leaves in pale light, and Vivienne felt a strange lift to her spirits.

It was years since she had traveled on public transport and she had quite forgotten the special pleasure of riding so high at the front of a London bus, able to see all around her and rediscover the beautiful city she took so much for granted these days. They progressed along Piccadilly, past the flaming torches of the In and Out Club at Palmerston House and on to Hyde Park Corner and the newly appointed Lanesborough Hotel, once St. George's Hospital, where as a child Vivienne had had her tonsils removed. Then on down Knightsbridge, familiar to her at street level yet so much more appealing now she was riding above the traffic and able to see the architectural details of the buildings and listen to the cheerful chitchat of people all around her.

She craned her neck to look down on the impressive sweep of Harrods' windows, then across toward Brompton Oratory and the Victoria and Albert Museum, as the bus swung left past South Kensington Underground station and into the Fulham Road. The sun was close to setting, tingeing everything with a mellow, golden glow, and the rain had soaked away entirely. The streets had thinned to a casual, meandering flow of people and, to her surprise, Vivienne found she was suddenly enjoying herself and was half inclined to stay on the bus past her stop and venture on to the wilds of Putney, or wherever it was headed.

Just before the lights by the ABC cinema on the corner, however, she rang the bell and descended. She crossed the road and went into the Pan bookshop for a brief browse before heading home. She loved this bookshop, perhaps the best in London, and bought an Anita Brookner novel and the new Elizabeth Jane Howard as well as the biography of Muriel Spark which she had been meaning to read for some time. That was something she could do this weekend; she could read. She could sit in the garden of her beautiful home and indulge her mind for a change, and if the rain returned, which it probably would, she could move into the conservatory on which she had lavished so much time and money.

Clutching her books along with her Harrods packages, Vivienne turned the corner into Gilston Road with a lighter step and a firmer resolution and smiled as she passed the great Victorian villas with their abundance of cherry blossom in full flower. This really was a marvelous city and she had the great good fortune to live in one of its most luxurious parts.

Enough of this sitting around at home, feeling sorry for herself and waiting for something which was unlikely now to happen. All of a sudden Eugene Appleby's genetic gift took over and Vivienne was gripped by a fierce determination to get out there before it was too late and live life to the full again.

Chapter Twenty-three

The line outside the V & A was so long and the weather so wet that Catherine gave up immediately and walked on instead to the Natural History Museum to take another look at the dinosaurs. She badly wanted to see the Fabergé exhibition but simply hadn't the strength to stand that long, particularly in drizzling rain that was already making her uncomfortable. Maybe she'd try again during the week, or some other day when the weather was a bit better, though these days trying to hit a fine day in London was about as futile as aiming for a hole in one. She would doubtless end up missing it altogether as she had so many other times in the past—exhibitions, films, plays—all through a basic lack of energy.

She loved the Natural History Museum, especially since its face-lift, and was content just to shuffle along inside its main hall, in another queue but one that was actively moving, looking up at the stained-glass windows and the wonderful detail of the interior now that it had all been cleaned up. She was surrounded by a group of schoolchildren, each with a backpack containing a sandwich lunch, and she tuned in to their conversations with a certain amount of pleasure, envying the enthusiasm and imagination that youth still held.

Ruth Ann would be pretty near grown up by now, possibly even with a baby of her own. Catherine could just see her, standing here beside her in the queue, listening to these children prattle and enjoying their high spirits as much as she did herself. What friends they would have been, mother and daughter, with the sort of close relationship Catherine had only ever dreamed of. She thought back to her years as a student nurse, rooming with the gang of other girls in Lambeth. That was the sort of closeness she would have known with her daughter, for she would never have allowed Ruth Ann to leave her side until she was properly adult and made the break of her own free will.

What happened to Catherine could never have happened to Ruth Ann. She would never have dreamed of leaving her own daughter stranded, alone in a strange country during her formative years, forced to grow up alone and make her own mistakes, without benefit of parental love or guidance. Ruth Ann would have grown up strong and fearless, safe in the knowledge that she could always run home to her mother for solace and support.

Nor would Catherine ever have allowed her own career to get in the way of being a proper mother. As soon as the pregnancy began to show she had planned to quit nursing, at least for the first few years, and devote herself entirely to raising her child and giving appropriate support to her husband and his career. They would have been a proper family in a permanent home. Any energy left over from child-raising would have gone into furbishing the love nest, building a secure and happy setting in which Ruth Ann could grow.

Eleanor had never known about Ruth Ann, the grandchild that never was and now never would be. Just occasionally, at moments of extreme exasperation, Catherine felt like throwing the whole sordid story in her face, if only to watch her disbelieving shock, but managed always to hold off at the last minute, which was probably just as well. Ruth Ann was part of Catherine's secret life, never to be shared by another living soul, particularly the demanding mother who had made her life such a living purgatory and was still quite capable, given an extra weapon, of grabbing it and using it to inflict the most excruciating pain.

Now that she had Sally to play with, Eleanor was behaving better, but who knew how long this latest phase would last. Sooner or later they were bound to fall out, Mama and her new little friend. As it was, Catherine wondered exactly what Sally's motives could be. No matter how sweet her nature, only a saint could endure the day-to-day contact with a selfish tyrant that had worn away at her own existence but which Sally seemed to find so diverting. Surely it wasn't the money she was after? Despite appearances, there was not a lot of it and Sally was far too free a spirit to be bothered with anything so mundane. No, most probably she was simply being kind and would one day grow bored and walk away. For the present, however, life at home was unusually serene and Catherine was taking full advantage of it.

They had reached the entrance to the dinosaur exhibition and were filing down a long, dimly lit corridor to the start of the display cases. The children all around her were questioning and exclaiming and Catherine found herself back in her own childhood, when the world was full of wonders and her patient, mild-mannered father would lead her round this very museum with the time to talk and listen and educate. How she missed him.

Even though she had seen this exhibition before, Catherine found it fascinating. It really was quite mindboggling to think that these vast creatures had roamed the earth more than sixty-five million years ago, a period impossible for the human mind to grasp, rather like counting the stars. When you set yourself to contemplating infinity, today's worries faded into insignificance, like the dull ache in her lower abdomen which had now returned and was quietly ticking on like incipient toothache. What a drag it was turning out to be. Catherine broke away from the queue and went to sit on a bench until the sudden spasm of queasiness had passed. Was she never going to be entirely well again? She feared that her operation at St. Anthony's had not done the trick. Instinct told her there was worse to follow.

Catherine's childhood had been dull but safe and she still retained fond memories of the brief periods they spent in London, in pampered surroundings with easy access to all the wonderful things the capital had to offer. Her father, when not preoccupied with diplomatic matters, had been an attentive parent and had treated Catherine like a tiny adult with whom he would have quite advanced conversations. They had walked for hours in Kensington Gardens, where J. M. Barrie had once exercised his dog, and the statue of Peter Pan was a favorite target for their Sunday strolls. Catherine still returned there quite often, when life was getting her down, to stroke the worn heads of the tiny bronze animals and try to recapture some of the magic she remembered from those childhood days.

Her early memories of her mother were rare and not at all distinct. Then Eleanor had been at the height of her fame, traveling long distances all over the world for a single performance in some grand opera house, heralded as the greatest soprano of her generation. Even at diplomatic functions, it was Eleanor who hogged the limelight. There was one much-recounted occasion when she even upstaged Princess Margaret with the sheer force of her physical presence.

Looking at their faded wedding pictures, Catherine often wondered how the flamboyant Eleanor Goddard had ended up marrying the quiet, mild-mannered Nicholas Palmer. In those days, when she was feted worldwide, they said she might have chosen whoever she liked, yet in her late thirties she had suddenly opted out of the main game and settled for marriage to a slightly stuffy, self-effacing diplomat, light-years away from the glittering galaxies to which she was accustomed.

And, even more remarkable, the marriage had worked.

All credit to her, Eleanor had made an exemplary diplomat's wife and had thrived on the sort of formal occasion that Catherine had always found so stifling. It was interesting how life ambitions varied. Catherine's own idea of heaven was comparatively modest: marriage to her one true love and the privilege—for that was what it would be—of taking care of him and raising his children. Money had never been a lure, perhaps because she had never really had to do without, and the memory of the tedium of the social occasions her mother had so much loved still filled her with a cloying sense of claustrophobia. God, but those people had been awful—fawning, insincere, terminally third-rate. Just thinking about them now and remembering added to her sudden feeling of faintness.

But Eleanor had survived and was still going strong, of that there was no doubt. In all probability, the way Catherine was feeling now, she would outlive even her daughter. More than anything, she loved to hold center stage and, once she achieved that, some of the beguiling qualities that must have ensnared a host of men in her youth rose again to the surface so that she could appear quite human. To outsiders, that was, to fans and opera buffs and casual acquaintances like Sally, who only ever got to see the charmer on the surface, never the monster beneath.

The rain had reduced itself to a depressing dampness when Catherine finally found the strength to leave her bench and hobble home. She hated Saturday afternoons with only Sunday to look forward to, two days cooped up alone with Mama and the prospect of another terrible row which Eleanor often used as a weapon to enliven the tedious weekend hours.

Catherine's sole break for freedom had come after the fiasco of the baby and her subsequent breakdown, and she still marveled that she had ever had the strength even to have thought of making a bolt for it. They had wanted her home in Vienna to recuperate from whatever it was that was troubling her, but for once she had dug in her heels and removed herself instead to a nursing home in Hastings from which she had taken long, dismal walks and gazed out at the metallic-looking sea, trying to come to terms with her life and make vague plans. The future, like the seascape, had been gray and despairing, and she might well have gone under altogether had it not been for a friendly Australian nurse who had sat with her in the garden, helping her with her therapeutic knitting and trying to rally her spirits by telling her tales of home.

"You really ought to go there," enthused the girl. "See it for yourself. You'd love it, especially after all this. It really is the land of opportunity, all sunshine and wide-open spaces and marvelous views across the harbor. And friendly people who would give you a proper welcome, not like these stuffy Poms, if you'll pardon the expression."

Catherine just stared at the sea with lackluster eyes, so her friend took things one step further and produced a copy of *Nursing Mirror,* which contained the advertisement which was to change her life, if only for a few short years.

"Nurses wanted for private clinic in Sydney, NSW," it ran. *"Two years minimum. SRN essential. All usual references."*

"Go on," said the girl. "Why don't you give it a go? There's nothing to keep you here and it might be fun. Can't be worse than rotting away in this godforsaken hole."

So she had done it and within a week received the offer of an interview. To her enormous surprise, she passed. Life had suddenly taken an upward curve and an element of bustle, and three weeks later, after a fast trip home to Vienna to see her parents, Catherine took off for Australia and a whole new future.

Of course they disapproved, at least her mother did, but Catherine was twenty-one and there was nothing now to keep her in London or, indeed, Vienna. Sir Nicholas had actually rather taken her side and slipped her a secret five thousand pounds as a running-away fund, in case she couldn't stand it when she got there and needed to come home in a hurry.

"You'll do fine," he told her confidently on one of their walks along the Danube. "Just don't go marrying an Australian. I must have my little girl back someday."

Alas, it was never to be, but neither of them could know that then.

The private clinic, in a suburb of Sydney, was attached to a convent. Catherine used to wander through the shady cloisters whenever she needed space to be alone and think. Somehow, now that she was so isolated from everything she knew and valued, Tom Harvey became an even greater presence in her mind, instead of fading into the background as she assimilated new experiences and generally broadened her horizons. She thought about him constantly and even kept up a correspondence with a couple of other nurses at St. Thomas's in the desperate hope of hearing news of him. Which, indeed, she did. Within a year of his arrival at Harvard, she heard, he had married a girl from Boston, rich they said and well connected; and later that he was doing well, shooting up the Harvard ladder and making quite a name for himself in surgical circles. Again she wept for him and Ruth Ann, for their aborted love and what might have been had Fate and her mother not intervened.

This secret sorrow ate away at Catherine's soul and added to her introspection. Australia was everything it had been cracked up to be—bright, full of sunshine and opportunity, warm and welcoming. But Catherine never really got into step there the whole time she worked in the clinic. She remained a sort of walking zombie, forever looking inward, impervious to the initial offers of friendship, which eventually died away.

On the whole she enjoyed the work. The patients were mainly young and some of them were troubled. Any spiritual reward she gained from this adventure came from nurturing those abandoned children, many of whom were homeless, and helping to build up their trust. Not for one second did she ever stop thinking of her own lost Ruth Ann and she poured all that thwarted maternal affection into caring for these damaged strangers.

Just as she was beginning to relax, to enjoy the freer atmosphere and charm of Australia, even cautiously to make a few friends, she received an unexpected summons from home. Sir Nicholas, still only in his early sixties, had had a fatal coronary and Eleanor had collapsed from the shock of it all. Catherine was forced to abandon her new career in order to return to Vienna to sort things out, to move them out of the embassy and back to London for a new life in sadly reduced circumstances.

The anguished widow and her downtrodden companion, that was what they had become. It was a role that seemed natural for Catherine. She had been playing it with quiet resentment ever since.

Chapter Twenty-four

The rain was still tipping down but Sally didn't care. She had the sort of hair that was only improved by the damp, and clear, healthy skin that looked its best in the British climate. She sat on a wooden bench outside a pub in Brook Green and waited while one of the boys got in a second round. They were a fun bunch these guys, Rory, Arthur, and was it Harry? They had picked her up in the pub on Thursday night and invited her out to their own local drinking joint. It was wet and a bit chilly but no one was going to mention it. Sally still sat there, just reveling in it. Her crazy denim hat kept some of the moisture from getting in her eyes and the jutting roof of the side veranda was protecting her from the worst of it. The blokes were not quite so fortunate but no one was going to be chicken enough to be the first to head inside.

"What time's the march start?" asked Rory at the bar, laying down fivers for the three pints of bitter and a gin and tonic and looking at the television mouthing wordlessly from the wall above his head.

"Two-thirty," said Arthur. "Or thereabouts. Where are we going to watch it, your place or mine?"

"And what d'you think's the chance," said Rory, "of getting her to join us?"

They both looked over their shoulder, out of the door to the bench where she still sat, surrounded by a group of stray men.

"If we go to your place," said Arthur, "we can do it in seven minutes, which means we've still got time for another round if we drink these quickly."

"By the look of her," said Rory, "she's a pretty dead cert wherever we go. Which means we can take it slowly and still score. Toss you for it."

Still guffawing, they carried the glasses back to Sally's table and were put out to find there was no longer room for them to sit. She laughed, graciously accepted the fresh glass, and went on talking to the group around her, entirely unconcerned.

Today had been a toss-up between staying in bed, which was her natural inclination, particularly on a Saturday morning after a hard Friday night; facing the pile of laundry which it was her turn to do; or striking off on her own, which had been her eventual choice, to this unknown pub in a different part of town, just for the sake of variety. One thing Sally never, ever lacked was invitations, and working in a bar put her in direct line for a lot of them. She'd always been able to pick and choose.

She was bored with her own particular group, so this gang would do as well as any other, at least for the time being. They lived in Hammersmith but liked to drink in the King's Road, and, as far as she had been able to suss, were all in the City, loosely speaking, scrabbling up the corporate ladder and trying to build their fortunes before they were thirty. Boys again, but amusing for the moment, so long as they paid for her drinks. But they were really too young and unworldly for her, so maybe, when she was good and ready, she'd introduce them to Georgy and then move on. How was that for altruism; she must be learning from Beth. Georgy wasn't exactly fun but she was clever and ambitious, like this lot. And the poor kid really deserved a break, mooning around as she did so much of the time, eating her heart out over an uncatchable man. If only she wasn't so sour so much of the time.

At least these expeditions to new watering holes took Sally out of range of Sam, with his great, moony sheep's eyes always on her. And Joe from the pub who was threatening to stifle her. Brook Green was quite a find; it was quiet and mellow and verdantly green on this dripping Saturday morning. She was more than ready for a change of scene so maybe she'd look for a place round here. It was classier than Lexham Gardens and farther from the Earls Court Road. And, from what she could see of the houses, ripe, she would suspect, for rich pickings.

Outside, a battered Bristol coupe drew up and two men sat talking and watching the pub from across the road. Denzil Davies, the driver, was swarthy and Welsh and middle-aged, while his companion, Kim, was a puckish, white-haired sixty, desperately hanging on to his fading youth in designer denim and aviator sunspecs. He had once been something in the fashion industry, only these days nobody remembered. They were both heavily hungover and bored. And fiercely debating this afternoon's projected trip to Cherbourg.

"What do you think?" asked Kim, staring over his tinted lenses the better to appraise the voluptuous bimbo seated, oblivious of the drizzling rain, amid a gang of hopeful hoorays.

"She'll do," said Denzil shortly. Saturday morning with a head on him like this was no time to be worrying about the comparative merits of female flesh. She was young, she was relatively toothsome, she was obviously available. One dolly was much the same as the next so far as he was concerned.

"Let's get on with it," he said, getting out of the car.

They called to her on her way back from the Ladies, stopping her in her tracks as she passed the fruit machine.

"Can I offer you something to drink? On a nasty wet morning like this one?"

Kim always got to do the initial pick-up; that was his specialty and he was an expert. He was slightly built, good-looking, and he dressed dead cool. Definitely worth a closer look. Sally strolled over to join them and plonked her butt on a spare bar stool. Kim grasped her hand in one simian paw as he tucked his aviator glasses in the top pocket of his denim shirt. Close up he was really rather dishy, though older than she had realized, with his chest hair turning white. She saw now why he preferred not to sit outside.

"A bottle of Dom Perignon, I think," he said to the startled barman, ignoring her request for another g and t. Then he settled back on his stool and looked her up and down appraisingly. She would indeed do, and slightly better than he had hoped. The body was excellent and the skin was good. He hardly needed to examine the teeth since they were very much on show in a wide, welcoming grin but, if need be, he would have done that too. He had been breeding horses for a long time now and could instantly spot a goer.

"Kim Butterfield," he said, "and this is my good friend, Denzil Davies. Up from the valleys for the match, you know, and looking for a little excitement in the great metropolis."

The Welshman nodded curtly, still looking a shade sour, slumped on his stool like an overblown walrus. Sally returned her attention to his sprightly companion. Bored as she was with all the young men, she thirsted for a spot of sophisticated company and this seemed to be as good as she'd get this damp Saturday afternoon when all they could talk about outside was rugby. She took off her soggy hat and raked strong fingers through her springing hair. Kim studied her breasts approvingly.

The champagne arrived, dusty from the cellar but already chilled, and the barman poured it into fluted glasses. Kim raised his in a toast to Sally.

"Here's to you, Sally Brown," he said, "and I hope you'll

join us for a spot of adventure this afternoon." He lingered on the breasts, making his meaning clear. "What do you say?"

Sally smiled. It was an obvious come-on but she had known worse. And she liked the way he looked and dressed, and noticed the expensive watch and the gold chains round his neck.

"What about the match?" she asked. She wasn't going to risk getting roped in to watch that.

"We thought we'd give it a miss. It worked as a wheeze to give Denzil's missus the slip but now we're here, we'd thought we'd do something a little more adult."

"Okay," she said, tasting her champagne. "I'm not doing anything else. What exactly do you have in mind?"

Denzil Davies raised one heavy eyebrow in surprise and dragged himself up into a less supine position. He could say this about Kim, he hadn't lost his touch. One brief flirtatious remark and a touch of the bubbly and the bird was snared. A looker, too. It hadn't been this easy in years; he was prepared to enjoy the rest of the weekend. Sally looked him up and down, for this was a two-way street. He had a gross beer belly but sensitive eyes and she guessed that in different circumstances he might be less of an obvious pain. In an odd way he complemented his lither, slicker companion, and she was glad.

"What we were thinking of doing," said Kim, "is taking my old tub from its moorings in Lymington and tootling over the Cherbourg this afternoon for a weekend's sailing. Care to join us?"

"Great!" said Sally. This sounded distinctly promising.

"Have you been on a boat before?" asked Denzil, wheezing painfully as he lit another cigarette. "Do you know what you're about with all those ropes and things?"

She grinned. *Don't patronize me, sucker.*

"My dad owns a boatyard in Tasmania," she said. "I was sailing practically before I could crawl."

Kim laughed and patted her knee. He liked her spirit already and looked forward to getting better acquainted with her firm young flesh. She was appealingly unworldly and deliciously naive. She'd do.

"Well," he said, when they'd finished the bottle, "guess we'd better get a move on. Do you live nearby? Is there anything you'll need?"

"Naah," said Sally. She had her hairbrush, her dark glasses, and a pack of condoms. What else could she need for just two days? A toothbrush she could pick up anywhere, or even borrow.

"Do I need a passport?"

"Naah," said Kim, patting her knee again. "You leave all that sort of thing to us." He winked at Denzil and they were away.

Sam was concerned when Sally hadn't gotten back by midnight, even more so next morning when he checked her room and the bed had not been slept in. Not that it was easy to tell; Sally lived the way she dressed, a consistent ragbag in a jackdaw's nest. But her shoulder bag was missing, and that awful hat. And the truth was, he'd lain awake till the small hours like an anxious parent but hadn't heard her key in the lock or her foot on the stair.

"What's it to you?" asked Jeremy icily, as he groped in the fridge for the milk. They had never actually had words about Sally but there had been a definite cooling-off since her arrival and both men knew they were rivals for her favors. But since the night of the opening of *Autumn Crocus*, when she'd dressed like a tart and managed to upset his friends, Jeremy had been having distinct second thoughts. Sexy was one thing but, where decent society was concerned, Sally was definitely beyond the pale. He had another girlfriend now which ought, by rights, to have left the way open for Sam. It didn't quite work like that, however, certainly not with these Brits. Jeremy seemed to assume automatic droit de seigneur no matter who else he might be screwing. He hadn't actually said as much but there was no need; Sam could see it from the contempt in his eye.

But Sam was actually less concerned about who she might be with than whether she was all right. She was very much a creature of impulse, his Sal, but she was just a girl, when all was said and done, with a disposition that was altogether too trusting and might easily lead her into trouble. He worried about her, couldn't help it. If he had his way, he'd be taking care of her properly. Since that first magical night she had only come to his bed occasionally, but his hope was undimmed and he remained bewitched.

He even lowered his pride that night to drop down to the pub and see if she was working. She was not and Joe was in a foul mood, not improved by the sight of Sam.

"Haven't seen her," he snarled, "and she didn't make the lunchtime shift either. If she does turn up, you can tell her she's fired. I can't run a pub without any staff."

The bar was packed, tribute no doubt to Sally, and Sam took his pint and sat miserably in a corner, hoping she'd come rolling in and that everything would turn out all right. He knew he hadn't the right to feel this way, that she was a creature of impulse who preferred to travel alone, but he couldn't help hoping. She was all he had ever wanted, so beautiful, so warm, so—vulnerable. Yes, that was it. She was like a friendly puppy who had never been kicked. She leaped up to everyone with a welcoming smile and Sam was terrified that one day someone really bad would try to take advantage of that innocence.

By ten-thirty she still hadn't appeared and Joe was making his feelings obvious by banging down glasses and generally making a noise. Humbly Sam approached him and offered to help but was greeted with such hostile rudeness that he decided to cut his losses and go home. Maybe she'd be there already. But, of course, she wasn't.

Sally rolled in on Tuesday night, suntanned, exuberant, and wearing a whole new set of clothes, with several glossy shopping bags swinging from her shoulder. She'd been to France, she told them, with some guys she had met in a bar, and really had one whale of a time, just look at the booty she'd acquired. Designer-cut pants and a couple of striped sweaters, plus a Hermès silk shirt and a strapless satin slip of a thing that even Sam could tell spelled big money.

"From Cherbourg?" he asked, suspiciously.

"No, Paris, you dope."

"How did you come to be there?" he asked. "I thought you said you were on a boat?"

"I went with Hector, a guy I met in Cherbourg," she explained patiently. "He brought me home in his motor-launch. He's a great guy. You must meet him."

"What happened to the original two?" persisted Sam. He knew he was overstepping the mark with all these questions but he just couldn't help it. She was incorrigible, and he was fascinated as well as repelled by her lifestyle.

"They got . . . mislaid," she said. "I lost them in Cherbourg."

"How come?"

She giggled, unable not to share the joke.

"The customs men were waiting when we arrived," she said. "And they picked them up. Isn't that a riot? It's a long story but I managed to lose myself in the crowd and luckily ran into Hector, who saved me by sweeping me off to Paris."

She really did think it was funny. Sam picked up the unread *Independent* and headed for his room. He didn't even hope she would join him there tonight. There were times when Sally's doings left him with a bad taste in the mouth. The sooner she settled down, the better. He'd have to give it some serious thought.

Chapter Twenty-five

Georgy was in Harrods the same Saturday as Vivienne, and also in Bond Street, but she didn't run into her again, which was probably just as well. She was shopping for a gift for Gus. She planned to surprise him with it later that night when she turned up at Orso's at his regular table, something to commemorate the success of *Autumn Crocus*. It was hard to know what to get for the man who had everything but Georgy was ingenious, and also a stayer. The Fabergé exhibition had given her the idea of jeweled flowers, but that was wildly beyond her means and also perhaps a touch inappropriate for a woman to give to a man. She thought about an engraved cigarette case but he didn't smoke, or an Edwardian snuff box, but he didn't do that either. She really wished he would, now she thought of it, because it would rather suit his Edwardian style.

She looked at cuff links but where on earth did you start? Antique ones, jeweled ones, sets with dress studs to match? Cartier, Tiffany, Calvin Klein? She had already trawled Camden Passage but all to no avail. There was no point in doing it at all unless they were exactly right and, now she came to think of it, Georgy had never actually seen Gus in sleeves that were not rolled up.

Her mind flicked over his elegant house and she contemplated tasteful objets d'art that might complement his impeccable taste, but here again she drew a blank. A piece of porcelain, an exquisite glass bowl, Dresden egg coddlers for the breakfast table? Just the thought of the scowl on the face of Karl the Kraut was enough to put her off that one; so where else could she look? Whenever Georgy thought about gifts for Gus, in her mind it had a habit of turning into a wedding list. What she really wanted to buy was the beginnings of a dinner service, or a deluxe Cuisinart, or something tasteful for the bedroom, and she found herself beating her head in frustration and thinking *if only, if only*.

In the end she settled for an arrangement of silk flowers—peonies and lilies in a plain glass bowl—which she arranged to have delivered to the house that afternoon, to avoid embarrassment at the restaurant. She hadn't actually been invited but that was where he always ate after the show and tonight of all nights surely called for some sort of a celebration. Maybe she'd take a bottle of champagne—or should she phone Orso's in advance and ask them to put some on ice?

That night Georgy dressed up for a change. She was so accustomed to wearing her working uniform of dungarees or jeans with a drab T-shirt or sweater that it was exciting to have a reason to rummage through her closet and choose something to make herself stand out and be appealing to Gus. Beth was no guideline at all, with her comfortable, frumpy clothes and flat shoes, but then she had been a back number all these years and Gus clearly preferred a more theatrical look.

In the main, Georgy's clothes were conservative. She had inherent good taste which led to cashmere and silk, with neat little Peter Pan collars and Chanel-style two-pieces, all suitable for a smart interview but not what she was seeking for tonight. She pulled out several outfits and laid them on the bed, then, in a flurry of agitated activity, tried each one on and gave it a negative vote. No, no, no. This was not the

Georgy Kirsch she wished to project. She wanted to look smart and zippy and stylish; there was nothing here that would suit.

By ten to five she was panicking so she grabbed her pocketbook and headed back west, desperate to find exactly the right thing before the stores closed at six. The King's Road, she had discovered, was a real no-go area. Full of tat and easy chic—cheerful, bright, and inexpensive—but not what Georgy was searching for today. It had to be Harvey Nichols or Browns, but was there time? She was standing on the edge of the Fulham Road, dithering about taking a cab and if so, where to, when she spotted a small boutique that looked her sort of place, and headed blindly through the door.

She still didn't know, but the girls were nice and some of the stock was great fun. *With your legs,* they told her, *you ought to wear something short,* and, before she knew it, they had her into something minuscule and strapless, made of scarlet silk, but striking—no doubt of that—and actually rather becoming. *Shoes?* they asked her, as she proffered her card. *There's a boutique two doors up that does just the thing.* So there she was, on the run again, with twenty minutes in hand, and ended up with Victorian satin ankle boots, high-heeled like a tart's and tightly laced.

There was time for a sit-down and a cup of tea when she got home, as well as a shower and a nap, since the show didn't end till ten-thirty. But Georgy, being a fusser, had to get it all on long before time and then pace agitatedly up and down, trying to decide whether she dared wear it. Her shoulders were a bit bony but she could always cover them up. A shawl, maybe—but she didn't have one.

"Hello, darling!" said the cabbie, when she finally left, and that very nearly sent her scuttling back home.

Orso's were polite but oddly puzzled when she swept in and asked for Mr. Hardy's table. She saw why the instant the waiter led her there; it was a table for ten and already full occupied.

"Hi, sweetie," said Beth in surprise, sitting next to Gus with Imogen on his other side. "Nobody told me you were coming or we'd have picked you up."

There was silence. Several pairs of eyes, most notably Marla's and Karl's, glared hostility at Georgy, while Gus gazed helplessly in all directions and for once failed to come up with an answer.

"Squeeze up, darling," said Beth cheerfully, quick to the rescue. "Look, there's plenty of room next to Imogen for another small one."

Georgy handed her sable jacket to the waiter and stood there revealed in all her satin splendor. Beth, she noted, was wearing a black linen smock over pants, and even Marla was more or less covered up. The rest of the gang were in workout clothes or jeans, as normal, and Gus wore his familiar denim. She had boobed—and in spades.

"What a gorgeous dress!" shrieked Imogen, as diplomatic as her ma, and Georgy squeezed herself into the extra chair provided by a disapproving waiter and tried valiantly to make the best of it. But inside, once again, she was bleeding.

"What am I going to do about it?" asked Gus, sitting at Beth's table the next day, head in hands. "I know it's my fault, you don't need to spell that out again, but *what am I going to do?*"

It was almost funny. Beth suppressed her grin. He was such a dope, her husband, and so incorrigibly vain. She stirred the mushroom soup and added a little dill. It would do him no harm to have to face someone else's feelings for a change. Maybe it would even help him to grow up.

"Overkill, that's probably the answer," she said, after a moment's thought. "Ever thought of pouncing on her and seeing what happens?"

"You're joking!" He was appalled.

"Not entirely." More *crème fraîche,* a touch more black pepper. Perhaps a little lemon juice.

"Your problem is you're always so much the gentleman. A touch of the old courtly love, that's what gets to them every time. It could go on forever unless you stop it now. Assuming that's what you want."

She stuck a teaspoon into her pot and waved it in front of his mouth. Like Imogen, Gus had grown to be an expert taster.

"It's hot," she warned.

"Mm," he said. Then: "You can't be serious. Pounce?"

"Either that, or propose. Only I'm pretty certain she'd accept. Could you cope with that?"

His eyes were anguished until he saw the laughter in hers, and they both collapsed on the table in a great guffaw of mirth.

"Seriously," he said, wiping his eyes. "It's getting far beyond a joke. If she turns up one more time uninvited, I can't be answerable for the consequences. I think Karl will kill her, I really do. He's barely restrainable now."

"Maybe then they'd lock him up and you could get on with a more normal life."

She was only half joking. She still loved him a lot and grieved at times for his unconventional lifestyle. Gay, she could handle, just—though she thought it a shame, particularly after all the good times they'd had together—but Karl was a lot to stomach. What men like Gus—handsome, intelligent, educated, and fortyish—could see in these callow boys defeated her. Yes, he had a delectable bum, she would grant him that, but didn't the initial lust wear off faster than this? And why couldn't Gus find someone more worthy? It was an ancient debate but it still troubled Beth. Why not an equal, one of his peers? The theater was packed with really wonderful men of a similar persuasion, so why Karl? *As soon ask me, Why Oliver?* she thought. Only she didn't think the two cases were at all comparable.

"If you were straight, you'd be a dirty old man," she commented as she stirred in the cream. Then they both screamed with laughter again until Imogen appeared accus-

ingly to tell them to shut up and to remind Gus he'd
promised to help her with her math.

"The thing is," said Gus carefully, as they strolled along the
bank of the canal, "things are not always as they seem."

One of the aspects of Georgy he particularly disliked was
her tendency to stand too close, to crowd his space. She
was doing it now, walking right up tight against him as if
they were lovers. Any minute now she'd be taking his hand
like Imogen.

He tried again.

"I mean, there they go"—he indicated ahead—"the two
lovely ladies in my life, to whom I am devoted, but that's
not really the point."

This was awful. He was getting nowhere. Up close, her
teeth were extraordinarily unattractive, small and pointed
and feral, like a ferret at bay. She was staring at him intently, her mouth slightly open, and he felt like wading into
the filthy water in order to make his escape. Beth and
Imogen, deep in conversation, strolled on oblivious of his
situation. He loved them both to distraction but he could
use a bit of assistance right now. Should he whistle or
what? On cue, Beth turned and waved but kept on walking.
Damn her, she knew exactly what he was trying to do, and
would she help him? Dream on!

"What I'm trying to say," he blundered on, "is that all is
not as it might seem."

Georgy's large gray eyes grew moist. This time she did
take his hand and squeezed it with sudden understanding.

"Gus, it's okay," she said. "I know what you're trying to
tell me and you don't have to worry. I know about Beth and
you, we're friends after all and discuss these things."
Georgy was proud of her new, close relationship with Beth.
It was a first for her, to have a female confidante. "Of
course I'd never do anything to come between you but she
tells me all that has been over for years. It's okay. But it's

darling of you to be so considerate. Most men wouldn't have given it a thought."

Cripes, this was even worse than he had feared. *Beth, where are you when I need you?*

"Look," he said, toughening up, stopping her in her tracks and turning her to face him. "There's something I have to say."

The eyes were still misty, the mouth all moist, almost as if she expected to be kissed. Suppressing a slight shudder, Gus took the plunge before things could get any worse or more out of hand.

"I am what I am and I can't do anything about it. You are a wonderful person and I love you like a sister but that's all there is. Or will ever be."

So help me, God.

"You mean there's somebody else?" The lip was beginning to tremble, any second now there'd be tears. He couldn't believe this, not in one who was usually so smart.

"Yes, if you like," he said, defeated. No point laboring a point if she didn't want to hear it. "And I'm sorry."

"You rat!"

She virtually spat at him, her eyes now ablaze, then turned abruptly on her heel and flounced away, back along the towpath in the direction they had come.

"What happened to Georgy?" asked Beth in genuine surprise when he caught them up.

"She went home," he said, linking both their arms in his and continuing with their afternoon stroll. Whew, but there were moments when he felt like giving it all up and entering a monastery.

Chapter Twenty-six

The tractor was giving him trouble and he cursed as he cranked it up one more time, his hand wrapped in an oily rag, the sun beating down on the back of his neck. So much plowing still waiting to be done and the whole of the Long Meadow to be seeded. One of these days he was going to have to let up a little and hire some help to replace the heirs he no longer could count on. He paused to wipe his brow and tilt the battered straw hat lower over his eyes. He was not as old as he looked but had weathered enough trouble to have put many a younger man into the ground.

Shimmering in the haze from the baking soil, a figure was approaching from the far end of the field, walking with a lightness of step and length of stride that were not familiar. He leaned against the hot metal bonnet of the tractor and shaded his eyes in an effort to see. The parched brown earth stretched for acres in all directions. Not a single other living thing was visible on the horizon. Now who was this, then, coming to make trouble?

"Hi, it's me."

For a full two minutes his mind was blank, so long had it been. The figure grew nearer.

"You didn't come to see me, so I thought I'd pay you a visit. Just for old times' sake."

As recognition dawned, he could scarcely believe what he was hearing—the voice of the damned; a visitor straight out of hell. Instinctively, he straightened and stepped back, holding one gnarled hand in front of his face to shade his eyes and shield them.

"You just stay away from here, do you hear me? You've caused enough damage already. I won't have you on my land."

He was a simple man, a farmer, with a quiet faith that had kept him going through all these long, tortured years. Not educated or even particularly clever; he knew right from wrong and kept himself to himself. And recognized evil even when it came disguised as kin.

"Oh, come on now, you can't mean what you're saying. Who have you got left now apart from me? Time to kiss and make up, don't you think?"

The smile was bright and mocking and the laughter light. He turned and stumbled away, back up the empty field away from this demon, the one being in the world he had sworn never to set eyes on again.

"Won't you even talk? I'm going away."

His ears were deaf to the voice of corruption and he didn't even turn when he heard the sound of the tractor's engine, reluctantly revving into life.

"Can't we just talk? One last time?" But he was having none of it.

The tractor caught him fair and square in the middle of the back and rolled over him, leaving him to die—alone, as he had lived for so long—in the center of the land that was all that was left to him of a ruined life.

Chapter Twenty-seven

Beth was sharpening knives. She had the full armory spread across the kitchen table as she worked away with her worn steel, using skill and good honest sweat in place of something more modern. Gus had once offered to buy her an electric sharpener but Beth had pooh-poohed the suggestion. Professionals, she had pointed out, always did it the old-fashioned way.

"You mean the hard way?"

She had smiled. Gus was such a perfectionist himself, it was satisfying for once to be able to act superior. And the truth was, once you had the knack, it was really no effort at all. Probably that was true of most things; a secret well kept.

The phone rang. It was Georgy again, this time with a long grouch against Gus. Beth listened silently, receiver tucked under her chin, and went on plying her steel. *Oh, tell me the old, old story.* There were times she was glad to be *hors de combat*, away from the exhausting business of love. A little hanky-panky on the side was quite enough for her, especially since she had gotten to know Vivienne slightly and seen the sad lines in her face and those haunted eyes. Great beauty could be an asset but it obviously wasn't enough. Beth's life might be patchy but at least she could say, with her hand on her heart, that it was satisfying. That was a woman who was clearly suffering, and it didn't make Beth feel good.

Imogen bounced into the kitchen, clutching her Snoopy pajamas and a toothbrush, anxious to get going with her own evening plans. She was growing so fast, they would soon be living separate lives. Tonight Beth had a date with Oliver, and Imogen was staying over with her friend Natalie. Imogen picked up the Chinese cleaver and waved it threateningly at her mother.

"Put that down! It's sharp!" warned Beth, then, "Sorry, Georgy, but I do have to go. I have this awful child capering around me, about to do herself or me some monstrous harm. I know, like father like daughter. Tell me about it! Talk to you soon."

She laughed at Georgy's blunt reaction, then hung up.

"Come along, pumpkin, let's get this show on the road. Oliver will be here in less than an hour and I'm nowhere near finished yet. And Natalie's mum will be expecting you."

"What are you doing?" asked Imogen curiously, surveying the warlike battery on the table.

"What does it look like? I've got a Greek wedding and a party of Japanese businessmen this week so I thought it was time for a little honing and polishing—just in case they ask for sushi."

"What, the Greeks?"

"No, idiot. Now, let's get cracking. Do you want me to run you there or will you walk?"

"I'll go on my blades. No sweat."

Imogen helped herself to a biscuit from the tin on the dresser, then sat down to lace up her boots. Gathering up her hardware and sticking the knives safely back into their slots in the block, Beth gazed at her daughter with rapt approval. She was a good kid and a joy to have around. That was one more blessing she had that rich, beautiful, oh-so-well-connected Vivienne Nugent lacked. But this was no time to be getting sentimental over her. Beth glanced at the kitchen clock. In forty minutes' time, if she were lucky, Vivienne's husband would be banging on her door, and, she devoutly hoped, God willing and barring accidents, banging her into the bargain not a long time later.

With Imogen safely packed off for the night, Beth sprinted up the stairs and turned on both bath taps full blast. Because she combined her career with being a full-time mother, she rarely had the luxury of a proper soak and a total workover before she met up with her lover. This was just a typical evening; forty minutes for bath, change of clothes, makeup job, the lot. One of her gossipy girlfriends, a Greek with more money than sense, had the irritating habit of ringing Beth for an inconsequential chat just as she was tearing around the house trying to get her act together.

"Now go and lie in a candlelit bathroom," Helena would end up soothingly, having wasted most of Beth's precious time with the solipsistic details of the minor crises of her life, "and be sure to relax properly before you meet him. Get yourself into a proper frame of mind."

You stupid twit! Beth always wanted to shout. *How can I when you have already consumed three-quarters of my getting-ready time? It was a maximum twenty minutes, now it's down to five. You've had all day to paint your nails, watch Australian soaps, nap, and shop, now you're treading on my space. Get real! Get yourself a life! Get lost!*

But she never did, of course. That was Beth all over. She would make soothing noises, fix a lunch date for two weeks' time which Helena would invariably cancel at the last minute, and promise to keep in touch. But, no doubt about it—and here was the point—she'd still choose, any day, the chaos and bustle of her own erratic life over the sterile emptiness of her rich friend's. Which brought her back, inevitably, to Vivienne Nugent.

Beth was back in the bedroom with the bath emptied and quickly rinsed round, frantically blow-drying the damp ends of her hair, when Oliver phoned to say he was going to be late. At least an hour and a half, he said; something to do with the bank.

Of course, she thought, what else but the bank? It wasn't a traffic accident, or a nuclear bomb, or an unscheduled cloud of locusts, or even another woman. Nothing as complicated as that. At least Oliver was consistent in his excuses. In an odd way, it gave her a certain security.

And it also gave her the breathing space she had just been longing for; time to run an iron over her less than immaculate linen shirt, to hunt for the cuff links that went really well with it, to pin up her hem, even stitch it. Time, if she judged it correctly, for a five-minute lie on the bed to unwind and think randy thoughts in readiness for the evening of passion she had been looking forward to all week.

One of the delights of illicit love, as Beth had observed before, was that you got the thrills without the drudgery, the gingerbread without the guilt. If you only saw someone sporadically, it was easy to present yourself always at your best. Life's little nastinesses, like period pains, cold sores, and unwaxed bikini lines, could be swept under the bed with the rest of the fluff balls. Beth stretched luxuriously on her white lace duvet, unwinding to Streisand's *Back to Broadway* and studying her less than perfect cuticles which she simply hadn't the energy to fix. Not after the hours she'd just spent laboring over a hot stove.

At nine Oliver rang again to say the meeting was still in progress and he wasn't sure what time he'd get away. He apologized and told her he loved her. He said he'd call the minute he could but urged her to have a snack, just in case. Beth made smooching noises over the phone and said it really wasn't a problem, that she'd still got plenty to do and would expect him when she saw him—then cursed and kicked the bedpost when he rang off. Shit, shit, shit. This was the downside of being a mistress, though how she loathed and detested that word, finding it archaic and degrading. The side it was easy to overlook when the going was good. She wrapped herself, cursing, in her silk kimono and sloped off downstairs to see what she could plunder from the fridge out of the advance preparations she had already made for Wednesday's Greek wedding.

With a plate of hummus and pita bread to keep her stomach from rumbling, and a whole bottle of chilled Chardonnay to wash it down, Beth settled in front of the telly to watch the end of the news and await Oliver's next call. Her golden mood was fast darkening round the edges, she had to admit, and she couldn't avoid a growing grievance at her situation, with a child safely parked and a whole evening wasted—for what?

Love without ties was a marvelous thing, far superior to the drudgery and bind of marriage, provided you were the one on the up end of the seesaw, the one who called the shots. While it was you with the burgeoning career and glorious future, financially solvent and answerable to no one, love without ties was a piece of cake. No messing. Happiness, romance, eternal optimism, and great orgasms were on the upside; the downside things like guilt and betrayal and loneliness and middle age and acting like a louse and betraying your friends you learned to push under the carpet.

Michael Fish gestured and smirked and made jokes about the weather while Beth, reflectively, poured herself another glass of wine. And, almost imperceptibly, a pale specter with extraordinary bone structure and haunted eyes slid into place beside her on the sofa.

While meeting Oliver had been the genuine thing, an instant *coup de foudre* that Beth could no more have ducked than a sudden thunderstorm out of a clear sky in an open field, loving Gus had been something altogether more low-key.

And as their parting had been so gentle, Beth and Gus had remained the best of buddies. They met only sporadically but stayed in touch and their youthful love matured into something more lasting, more like the empathy between siblings. Gus would always be there for her and Imogen and she for him. It was a comfortable love, a more enduring one—better by far than something explosive like the love Beth had for Oliver.

Who had still not rung. She carried the empty bottle into the darkened kitchen and pulled the cork of another. The clock said ten to eleven and she had an early start in the morning. What the hell, her mood of erotic anticipation was long since dissipated so she might as well be blotto whether he turned up or not. This was the aspect of illicit love she really hated, it made her feel grubby and ashamed. Oliver had swept her off her feet with his glamour and raw need, after years of noninvolvement and a series of casual relationships that would not threaten her child, but lately his increasing absences had made Beth realize what she was having to do without. Now, while she was still at her best and her child was rapidly growing up and gaining her own independence.

The phone finally rang at ten past and, by mutual agreement, they decided the night was shot. He told her again that he loved her, repeated his regrets, promised to call in the morning and that he would make up for it.

Beth grunted and sank another glass of Chardonnay as she crashed down the receiver in the sleeping kitchen. Then, gripped by a sudden unspeakable rage, she grabbed hold of one of her newly sharpened knives and flicked it, with the deadly precision of a circus performer, across the room and into the scrubbed pine surface of the table, where it bit with a quivering thwang.

Sod off, Oliver Nugent, I deserve better! she thought— and somewhere in the lurking shadows the sad-eyed specter responded with a tight-lipped smile.

Chapter Twenty-eight

Vivienne's house meant more to her than anything. She hadn't started off domesticated, it had grown on her over the years since they had bought this wonderful place. To begin with it had been something of an extravagant gesture, a sign to the world that the Nugents were upwardly mobile, but lately, with Oliver's increasing absences abroad, the house had become Vivienne's fortress, her retreat from what she felt to be an increasingly hostile world. Here only Dorabella and the cats could see her as she drifted inconsequentially from room to room, and when Dorabella was off duty, she spent more and more time shut away in the sanctuary of her bedroom.

They used to entertain a lot as a couple and at one time Vivienne's soirees had been the hottest ticket in town. She had had dinners for thirty on a regular basis, with tables laid out in the candlelit conservatory and live music in the first-floor drawing room, while guests carried their plates to sit on the stairs and listen. Ashkenazy had played here, and Itzhak Perlman, and she'd even persuaded Pavarotti, because he admired her beautiful eyes, to come around one evening after they'd eaten and sing a couple of arias to go with the brandy and cigars. If she'd known Eleanor Palmer, she'd doubtless have invited her too.

These days, however, their socializing had died except for the occasions when bank business intervened and Vivienne was obliged to reinvent herself as a hostess and throw sterile dinners for people she didn't much like, who lacked the glamour and wit of her own chosen circle. Oliver was away too often and Vivienne simply hadn't the energy to put it all together anymore. She began to see the shallowness of many of her acquaintances, people who only cultivated her in order to get onto her dinner list, and she had entirely lost the zest for empty conversation. What she yearned for these days was friends, but how on earth did you set about finding them?

Meeting Georgy in Harrods had given Vivienne quite a jolt. She had tried to shut her mind to that unpleasant business, and coming face-to-face with the American girl had been an unwelcome reminder. Besides, she found Georgy querulous and rather pushy and hadn't much warmed to her. There was something about native New Yorkers that set Vivienne's sensitivities on edge. Georgy was simply too loud, too abrasive, and altogether too forthright to be a natural friend. She was also at least fifteen years younger and therefore something of a threat.

In retrospect, however, Vivienne had to admit she had quite enjoyed her brief stay in hospital. She was not used to the easy chat of a bunch of other women and had found it at first intrusive. Until her adventure of entering a public ward, she could not have tolerated the idea of not being entirely private, but after a bit she had found that the presence of the other women had actually helped. She remembered the laughter and the slightly coarse cheerfulness that was always there in the background and on which she had begun to rely, a morale-booster rather than a deterrent. It put her in mind of the famous wartime spirit, and she missed it.

More than anything, however, she was finding she missed Beth. She had not forgotten her kindness and the rallying words from beyond the curtain before she was wheeled off down to the theater. She longed to be able to pick up the phone and invite her to lunch, but something still stopped her. It was absurd, but Vivienne was frightened of being snubbed; Beth was so warm and outgoing, so friendly and natural with everyone around her, yet Vivienne sensed some evasion, something she did not understand. So she compromised and rang Catherine instead, suggesting they meet for tea one afternoon at Fortnum & Mason.

Vivienne was shocked when she saw how Catherine seemed to have shrunk since leaving the hospital. Though always slight, her clothes now hung on her and her pale skin, stretched too tightly over her bones, seemed almost transparent. Her cup rattled slightly as she placed it in its saucer and Vivienne found herself stroking her hand.

"How are you, my dear?" she asked with real concern.

"Not terribly good," Catherine admitted and told her about the continuing dull pain in her lower abdomen, where the doctor had made his investigatory incision.

"What was it exactly?" Vivienne loathed the subject but felt she had to show interest.

"Ovary," said Catherine, coloring faintly. "I had a cyst which they removed successfully. What I'm feeling now is just the results of the surgery, adhesions or something, so they said."

Then why does your skin look like fish scales? thought Vivienne. *And your hair so lifeless and dull?*

She changed the subject. How were their fellow patients? she inquired. Had Catherine kept up with any of them? A flush of life returned to Catherine's pallid cheeks and she visibly perked up. She did see Sally, she said, who dropped by quite often to visit her mother. And Sally saw Beth. And Beth saw Georgy.

"I like Beth," said Vivienne cautiously. "I admire her spirit. I'd quite like to see her again. Do you think we could all have lunch—or are women with careers like that always rushed off their feet?"

"Don't know," said Catherine. "I suppose it depends. Sally knows the lowdown. I think Beth mostly does lunchtime affairs—business do's in the City, stuff like that—but when she has a run of working in the evenings, then she alters her hours and takes some time off. That's the joy of being your own boss. Shall I ask Sally?"

"Would you?"

San Lorenzo, thought Vivienne, *or the Fifth Floor at Harvey Nichols.* Or perhaps Dorabella could whip up something simple so she could invite them to the house. But hang on, Beth was a professional cook. Would Dorabella's basic cooking be impressive enough? she wondered.

"What about Sally?" asked Catherine. "Do you want to include her as well? She works part-time at that pub near the World's End. I know she's often free at lunchtime because that's when she comes to sit with Mama."

"Why not?" said Vivienne, expansively. "And the American girl too, I've forgotten her name. Let's have them all. Are you in touch with her?"

"I'm not but Beth is. Sally will know."

What fun! An all-girl lunch party after all these sterile months. Vivienne was already cheering up. Something to plan for; more important, something to look forward to. Nothing too fussy, keep it simple; don't risk frightening them off. Light, delicious food and a lot of wine, time to linger and gossip and catch up; to do the things women did in groups and get to know each other better.

"I'll tell you what!" she said gaily, touching Catherine's fragile wrist with one manicured nail. "Why don't I ask Addison Harvey too, just for a lark. He's by way of being a bit of a family friend. His wife and I sit on committees together and he plays squash with my husband. What do you think? If we're going to have a reunion, why not make it complete!"

It was meant to be a joke, but failed abysmally. The blood drained from Catherine's face, she knocked over her teacup, and Vivienne was just in time to prevent her from falling to the floor. What had she said?

"Catherine? Catherine?" she whispered, propping the life-

less woman back on to her chair and urgently fanning her
with the menu. "No, it's quite all right," she added in her society voice to the gawkers at the next tables and the anxious
waitress who was hovering. "She's just feeling a tiny bit
faint. More tea, please, and a fresh cup."

"I'm sorry," croaked Catherine after a while, wiping her
streaming forehead with a sad lace hankie and pulling ineffectually at the strands of damp hair that clung to her neck.
"Too embarrassing . . . I'm all right really."

"Are you quite sure?" Vivienne was genuinely alarmed
and the waitress still hovered.

"Yes, I'm sorry."

Catherine was almost weeping with consternation and the
chatterers at the adjoining tables had fallen ominously silent.
Vivienne swept them with an imperious eye and it worked
like magic. Conversation flowed again around them and
they could, at last, have a private word.

"Is there something you want to tell me?"

"No." Catherine faltered.

How could she explain? It was something she had never
spoken of to anyone, and Vivienne, for all her kindness, was
not the coziest of people nor the most accessible. And she
knew his wife, she said.

"I am so sorry," she said again, mopping her face. "I
shouldn't have come."

And then, miraculously, a fresh pot of tea arrived with
clean cups and saucers, and the bill.

"My dear, she was positively reeling!"

Vivienne was on the phone to Beth, describing the
events of the previous week. "Do you suppose she's all
right? Or might she be iller than she realizes? More important, is there anything we can do? I feel so helpless
. . . so responsible somehow."

She would ask Phoebe to check with Addison but assumed he wouldn't tell; not if he maintained the professional discretion she was relying on. Beth answered

monosyllabically. She was, as usual, in her kitchen, furiously concentrating on marinating two dozen quails, with one eye on the Aga and the other on the clock. This woman certainly did go on. Didn't she know about deadlines and life in the fast lane? Obviously not. Plus Beth had no desire to get too girly with her; the embarrassment factor put anything like that firmly out of court.

"Anyhow," went on Vivienne, on a lighter note, "I am so glad Catherine was well enough to pass on my message and I do hope you'll be able to join us on Thursday week. Nothing special, I assure you, just a snack and a glass of something at my place, to catch up on old times. Shall we say twelve-fifteen or twelve-thirty? Quite informal . . ."

Oh, Lord, now what was she to do?

"I'm afraid it's not as easy as all that. I do have a full-time job, you know, and can rarely get away for social lunches."

It was more or less the truth. The fact that she did not work every day need never be divulged. The last thing in the world Beth needed was the extra complication in her life of having to pretend friendship to a woman she was betraying. The slightly plummy voice had fallen silent and Beth, still tasting and adjusting, realized she was being less than polite. She pulled herself together. If anyone was at fault, it certainly wasn't Vivienne, and there was no call to be rude or even offhand.

"How nice," she said, with an enthusiasm she was far from feeling. "I'll certainly come if I can. I'm sure I can rearrange things. Anything I can do to help?"

And, while Vivienne whittered on about it just being a few old pals informally round the table in the conservatory, her inner voice said, *Cripes! What in hell's name do I wear?*

What *did* you wear, for lunch with your lover's wife, in his own house, in his absence?

"Sackcloth and ashes," said Deirdre, disapprovingly.

"A dagger in your sock and keep both hands in view," said Jane, who was married to a Highlander.

"A gumshield and a gun," said Sally, ever the practical one.

Vivienne's house, when she got there, turned out to be gorgeous. Beth had driven past on a number of occasions, of course she had, but had never dared loiter or even give it more than a passing glance. Now she pulled up outside, in full view of anyone who happened to be watching, and sat for a while just gazing before she undid her seat belt and got out. It was early Victorian and stucco-fronted, gleaming white in the morning sunshine and counterpointed by a magnificent magnolia tree in full flower. The Boltons was a beautiful garden square with a church in the middle, as quiet and immaculate as Beth's own picturesque enclave off Ladbroke Grove. After a quick check in the car mirror that she wasn't too much of a wreck after her hectic morning, Beth walked up the immaculate path and banged on the gleaming knocker.

A smiling woman with smooth brown skin and blue-black hair opened the door. She wore a blue cotton uniform and starched white apron. It wasn't often, Beth reflected, that you encountered liveried servants these days in London. She followed her across a black and white marble floor into an inner hallway dominated by an immense rococo-style gilt mirror and marble-topped console table.

Vivienne appeared at the top of the stairs, smiling and holding out her hands.

"Beth, my dear, how nice to see you!"

She wore a plain silk shirt in dramatic gentian blue over narrow black pants, and sapphire earrings that would have been able to breathe more easily in a bank vault. Beth, aware of the turmeric stains on her own baggy sweater, swallowed nervously and smiled back.

"Nice of you to invite me. Hope I'm not the last."

She ran up the stairs and they kissed lightly on each cheek before Vivienne led her into a vast sunny drawing room overlooking the square. Catherine was there already, prim on a Regency chair covered in golden watered silk and toying with a glass of sherry. She was clearly relieved to see another person.

She does look bad, thought Beth sympathetically.

"What a gorgeous room!" she said. "Like Versailles. I'm surprised you let hoi polloi pollute it."

Vivienne smiled. She was used to this sort of comment and occasionally wondered if a slightly less formal sitting room might be an idea, for gatherings such as this. A den—or was it a rumpus room the Americans called it? She'd give it some thought. They certainly had enough space.

"So how've we all been?" asked Beth, accepting a glass of chilled Chablis and reclining into the cushions. "All better, I hope?"

Vivienne nodded, hoping to glide over the subject, but Catherine hesitated.

"I'm still in quite a lot of pain," she said apologetically, "something to do with the aftereffects of surgery."

"And running around after that terrible old mother of yours," remarked Vivienne, offering salted cashew nuts in a silver dish.

There were voices in the hall and Dorabella showed Sally into the room. She wore her familiar patched jeans and scruffy boots, surmounted by a striped poncho, over a man's denim shirt with the sleeves rolled up to the elbow. She looked enchanting, positively edible.

"Hi there, folks, g'day!" she said, pecking Vivienne on the cheek as she passed and crossing the room to give Beth a sloppy kiss. "Isn't this just ace!"

She gazed round Vivienne's palatial room like Alice in Wonderland, childishly delighted by so much splendor. Beth relaxed, prepared at last to enjoy herself. When Sally entered a room, she brought the sunshine with her.

Georgy arrived late and flustered, laden down with cameras and complaining. Vivienne shook the outstretched hand, gave her a flickering smile, then led them all down to

the garden room, a huge, glass-walled conservatory filled
with running water and luscious plants.

"Oh, boy!" breathed Sally, standing on the threshold and
soaking in the warm, damp, heavily scented air. "This is
some place you've got here, Viv. You ought to charge the
public a fiver a time to see over it. You'd soon make the running costs back. I bet where Georgy comes from they'd
have coach tours to a house like this."

A table draped with a pink linen cloth was set for five
next to a shallow indoor pool where huge goldfish lazed in
deep green water, illuminated from beneath. Dorabella
placed cold mineral water and another bottle of Chablis in
the ice bucket beside Vivienne's chair, then withdrew to the
trolley to serve the food.

"Well," said Beth. "This was such a good idea. How great
to see you all again, looking so much better."

And she found she really meant it, despite her original
misgivings.

They smiled at each other, pleased to be together again.

"Thought I wouldn't recognize you in your clothes,"
cracked Sally, and even Vivienne smiled as she poured the
wine.

"It seemed a good idea, a little reunion. To see how you
all were doing; to catch up on the news."

Mustn't let on how relieved she was they had all turned
up; at all costs, mustn't let the loneliness and panic show
through.

"I've gotta be out of here by three," said Georgy, as if
reading her.

"Me too," said Beth, glancing at her watch. "We working
girls, you know."

"I've got a shoot on the South Bank. A new ballet company from Hong Kong, opening next week in *Les
Sylphides*."

"How fascinating," said Vivienne in her best society
voice. "What lives you girls do have. Unlike me who's little
more than a housewife, I'm afraid."

Some housewife. Chatelaine of a castle more like, thought Beth.

Dorabella had made omelettes which melted in the mouth like butter, and a crisp green salad. Beth took a forkful, then raised her hand in the air with finger and thumb joined in appreciation. Bravo!

"Exquisite!" she breathed. "With cooking like this at home, who needs to go out?"

Or stray, she thought. *Even less understandable.*

"Oh, it's all Dorabella's doing," said Vivienne, handing them a silver dish covered with a linen cloth, containing warm rolls. "The kitchen is her preserve entirely."

"Well, when she gets bored with luxury living," said Beth with a smile, "tell her there's always a humdrum job for her with me."

They chattered on, catching up on each other's lives, then Dorabella wheeled in fresh strawberries and a pot of coffee.

"Anyone want cream?" asked Vivienne. "No, didn't think so. Everyone's so healthy these days."

"Except for me," said Georgy, lighting up a fag in that selfish way Americans had. Catherine hesitated just for a second, then rummaged in her handbag for her own packet. Vivienne let it go. Normally she hated people smoking in her house, but what the hell. Friendship was what counted; all of a sudden she was beginning to reassess her priorities.

The conversation shifted back to hospital, specifically to their suave consultant.

"He's not really handsome," said Georgy, "but he sure as hell is glamorous."

"It's power what does it," said Beth. "That's always a killer. Combined with money, of course. He must be making a pretty packet."

"We know him socially," confessed Vivienne, "at least, I know his wife and Oliver plays squash with him at one of his clubs."

Her secret must be safe, she had decided that some time

ago. His medical ethics must surely protect her, and certainly Oliver had never said a word.   .

Catherine fell silent and Beth saw she had grown unnaturally pale.

"Do you still see him, Catherine?" Something was wrong.

"He's been to the flat a couple of times."

Then she is iller than she's letting on, thought Beth with compassion. *Poor soul. How brave she is.*

"Probably fancies you," said Sally with a grin. "I don't mind telling you, I wouldn't say no to a bit of that myself. You can tell he has a roving eye. Doctors always do."

Vivienne was reaching for the coffeepot when there was a crash and Catherine hit the floor. She had fainted clean out.

"Crikey," gasped Georgy, "do something."

But Beth and Sally were already there, one on each arm, helping her up.

"I'm sorry, I'm sorry," muttered the poor woman in confusion as she regained her senses. "I really don't know what happened. I don't think I've had too much to drink."

"You're ill, that's what," said Beth firmly, "and we are going to take you home."

She glanced at Sally and together they helped Catherine to her feet and across the conservatory to the door.

"Sorry about this," mouthed Beth to Vivienne, "but I think she probably needs to be in her own bed."

In the hall they came face-to-face with Oliver, returned home unexpectedly early, but scarcely a glance passed between him and Beth. With astonishing cool, all he did was open the heavy front door and stand aside to let them pass. In the street, his Mercedes was drawn up right behind Beth's Volvo.

Bet that gave him a bit of a turn, she thought as they helped Catherine into the passenger seat.

Chapter Twenty-nine

Catherine was shaking and weeping, both at the same time, and when they drew up at Albert Hall Mansions, Sally had almost to carry her from the car. It was no great chore; the poor creature was little more than skin and bone.

"Let me," she said, ringing the doorbell. "This could be tricky but I reckon I can swing it. You've no idea what we are dealing with here."

After a long wait, just as Beth was beginning to fear there was no one at home, the metal cover behind the pinhole eyeglass was pushed aside.

"Who is it?" demanded an imperious voice.

"It's Sal, Lady Palmer," called back Sally. "With Catherine, back from lunch."

There was a further pause while the cover was replaced and they could hear the scrape of the chain being removed. Then the door slowly opened and there stood Eleanor, wrapped in a patterned silk kimono, with all her war paint on. She had obviously been lying in wait.

"At last," she said ungraciously. "Whatever time do you call this?"

"Catherine's sick, Lady Palmer," said Beth, ushering her inside. "She needs to lie down and I think we should call the doctor."

Eleanor appeared unmoved but shuffled ahead of them down the musty corridor toward Catherine's dimly lit room at the rear. There was something slightly touching, Beth thought, about the girlish bedroom with its faded quilt and a row of childhood books, still in their musty dust jackets, lined up in a narrow bookcase next to the bed. She half expected to see one of those Beatrix Potter lamps but the one on the bedside table was quite plain, a faded dusky rose with a fringed shade.

"What on earth's the problem?" asked Eleanor, annoyed at having her own thunder eclipsed. "Too much to drink at lunch, I'll be bound. Catherine can be very silly."

Beth ignored her. She and Sally helped Catherine onto the bed and Beth wiped her damp forehead with a clean tissue.

"How're you feeling now?" she asked softly, reaching for Catherine's pulse and not liking what she felt.

"I'm all right," muttered Catherine, overwhelmed with shame. "I feel such a fool for spoiling the party."

"You didn't spoil it," said Beth, fluffing up the pillows so that she could lie back more comfortably. "We were about to go in any case."

"I think we should leave her to rest," she said to Eleanor and, brooking no argument, ushered both her and Sally from the room.

"Exactly how sick is she?" demanded Beth, when they were seated together in the airless front room, where dusty sunlight filtered through heavy net curtains that were none too clean.

Eleanor flicked one plump hand in the air in a theatrical gesture.

"Oh, it's nothing really," she said dismissively. "Catherine always was a sickly child. No stamina, that's the problem, just like her father. He died and left me when I needed him most, right at the height of my career with the world at my feet. I had to leave the Embassy and all my friends in Vienna and come back here to live on a widow's pittance. Catherine, of course, came home to be with me, as was only proper. She was skulking in Australia at the time, doing a little nursing job, but her heart was never really in it, I knew that. She wasn't a lot of help to me either, I can tell you, not when I was trying to pull together the ruins of my life."

Miserable old cow, thought Beth grimly but Sally brought them down to earth by bouncing to her feet and offering to call the doctor.

"Does she still see Mr. Harvey?" she asked. "Or is there a local GP who would come?"

Eleanor shook her head in horror. A local GP—too vulgar for words. Nothing less than the consultant gynecologist would do, but she still looked doubtful. She always suspected her daughter of making a fuss, though she had to admit she did look peaky today.

"If you think it's really necessary," she said grudgingly. "He is very expensive. Harley Street, you know."

"Not if you see him on the National Health," said Beth patiently, aware that Lady Palmer had not once shown her face in the hospital. She nodded to Sally to make the call. "And Catherine is obviously pretty poorly. Anyone can see that."

Anyone with half an eye, was what she meant—anyone but her mother, now preening in front of the clouded antique mirror at the prospect of receiving such a distinguished visitor. She looked like Madame Butterfly with her chalk-white makeup and heavily accentuated eyes, and the piled-up boot-black hair that needed only a pair of knitting needles to complete the effect. *She's ridiculous,* thought Beth, *a vain, pampered, totally self-absorbed old woman. A creature from another age.* What she needed, literally, was a breath of fresh air in her suffocating, self-indulgent life. Beth longed to rip aside those musty Miss Havisham curtains and throw open the windows.

"He'll be here within the hour," announced Sally. "He's

just winding up in his consulting rooms and says he'll drop by on his way home."

They were lucky, Beth realized. It was not easy to get a consultant to call, and so promptly too. Either the Palmer name still meant something in posh circles or Catherine was a lot more sick than they realized. Probably both. Beth glanced at her watch but Sally said she'd stay. Her hours at the pub were fairly flexible and she knew Joe wouldn't mind if she were late for a change. Beth turned to her with a smile of relief and kissed her cheek. The breath of fresh air was here already; lucky Eleanor. Lucky Catherine.

"You know something, I think he does fancy you," said Sally later, sitting at Catherine's bedside after the doctor had withdrawn, stroking her hand as she tried to get some sleep. "You should have seen his eyes while he was examining you, full of compassion and concern—really caring."

The examination was over and Eleanor had summoned Addison Harvey in her usual imperious manner and was now incarcerated alone with him in her womblike drawing room. Sally, who was getting to know the old lady well, half expected to hear the notes of the piano at any moment and the diva begin to warble. She had absolutely no compassion, that terrible old woman. It was something with which Sally empathized entirely.

The confrontation in the drawing room was, however, not at all as Sally imagined. When Addison Harvey, flushed and concerned, walked in and found himself facing the old lady, done up like a Japanese geisha and waiting for him enthroned in a high-backed chair, all they could do was stare at each other and gasp.

"You!"

"Great heavens! I never imagined such a thing! Wherever did you come from?"

"From Harley Street. I'm your daughter's gynecologist, or weren't you aware of that?"

Even after all these years, the mutual dislike was as fresh as ever, as tangible as a sexual frisson.

"But your name? You've changed it?"

"My mother's. It seemed more . . . fitting."

Eleanor gave a vulgar chuckle, relaxing her guard for the first time.

"Trying to be posh—eh? I must say you've improved a little, without the pit village accent." She waved one hand vaguely in the direction of the sideboard. "Go over there and pour us both a port. I feel we need it after all this. My goodness, whoever would have thought it."

She sat and clucked and shook her head as Addison, like an automaton, did as he was bid. He selected from the cupboard a pair of fine embossed glasses which he dusted off and half filled with port. His head was reeling with shock. The truth was, until this moment he had not recognized his patient, and it was all proving too much for him. He was not as young as he once had been; his heart was working overtime and he felt an attack of asthma threatening. He needed, more than anything, to regain his self-control, time on his own to think before he had to answer any questions.

"Well, you seem to have done all right for yourself," she pronounced, once the glass was in her hand and he was seated. "Better than I would have expected."

With an experienced eye, she noted the cut of his suit and handmade shirt; the designer haircut and heavy gold signet ring. She might be old now and fairly infirm but her connoisseur's eye was as sharp as ever and her standards hadn't slipped.

"I've been lucky." He stared into his glass. Modesty did not sit well on him but he was still severely shaken by this confrontation; running his mental eye rapidly over Catherine's notes, shocked by what he now knew, shaken to the core by the implications.

"I saw you at the theater," announced Eleanor. "I recognized you then but Catherine didn't. I thought it best to say nothing. Does she know it's you?"

He shook his head. "I don't think so. She's really pretty ill and her mind seems to be wandering."

How could he admit to her mother that he hadn't even recognized her, hadn't given her a second thought for twenty years?

"You never did have much backbone," said Eleanor, with satisfaction.

Which was surely the understatement of the century.

Catherine's pale eyes flickered with renewed hope and she leaned across to the dressing table mirror to try to see how she looked. Not too bad, all things considered. The flush his visit had brought to her cheeks was not unbecoming and Sally had brushed her hair and helped her with a flick of lipstick and a dusting of powder before he arrived. Sally would have made an excellent nurse. She had the right instincts regarding a patient's comfort as well as a genuine caring, something Catherine had always been aware she herself lacked.

"You're a dear," she said, touching Sally's hand. "But what makes you think a man like that would take notice of a wreck like me?"

"I was watching him." Sally's vigorous nod brought a ghostly smile to Catherine's lips. "If that wasn't lust in his eyes then I'm still a virgin. Hurry up and get well so that he can have his wicked way with you."

After Sally had gone with a lascivious wink, back to the pub to do her evening stint, Catherine lay in the semi-darkness and thought about Tom. He hadn't said so in so many words but she knew it was him come back to save her. She'd allow him his little surprise. He had given her some pills which were making her feel luxuriously drowsy and, for the first time in weeks, the ache in her abdomen had abated. Tom Harvey. Back at last, just as she had always known he would be, more successful than ever but every bit as charming, with the genius in his healing hands to make her well again. It was funny really. Throughout her recent illness, she had felt his presence hovering near. Now she knew for certain it wasn't an illusion; she had been right all the time.

She was wearing her faded Viyella nightgown, which Sally had hastily snatched from a drawer, the one with the high lace-edged collar and three-quarter sleeves and a motif of tiny green and white apple blossoms on a white background. He had asked Sally to stay while he lifted the nightgown and probed her stomach with the strong, cool fingers she remembered so well and had dreamed of all these years. Then he had slipped on thin rubber gloves and examined her internally; just feeling his fingers inside her again had made her want to cry out in happiness, despite the pain.

He had come back, her beloved, and all the lost years of hopeless longing and despair faded into insignificance. It had all been worth it now that she had seen him again. Her love burned as fiercely as ever and this time she knew he would not abandon her. It just went to show what God could do if you kept the faith. With hope in her heart and a soft smile on her lips, Catherine closed her eyes and slept.

Outside in Prince Consort Road, Addison Harvey sat at the wheel of his silver Corniche with his head in his hands, a wrecked man. The nightmare he had dreaded had finally caught up with him, just when he thought he was finally home and dry, with royal patronage beckoning. Yet the instant he found himself face-to-face with that singer, the years had simply melted away. Catherine Palmer—how was it possible he had been able to forget her so completely? The name had rung a distant bell when he saw it on her medical notes, but it had all happened so many years ago, he had failed to make the connection. So much had happened since that fateful night, he might be forgiven for having eclipsed her. So many patients, so much hard work; everything he had striven for and achieved, all thrown into jeopardy by one foolish act more than twenty years ago.

"I'm going to have a baby!" she had said, running to him with tears in her eyes, blind with infatuation, confident he would take her in his arms and give her the comfort she desired. Poor fool. Instead, he recoiled in horror and pushed her roughly away. Who did she think she was kidding? He had just been royally humiliated by her bitch of a mother. Did she really believe her sniveling was going to work with him now?

"You stupid little fool!" he said. "Don't you know enough not to let these accidents happen? You work in a hospital, for Christ's sake. Have you learned nothing about the facts of life?"

He left then, in a towering rage, and went home to sink a bottle of Johnny Walker and try to forget his humiliation. When Nancy, the roommate, called to tell him about Catherine's attempted suicide, he had been in no state to understand, let alone do anything about it.

Oh God. Addison wiped his face with a silk handkerchief and lit a cigar. The next part was even worse. He ought to be thinking about going home but hadn't the strength; besides, he couldn't bear the thought of Phoebe seeing him in this state.

Just thinking about it brought him out in a sweat. The afternoon of the men's finals at Wimbledon, while the whole world was otherwise engrossed, he remembered the deserted theater with its makeshift lights and the gowned and masked figure of that nurse—the roommate—standing mutely by, scared witless as he was, assisting him. While he, the boy surgeon, not yet fully qualified and lacking proper experience, wielded his knife and broke every ethical code by cutting away his own fetus—the daughter he had never managed to replicate—and dropping it, still pulsating bloodily, into the kidney bowl.

Nancy's reward was to have been to share his future. How foolish women could be; how trusting, even the canniest among them. She had been a good friend to Catherine, had stood by her, but the law of the jungle prevailed when it came to catching a man and she had been the first to agree that Catherine was bound to get over it; would find someone worthier to love one day, someone more of her own kind. Nancy and Tom were two of a kind, with their rough upbringing and working-class roots. He was already safe in Boston, making plans to dump her too, when he heard news of her fatal road crash. Once again, the luck of the Harveys held, leaving our hero free—to proceed with his upward scramble without so much as a backward glance at the wreckage strewn behind him.

But that had been the pattern of Tom's life. It was luck rather than brilliance that had set him on his way, first in London, courtesy of a scholarship, later in the States. It was charm rather than brains that had won him the right wife, with social connections to enhance his surgical skills and oil his way up the ladder to the glittering prizes of the medical world. His youthful ideals were long since forgotten; these days money and social position came first. After fifteen years at the top of his profession in New England, he had returned to set up a lucrative private practice in Harley Street plus, with an eye to a future gong, a spot of National Health work thrown in on the side, a salve to his famously liberal conscience. On the right occasions, he swanked about his humble origins though the hint of Durham Catherine had once found so beguiling was no longer detectable in those smooth, mid-Atlantic tones. Each year he went back to Consett to visit his folks, though he almost never invited them back to his affluent riverside home in Sunningdale.

"They just wouldn't feel comfortable," he explained to Phoebe. "Dad likes his walk down the hill of an evening to the Union for a couple of jars, while Mum would miss her regular brew and her chats over the garden fence to those nosy neighbors."

The truth was he was ashamed, and no longer felt at ease in the company of his father, who had devoted his life to the defense of his workingman's ideals and had sacrificed so much in order to educate his son. Nothing gave the old man greater pleasure, on those rare occasions when Tom actually did come home, than to take him into the Miners' Union for a pint, in order to show him off to the men who had known him all his life.

"Here's our Tom," he'd say with pride. "Got his gold medal and his Fellowship of the Royal College of Surgeons. There's nowt can stop him now, I reckon. He's always been set on saving lives, right from when he was a nipper."

"Happen he ought to stay here," growled one old man, lighting his pipe with difficulty due to one arm being amputated at the elbow. "Here, where his roots are, and put his skills to mending bones and saving workingmen's lives."

Tom had got them all another round and endeavored to change the subject. He knew about the Harvard fellowship but had not yet broken the news. His mum and dad had struggled so hard to set him on his way, they would never be able to understand why he was abandoning them for America. Nor could he tell his gruff old dad, who had spent all these years risking his life on the pitface, about his chosen area of specialization, gynecology. It was more lucrative and would bring him into contact with a better class of patient.

So he had slipped away and sold them down the river, married the Boston heiress, built himself a new, cushy life, and only returned to his native England when his boys were growing and he wanted to enroll them at Harrow. Old traditions die hard and Tom had always been a secret snob. Fortune had continued to smile on him and life to treat him well. He was unfaithful to his wife, but not excessively, and he was proud of his place in the community. There was a lot wrong with the British medical system, which he felt lagged light-years behind the States, but it was a comfortable life and he had few complaints.

Twenty years ago he had acted as he did out of panic linked to ambition. Faced with a threatening dilemma, he had chosen to save the career he had worked so hard to achieve and abandoned the Ambassador's daughter and her child. Yet now, right under his nose, lay clear evidence of his ancient crime, come back after all these years to haunt him. Catherine might have changed but the X-rays would reveal all and the plates now locked in his office safe were potentially lethal.

For Catherine was dying of an ovarian tumor caused, almost certainly, by that bungled abortion twenty years ago. Her life was ebbing away and she seemed not to want to fight. He had an uneasy feeling she was fully aware of who he was but was not letting on. That would certainly be in keeping with the shy, pretty nurse he had known so long ago and callously trifled with, thinking that she might help to further his social career. But the bitch of a mother had put an end to all that.

Yes, she knew. The more he thought about it, the more certain he became. She had recognized him and had forgiven him. That was the hardest part of all to bear. At the prospect of what he now stood to lose, Addison Harvey put his head back in his hands and wept.

Chapter Thirty

Sally had really liked working at the pub, but now Joe was getting rather heavy and she found that a real drag. After losing his temper when she had abandoned him for Paris, she had sweetened him up with some all-night sex. He was cute enough and good in the sack and he made her laugh. That should have been enough, but lately he was growing possessive and that was always the beginning of the end as far as Sally was concerned. She simply wasn't ready to settle down, not in this country, and although she thought she would quite like a kid one day, she didn't particularly want it to have mixed blood, and besides, there was plenty of time. She was not long past thirty; these days that was nothing.

"Don't even think about it," cautioned Beth. "Not yet, not until you have some prospects and some money put away for a rainy day."

"You sound like Dreardre," said Sally with a grin.

"I know I do, but on this one subject I know whereof I speak. You have to want it a lot to make it worth doing and I honestly don't think you're ready yet."

"Not until the right man comes along, huh?" said Sally.

"Well, I never know with you. That never seems to be a problem."

"Thanks a bunch."

"I mean it. One of these days I hope you'll fall in love and then you'll suddenly know what life is really about."

"How do you know I haven't been in love already?"

"I know."

"Well, it's all a lot of rubbish if you ask me. Look at you and Gus. That didn't work. Look at you and Oliver."

"I know. I'm not saying do as I do, only as I say. And I love you enough to want the best for you. You're my little mate."

Sally went and put her arms around Beth, touched. Beth pushed her away. She was, as always, cooking and had reached a tricky part. Sally was just like Imogen at times, as guileless and as immature. And every bit as lovable.

"No, I am going to be the Bad Fairy in your life and wish that you fall in love. You can't stop me, the spell is already cast. And you're far too special not to hold out for the best. Wait and see."

"What do you think of Joe? Or Sam? Or Jeremy? Not good enough for you, huh?"

"They're just boys, you need a man. You'll know him when you meet him, believe me."

"Besides," said Beth later, wiping down the kitchen table with a damp cloth, which she then hung on the rail of the stove to dry, "it did work with Gus. And with Oliver. Relationships are all different and have their own course to run, and now that we all live so much longer, you can't expect to be faithful and loving till death do you part. It's simply not realistic."

"How *is* Oliver? Do you still see him?"

"Yes, I think so. Not for a week or so, though."

Not since Vivienne's lunch party, if she were honest, and that frightful unexpected confrontation in the hall. Oliver had called her later to demand what she was doing in his house and why he didn't know about it.

"Ask Vivienne, it was all her idea. Besides, you weren't around," she explained. "You were in Strasbourg when she rang and I couldn't really get out of it. Not without it look-ing very strange and making her suspicious."

What were you *doing, come to that?* she should have asked. *Home in the afternoon without ever telling me? Having a bit of nookie with the wife on the sly, I shouldn't be at all surprised.*

She had felt enough of a bitch as it was, blatantly sitting there in Oliver's house, smiling at his wife and acting like a friend. It was all wrong, it wasn't Beth's style. Something would have to be done but she wasn't quite sure what. Next time Oliver called for a date, she surprised them both by taking a rain check, with the bald excuse that she had too much work to do and was tired. And when she phoned Vivienne to thank her for lunch, she said they must do it again, quite soon, next time on her own turf. She didn't re-ally want Vivienne in her life but something deep inside her, some elementary sense of fair play, made her feel she should put out some sort of a hostage to fortune. Even if Oliver was willing to go on playing the adulterer, the role didn't sit eas-ily with Beth.

"Now Oliver," said Sally shrewdly, reading her thoughts. "He's a man." She had only seen him that one time but he had left his mark.

"Perhaps," said Beth reflectively.

Beth's words came back and hit Sally with a resounding thwang next time she strolled into Albert Hall Mansions and found Eleanor taking tea with Duncan, the vet. He was leaning back in a tiny, uncomfortable chair, completely at his ease, and he rose to his feet when Sally arrived and shook her hand with a lazy smile.

Wow, thought Sally, rebounding from the force of the im-pact. *He really is a hunk. How come nobody warned me?*

Eleanor clearly thought so too and was much less wel-coming than usual. She was all decked out in her fancy best so she must have been expecting him. She fixed Sally with a baleful stare, willing her to leave. She was a wily old bird and very competitive. Sally grinned companionably and thwarted her by helping herself to a cup from the kitchen and settling down to spoil their tête-à-tête.

"Don't you want to look in on Catherine?" asked Eleanor in her diva's voice.

"She was asleep when I left her," said Duncan helpfully.

"Then I won't," said Sally. She liked this man.

He wore jeans and a denim jacket and his hair was brown and longish for a man of his age, covering his ears and merging with his beard, which was already streaked with gray. His eyes were a clear, searching blue. Sally felt them scanning into her soul and turned away, discomfited.

"Who's minding the shop while you're away?"

She rose and paced the room, looking at Eleanor's knick-knacks which she had examined so often before. She was ill at ease and didn't know why. It was a feeling entirely alien to Sally, who normally kept on top of things.

"Vanessa. I told her I'd be back soon."

His voice was warm and soothing and reminded her of sunshine and the great Australian outback. His hand, lying idly on the arm of his chair, was brown and capable; his wrists were strong. Sally had an overpowering desire to climb up on to his knee and rest her head against that powerful chest. With difficulty, she resisted. He was looking at her strangely, almost as if he could tell.

As was Eleanor, with open hostility now in her aging eyes.

Well, at least I'm making an impact, thought Sally. When Duncan said it was time he was going, Sally said she would stroll along with him.

"Give Catherine my love," she said, forgiving Eleanor enough to peck her on the cheek. "Tell her I'll be back soon when she's awake."

"And where do you fit in?" asked Duncan as they walked past the Royal College of Music and down toward the Gloucester Road and Duncan's surgery.

"Hospital," said Sally.

"But you don't come from these parts. You're an Aussie like me."

Sally stared at him. He had a good ear.

"Actually, I'm a Kiwi," she said but she felt uncomfortable.

"But the accent?"

Sally just grinned. "I've knocked around the world a bit. Guess I've just mixed too much with Aussies. Bit of a mongrel these days, I suppose. That's what comes of living in Kangaroo Valley."

"What do your folks do?"

"I don't have any folks," said Sally. "They're dead. But my dad was a doctor, internationally known."

Duncan looked at her shrewdly but didn't pursue it.

"In New Zealand?"

"In Auckland."

"So now you're traveling the world, seeking your fortune?"

It sounded a touch patronizing but he was simply being kind.

"Something like that."

He was tall and athletic and even Sally, with her vigorous stride, had trouble keeping up with him. An awful urge came over her; she badly wanted to hold his hand.

"Catherine's very sick," he said after a while. "She's beginning to ramble on about the past. Beats me why her mother keeps her at home. She really should be in hospital, being properly nursed. That old woman's in no condition to look after her. Sometimes I don't understand the Brits, particularly the ones who can afford it."

Sally listened but said nothing. From what she had seen, she had an idea there was some sort of collusion between Eleanor and Addison Harvey but she didn't know for sure and it was not her business.

"It's always a sign of a fading mind, like somebody drowning. On and on she goes about things that happened whole decades ago, as if she's confusing then with now. About this doctor, sometimes I think she confuses me with him. It's almost embarrassing the things she says, poor love. If only that old harridan were a shade more maternal and sympathetic."

"I know that doctor," said Sally after a pause. "He was my doctor too. He's rich and vain and condescending, and furthermore he doesn't give a damn, not about his patients. He just notches them up as one more item on his hefty bill."

Duncan was surprised at her vehemence. Sally too.

"No, the one I'm talking about has been around quite a while," he said. "Right from her nursing days, before she went to Sydney. Some guy she knew and loved when he was still a student."

Sally was startled.

"Addison Harvey?" she said. "The posh Harley Street gynecologist we were lucky enough to get on the National Health?"

"That's the one. But I promise you, she knew him before, it's all she talks about when I sit at her bedside. That, mixed in with a lot of other extraneous stuff, about Australia and freedom before her ma got her back into her clutches."

"She did?" It was news to Sally. And disturbing. In the past few weeks she had spent a lot of time with Catherine, listening to her ramble on, but she had never dropped a word about knowing Addison Harvey so well. Or, for that matter, anything else relating to her past.

They reached Duncan's street and he squeezed Sally's arm in a friend's embrace and said he imagined he'd be seeing her around.

"Take care," he said as he crossed the road.

But he doesn't really mean it, she thought woefully, watching his long easy stride as he crossed the cobbles to his own front door. *He's not going to give me a single thought.* For the first time she could remember, Sally

Brown felt distinctly out of control, positively lightheaded, as if she were coming down with something.

Help, she thought, remembering Beth's prophecy. *Could this be what she was talking about?*

There was no doubt about it, Duncan Ross was a man. With a capital M. And Sally, for the first time ever, wasn't at all sure she was going to be able to cope.

Joe was cranky and trade was slow, so Sally said she had a headache and was going home. She was still feeling very strange and badly needed to think. She strolled up to Brompton Cemetery and set herself down on a secluded seat among the strange Victorian tombs. It was mid-evening and the sun was going down, slanting shafts of orange light along the avenues of graves. She loved this place, it was so still and otherworldly, and the only people she was likely to meet among its weird ornate structures and overgrown foliage were solitary men, loitering—customers, no doubt, of the famous gay pub at the other end of the cemetery, a few yards to the right along the Brompton Road.

Georgy lived somewhere close, she knew, and at any other time Sally might have dropped by and taken a glass or two off her. Goodness knows, she had done it often enough before when she felt in the mood, but the American girl was not the easiest of company and Sally could never be sure whether Georgy liked her or not. She had the brittle, uncompromising exterior of the driven New Yorker, suspicious of other women and poles apart from Sally's own laid-back disposition and outlook. Yet Sally had no particular ax to grind and they were, as Beth was fond of pointing out, two strangers displaced. Maybe, one of these days, she'd give it another go.

Tonight, however, she had other things on her mind. Duncan Ross had reached her in a way she had not believed possible and she needed time to think and compose herself before she went home and had to confront that mob. Of *boys.* There Beth had been right.

The bench was cold so she rose and strolled along the main avenue, stopping to read the gravestones and study the funny little houses people had built for their lamented dead. There was a feeling of such peace here that Sally was lulled back into calm. Many people would be scared of such intimacy with the dead when the light was fast fading, but it reminded her of the convent and she felt strangely at home. As well she might, for she'd scarcely known any other.

She couldn't stop thinking about Duncan. He was hunky, he was delicious, he was quite a bit older, and for some indefinable reason he scared her half to death. Sally couldn't understand it; she had never been along this path before. The one talent she had ever really had, apart from survival, was for pulling men, right from an early age, which was one of the reasons she was constantly in trouble at the convent. But what was happening now, the changes she felt throughout her body, was something uncharted. For the first time in her life Sally Brown was seriously nonplussed—not to put too fine a point on it, scared shitless.

He was unattached, he was heterosexual, he was nice to Catherine (and her mother), yet not involved. He had smiled with appreciation when Sally entered the room and his eyes told her he admired her beauty, responded to her animal magnetism in the normal way. A *cinch*, she had thought—except it turned out it wasn't. He had chatted to her, asked her questions, then walked away without a backward glance, and instinct warned her he would not be calling. It ought not to matter but it did. Dead right, it did. Sally Brown was not used to being thwarted.

Added to which, he really rattled her. Those calm eyes seemed to be all-seeing and she sensed he had her number. That was the scariest part of all and yet, for once, she felt no urge to run. Quite the reverse, in fact.

No one but Dave was home when she finally got there. He was watching the football while he pored over financial papers, the remains of a beer and a takeaway Chinese on the floor by his feet. He was sweaty and unshaven and had garlic on his breath but she lured him to bed anyhow because she needed to be held. But even more urgent than that, she wanted not to think.

"I'll sit with her tonight, no sweat."

Sally was at her most beguiling and could hear Eleanor beginning to soften. *Silly old fool,* she thought fondly, *I know she's got a recital tonight and someone really needs to be with Catherine.*

On an impulse, Sally had called in sick and so was free.

"I can be there by six, if you like. Just say the word."

"Be prompt. It is imperative I leave by six-ten at the latest."

Eleanor's voice was pinched and haughty; it must have cost her a lot to climb down but it meant she was forgiven. Sally could imagine her standing in the hall, holding the old-fashioned earpiece at arm's length in order not to spoil her elaborate coiffeur. It was only Croydon but at least it was live. Good luck to the old duck if that was what made her happy. It was certainly preferable to the geriatric ward.

"Don't worry about Catherine," she said later, over a sherry with Eleanor in the drawing room. "I'll see she gets to sleep and I'll tuck her in. And I'll stay till you get back if she wants me to."

"And if necessary," she said as an afterthought, "I'll give her her pills, though I'm sure she won't need them as she seems so much better. And I'll call Mr. Harvey," she added on a lower note, "if anything at all should go wrong."

"Don't worry about that, he'll probably drop by anyhow. He said he might."

Eleanor sighed and closed her eyes with fatigue. It was all so trying, this illness business. At her time of life, she really didn't need it. If only Catherine would pull herself together. But it was nice of this child to offer to sit. She might be wayward but she was clearly good at heart. She beamed at Sally through eyes that were suspiciously bright, then rose in stately fashion to check her mascara in the glass.

"It's all too much for me," she murmured as she licked a finger and smoothed her eyebrows into shape. Thank goodness she had the doctor eating out of her hand and agreeing to pay regular house calls so that he wouldn't have to admit her to hospital. What a piece of luck that had been, running into him again after all these years. He was obviously still embarrassed by what had happened between them so long ago, and that worked marvelously into Eleanor's selfish plan.

But Sally wasn't listening. She was thinking about Catherine, who was obviously very ill. Thinking about Duncan, too. With a bit of luck, maybe he'd drop by. If she concentrated hard and willed it to happen, wasn't that what she had read? He was a kind man with a good heart and he did, after all, work just around the corner. Didn't she deserve some brownie points for being here at all this evening? (And did she really want to see him, to let him know how she felt? She still had mixed feelings about that.) And what else would he be doing on a Thursday night after he had closed the surgery?

Yeah, yeah, said the cynical voice in Sally's head. *A guy like that in a city full of voracious women?*

But Beth had told her it could happen and Beth was her Fairy Godmother who would never lie.

The doorbell rang from downstairs.

"That's the car," said Eleanor, snatching up her wrap and checking in her beaded bag that she had all her necessities.

"Break a leg," said Sally cheerfully, seeing her out. "And don't fret about a thing. I'll be here."

Catherine did indeed look a poor, sad thing when Sally, having washed the glasses, stole in and took up her seat at the bedside. The room was in deep gloom and all Sally could make out was the waxen face on the pillow.

"Tom?" said Catherine feebly. "Is that you?"

Sally realized that Catherine must be talking about Addison Harvey—she'd been referring to him as "Tom" ever since she fell ill. She paused a second, tempted to lie. What harm could it do and it might bring a flutter of hope to the wasted creature in the bed. She had always been a skilled impersonator and it was possible, in this light, that Catherine wouldn't know the difference. Then she saw the potential danger and stopped herself in time.

"No, it's me—Sal," she said, patting Catherine's hand. "Probably he'll be here soon. I bet he finds it hard to stay away."

Catherine smiled. Sally could just make it out in the half-light.

"He never leaves me," she confided, in the same low voice. "Always here by my side, night and day, dear man."

Sally leaned over and plumped up the pillows.

"I told you he fancied you," she said brightly. "All you've got to do now is get well so that you can give him a proper run for his money."

"He's most probably doing a gig," murmured Catherine. "Out on the town with the Sawbones Seven. He's a marvelous clarinetist, you know, he could have turned professional."

Sally was surprised. Here was a turn-up for the books indeed, if it were true; staid old Mr. Harvey playing in a band, whoever would have thought it? Or was it just another sick fantasy of a fading mind? She thought of the middle-aged man with his thickening waist and slightly stooped shoulders, due, no doubt, to a lifetime in the operating theater, hacking his way through human gristle and fat. And the graying hair and disillusioned eyes. It was hard to see him as a youthful Lothario but these days all Sally could think about was a pair of straight-shooting blue eyes that were beginning to haunt her dreams.

She smoothed Catherine's forehead and felt that it was clammy.

"I'll get you a cup of chamomile tea," she said. "And I'll sit with you awhile until you're ready to sleep."

She went into the kitchen and switched on the kettle, then on into the bathroom, where she rummaged in the medicine cabinet and found Catherine's prescribed pills. Either the leprechauns, or Addison Harvey, would see she got them. Sally wasn't particularly bothered; she had a date. Catherine smiled faintly but her eyes were already beginning to close. It wouldn't be long now. Sally sneaked a look at her watch. It was almost ten and she didn't want to be late.

As it was, she needn't have worried. At five past ten Addison Harvey arrived, letting himself in with his own key.

"Still here," he said, clearly surprised to see her and not altogether pleased. "And how's my patient this evening?"

Sally was flabbergasted. So Catherine's murmurings were not, after all, simply the product of a sick mind. If he had his own key, he must really feel something for her. Well, well, well; her jokes had been more on target than she thought.

"Not so good," she said. "She seems a little feverish but she's sleeping now. I was wondering whether to give her her pills but thought I ought to wait until the proper time." She put the bottle into his hand. "Is there anything else I should do or is it all right if I go now?"

"Run along," said Addison distractedly. He was doing this for Eleanor, as part of their bargain, but he wasn't at all easy about it. Particularly if this bright young woman was going to be snooping around and knew how often he was beginning to make house calls. They'd have to have a further talk, Eleanor and he. The situation was growing unbearably complicated but right at the moment there was not a lot he could do about it. She had him over a barrel, that ruthless old woman, and she was well aware of it.

Luckily she only knew part of the truth. He intended to keep it that way.

Chapter Thirty-one

Georgy was bursting with marvelous news but who in this town was she going to tell? At times like this she realized just how alone in London she really was. At least in New York there were friends she could ring but here, well, here was different. For momentous news, she normally called her mother back home on Long Island but on this occasion Myra would scarcely appreciate it. She tried Gus, with whom she was still obsessed, but the Tiresome Kraut answered, as he nearly always did, so she hung up. *No way, José.* Karl made it abundantly clear that he couldn't abide Georgy on any level and went out of his way to make her feel *de trop* on the rare occasions that their paths did accidentally cross.

Bigot! thought Georgy. *Racist! Just because I'm Jewish ... but who on earth is he to talk? The Germans hardly came out of it squeaky clean. If it hadn't been for them, I wouldn't be American.*

So instead she called Beth and, as always, caught her cooking but not too busy to listen to Georgy's news.

"My father's coming to London next month. Isn't that great?"

"Terrific, sweetie!" said Beth, the receiver jammed under her chin while she stirred the hollandaise sauce and tested its consistency. "Do we get to meet him? How long's he here?"

"I really don't know. Not long. He's on a case." Of course.

"That does sound important. Listen, I can't really talk now or this sauce will congeal. I'll call you tomorrow and we'll make some plans. Can't wait to meet him!"

"Georgy's dad's coming to town," she explained to Imogen, who was half listening with her nose in the evening paper.

"Big deal!"

"Now don't be beastly, darling. For Georgy it *is* exciting. She idolizes her dad."

"I thought it was *my* dad she idolized," said Imogen sarcastically, and Beth grinned to herself and gave her daughter the spoon to lick.

"Yes, well maybe. But it all comes to the same thing if you think about it."

Georgy stood in the doorway of her darkroom and groaned. Even if she removed her photographic equipment and developing trays, there was hardly room to swing a cat, let alone a major criminal psychologist with big ideas and a fat expense account to match. She would love to have her father stay here so that she could lavish on him some of the attention she had been missing all these years, but it just wasn't feasible. In any case, Fulham was too far from the center for Dad on one of his whistle-stop visits. Claridge's was right in the heart of things and a real home away from home to Emmanuel Kirsch.

Looking at this small cramped space through her father's eyes, Georgy found herself suddenly discontented. The Hunters' bijou residence was all very convenient as a temporary London pad but not nearly spacious enough for a professional photographer who wanted to work from home, not one with as many assignments as Georgy was beginning to amass. Dreams, too. She longed for a real studio somewhere but knew she could never afford one.

Mostly she did her work in the field, wherever it took her, but there were times when that was simply not convenient, when Georgy would have liked sufficient space of her own so that she could take her time and get the lighting and background effects just right. And buy herself the Hasselblad she dreamed of, with space in which to use it properly, without having to be out at all times and in all weather, lugging enormously heavy gear because she couldn't afford an assistant to do it for her.

"Dream on!" she told herself ruefully, as she closed the door to the bathroom which smelled of chemicals and from which she had removed the light bulbs, and edged her way along the side of the crowded room to the window, with its blinds firmly pinned into place in order to cut out the light. She would need a professional cleaner to put this place back into shape before the Hunters reclaimed it, but luckily Josh seemed settled in Paris, at least for the time being, and showed no signs of wanting to return to London.

It was amazing how a person's needs could expand to fit any space. Six months ago, when she first took it over, this house had seemed wonderfully roomy, particularly for just one person, but take a look at it now. It was depressing really. The only good thing was that Georgy had so far been so busy, she had not yet had time to do much serious shopping, so the bedroom was not as cluttered as it might be. But still.

Her mind flew, by automatic reflex, to Ripplevale Grove and Gus's spacious house . . . but that way lay only bitterness so she shut off her dream and ran downstairs. She would not allow that German to spoil things for her. She would make a plan and carry it through but was not yet sure what she wanted to do. She only knew she lived for her work and Gus Hardy. Sometimes she frightened herself with the intensity of that emotion.

Nights she couldn't sleep, which were frequent, Georgy

would lie in bed with the telephone cradled on her chest and dial his number, over and over again, content just to hear it ring in his empty house. Sometimes it would be answered, usually by a bad-tempered Karl but occasionally by Gus himself, and then Georgy would hold her breath and listen to her heart beating in terror lest she be discovered.

Once Karl had even challenged her by name—*"Is that you, Georgy, you cunt!"*—and she had rapidly hung up. Then cursed herself for her foolishness in so feebly giving the game away. For several weeks she had left them alone but the compulsion did not go away. Karl's aggression, she told herself, must mean something. If he was that scared, surely that meant there was still hope for her. Maybe Gus did care for her after all. Maybe his cruel confession by the canal had been nothing more than a cover-up, because his feelings for her were actually so strong.

She had tried pumping Beth but found it impossible to get hold of anything concrete. Beth simply smiled and uttered evasions and encouraged Georgy on to safer subjects. And occasionally set her up on blind dates which patently did not work. And Imogen was worse than useless since she was just a kid who broke into foolish giggles whenever Georgy brought Gus into the conversation, no matter how subtly.

She wondered what her father would make of Gus and if she dared introduce them. She rather fancied Emmanuel would disapprove. He was highly protective of all his daughters, detached though he might be these days with his work and his brand-new family, and basically frowned on what he termed the arty types Georgy hung around with. He didn't go so far as Myra, who prayed nightly for a dentist or accountant to sweep her eldest daughter off to Scarsdale, but viewed with suspicion anyone who did not have a regular job with proper hours. A real *mensch* was what he was looking for for Georgy but they were not that easily come by. Not, at least, in Georgy's experience.

It was nine-thirty already and time to get going. Today
Georgy was going backstage to photograph the Bolshoi
Ballet who were newly arrived in London and shortly to
open at the Albert Hall. It was a great assignment and she
was lucky to have got it, thanks to a friendly picture editor
on the *Telegraph Magazine* who had used her a lot, admired her work, and thought she deserved a break. Georgy
was a professional through and through and, once on a job,
tried always to deliver the goods. If she'd only had the
confidence to recognize it, her work was every bit good
enough to stand up for itself and a lot of this basic angst
was really uncalled for. But that was Georgy's nature, part
and parcel of her inherent talent. If she had been able to
relax, she might have lost her edge. If she lost her edge,
then she was no better than the other million photographers, all fighting for a living. It was a vicious circle.

She was due at the Albert Hall at ten-fifteen and the
shoot was likely to last all day, or at least until the dancers
were ready to quit. Then she thought she might pop round
the corner and look in on poor old Catherine who was,
they told her, not at all well and apparently not improving.
Georgy felt a twinge of conscience whenever she thought
of Catherine. She knew Sally saw her regularly and also,
occasionally, Beth. Ever since that awful day at Vivienne's
when Catherine had scared them all so much by collaps-
ing, she had meant to do something herself but had never
quite got round to it.

Flowers might be nice, or at least a card. Or some
smoked salmon or something like that, for her to nibble
when she didn't feel up to a proper meal. Or a book,
maybe, if only she knew what Catherine liked. Myra
would have made her chicken soup but that wasn't
Georgy's thing at all. In truth, she scarcely knew her even
though they had shared a hospital ward. Then Georgy remembered that dreadful New Year's Eve and how lonely
she had felt when she collapsed at King's Cross. Lonely,
vulnerable, and longing only to die. She would definitely

do something, if only she could find the time. She'd make a note to remind herself on the bulletin board in the kitchen.

The Bolshoi Ballet were doing a major gala season and Georgy was aware what a plum of a job she had landed. During the four weeks they were in London, their repertoire was to include a wide range of classical ballet, ranging from *Sleeping Beauty* and *Swan Lake* to *Spartacus* and *The Stone Flower*. This would mean a number of photo calls, so her schedule was fairly hectic. But it should be well worth it. Apart from the *Telegraph,* she had a number of other interests too in this particular spread and high hopes of selling her pictures around the world.

One of these days, if she stayed on in London, she really ought to be thinking about getting herself an agent, but good agents were hard to come by and she was still too much of a newcomer to know who to go to. She would ask her magazine contacts what they recommended. It was too much for her to cope with and at times made her quite ill with anxiety.

But the dancers were amazing and as the music got to her, Georgy relaxed and let herself be swept along with the passion and excitement of Tchaikovsky. She shot film after film, in both color and black and white, and the more they danced, the more she got involved until she was at one with the music, throwing herself into it and expending so much energy she found herself trembling and quite wrung out with sweat.

It was after seven by the time Georgy managed to drag herself home, as exhausted as if she had been dancing the *Nutcracker* herself, wanting only to dump her heavy equipment on the living room floor and go soak in a long, hot bath with a tumbler of Jack Daniel's to help ease the pain. She was nibbling a cracker and waiting for the tub to fill when the telephone rang. She thought about not answering it, she was so exhausted she couldn't face anything new tonight. But it might have been Dad or even Gus and she couldn't afford to risk it.

It was Beth, sounding sober and subdued. Catherine was dead, she told her. Late the night before, in her sleep. Alone.

Part
Four

Chapter Thirty-two

The seafood restaurant on Fisherman's Wharf was a welcome relief after the conference. Large plate-glass windows pivoted open to let in the cooling sea breezes and light flashed off the harbor, reminding him of home. He ordered champagne to celebrate his recent marriage and his colleagues joined him in a toast.

"Not a bad way to spend a honeymoon."

"Not when it's all expenses paid."

A waiter approached.

"Call for you, Dr. Dawson."

"Here?" Who could have tracked him down; who knew where he would be?

"Wifey missing you already?" joked one of the others.

"More likely run out of traveler's checks."

He crossed the airy room to the corridor outside, where the waiter indicated a row of telephone booths, all but one of them empty.

"Dawson."

"You probably don't remember me."

The voice was pleasant and entirely unthreatening. He relaxed. It was amazing how patients could track you down, even here, thousands of miles from home. It could be irritating but was part of the celebrity being a successful surgeon bestowed. He glanced at his watch. *Mustn't keep them waiting.* The meetings were due to start again at two. There wasn't a lot of time.

"So what can I do for you?"

"One moment, Dr. Dawson. If you'll forgive me."

A pause, then light footsteps. A shadow darkened the opening to the booth where a stranger stood blocking the spectacular view.

"Dr. Dawson? You don't remember me, do you? But then, why on earth should you, after all these years?"

A pleasant face, not especially memorable. Casually dressed with a friendly smile. Again he glanced at his watch.

"Yes?"

The knife-thrust when it caught him was done so skillfully, in and under and up beneath the rib cage, straight to the heart, that he would have been impressed by the speed and the sheer professionalism.

If only he'd had the time.

Chapter Thirty-three

They buried Catherine on a warm Saturday afternoon in early May. The service was at Holy Trinity, Brompton, to be followed by internment across the river at Putney Vale Cemetery because Lady Palmer, when it came to it, could not endure the thought of her sole remaining flesh being consumed by fire and preferred that her daughter should lie in peace beside her father.

It was the first really springlike day of the year—the British climate grew more erratic by the minute—and Beth and Imogen, having arrived early in order to ensure they could park, had time to stroll in the shady gardens behind the church and listen to the full-throated birdsong issuing from the chestnut trees. The air was thick with the sweet, nostalgic smell of freshly cut grass and the paths were edged with pale harebells and blue aubretia.

Poor Catherine, thought Beth as they perched on a bench next to an imposing Victorian tomb surmounted by a gray stone funerary urn swathed in carved cloth. *Just her luck to miss the best of the weather.* From the little Beth knew of her, it seemed to sum up most of Catherine's all-too-short life. As more cars began to arrive and park in the forecourt immediately behind the vast domed splendor of the famous Oratory, Beth and Imogen walked back across the lawn to take their places in the church; not so far forward as to be conspicuous yet close enough to get a good view of what was going on. On this sort of occasion it was hard to know the exact pecking order among the mourners but if need be, thought Beth, and vast numbers of the Palmer family were to show up, they could easily move.

She need not have worried. By the time the service was actually under way, the church was less than a quarter full. First a handful of elderly ladies in hats, carrying large, square handbags, with their slightly doddery husbands in tow, wandered noisily up the outer aisles, chattering like a flock of starlings, residents no doubt of Albert Hall Mansions, come *en bloc* to show their respects. Next, a clutch of slightly seedy, similarly elderly theatricals, with dyed hair—the men as well as the women—and unusually pale skin, as if the light of day, let alone this glorious spring sunshine, rarely touched it. They were dressed in dusty black, every one of them, and Beth loved them on sight. They were like walk-on parts from her beloved Nottingham Playhouse. One even sported a feather boa that had certainly seen better days.

Oh goody, she thought, grinning to herself. *The opera groupies are here in force! Let the play commence!* Imogen, sensing the grin, turned slightly in the pew to fix her with a stern look which warned her to behave. The organ started to play a melancholy threnody in a minor key and the grin was wiped from Beth's face as Vivienne Nugent swept past up the center aisle, followed at a respectable pace by her husband.

It was several weeks since Beth had last seen Oliver and it simply hadn't occurred to her that he might appear at Catherine's funeral. After all, as far as Beth knew, he had only met the poor soul once and then only fleetingly, and since he could not, by the wildest stretch of imagination, ever be thought of as a dutiful husband, it was extraordinary he should be here today. She had to admit he was looking particularly tasty, in an expensive Italian silk suit that subtly enhanced the slate-gray eyes, and against her better instincts, she felt the familiar tug of desire in her lower regions. Oh dear. Would this feeling never go away? She would almost certainly have to face him once the service was over, though what on earth she was going to say, she hadn't the faintest idea.

It never even entered Beth's mind that Oliver had contrived to be here today purely in order to see her. Though he would scarcely admit it even to himself, he had missed Beth these past four weeks and was irritated and slightly rattled by her continuing unavailability. What they had together was good, at least that was what he had always thought, and today's excursion was a bald attempt to confront her in order to deduce at first hand exactly what might be going on. Oliver was not used to this sort of treatment; in fact, he had never experienced it before. He needed some answers and he meant to get them, even if it did mean having to sit through this dreary funeral.

The Nugents slid into a pew several rows ahead of Beth and Imogen and Vivienne glanced back at them and smiled. She was wearing a neat little navy suit with the minimalist stamp of high couture, and her glossy black hair was short and sleek, setting off to perfection her exquisite bone structure. They were a classy pair, the Nugents, no doubt about that, and Beth felt a warm glow of pride as she studied the back of Oliver's unyielding head as he sat reading his service sheet. She could tell he was cross. She knew him that well.

Since the debacle of Vivienne's lunch party, Beth had been avoiding Oliver, though she was still not entirely sure why. After all, they had been together for two passionate years and it was not as though she had not known right from the start that he was married. No, it was due more to some primordial sense of what was right—the instinct that had caused her to let go of Gus all those years ago, even to stand joyfully by and watch him flex his wings and fly away, knowing he would soar that much higher without the ballast of her and the baby on board.

In her way, Beth loved Oliver, she truly did, and the years

they had spent together had possessed their own special magic, as well as doing no end of good to her self-esteem as a working girl and single mother, past the first flush of youth.

But he didn't belong to her, it was that simple, and meeting Vivienne in the hospital and sensing her loneliness and quiet despair had put an end to any future ecstasy as far as Beth was concerned. That was the hard truth and only now was she facing up to it. Call it northern puritanism or whatever, she knew she could not go on. It simply wasn't right.

Georgy arrived alone and stood for one panicked moment on the threshold, daunted by the huge interior of the unfamiliar High Anglican church, longing only to run and hide. She slipped unobtrusively into the back pew, fervently hoping she would not have to take part in the actual service. The interior of Holy Trinity, illuminated by bright daylight filtering through stained glass, was vast and impressive and served to remind Georgy one more time how much she needed a studio of her own. This church would suit her needs exactly. A thin smile tugged at the corners of her mouth as she imagined a troupe of Bolshoi dancers tippy-toeing across the space up front which seemed to be where the action lay. A cute choirboy in a frilly white collar was solemnly lighting the candles and there was a rustling in the choir stalls as his confreres took their places.

The organist switched to a more robust dirge and up the central aisle processed six black-clad undertakers followed by the main funeral party. The congregation rose to its feet, and watched in silence the sad little straggle of mourners. First came Eleanor, heavily veiled and looking suddenly shockingly frail, leaning on the arm of a tall man in gray who seemed vaguely familiar, though Beth could not immediately place him. Right behind, as dutiful as a daughter, came Sally, for once rather charmingly demure in a short denim skirt with matching top, her mass of hair restrained by one of her awful hats. They were followed by a further clutch of elderly folk, as frail and doddery as Eleanor herself, and that appeared to be it. *Le tout ensemble.* A surpliced server carrying the cross led the vicar and his entourage to their places in front of the altar and the service began.

Once in place, Sally turned and waved and Beth, amused by her lack of reverence, gaily blew her a kiss. She glanced around the church. Not much of a turnout, with scarcely anyone of Catherine's own age apart from herself and the Nugents, and a rather blowsy young woman in red who was probably Vanessa, the other receptionist. *Poor Catherine,* thought Beth again. Was this all she had to show for a life? No friends of her own age, just acquaintances from the hospital, and apparently no close relatives either, other than the harridan who had dominated her life and probably helped to shorten it. Eleanor was still holding center stage, sniveling into a flimsy lace handkerchief, as well she might, at the front of the church in full view of everyone. Poor Catherine indeed. No child, no husband, no love of her own. Instinctively Beth squeezed Imogen's hand and drew her closer while her eyes strayed involuntarily to the back of Oliver's head. If she, Beth, were ever to die prematurely, she would, at the very least, know she had been amply loved. For that she was grateful.

The church door opened again and Beth watched the thickening figure of Addison Harvey sliding into the pew alongside Georgy. About time too; the very least he could do for Catherine was turn up. Beth had only the vaguest idea of the part he had played in Catherine's life but she did know from Sally that in her last, tormented days the poor woman had seemed possessed by him and talked of very little else. Possessed, that was it; she stole another look.

Harvey was slightly red in the face as if he had been hurrying, mopping his forehead as he fumbled in his hymnbook for the appropriate page. He was expensively, even foppishly, turned out in a two-thousand-pound three-piece suit, more suitable for a wedding than a funeral, and his graying hair was cut as stylishly as any television personality's. A man not handsome but distinguished. And, to judge from his face, not happy either.

I wonder, thought Beth, _what's he got on his conscience. Did he know she was dying and was there nothing he could do? It can't be easy being a doctor, particularly a surgeon with so much responsibility if anything should go wrong. I make mistakes, of course I do, but if I make a mess of a recipe, I can always get new ingredients and start again. Not so when it's human life you are tinkering with—and everyone, surely, is allowed an off day._

Poor sod, she thought, _rather him than me._

The service droned on and the vicar rose to give his oration. Fine words, noble sentiments but was this the Catherine Palmer any of them knew whose virtues he was so lavishly extolling? Had he, Beth wondered, ever even met her? She was growing fidgety, as she always did in church, so she switched her attention to the rest of the congregation to avoid incurring another of Imogen's glares. This child was turning into a regular tartar: if Beth weren't careful, she'd grow up to be another Eleanor Palmer.

Which drew her attention back to the front pew and the fine-looking man seated between Eleanor and Sally. As if sensing her eyes upon him, he turned slightly in his seat and it all came back in a flash. Of course, the vet. However could she possibly have forgotten? She remembered him clearly now from the hospital, and how much she had admired him then. The unfamiliar groomed look had thrown her off the scent. In sober suit and tie, with his hair and beard well combed, he looked less like Wild Aboriginal Man but every bit as hunky.

Duncan Ross indeed, the Australian who had been so kind to Catherine in these last harrowing weeks, and was obviously now doing a prop-up job for her mother. But, then, anyone who would devote his life to healing sick animals must be a bit special. Beth wasn't in any way an animal freak herself, could take them or leave them, but always respected selfless devotion. Unlike those entirely in thrall to Mammon . . . and her eyes flicked back to Oliver in his elegant suit with the exquisite unhappy wife by his side. The comparison might be unkind but it was fair. Next to that fine, upstanding man, the Nugents seemed like creatures from another planet.

Sitting right at the front of things, her arm pressed tightly against Duncan's, Sally was in seventh heaven. She knew she should be feeling something for the dead, but God wasn't listening, and anyhow Catherine had been sick; even at its best her life couldn't have been that much fun. Face it, she was a loser. In absolute truth, it was a happy release, though no one so far had had the guts to say so. Despite her schooling, Sally did not believe in an afterlife or retribution beyond the grave or any of the other rot the priest was spouting from his pulpit. Life was for the living; there was nothing more.

It was a shame about Catherine, who had seemed nice enough, but all this sermon was giving Sally was renewed determination to get out there and live a bit while there was still time. Nobody really cared about Catherine's death, other than that selfish cow of a mother, and then for all the wrong reasons. Sally didn't believe she had ever really loved her, not deep down, but was putting on all this show for the benefit of the audience. And because she was dead scared of ending up alone, as well she might be.

Maybe now that Catherine, her prop, had bitten the dust, the old trout would finally get her act together and start living a proper life again. After all, there was nothing really wrong with her; Sally had sussed that out right from the start. She liked the old girl and respected her, recognizing another con artist when she saw one. In her prime, Eleanor Palmer must have been a truly foxy lady, worth a dozen of her namby-pamby daughter. Sally found her amusing and something of a challenge. And by following her instincts and sticking around for the fun, look where she was sitting now, right up next to this sensational man whose strong, suntanned hand lay so close to hers she could feel it radiating warmth. She had to resist a burning urge to lean across and lick it.

It was a first for Sally, and she had a nasty feeling Beth had been right all along, that this was the one she had been waiting for. Her defenses were always in place and her baggage mentally packed, then right out of the blue along came Duncan Ross, the wild Australian vet, and alarm bells started to ring.

She felt his hand on her arm.

"All right?" The blue eyes were concerned though the smile was reassuring. She felt like a wounded hedgehog and wanted to curl up under his chin and lose herself in the safety of his beard.

She beamed from under the brim of her Garbo-esque hat.

"I'm fine."

The blue eyes crinkled, the grip on her arm tightened fractionally, and then—goddammit—he switched his attention away from her, back to the old bat on his other side.

Addison Harvey was perspiring heavily, not only because of the sprint from his golf game in Sunningdale to get to this service in the heart of the West End on one of the busiest Saturdays of the year, but also from the weight of his conscience that was threatening to bring him down. He had had to come and if it had not been for the fact that his partner this morning was president of a major Japanese pharmaceutical company, he would have ducked out of the game altogether. He hated funerals, particularly those of patients, but duty obliged and there were certain occasions decorum forbade you to miss.

But for more reasons than one, most of them still churning around in his brain, Addison needed to be here today, to see Catherine decently laid to rest and to grieve a little for her in public while he dared not do so in private. Phoebe had tuned in to his mental turmoil but did not know what it was about. It had been hard shutting her out, though he was in the habit of doing so. Phoebe was a dear soul, quite the best thing to have happened to him even apart from the money, and he knew he had never deserved her. But there were areas of his life even Phoebe could not be permitted to share and this was definitely one of them. My God, if she only knew.

She had hovered over him at breakfast, aware of something troubling him, concern in her eyes. "Are you all right, hon?"

"Fine, just fine. Where are my socks, the ones that go with this Lacoste shirt? Not that it matters, of course, but I'm going to be late and Hideo Yosaki controls more than a billion dollars' worth of drugs. Do you realize what that means to the likes of us?"

Phoebe found his socks, then folded him in a quick embrace.

"I know something's bothering you but I don't know what. Drive carefully, dear heart. It's only a game and I don't care how many drugs he controls, I want my husband back alive."

As she stood in the doorway of their beautiful mock-Georgian mansion, she asked what time he'd be home for lunch. Or did golf with a drug king on a Saturday morning, when he ought rightly to be cutting the grass, also include giving him lunch?

"Didn't I tell you?" Addison was stricken. "I won't be back, at least till late. There's something I have to do at the hospital."

If he told her the truth she'd want to come too, and he could not bear the thought of her witnessing one of his mistakes. Not that she'd judge him, of course. He knew Phoebe well enough to know she would only love him more, and that he couldn't take. Cursing himself for his ineptness, he watched the familiar shutters click down over the eyes of the only woman he had ever remotely loved, however inadequately.

Why do I have to lie? he asked himself, as the Rolls pulled away down the curving drive. *She'll only think it's another woman.*

Which, of course, in a kind of way it was. Catherine Palmer lay heavily on his mind and, now that it was too late to make amends, he knew she would also haunt his conscience. All the way up to London, as he purred along the motorway in his expensive car, he thought about her death and whether it could have been avoided. She had been going to die in any case, he'd known that since he first saw her X-rays, but at that point she'd been nothing more to him than a faceless patient, not the girl he had so tragically betrayed all those years ago.

He tried to blame her mother but knew he was fudging the issue. Eleanor had called him spineless and, although it stung, he knew there was truth in what she said. The ideals he once had, that Catherine had so much admired, were long ago vanished, subsumed into a much more powerful drive, ambition. He had worked hard for what he had gotten and wasn't about to risk it. The call from the Palace could come at any moment. With that promise hanging over him, he would keep his guilt to himself and, if his luck continued to hold, no one would ever know what part he had actually played in Catherine Palmer's death.

"For all the saints," sang the congregation, and Beth, heart brimming, rose on her toes to give it her very best. This was terrific, she loved this hymn; in her eyes this was what church was all about. They had sung it at school, on special occasions, and it awoke all sorts of memories, stirring and good. Duncan Ross, at the front of the church, heard her soaring, melodious voice and glanced back with instinctive pleasure. Now *that* was a woman for a man to look at twice; feisty, clear-eyed, unafraid, and in her prime. Generous and entirely unaware of just how attractive she really was. This positive assessment, based on just a couple of fast looks, surprised even Duncan. He had been too long in this town, away from the sunshine and the simple life, and his tastes were growing jaded. This woman, Catherine's friend, singing like a lark from the middle pew, reached out to him in some subtle way and reminded him of all he had been missing.

Better watch it, he warned himself as he followed the old

lady out of the pew and down the center aisle. *Or before you know it, you'll be in big trouble.*

"Hi," was all he said later in the forecourt, coming over to greet her with outstretched hand. "I'm Duncan Ross. I don't believe we've met."

"Beth Hardy." She wiped her damp hand on her skirt before taking his, to disguise her nervousness. "And this is Imogen Hardy, my daughter."

His blue eyes met her gray ones and liked what they saw. Liked the look of the daughter too, standing there quiet and well behaved, waiting for her mother to be through, hiding her boredom.

They beamed at each other and something intangible flashed between them like summer lightning, full of promise.

Oliver was seething. Vivienne could feel pure rage radiating through his sleeve, though for the life of her she could not fathom why this should be. She had not forced him to accompany her to this rather dreary funeral, far from it. She had not even suggested it, in fact, since he did not know the dead woman and Vivienne herself had intended to make only a fleeting appearance out of solidarity for the five of them in hospital together. But all of a sudden, just as she was dressing, Oliver had appeared and announced that he thought he would drive her there. It was not very far, she had said, concentrating on her eyeliner, just along the road, in fact, but he said that was okay. He hadn't anything else he particularly wanted to do and since it was a funeral, it would be fitting. They should do more things together as a couple. They were in danger of drifting apart.

Vivienne said nothing as she outlined her lips and blotted them dry but she was pleased, very pleased. And she smiled inside, careful not to show too much emotion for fear of scaring him off. She was learning. And maybe there was a vestige of life yet in this tired old marriage.

Now, however, that mood of optimism had flown right out of the window and things were back to normal, with a vengeance. Oliver was in a rage, which was rare, and she really didn't know why. He was fiddling with his car keys and saying they had to be going, while the congregation was still pouring out of the doors and there was the burial still to be got through, across the river in Putney. He had had a brief word with his old pal, Addison, and now was glancing at his watch at ten-second intervals and muttering something about a meeting he had just remembered in the City. On a Saturday afternoon too, when previously he had told her he had a clear weekend.

Well, go and do it! thought Vivienne viciously, and then she caught a glimpse of Lady Palmer, all scrunched up with grief and supported by the vet and that nice girl, Sally. And Beth was standing right by with her daughter and Georgy— and all of a sudden she knew where she wanted to be. In level tones, she told her husband he could leave, that she would be all right. Then she walked across the churchyard in shoes that had only ever trod carpet before, and joined the group.

They had lowered the coffin and spoken a prayer and watched Eleanor, aided by Duncan, as she feebly shoveled earth. And now they were slowly dispersing, Sally with her arms around the sad old lady as she leaned heavily on Duncan's arm, with Beth and her daughter standing by. Vivienne, her chic Italian shoes all crusted with mud, stood on the edge of things, looking on and wishing there was something she could do to help. Then she noticed Georgy, also standing alone, a similar hesitation writ clearly on her face.

Why, thought Vivienne, *she is as lonely as I.*

And without further thought she stepped forward and tapped the American girl lightly on the arm.

"I'm going to grab a cab back to Kensington," she said. "Care to share it and come home for a cup of tea? I rather think we've earned it, don't you?"

Chapter Thirty-four

Vivienne and Georgy were sitting in the conservatory drinking killer martinis, on the rocks. Vivienne actually preferred her Stolichnaya neat but Georgy, in her forceful way, reminded her she was with an American now and insisted on making cocktails New York style—tons of crushed ice, a hefty slug of vodka, and just a whisper of extra-dry vermouth as a garnish.

"After this you'll never look at another gin and tonic, I guarantee," said Georgy, handing one glass to her hostess.

It was only ten to five but no one was there to judge them and anyway, Vivienne had long ago become immune to what people thought. When she wanted a drink, she had one. Only when Oliver was around did she try to put any sort of restraint on her intake.

"*L'chayim!*" said Georgy gutturally, raising her glass in a toast.

"Your very good health!" responded Vivienne, taking a sip and visibly wincing. Wow! Her eyes widened with pleasure as the dryness of the martini hit her taste buds.

"Mm, you weren't exaggerating. Not bad at all. Though usually I prefer my poison undiluted. Does the job that much quicker, I find."

Georgy wrinkled her nose in pleasure. This classy lady

was proving to be quite a revelation. She had not warmed to her in hospital and was still finding it hard to shrug off that blatant snub in Harrods. Yet here she sat in her majestic home, letting her inhibitions slide just like a regular person, and she was generous too. And the house was to die for, there was no question of that. Ever since that lunch, Georgy had longed for an excuse to see it again and now here she was, comfortably ensconced in a white wickerwork two-seater, upholstered in a subtle mix of turquoise and emerald which blended beautifully with the lush greenery and cascading water. The lady had taste as well as money. In a different scenario, she might have made it as a professional designer.

"Yes," she said, leaning back. "This is definitely the life."

Vivienne was pleased. She watched the admiration in Georgy's eyes and her battered ego preened. Her first impressions of Georgy had been similarly offputting. In fact, she had not liked the American one bit, finding her pushy and aggressive and altogether too loud. But since she had recognized the girl's innate loneliness, reflected in her own, she realized that the brash manner was no more than a social barrier. They said rude people were often simply shy but Vivienne had always dismissed that as just so much claptrap, though often kindly meant. Yet here was a kindred spirit sitting smiling at her and, what was more, appreciating her house, always the clincher where Vivienne was concerned.

Georgy, her inhibitions draining away with the combined onslaught of the martini and the humid, almost tropical, earthy smell of the vegetation, was gazing around the magnificent room and thinking, *Wow! What couldn't I do with a space like this!* It was only a pity Vivienne didn't have a son. He would be young yet, but well worth waiting for, even if she had to abduct him from kindergarten in order to have her wicked way with him.

"Do you have any children?" she asked idly, and saw Vivienne stiffen and the shutters clang down.

"No."

A flash of something like pain shot across her face, to be rapidly concealed behind a tight, social smile.

Oh-oh, thought Georgy, cursing herself for not thinking. With all this money and nothing apparently to do all day except dream up new color schemes for her showcase of a house, there had to be something. With half a brain she should have sussed that the lack of tiny pattering feet was more than just an oversight. Rich Brits liked to breed; that, surely, went with the deal.

"We never got around to it," said Vivienne after a pause, twirling her long-stemmed glass and avoiding Georgy's eye. What she was too ashamed to add was the real truth, that for too many years she had put off conceiving for fear of ruining her knockout figure. A goddess without a heart; how true that was. She reached for the vodka bottle but Georgy had got there first.

"Let me," she said, jumping up. "I'm butler today, remember?"

"And now it's too late," said Vivienne despondently. "Since this latest little hiccup."

Me and my big mouth . . . Of course, she'd had a hysterectomy and Georgy simply hadn't thought. How awful! Imagine being told you could no longer conceive, no matter what, particularly when you had a solid marriage and a house like this . . . unbelievable. Hung up as she was herself about finding Mr. Right and settling down before she was too old—which to Georgy meant before she was thirty—she could not imagine a more frightful scenario. Especially with a husband as dishy as that who must surely want a son.

Thoughts of Gus, superimposed by the enchanting Imogen, flashed across the screen in Georgy's brain as they did so often, but this time she expunged them. Not now; now was not the time. She might have her fantasies but this sad

lady was seriously hurting and the least she could do was try
to lighten things up. So she told Vivienne instead about the
Bolshoi Ballet and the work she was doing backstage and, as
she warmed to her subject, she was relieved to see the finely
etched lines gradually ease themselves away from Vivienne's
beautiful face.

Oliver, more put out than he could ever remember, stormed
off to his office in Bishopgate even though he had no real
reason for going there on a Saturday, when the markets
were not trading. He just needed to absent himself from his
wife and the spectacle of Beth, looking more luscious than
ever, making herself agreeable to a bunch of geriatrics and
some hairy Antipodean who looked like an outtake from a
Harrison Ford movie. All he wanted was to elbow his way
through the pathetic crowd and carry her away; instead he
roared off in his Mercedes to the City, to cool his heels in
the empty halls and endeavor to regain his equanimity. He
wished now he had never offered to involve himself in that
depressing funeral of some sad sack he had scarcely met
and whose name he had already forgotten. But Vivienne
had let slip that Beth would be there and that, where Oliver
was concerned, was like aniseed to a dog.

   He needed to know exactly what was going on. Things
had proceeded so swimmingly right from the start that he
could not accept she could be giving him the runaround
now, not after all this time. To begin with, it wasn't Beth's
style, and what possible motive could she have? Their
union had always been gloriously straightforward, which
was why it had lasted, and had so far run without a hitch.
They loved each other, he knew that for a fact, and got on
famously in bed. He saw her whenever it was convenient
and didn't get in the way of her having a life of her own.
The great thing about Beth was that she never whined or
clung, never talked about permanence or laid down ultima-
tums. They were both far too mature. She had even done

her child-rearing early so the old hormones were safely under control.

Beth had entered his life like a breath of fresh air with her gutsy outlook, her humor, and her determination to stand alone and not be dependent on anyone. He liked her kid, too; Beth was an excellent mother. In fact, he liked everything about her, including the fact that she refused to be hamstrung by fashion and was quite relaxed about being slightly overweight. Beth was a modern woman, the exact opposite of the beautiful trophy wife he had married and then grown so rapidly weary of.

Oliver liked order in his life and Beth suited him down to the ground, as tactful and compliant as a first-class secretary. She was entirely accommodating, happy to see him when it suited him yet never cloying or tedious. She was sexy, loving, and loyal—all the things he desired in a mistress—and even when they had come face-to-face in his own hallway in front of his wife, she had not betrayed him by so much as a flicker.

So what could possibly have gone wrong now? He genuinely hadn't a clue. To begin with, he had been rattled at the idea of Vivienne knowing Beth socially. It had all seemed too much of a coincidence, far too close to home for comfort. But when it had all been explained by Beth (Vivienne stuck to her story about them meeting on some fund-raising committee for a local hospital) he could see it was no one's fault. Fair's fair, after all, and Oliver—with his public-school upbringing—was as sporting as the next man and knew how these women's complaints did have a tendency to draw the fluffy little things together. Also he was a gambling man and enjoyed an element of risk. If anyone *was* at fault it was Vivienne, for sneaking off to hospital without telling him, and an NHS one at that. But since she had not mentioned it, he was officially still in the dark.

Apart, of course, from the odd involvement of his old mate, Addison Harvey, with whom he played squash at the RAC Club. Harvey was a professional man, one of the best, they said, so naturally he would not spill the beans about Vivienne's little secret. All he would reveal, with half-closed eyes and a knowing nod and the reassuring elbow squeeze that went with being an eminent doctor, was not to worry because all was in order. So Oliver had put it out of his mind. Harvey was a good bloke, with a deadly back-hand that could put the most amazing topspin on his balls, and he was reassured that whatever Vivienne's little problem might have been, she had been in the best possible hands. And, furthermore, her bizarre desire for secrecy meant it had not cost him a bean, making him a winner all round.

Odd how the two women in his life had met, introduced quite fortuitously by the NHS, another instance of that tired old cliché about the smallness of the world. And Viv obviously had no suspicion that he knew Beth, so Oliver had been able to abandon his paranoia and breathe freely again. Except that Beth now seemed to be avoiding him and that was something he could not lightly dismiss. He had racked his brains but come up with nothing. Yet it was fully four weeks since they had last made love and although she always produced excuses, they were never very convincing. Oliver was on the edge of becoming very annoyed indeed.

Today's little fiasco had been the ultimate straw. He had gone there solely to see her, she must have known that, yet there she was, done up to the nines and as breezy as you please, flashing that great big inviting smile and allowing some hairy creep to monopolize her just when he, Oliver, was trying to get her on her own for a quiet word. Whatever sort of game did she think she was playing? And who the hell did she think she was?

Beth and Imogen had gone back to Albert Hall Mansions with the grieving Eleanor and a straggle of neighbors, plus Sally and Duncan, who seemed to be acting as the hired help. They were standing now in small groups in the large, gloomy drawing room, sipping weak tea and talking in low voices, Beth all the time wondering what was coming next and how on earth they could politely slip away. Imogen was behaving wonderfully. She hadn't said a word but her eyes, when she turned them to Beth, were stricken. *A treat for you, my girl, when we finally get home,* thought Beth. *You certainly deserve it, so that's what you're going to get.*

Beth was horrified at the change in Eleanor who seemed, in the space of just a few days, to have physically shrunk within the whaleboned bastion of her posh frock, suited more to a concert before hundreds than a few sad friends in for a funeral tea.

Sally was being splendid but that was exactly what you would expect from her, fetching and carrying like a daughter and now coercing Imogen into the kitchen to help with the washing-up. Beth wandered in there to see how they were coping and was instantly depressed by the faded cream walls and shabby chintz curtains, and the shadowed vastness of the ceiling that had seen neither mop nor duster for decades. What a life Catherine must have led in this airless, joyless place; an unpaid servant with no hopes or prospects of her own. And now it was over, far too soon. Depressed, Beth left them to it and wandered back to the drawing room.

One of the saddest aspects of her prematurely snuffed-out life was that, along the crowded mantelpieces and table-tops of the cluttered flat, Beth was unable to detect a trace of Catherine, apart from one old photograph of her on a pony at some church gymkhana, smiling broadly with a gap in her teeth and her hair sticking stiffly out in two thin plaits. The rest of the pictures, which were ranged in rows upon every available surface, were of either Sir Nicholas and Lady Palmer in ceremonial dress or else of the diva alone, dressed for one of her many performances in full theatrical fig with stage makeup.

Poor Catherine. It was all so solipsistic, it was sickening. Beth shuddered and turned to find herself being studied from a distance by an amused Duncan Ross.

"No need to tell me what you were thinking," he said, joining her. "It's written all over your face."

"Lord, I hope not!" said Beth in horror, startled to find herself so minutely observed.

"Only to someone who's really looking. The rest of them here are as self-absorbed as she is."

Beth smiled in relief; he understood. Duncan, on the other hand, felt a compelling urge to kiss her. He took a firm grip on himself and compromised by giving her shoulder a friendly squeeze. The rest could come later; he sensed there was no hurry. He relieved her of her empty cup and placed it on the piano for Sally to clear. He liked this woman with her frank approach. She was his sort of person, all too rare, particularly here in London.

"What a wicked waste of a life," said Beth. "Acting servant to that vile old woman. It must surely have shortened her life. I'd be tempted to die young too, if only to escape the tedium of it all."

"She did have a job," said Duncan, "with me. Though she wasn't in it very long, more's the pity."

He reviewed the remaining company. Eleanor, a parody of Queen Mary in her antique lace and rows of simulated pearls, had regained her composure sufficiently to be helped to the piano, where she was holding court.

"In a moment she's going to sing," said Beth. "Just watch her. I don't think I can bear it." There was admiration mixed with her disbelief. Eleanor needed only a potted aspidistra to complete the Victorian tableau. Duncan beamed, enraptured.

"They're okay, this group," he said benevolently. "Just lonely folk, a little out of their time, trying to make the best of it. Not a lot wrong with that."

What a nice, nice man. Beth felt ashamed of her own mean spirit and longed more than anything to be held against that strong chest by those capable arms and not to have to worry about anything again. She grinned apologetically. He was watching her in a knowing way and she felt herself blush.

Other eyes were upon her from across the room and she turned, with a feeling that was almost relief, to see Sally standing in the doorway. *Oh-oh.* Hadn't she left them doing the tea things, and wasn't she supposed to be lending a hand?

"Sal, come join us!" she called, beckoning lavishly, but Sally had turned and headed back to the kitchen.

"Sally?" Beth was startled. She went to follow her but Duncan placed a hand on her arm that forbade her to move.

"In a minute it'll be all right to leave," he said. "Come with me. I'll drive you home."

"I've got my own car outside," she said defensively. "And a kid in the kitchen."

He grinned, nice and easy. "Then you can drop me, no sweat."

She laughed in delight. "That's crazy!"

"I'm just around the corner; I'll pick my car up tomorrow. I've got some new kittens at the surgery. Why don't you both come by and see them?"

Vivienne and Georgy were into their fourth martinis and Georgy was beginning to feel a little the worse for wear. She was seriously in love with Vivienne's cats. As the hour grew later and the temperature dropped, they had moved upstairs to the drawing room where Ferdinand and Isabella were busy showing off.

"They're not allowed in the conservatory," explained Vivienne, "because of the fish."

They really were extraordinarily beautiful, as lithe and perfect as ballet dancers. Georgy was not by any means an animal person but these cats—well, these cats were something else entirely. Isabella had settled cozily into her lap and was kneading her delicate, ten-denier tights with gentle, rhythmic paws while Ferdinand was executing giant Nijinsky leaps in pursuit of an invisible fly. Enchanting.

"I'd love to photograph them," said Georgy.

"You would? You're not just being polite?" Vivienne was thrilled. "I'd really like that. They're my babies. I thought of having them painted but doubt they would ever sit still that long. Photographs would be as good. Better in fact," she corrected herself, remembering her manners.

Georgy laughed. She was teetering on the brink of being half-cut, though Vivienne still appeared entirely sober.

"Look, how's about I show you some of my work? Then you can judge for yourself whether I'm good enough. I usually take dancers but these guys have a lot of the same attributes, without the temperament, of course."

Ferdinand, tired of his fly, was watching them from the top of a tall china cabinet next to a priceless Ming vase.

"Doesn't that scare you?" asked Georgy. "I know I'd freak if it were my apartment."

Vivienne shrugged. "Oh, they never break anything," she said with confidence, swinging Isabella up by her paws and kissing the ice-cold nose. "As kittens they practically wrecked the joint but now they have grown into a state of grace."

"Which is why," said Georgy, "I've simply got to get them on film."

It was almost eight and Georgy realized she was starving. How rude, to have stayed so long.

"Don't leave!" said Vivienne as Georgy drained her glass and made as if to go. There was still no sign of Oliver and she hated to be alone on Saturday night. Throwback to the sixties it might be, but she couldn't ignore it.

"Stay and eat. I'm sure I can rustle up something in the kitchen, or else we can go round the corner to the Star of India."

"Are you sure?" But the question was rhetorical. Georgy was feeling very comfortable, and besides, she had nowhere else to go.

In the end they settled for duck pâté and French bread in the kitchen, with a bottle of Beaujolais for Georgy while

Vivienne stuck to straight Stoli, having abandoned the ice. It was like a picnic but without the flies and the two of them giggled like schoolgirls having a dorm feast. Bit by bit, Georgy told Vivienne her life story—her childhood dream of becoming a dancer, her place at Juilliard, and her ultimate disappointment when they told her six years later that she simply didn't have that extra something.

"So then what?" asked Vivienne, her eyes bright.

"My dad bought me a fancy camera," gulped Georgy.

"And?"

"I started taking pictures."

"That's it?"

"That's it."

Georgy shrugged. Put like that it sounded so simple. No need to dwell on the long, long hours and the hard, back-breaking work. Or the courses she had taken at NYU, the apprenticeship to a legendary photographer on the *National Geographic* (fixed via a family connection) which had involved little more than toting heavy equipment, being up at all hours and in all weather, running errands, cleaning up and making coffee. But learning, always learning.

"I think that's a wonderful story," said Vivienne, her sapphire eyes now awash.

Georgy nodded.

"And you'll take my cats?"

Another nod. They were friends, they were sisters, this had been a wonderful night. Silently they embraced.

Footsteps sounded along the passageway and Oliver stood at the door, surveying the scene. He was hungry, still immaculate, and as irritated as hell. The table was strewn enticingly with fresh bread, succulent tomatoes, pâté, peaches, and figs. And an empty wine bottle. A homely scene, a cozy one with two women hugging with tears in their eyes and their mascara all smudged. It was altogether too much.

"You're drunk!" he snapped, and went upstairs to bed.

Chapter Thirty-five

When she saw how Duncan was looking at Beth, Sally was seriously put out. She had the easiest, most happy-go-lucky nature in the world yet here was the man she had been dreaming about gazing with moonstruck eyes at a fat woman who was pushing forty and already had a kid in tow. She couldn't believe it. Okay, Beth was a doll when you got to know her, but still . . . Besides, Beth already had Oliver—Gus too, after a fashion—so it was doubly unfair. The question was: what could Sally do about it?

For the first time in her life she felt jealous and her confidence in her sexual allure took a serious knock. She carried a pile of tea things into the kitchen, where Imogen was still sloshing around in the sink, and slammed them down on the draining board.

"What's up?" Imogen was visibly startled. She had never known Sally in a mood before.

"Oh, I don't know. Just bored, I guess. Time I got out of this dump, the atmosphere's beginning to stifle me."

It wasn't clear if she meant London or merely Albert Hall Mansions; Imogen didn't ask.

Just then Beth stuck her head around the door and smiled.

"All set?"

She looked around with approval at the gleaming surfaces and stacks of clean cups and saucers waiting to be put away.

"Great stuff, girls! Here, let me give you a hand."

She started to sort out the various china patterns but Sally waved her off. She looked tired and tetchy, not at all her usual smiling self.

"I'll do it. I know where it all goes."

Beth caught her daughter's eye and Imogen pulled a face. Sally out of sorts, whatever next? Beth took the cloth out of Imogen's hand and hung it up to dry without a word. Obviously overdoing things, so it wasn't surprising she was on edge. Look how marvelous she had been to Eleanor these past few days. The poor sweet must be knackered.

"Okay," she said brightly. "As long as you're sure, we'll be off then. Any chance of seeing you tomorrow? You know there's always a place for you at our table."

Sally stood with her back turned, running water over her finger until it was hot enough for the final batch.

"I'll see how I feel," she said stiffly, after a pause. "Why don't I give you a buzz in the morning?"

"Just as you like. Take care." Beth kissed her lightly on the cheek, then ushered Imogen out of the room.

"What's eating her?"

"Don't know. The mood just suddenly descended about half an hour ago. Probably getting her period or something."

Beth laughed and ruffled her daughter's hair. That, currently, was Imogen's catch-all for most conditions. She didn't dispute the diagnosis but secretly was disturbed. She loved Sally like a younger sister and hated to see her out of sorts. No doubt the shock of Catherine's death was beginning to take its toll. And why indeed not? After all the time Sally had spent recently with both mother and daughter, she would not be human if she didn't feel something; it was a lot for someone of her age to shoulder.

It didn't take Sally very long to pull herself together. By the time she had finished drying the tea things and stacked the clean china in the pantry, her gray mood was already beginning to lift. Goddammit, when all was said and done, he was only a man. There were plenty more where he came from and Sally prided herself she could pull any man she set her sights on. Any man at all.

Eleanor, as Beth had predicted, was already seated at the piano, her elderly acolytes clustered around her, set to embark on some muted Schubert lieder, in keeping with the solemnity of the occasion. Beth had left and so, apparently, had Duncan. Sally gritted her teeth and threaded her way through the admirers to kiss Eleanor's floury cheek, relieved not to have to stay for what would undoubtedly develop into a geriatric rave-up. She had to hand it to the old girl, she was certainly a goer. Nothing defeated Eleanor Palmer for more than a minute. It was this spirit that Sally admired and that kept her coming back. Under the skin, she felt they were really two of a kind. It had been sad for Catherine that she had not inherited some of her mother's ruthlessness.

"'Bye, sweetie," whispered Sally into the aged ear. "Keep your pecker up and I'll see you very soon."

Eleanor, her eyes on the keyboard, let it be known with a queenly wave that Sally was dismissed, and launched herself into song.

All three of her flatmates were there when Sally arrived home, huddled disconsolately in the kitchen, in the throes of one of their interminable discussions about how to spend the evening. They brightened visibly when Sally rolled in. She supposed it was flattering, this puppyish devotion, but it was seriously beginning to get on her nerves. God, but they were boring. As usual, Beth had been right. They were

boys, not men, and these days Sally wanted something a lot
more challenging.

It was a toss-up between *Aliens, Superman II,* or bowling
in Streatham. *(Please!)* Or a quick trot down the road to the
Hansom Cab which was, of course, Jeremy's choice. Once
Sally would not have hesitated to fall in at his heels but
tonight she was simply not in the mood. She told them to
go without her as she wanted to wash her hair then, brushing aside their incredulous looks, grabbed the radio and an
apple and stomped upstairs to her room to read
Cosmopolitan and brood.

Lovesick, that was what she was. She'd read about it
often enough, usually in these pages, but had always dismissed the concept as being a bit of a myth, the product of
some cynical adman's brain, aimed at boosting infinite
sales of pheromone-related junk. The one thing Sally had
never lacked, throughout her troubled adolescence, was
confidence in her own extraordinary pulling power. The
highlight of her time at the convent had to do with a wild
break for freedom one giddy summer weekend, when the
police had intercepted her hitchhiking and returned her, not
a bit contrite, to the disapproving hand-wringing of her
veiled jailors. But that was just a lark, put down to adolescent high spirits and eventually forgiven.

Whereas here she sat now, a crumpled mass of indeci-
sion, heart pounding, stomach churning, ears on red alert
for a telephone that never rang and definitely off her food.
Pathetic. She lobbed the half-chewed apple into the indus-
trial-size Maxwell House tin that served her as a wastepa-
per basket, curled herself up under the duvet and cried.

By lunchtime next day Sally and Beth were best friends
again, as was inevitable, and Sally was sitting in Beth's
kitchen, feet up on the Aga, telling funny stories and acting
normal. Probably the greatest gift Beth had given her was
this insight into female friendship, something Sally had
never ever encountered before. Beth believed her close

women friends should come first and that no man was
worth falling out over. She believed in sisterhood and fair
play and now she was demonstrating both those ideals.
Look at her and Georgy; look at her and Vivienne. What a
saint!

There was nothing remotely dog-in-the-mangerish about
Beth, that was one of her special qualities. She loved Gus
and always would but lost no sleep over Georgy's frenzied
pursuit of him, other than her concern about Georgy getting
hurt. In the gentlest of ways, she had tried to head Georgy
off but Georgy was too thick-skinned to take notice, so all
Beth could do now was listen, and be on hand with a box of
tissues when the shit hit the inevitable fan. Sally thought
she was a sucker, but that was Beth's business.

And the same, oddly enough, applied to Vivienne. To
Sally's way of thinking Beth had every reason to detest
Oliver's wife, to avoid her at all costs and block her out of
her life. Yet it had only taken one social occasion to turn
her into a friend and now, unbelievably, Beth was actually
talking about damping down the affair out of an idiot feeling of misplaced guilt and not wanting to hurt a woman she
scarcely knew, who was too obtuse to recognize what was
going on right under her own selfish nose. *Weird,* as
Imogen would say.

Sally's own philosophy was starkly simple. If a woman
couldn't keep her man happy, then he was fair game. She
did not believe in monogamy or permanence and worked
on the principle that if she fancied it, she'd screw it—no
sweat. What was wrong with grabbing a little animal pleasure along the way? If God had intended us not to fornicate,
he would not have created the coil or the Pill.

But none of this need she mention to Beth, who was free
to dream on if that was how she got her kicks. And she had
to admit, to her own surprise, that some of her happiest moments had been spent here in Beth's kitchen. For Beth, food
was an all-embracing panacea; Gus always joked that in
some earlier life she must have been a Jewish mother. The

moment the doorbell rang, no matter what the hour, Beth was poised with corkscrew in hand and a plate of some homemade delicacy to fill the gap while she threw together a delicious meal.

Today was no exception. It was Sunday morning and although Sally had only called less than an hour ago, the room was filled with the most wondrously appetizing aromas and the table already set for five. Sally leaned back, a drink and a homemade cheese straw in either hand, and watched Beth cook. A Mozart flute concerto was playing on the hi-fi, the church bells were ringing from across the close and all seemed very much right with the world. Just for now.

The wicket gate creaked and impatient fingers drummed an urgent tattoo on the window. Imogen looked up from her Sunday supplement and dived to the door with a yelp of delight. Sally turned with a welcoming grin, expecting to see Gus, whom she liked a lot, then froze to find Duncan looming in the doorway, beaming down benevolently at all of them.

"Hi there!" Beth at the stove wagged an oven glove at him and stretched out her cheek to receive his kiss, while Imogen jumped excitedly up and down, bombarding him with questions about some wretched kittens. Sally stayed right where she was, frozen into silence.

Duncan produced from the pockets of his battered leather jacket a couple of bottles of fine red burgundy and placed them on the table.

"You did say red?" He looked round for a corkscrew so that he could let them breathe.

"Mmm, nice," said Beth approvingly as she glanced at the labels. "Australian."

"Got to back the old country," said Duncan, tossing his jacket on to the window seat and rolling up his denim sleeves.

Sally was mesmerized, glad she had had the foresight to wash her hair. Close to, he really was the most extraordinarily attractive man, with his smooth brown skin, shaggy hair, and those searching blue eyes she found so disconcerting. He was wearing faded jeans and boots like hers and she could not drag her eyes from the power of his wrists as he eased out the corks with the minimum of effort. Then she glanced up and saw how he was looking at Beth. She had not been wrong; it was clear on his face.

Beth, wrapped in an enveloping chef's apron of white cotton, was working away at the stove basting the beef, shoving loose strands of hair from her sweaty forehead, flushed with the heat from the open oven door. She looked gross to Sally—fat and frumpy, frankly middle-aged. Yet Duncan looked as if he would like to eat her. A cold hand clutched at Sally's heart and she banged off upstairs to the loo.

Duncan settled into a sturdy leather chair and stretched out his long legs on the other side of the stove, skillfully balancing himself with the toe of one boot resting lightly on the rail. They had only spoken for the first time yesterday, yet he looked as though he had been at home here all his life. The thing about Duncan was that he seemed always to be laughing. Merriment creased the corners of his eyes, turning them into cobalt slits, and his teeth shone white from his grizzled beard as he lazily watched his woman doing her virtuoso best with a gleaming joint of beef. Cooking, as only Beth knew how, for the people she loved most in the world.

"How is everyone's glass?" she asked. "Duncan, help yourself. Lunch will be ready in twenty minutes so there's time for another one all round if you'd care to fix them. Vodka's on the side, Clamato juice is in the fridge and Worcester sauce and Tabasco and all the other gubbins are lined up on the dresser."

She turned to smile at him, pushing back her hair with the back of one hand.

"I assume you know how to do it," she said.

"Me? I'll have you know I've hung out in some of the best bars of the world. Worked in them too."

Duncan set to work.

"Imogen has a Virgin," warned Beth. "Everything else but hold the vodka."

"Mum!" objected Imogen.

"Not till you're older, you know the rules. You can have a glass of Duncan's wine with your lunch."

Sally was back and watching. *Bloody hell!* a voice in her head was screeching. *He loves her, I can see it in his eyes. I could kill him for this. Or her.*

"Is Gus coming?" she asked hopefully, eyeing the five set places.

"No, only Georgy," said Beth, heaving the meat back into the inferno. "She called just before you did."

When they were all seated round the plain pine table and Beth had served the roast, with sweet-glazed carrots, fresh garden peas with mint, and butter-crisp new potatoes, Duncan gave them Eleanor's news.

"I'm sorry to be the bearer of rotten tidings," he said, "but I'm afraid I've just heard something fairly grim."

All eyes turned to him. He sat playing with the pepper mill as he groped for words.

"It seems Catherine's death was not entirely natural." His eyes focused on each of them in turn. "She was dying, but not quite yet."

Dead silence round the table; even Imogen stopped chewing.

"What happened?" asked Beth.

"She took an overdose of the morphine sulphate she was given to ease the pain."

"Cripes!" said Imogen, mouth full. "You mean she topped herself?"

Beth, incredibly shocked, leaned forward and reached out a restraining hand. Duncan was still fiddling with the pepper mill; there was obviously more to come.

"I popped in to see Eleanor this morning," he said, "when I picked up the car. The pills were safely in the cabinet in the bathroom when Eleanor left, just after six, for a concert at the Fairfield Hall, but the bottle was there on her bedside table next morning. Half empty. And Catherine was dead. Eleanor looked in on her at midnight when she got home but she seemed to be sleeping so she didn't disturb her. She didn't even turn on the light."

His eyes are like cornflowers, thought Sally as Duncan looked at them each in turn. Everyone was silent. Catherine's death had been shocking enough; this was worse.

Beth turned to Sally in surprise.

"But I thought you were with her that last night, Sal. How come you weren't there when Eleanor got home?"

Sally hesitated.

"Well, I was and I wasn't," she said cautiously, choosing her words.

"What do you mean?" Beth's tone was unusually sharp.

"Well, I know I promised Eleanor I'd hang on there till she got back from her concert, and I really meant to do that even though . . ."

Beth raised one eyebrow in query, her eyes suddenly cold.

". . . even though I had a date," said Sally lamely. "She was very restless so I made her some chamomile tea and was wondering whether to give her a couple of those painkillers a bit early, to see if they would help her sleep. I couldn't see it would make much difference, she was so sick, poor darling. I mean, for pity's sake, she was dying."

She turned to Duncan, suddenly close to tears, but he was looking at Beth.

"And then?" asked Beth, dispassionate as a judge.

"And then," said Sally slowly, "someone else showed up."

They all stared but Sally, suddenly milking the situation for all it was worth, was not going to be hurried.

"She had told me she was expecting someone, a late-night visitor. Got herself all dolled up for him she did, with blusher, eyeliner, the lot. So I thought I'd give her a break. Poor love, she didn't have much fun at the best of times. The least I could do was help her indulge a fantasy."

"But it wasn't a fantasy?"

"No. It was someone who let himself in with his own key just as she said he would. I was amazed."

They all stared at her. "Who?"

Sally paused dramatically. "Who do you think?" She looked at their spellbound faces and laughed. "Addison Harvey, of course. Who else? The one true love of poor old Catherine's life. Only she called him Tom."

"And then?"

"I said I would hang on till Eleanor got home but he said not to bother. So I handed him the pills and left. After all, why keep a doctor and bark yourself?"

"So how come he's not said anything? And why was Catherine alone when her mother did get back?" asked Beth.

"Don't know. It did seem a bit odd at the time, him being so much at home there and having his own key, but he was so authoritative I didn't question it. And besides . . ."

"You had a date."

She nodded.

"He did say something to Eleanor," said Duncan. "But not until the next day when she called him in hysterics and he came over to confirm the cause of death. He told her Catherine had ODed on morphine sulphate but not, as far as I know, that he had been there that night."

They all looked at each other and shrugged. The truth was, it really wasn't their business. If the doctor and the mother were *au fait* with the situation, then let it rest. Only one thing was certain; whatever had happened in Catherine's final hours had been for the best, there could be no doubting that.

"Was she telling the truth?" asked Beth much later. "And if so, shouldn't someone be informing the police?"

Duncan shifted her weight slightly off his right arm, which was getting cramped.

"No," he said after a moment's thought. "What's done's done and the poor woman was dying anyway. Why put Eleanor through any more distress? If Harvey chose to take the law into his own hands, then that's a doctor's prerogative. It was a medical decision and a brave one in the circumstances. Don't you agree?"

He bent his head slightly to kiss her on the nose.

"Maybe Catherine even colluded. They were pretty close. We'll never know, so let's keep it to ourselves."

The others were long gone, Imogen on her rollerblades to the park with Sally, Georgy to sleep off her gargantuan hangover from the night before. Beth and Duncan had cleared the debris from the table, rinsed the dishes, and were now stretched out comfortably on the kitchen sofa, her head resting on his chest, listening to the comforting background thrum of the dishwasher.

"Happy?" he asked after a while, tightening his grip and blowing gently into her hair.

"Blissful." She breathed in his warm, clean, masculine smell and felt an ache of desire course right through her.

So why don't you take me to bed?

But she knew that this time there was no rush. Because, at last, she had found a real man, one she could trust. And that was worth waiting any amount of time for.

Chapter Thirty-six

Sylvia Kirsch pushed aside the plate-glass patio doors and stepped barefoot onto the lawn. Even at seven in the morning, the heat that was rising though the grass was still deliciously cool with the damp from the sprinklers that were spraying shimmering spider's webs of silver over the lawn and its surrounding beds. She walked the few yards to the poolside table where the pool boy was opening a yellow and white umbrella to protect the breakfasters from the sun, while a Mexican maid in a blue linen dress arranged coffee, croissants, and freshly squeezed orange juice on a crisp white cloth. By nine the sun would be at its hottest. Now was the time to enjoy breakfast al fresco.

Sylvia relaxed with her juice and the papers and watched the lone swimmer finishing his fifty laps. At sixty-two, her husband was still in excellent shape and she loved to watch this early-morning workout on the rare occasions their timetables coincided long enough for them to snatch a meal together. Emmanuel Kirsch rose powerful and dripping from the pool, snatched a towel from the tiles as he climbed up the steps, and stood in front of his wife like a great shaggy beast, shaking cold drops all over her linen shorts from his thick silver hair. She laughed and fended him off as he bent his dripping head to nuzzle her cheek.

"Lay off, will you! I just had my hair done!" Then, more soberly, "What time's your flight?"

Emmanuel slung the towel around his burly neck, slid his shoulders into a toweling wrap, and sank into a canvas chair while Sylvia poured his coffee. He liked it hot and strong and he savored this first cup more than any other, particularly since the doctor had made him cut down his daily intake and had put him on a rigid low-cholesterol diet. He glanced at his silver Rolex.

"Noon. I'm dining at the Yale Club tonight with Ed, then hotfooting it down to Washington tomorrow for the hearing. Should be there—oh, three, four days—and all being well, on a flight to London before the end of the week."

"And how long will you be there?" He traveled so much, it was a joke between them. Sometimes, she said, he sounded like a PanAm pilot. She longed to go with him but knew enough, after nine years, not to suggest it; not when he was on a case as serious as this. Already his mind was veering away from her, occupied with the complexities of the latest murder case and the witnesses he hoped to be able to interview in Europe.

"As long as it takes. Hopefully just a few days, but you never can tell. If you'd wanted a nine-to-five old man you should have married an accountant. Or a PanAm pilot."

He leaned across to kiss her cheek.

"I've got to get back for the judicial hearings on Thursday week. Right now, that's about as precise as I can be."

Emmanuel was at the height of his career and showed no signs of ever slacking off. Despite the heart murmur and the cholesterol scare, Sylvia had no intention of nagging him to slow down, because that was the essence of the man she had married, the man who had swept her off her feet in one dramatic meeting.

"Well," he said, draining his cup and rising to his feet, "time to get this show on the road. Where's that goddamn kid? Always underfoot but never here when he's wanted."

"If you are referring to your son and heir," said Sylvia, "he was up with the dawn chorus and off to the stables to help them muck out before you were even stirring."

Emmanuel grinned. "He's some kid, what? Eight years old and already living like a cowboy. My son, the champion jockey! He'll have his own stud by the time he's eighteen, mark my words!"

Sylvia smiled to see her husband so enthusiastic about his youngest child. Ariel had been born when she was over forty and she had been apprehensive in case he would prove too much of a burden to his father, who had washed his hands of child-rearing years before. She need not have worried. Ariel was the son Emmanuel had always yearned for; a sparky, spirited, cut-down version of his father, already a handful at only eight years old. With the same darting dark eyes and hyperactive mind; the same energy, fearlessness, and breathtaking charm. No wonder Emmanuel worshiped him; she did too. But she was also aware that Ariel was hogging the attention his older half-sisters lacked. That, she knew, was one of the grievances Myra still held against her, even though there had been another wife in between.

"Will you get a chance to look in on Georgy?" she asked, sipping her juice as she followed him into the house. There was nothing he needed her to do—her husband was a man with a regimen honed to almost military precision—but Sylvia liked to share with him as much as she could, knowing how she would suffer from his glaring absence over the next few days.

At thirty-nine, Sylvia had been a power in her own right, a top-notch journalist on the *Los Angeles Times* who had given up everything for this charismatic man she had met at a time when she was beginning to give up hope of ever having a settled life. She still kept her hand in, of course, writing an occasional column for the paper when they needed one, but her main energies these days were spent supervising their comfortable lifestyle and raising their son;

that and keeping a firm eye on her husband's well-being by trying to cushion him from any potential damage from his punishing work schedule.

"If there's time, of course I will," he said, stooping slightly to catch the appropriate angle in the mirror as he knotted his tie. "What, go to London and not find time to see my Little Princess? Besides, I'm keen to see how she's making out without her mother forever breathing down her neck."

Sylvia laughed. Myra's suffocating protectiveness was another of their jokes.

"She'll be fine, you'll see. How old is she, nearly thirty? Come on, that's practically middle-aged."

Emmanuel silently calculated.

"Twenty-six, actually, last September. Four years older than Risa. My, how time certainly does fly. I keep seeing her as a bony kid with braces, and now she's quite a woman."

Sylvia nodded. To her, Georgy, her eldest stepchild, was still that bony kid, nervy and unpredictable, not at all easy to get along with, hard to love.

"Well, be sure and give her my love," was all she said. "And find out when she's going to deign to visit Newport Beach."

"It's the old problem, the time factor. You know how frenetic she usually is. Can't even make it back to New York these days, except for weddings."

Sylvia laughed. "And I wonder who she gets that from."

She sat on the bed in the airy, Spanish-style room, with its views over the orange groves to the wide Pacific Ocean, and watched him button the starched blue shirt which set off his tan so well, then shrug himself into the jacket of his well-cut lightweight suit. Two more suits, of a heavier fabric, hung in their bag on the closet door and a pair of polished black wingtips were waiting to replace the snakeskin loafers he wore in California.

"Don't forget your Burberry," teased his wife.

"No, Myra," he said gruffly, reaching for a long-handled brush and flicking imaginary dust off his immaculate shoulders. He looked good and he knew it, every inch the celebrated criminal psychologist. Sylvia's heart softened with tenderness as she slid smooth hands over the back of his neck and tidied the hair that was beginning to curl over his collar. God, how she loved this man. Sometimes the sheer intensity of her feelings scared her. He was everything, and more, that she had ever dreamed of and, having waited so long to find him, partings like this frightened her more than he could know. In her gloomier moments she faced up to the facts; in his sixties he was as attractive as ever, while she was one of a number of wives, and aging. And at least one week in four they spent apart, often on different continents. Then she pulled herself together, for that way lay madness. She was, after all, the mother of his son, of all his four children the one most like him and also the most loved. She knew it had been hard on Georgy when Ariel had come along, when she was already grown up, but she hoped one day she could bring all Emmanuel's children together and get them to love each other as proper siblings. But that would have to wait for a later date, when Ariel was older and his father a little less pressured.

"Get a haircut in London, sweetie," was all she said.

"Don't fuss, woman."

He bent to kiss her lightly on the lips, patted her bottom as he reached for the suitbag, and was on his way down the stairs, shouting to his driver to bring the car round.

Georgy was sitting with Vivienne on the sofa, her leather portfolio open between them. Sheets and sheets of contact prints, both color and black and white, spilled out all around them, on the coffee table, the sofa, and round their feet on the carpet. Isabella was draped round Georgy's shoulders like a sable scarf, purring profoundly with a quiet contentment, but the luckless Ferdinand had been banished to the kitchen because he could not resist licking the shiny

prints with his rough little tongue. Georgy had already conquered her natural nervousness of animals, to the extent of
being able to function quite normally with this warm, furry
thing round her neck.

Vivienne was astonished by the power of the photography. The pictures were infinitely better than she had imagined and, as a result, Georgy had shot right up in her
estimation. This girl was a true artist, of that there was no
doubt. Behind her snappy manner and paranoid outlook lay
a real sense of poetry and a true eye for beauty which
somehow she managed to capture on film. Quite amazing.
Vivienne moved slowly from transparency to transparency,
holding each one up in turn to the window, then laying
them next to each other along the glass top of the table.

"You really need a lightbox to see them properly," fretted
Georgy, never satisfied yet pleased by Vivienne's flattering
response. "Just one more thing I'll need to save up for once
I can afford the space."

Vivienne sat in silence, sucked into Georgy's magical
world of ballet. Somehow she had managed to capture
more than just the grace and fluid movement of the dancers
so that Vivienne felt she could hear the music and share the
electrifying atmosphere inside the Albert Hall.

"These are truly spectacular," she said at last, tidying
them loosely into a pile. "What a talent you have, to be
sure. If I had a fraction of what you've got I would consider
myself truly blessed."

Georgy was pleased but still not entirely convinced.

"I'd far rather dance than simply record it," she said, col-
lecting her pictures and shoving them back into their case.
"Photography's not entirely a respectable profession, you
know; not considered to be an art at all. Not like going out
there onstage and putting everything you've got into it,
with real blood, sweat, and tears."

"Don't put yourself down!" Vivienne had heard it all before but simply didn't agree. How could she, with all this
evidence of a powerful talent right here in front of her?

Vivienne herself had impeccable taste and the money to indulge it, yet Georgy made her feel quite humble. What wouldn't she give for a daughter like this; if only she had not been so selfish and allowed her vanity to get in the way of motherhood. She wanted to grab hold of Georgy and shake her.

"Look at it like this," she said. "A performance lasts just as long as the music is playing, whereas your pictures will survive forever. In a hundred years' time, if they are properly preserved, people will still get pleasure and inspiration from looking at what you have created here, your own unique way of seeing things. Like Toulouse-Lautrec with the Folies Bergère; like Cartier-Bresson. What a truly marvelous legacy to be able to hand down. I envy you."

"I don't know." Georgy still had doubts. For so many years she had dreamed of being a dancer, had practiced and sweated and starved herself to that sole end, only to be told at the crucial age of sixteen that she just didn't have what it took—that extra intangible something that separates the stars from the rest. And for any child of Emmanuel Kirsch, less than best meant second-rate. Instead of supporting her and telling her it didn't matter, what had her father done? Turned his back on his real children once more and married for the fourth time, this time begetting the son Myra had always claimed was the one thing he wanted from life, thereby compounding Georgy's misery and guilt. *If you, my firstborn, can't make it work,* he seemed to be saying, *then I'll simply create perfection in your place.*

"Not every dancer can make it to world status," said Vivienne, watching Georgy's suddenly closed face and remembering herself, a chubby Shirley Temple lookalike, decked out for those excruciating ballet classes which her father had forced her into at three then mercifully allowed her to drop at seven. "It's like tennis. What about other sorts of dancing? Something more popular, perhaps?"

"Dancing is dancing," said Georgy stubbornly. "I only ever wanted to be the best. I didn't want to settle for musical comedy or, worse still, a touring company. Can you imagine anything worse than Sticksville, USA, playing to audiences of housewives and Shriners' nights, in towns where the locals know diddley-squat about quality?"

Gus did it, said a voice in her head, but she brushed it aside. Gus was different; he started off a genius.

"No, I'd sooner settle for second best than be lumbered with a third-rate career and arthritis by the time I reach forty."

Deeply moved by her honesty, Vivienne reached for Georgy's hand in a spontaneous gesture of solidarity and was pleased to feel Georgy's fingers close tightly over her own. Today she was wearing her hair drawn severely back, which accentuated her fierce little face with its assertive nose.

"Sweetie, you're by no means second best," said Vivienne. "You must never for a moment believe that. These photographs are quite extraordinary. I'm certainly no expert but I do know quality when I see it and you are very special. Why do you think they sent you here in the first place? Are you really telling me a magazine like that would waste good money if they could get the job done on the spot? We do have our own photographers, you know. Our Queen's sister married one."

At least she had Georgy smiling. Vivienne could be quite a tonic at times; she felt the spiky resistance beginning to crumble. As they cleared away the pictures and straightened up the room, Georgy talked more about herself—about Myra and her sisters and the comfortable home on Long Island that stifled her but which, at the same time, she often missed so badly. And the famous father she saw rarely but whose approval she had always worked so hard to win. Whose favorite child she once had been until she grew into a gawky teenager and he had replaced her with the son he had always longed for.

She sat back lithely on her heels as she talked and a glow came into her sallow cheeks. He was the one who had taught her to pick herself up when the going got tough and get right back in there. Because, at the final count, it wasn't the game that mattered, it was winning.

"What's more," she said with childish enthusiasm, "he's probably going to be here next week."

At the prospect of seeing her father again, the birdlike features softened so that Vivienne could see she possessed an unusual beauty all of her own.

Why, she thought, seeing the flush on Georgy's cheek and the sudden light in her eye, *she's in love with him and doesn't even know it.*

Chapter Thirty-seven

Oliver whacked the ball into the corner of the court, scoring points off his opponent and bringing the game to an end. He was seeing Beth this evening and the prospect had lent an edge to his performance. Addison, thirty pounds heavier and clearly out of condition, dropped his racquet and bent double with exhaustion as he picked up his towel to mop his neck.

"Christ, old boy, I'm certainly not the man I once was. This old ticker just can't take it anymore. Not that you didn't play brilliantly," he added somewhat grudgingly.

Oliver laughed and pushed back his damp sweaty hair.

"Physician, heal thyself!" he said. "There's nothing wrong with you that fewer lunches and a bit more exercise wouldn't fix."

Addison grinned. It was shameful, really, but the man had a point. Constantly advising patients, and at a price too, to cut their intake of fat and cigarettes and increase their daily exercise, while here he was, a top-ranking doctor, breaking all the rules as a matter of course.

"It's the drug peddlers," he explained as they headed toward the showers. He was panting for a cigar but that would have to wait. "Once they get their teeth into you, there's no escaping . . . and it's such a delicious way to die!"

"The thing about the City," said Oliver, "is that no one's doing it anymore. The power lunch is out. All we ever do these days is nibble a plate of smoked salmon and drink a glass of fizzy water."

"Lunch is for wimps."

"Something like that. It's refreshing, in a way. Means the young Turks spend more time on the floor and make that much more money, but it's also depressing. A lot of the fun has gone out of the game. When you end up doing it solely for the rewards, well, it begins to defeat its purpose."

Addison glanced at the other man with interest. They were roughly the same age, yet if he were honest he could give Oliver a good ten years. Standing under the shower, with the water streaming over him, he was an enviable specimen with his smooth chest and flat stomach, the body of a much younger man. No wonder the birds fancied him; Addison thought of the delectable wife and lusted.

"You sound somewhat jaded," he said. "Nothing wrong, I hope."

"Nothing that a good shag won't cure," said Oliver honestly, flashing his rare smile as he stepped from under the water jet and toweled his hair.

Addison was thunderstruck. Well, you just never knew. There he went, envying Oliver his happy little love nest, and all the time it was a sham. He longed to ask questions but professional caution warned him to tread carefully. Chaps didn't invade each other's privacy like that and, more alarming, confidences were expected to work two ways. He couldn't resist a tiny pry, however, as he stepped back into his lovat tweeds and zipped up his pants.

"Got a date?"

"You could say that."

Oliver was at the mirror, combing his sleek black hair into place, fingering his firm chin to check if he needed a shave.

"With the missus?" Doctors ought not to do this but Addison dared. If anyone asked him a similar question, he'd come clean. He wasn't sure about Oliver, who had always seemed a bit of a dark horse, but in his own chosen profession something on the side was considered par for the course.

Oliver laughed, displaying immaculate teeth.

"Not tonight. Are you kidding?" He glanced at his watch. "No, I'm meeting her in forty minutes so we've time for a fast jar if you're game."

Lucky sod, thought Addison sourly, as he knotted his tie and tucked it into the top of his waistcoat. Lately he had not been doing so well in the girlie stakes. Either his libido was lessening or else he was losing his touch. He thought of faithful Phoebe, waiting so trustingly in Sunningdale, and felt a trace of bleakness. She was a dear and he did not forget his good fortune at finding her just when he needed her most, but when all was said and done it had to be faced, a leg-up was not the same as a leg-over. And this smarmy bastard preening himself at the mirror appeared to have it all ways. Made money, married money, and still playing the field. And with a wife at home any healthy male worth his oats would give a lot to get into the sack.

All libidinous thoughts were knocked out of Addison's head by Oliver's abrupt change of conversation as he set up the drinks.

"What's the real truth behind Catherine Palmer's death? We were discussing it last night and it still seems pretty baffling."

Addison took a fast swallow of his gin and tonic while the cogs within his brain went into overdrive. The one subject he wanted to avoid; even thinking of her now brought a chill sweat to his brow and a distinct palpitation to his heart.

"What exactly is your question?" he asked carefully. "It was an overdose. I thought you realized that."

"Yes, I know. But Vivienne seemed to think there might be more to it than actually came out in public. Something she heard from Beth, something the old girl is reputed to have told the vet."

"The vet?" This conversation was getting crazier by the minute and the last person Addison needed invading his scenario was anyone else with the remotest knowledge of medicine.

"That hairy Australian," said Oliver with venom. "The one who's always hanging around my wife." *And not just my wife, either. That's only the half of it.* "The one Catherine Palmer used to work for."

God, the vet.

"I'd forgotten that," said Addison lamely, and the strange thing was, he had. He knew she worked locally, enjoyed what she was doing, but had never really focused on what she actually did or, come to that, anything much about her at all other than the time bomb ticking on inside. This one could be tricky. These horse doctors often had more arrogance than sense, and an Australian, to boot. Addison hated Australians on principle. In his eyes they were definitely second-raters, no question about it, and the fewer he encountered, the better. He thought fast.

"She took the morphine sulphate I left to assuage the pain. It was a shame really, though in any case she hadn't long to go. These things do happen. Whether she knew what she was doing isn't clear, but *in extremis* people should be allowed to think for themselves."

He emptied his glass.

"Don't you agree?"

Oliver watched him shrewdly. There was no doubt Addison was holding something back but it wasn't his right to push any harder. He'd scarcely known the woman, after all, and come to that, neither had Viv. If Addison had helped her on her way, then that was his business and doubtless an act of mercy. One thing Oliver was profoundly glad of was that he didn't have to make decisions like that. Money was one thing, and he had often watched lives collapse through mismanagement, but at least if he ever made a faulty diagnosis, it was not exactly life-threatening. Or, at least, not often.

The clock over the bar was pointing to eight.

"Must go," he said. "Same time next week?"

"I really don't know how I'm going to handle it," said Beth, phone tucked under her chin as she tried to do something last-minute to her hair. Oliver was already late so she was grabbing the time for a swift consultation with Jane.

"I don't know how I feel about him anymore, for one thing, and I just don't want to go to bed with him. Not now. Not since Duncan." There, it was out. It did sound faintly wet, she realized, but that was how she was. And Jane was her best friend and would understand.

The last thing comfortably married Jane wanted to do was promote the cause of Oliver, but it was still early days, and a bird in the hand . . .

"What exactly is happening with Duncan?" she asked. She had not yet been allowed to meet Mr. Wonderful but he was all Beth talked about these days.

"Really not a lot." One of Beth's endearing traits was her total honesty. "But I think he likes me."

Which had to be the understatement of the year but that was something she needed to keep to herself, at least until she had some evidence to share with her friend.

"He rings a lot. And he's nice to Imogen. And we make each other laugh."

And he makes my knees shake and my knickers damp just thinking about him and all I can think of, day and night, is the thought of being in his arms, his bed, his life forevermore.

"How does he kiss? Or don't you know?"

Beth laughed.

"It's not quite that dire, thank you very much. We're beyond playing doctors and nurses, I'm happy to tell you."

But it was a bit of a puzzle. She fell silent and thought about it, feeling the familiar swoop of excitement in the pit of her stomach. Duncan's kisses were all she lived for now, too incredibly exciting even to begin to describe.

"Not at all bad," she admitted. "Or else I'd begin to think he was gay."

"Well, there must be something wrong." Jane was a pragmatist. "Or what's he waiting for? Is he married, do you think? Or perhaps it's Imogen he's after. You want to watch these men. Nowadays almost anything goes."

Beth gurgled with delight. "Maybe he's a Hare Krishna. Or do I mean a Mormon?"

"That wouldn't get in the way of lust," said Jane. "Grist to his mill, in fact. You could simply join the team. Nights off to wash your hair while he was otherwise occupied, stuff like that. But do they have them down under?"

The doorbell rang.

"Cripes, he's here. Oliver, I mean. What *am* I going to do? You still haven't told me. Quick!"

"Have a headache. Or a period. Or genital herpes, take your pick. But remember—anything that's coming to him he richly deserves, so whatever you do, take no hostages. And ring me back the second he's gone. Otherwise I shall know he won."

Oliver sat with his head in his hands, more moved than Beth had expected. This was quite a revelation but it came too late. It seemed this man really did care for her, in his own somewhat detached manner. That, or else he was a bloody fine actor. She longed to cross the room to him but stuck to her chair and her guns. It was proving quite upsetting, particularly since she had nothing really to tell him to make things easier to swallow. And that mattered: Beth was a creature of conscience.

I've met this bloke I fancy. Put that way, it would sound too wet for words.

"I never pretended to be anything but married," said Oliver eventually, in a low voice. He raised his head and stared at her with reproachful eyes. What was going on here?

Was she turning broody all of a sudden? Beth, of all people? It didn't bear contemplating.

She shuffled awkwardly and picked at the pewter roses, longing to find a fly. Was he going soft?

"I know," she said. "It isn't that. You've never promised anything you couldn't deliver. I respect you for that."

"Then what? Bed is good, isn't it? I always felt we shared at least that."

She glanced at his stricken face and felt even more of a heel. Oh, Lord, what was she to do? Leaving Gus had been bad enough but at least he had wanted his freedom. She had always felt, deep down, that Oliver could take it or leave it, which was part of his attraction; kept her keen. Now she wasn't so sure. She took a deep breath and pretended to level with him. It might sound a touch naive but it was easier than the truth.

"It's Vivienne," she said. "I like your wife."

"Well, I'm glad. So do I. But what difference can that possibly make to us? She has nothing to do with you and me. She's another part of my life entirely and what she doesn't know can't hurt her."

Beth's anguish eased a little. *Bastard.* Now he was talking like a man; her feet touched bottom and she braced herself.

"It matters to me. While I didn't know her, I could only imagine, but now all that has changed. The monstrous Her Inside who gave you such a terrible home life has gone and all I see now is that fragile, frightened woman who always seems so sad."

She knew she was enraging him but it couldn't be helped. It was true what they said; men were pigs. She had started, so she would have to finish, and now was the moment for the coup de grâce, even though it could mean she would spend the rest of her life regretting. And alone.

Oliver got up, his hands wide in helpless exasperation, and paced the room. Beth, curled in her chair, watched him in silence. There was no answer to this one, none that she could see. He turned to her, pleading, and dragged her into his arms. Normally his fierce kisses reduced her to putty but tonight something magical had happened to her hormones. They just weren't functioning; he left her cold. Even the seductive scent of his aftershave failed to thrill her. All he was, she saw now with ice-cold clarity, was a beautiful, sexy, selfish man without an ounce of humor or understanding.

"Come to bed," he whispered, sticking his tongue down her throat. "And I'll show you what you'd lose if you ever let me go."

She gently disengaged his hands and moved away.

"What it boils down to," she told Gus the following morning as they strolled arm in arm through the new Whiteleys complex, watching Imogen dodge excitedly among the Saturday shoppers like a dog let off its lead, "is that I am a free agent and what I want goes."

Gus squeezed her arm and laughed. This was Beth at her heady best and he thoroughly approved, even if these days she did scare him slightly. They wandered into a bookshop and stood together, companionably leafing through the new publications.

"I'm sorry if it upsets you in any way," he said. "But I have a strong feeling it doesn't."

She grinned wryly.

"You know me. Never content with what I've got."

Imogen joined them and Beth drew them both into a tight three-way hug.

"Well, that's not entirely true," she added. "What I've got is here and that's really all that matters."

Gus shook his head in exaggerated wonder and followed her out of the shop.

"Women!" he whispered to his daughter, tucking her hand into his sleeve and stepping forward to grab her mother. "I'll never understand them, but I guess that's all part of the fun."

Chapter Thirty-eight

Oliver came home in the worst possible temper but for once Vivienne was in no mood to humor him.

"You're late!" she snarled from the bathtub as he burst into the bedroom, and she didn't even bother to hide the glass.

"And what's that to you?" he demanded with equal *froideur,* even though he was fighting mad and fit to punch the first thing that came to hand, which happened to be her. He ripped off his tie and then his jacket and flung both on the floor in a childish attitude of rebellion. What he wanted more than anything was a drink. He kicked off his shoes and pounded downstairs in his socks but Vivienne had removed the Stolichnaya to the privacy of the bathroom, so he poured a large brandy instead.

Women. He had had it up to here with them. He was too agitated to work so returned to the bedroom, the only lighted beacon in the house, and threw himself onto the bed. There was silence. In the bathroom the water moved slightly as Vivienne sat up and craned round the door in a fit of curiosity to see what was biting him. All she could see were his feet, dangling over the edge of the bed, and bits and pieces of his clothing strewn across the floor. Most interesting. Despite herself, something moved deep within her and she automatically checked out her appearance in the mirrored wall to see that she was not looking too much of a fright.

"Oliver?" she tried tentatively as she drained her glass, but there was silence.

She pushed herself upward out of the foam, wrapped a vast white bathsheet round her as she stepped onto the monogrammed mat, checked her eyes for smudged mascara, and advanced into the room.

"Oliver?"

He lay supine, staring up at the ceiling, and his eyes were open but not focused. The top two buttons of his lavender shirt were undone and he smelled divine as she leaned across to check his pulse, then caught his fishy eye upon her and giggled suddenly like a schoolgirl.

"Oliver!" she breathed as he caught her in a sudden snatch and ripped away the towel, rough hands working her breasts, harsh tongue burrowing into her cleavage. Suddenly awake and as hard and ferocious as a tiger, he was on top of her, pinning her wrists to the pillow, tearing, pummeling, thrusting into her flesh until she wanted to scream out with pain. With the terrifying, unexpected, exquisite pain of it all—pain she had long dreamed of; pain that was almost forgotten.

"Oliver," she murmured again when he was through, smoothing back the wild damp hair and kissing the eyelids closed in exhaustion, with lashes like a cat's fanned softly across his cheek.

For a long time she lay, spent with emotion, his weight pressing down on her, the damp from the bath drying on her skin, a sharp, sweet, long-forgotten ache issuing from between her legs. Tomorrow she would be sore; just as well she was not going horse-riding. Like an old movie projected on the ceiling, it all came back in sharp, clear focus, that night at the Clermont when she was still just a silly girl and had first set eyes on this man at the gaming table. The night arranged by Fate which had altered the course of both their lives.

And, once again, she found herself remembering Celia Hartley.

Vivienne had only actually seen her once, the girl it was widely rumored Oliver Nugent was set to marry. She was a slight, fey slip of a thing in old-fashioned ivory lace, with her hair coiled heavily on the back of her head like an Edwardian heroine and a frowning mama in heavy whale-boned silk like the Duchess in *Alice in Wonderland*. Vivienne had refused to take her seriously. She might be filthy rich—her family originated in Bristol and founded their huge fortune on the slave trade—but she was certainly no match for a man as lusty as Oliver or, come to that, an opponent with real fire in her belly like Vivienne. At first Vivienne had been wary of Celia, for the fortune which was greater than anything her father had yet amassed, and the sickly breeding which spoke out of every fine bone in her face. But once she had caught Oliver's eye and seen the visible quickening of his pulse whenever she was near, the other girl had failed to exist as anything more than an irritation; certainly not a threat.

From the moment of that fateful dinner in Sherborne, Vivienne knew she had won—it was just a matter of waiting it out. From that point on, she had acted as if Oliver were already hers, with not a single thought for the gentle, ailing Celia languishing in her rose-scented bedroom, waiting for him to make their union official. Raised by Eugene to go out and grab what she wanted, Vivienne had made it her aim always to be firmly in the center of Oliver's attention. Whereas a nicer girl might have held back and reminded him of his existing commitments, Vivienne had brushed aside all mention of Celia as being just too boring for words.

The courtship was short and heady, with a roller-coaster intensity from which neither of them ever drew breath. Yet, at the same time, Oliver did not forget his duty toward his erstwhile sweetheart. He wanted to let her down gently, not to hurt her more than was necessary. She was, after all, entirely blameless, the sometime future wife who would have suited him perfectly, had not passion come thrusting rudely in in the shape of Vivienne Appleby.

But Vivienne's birthday was looming and one of her life's ambitions had always been to be engaged by the time she was twenty-one. Her parents offered her a dance at the Dorchester but, having more or less snared her man, Vivienne preferred a slightly less formal occasion, celebrating with friends in the family home in Gloucestershire. She begged Oliver to break his silence and let her put the announcement in *The Times* on the day of the party, but he refused. Some things, he told her sternly, had to be done in the proper way. He would sort out the Celia situation at his own speed, when he was good and ready. She knew she had his heart; the formal announcement that he had won her hand would simply have to wait until a respectable period had elapsed.

Vivienne was not used to hearing the word no. She went into a sulk, then roared into action in her usual self-centered way. She turned for help to her new best pal, Sukey Portillo, to whom she had already offered the honor of being principal bridesmaid.

"Sukey, sweetie," she had said, one week before the party, to which she had invited three hundred close friends plus a sprinkling of prestigious oldies her father wanted to impress. "We are a little light on the glamour stakes as far as the men are concerned. How's about bringing that delicious young man I saw you with at Annabel's last week? The tall, faun-faced one with the curly hair."

"Richard Compton Miller?"

"That's him. Didn't you mention he works for a newspaper or something?"

Sukey snorted with derision. "You know darned well he's on the Hickey column. And I'll bring him if he's free.

He's so much in demand these days but he does like to party."

Thus it was that the morning after the party, which was a glittering success, Vivienne opened her *Daily Express* to find herself blazoned across the diary column, hand in hand with a grinning Oliver, above the caption: *Deb of the Year to Wed?* It was only minutes before the rest of the pack were upon her and Vivienne spent one of the most enjoyable mornings of her life, taking calls from reporters and refuting the rumors.

"No comment," she said blithely to all and sundry but the lilt in her voice told another story entirely.

When he got over her impetuousness, Oliver could not stay cross for long and, with Vivienne in his arms as he drowned in the perfume of her hair, he promised to call on Celia first thing next morning to try and limit the damage caused by the newspaper report. It was not something he looked forward to but there were things incumbent on a gentleman, particularly one who had just been publicly made to look an utter heel. Vivienne's behavior had been right out of line but he had to admit he was also at fault for allowing the Celia situation to drift on unresolved for so long. He hoped she would understand and might even be able to forgive him; among the reasons for his long attachment to the frail girl was her exceedingly sweet nature.

Alas, he was too late. Even while Vivienne was lying on her bed, luxuriating in the excitement her rumored engagement was causing, poor Celia—pushed to the brink by despair—looped a length of curtain cord around her fragile, aristocratic neck and leaped from the top of the ornate staircase in her family's Belgravia mansion. The butler discovered her broken body, swaying gently over the stairwell, when he came to summon the family to dinner.

She was buried discreetly in the family churchyard near Bristol and the Hartley clan closed ranks and vowed vengeance on the Nugents. A sister, perhaps as precariously balanced as Celia herself, made it her duty to target the one she accurately considered to be the true cause of Celia's suicide. Each year since Celia's death, Vivienne had received a brief, handwritten note to remind her of the anniversary. As if she could ever forget.

Oliver was still fast asleep, snoring now in an unattractive way, the brandy on his breath mixing unappealingly with the smell of stale semen. Vivienne shook herself out of his slack embrace and returned to the sanctity of the bathroom for a shower and another slug of Stoli before gliding off upstairs to one of the guest rooms so that she could sleep alone. Suddenly his presence in her bed offended her. She felt violated by what had happened; sickened to contemplate how the passion they once shared had reduced itself to such a travesty.

The floor above was one they rarely used, containing two separate guest rooms, both with *en suite* bathrooms, and a large, empty, bay-windowed room which they had once designated as the nursery. Wearing a full-length nightgown in soft white linen, with sleeves and a high neck, she opened the door of this neglected room and stood barefoot on the polished boards, staring at the space that had for so many years remained unused. Apart from elaborately swathed curtains, in pale blue sprigged with cream, it was entirely unfurnished, and the cream and blue Laura Ashley wallpaper was as fresh and immaculate as when she had first put it up, eight years ago.

It was a beautiful room, lavishly proportioned, with a high ceiling and wide sash windows; in all, a criminal waste of space. Vivienne stood there for a long while, watching the patterns cast by the streetlamps shining through the swaying branches of the trees outside, and all of a sudden it came to her; she knew what she wanted to do. She switched off the light and closed the door softly, moving like a ghost across the thick carpet and into one of the guest suites. A pretty room, quite without character, its single bed was already made up in readiness for the unexpected guest, with clean towels in the pristine bathroom, the latest Muriel Spark and a book of flower prints on the bedside table, alongside a bottle of Malvern water and a box of digestive biscuits.

Grateful at last to be on her own, Vivienne slipped between cool, starched sheets and prepared to sleep. But before she did all that, she locked the door.

Dorabella was surprised when she entered Vivienne's bedroom next morning with her breakfast tray and found her up and already on the telephone. Oliver was long since gone to the office and the fact that they had not actually shared a bed was not apparent. Even alone, he managed to turn the room into a tip. Dorabella was well used to clearing up after both of them.

"Put it there," mimed Vivienne, one hand over the mouthpiece, then smiled an unexpectedly brilliant smile for one who normally found it so hard to come to terms with the world at this hour in the morning. She was talking to Phoebe; it was still not quite nine.

"The way I see it is this," she was saying. "You've got the clout, I've got the money and connections, and she's got the talent—and boy, do I mean talent. Wait till you see what she can do. You ain't seen nothing yet, I'm telling you!"

She laughed. Life had suddenly broken out from behind the clouds and this morning Vivienne was seeing things quite differently. Out of adversity came revival; either it wrecked you or you lived to fight again. Phoebe was as surprised as Dorabella but delighted that her husband's small favor seemed to be paying such dividends. Vivienne Nugent was a good sort really, she had always suspected it, and if the result of Addison's having sorted out her small medical worry was to turn her into a mover and shaker, Phoebe was all in favor. And would do her darnedest to give her whatever support she needed.

Downstairs the door knocker clanged and Dorabella put her head round the door.

"Miss Georgy," she announced.

"There she is now," said Vivienne into the phone. "Have to go, sweetheart. Try and get here soon, while I tell Georgy my plan."

Georgy, too, looked radiant when Vivienne burst into the drawing room where she was waiting. This morning she wore her hair on top, which really suited her, and a pillar-box-red jacket with black flares and high-heeled boots. Vivienne approved. When she bothered, her little American friend had quite a distinct style; it all boded well for what Vivienne had in mind.

They kissed.

"See what I've brought you," said Georgy, smiling broadly. "Fresh from the darkroom."

She spread glossy prints all over the glass table, then stepped back so that Vivienne could examine her handiwork. They were superb. The grace, the balletic subtlety, the sense of airborne agility that had given Georgy's Bolshoi photographs such distinction, she had brought to these portraits of the cats. Vivienne took each print by its corners and shrieked her approval.

"Georgy, dear heart, these are sensational! How on earth do you do it?"

Even though she had been present while the pictures were being taken, she had not anticipated results as outstanding as this. Burmese cats are natural beauties, with the feel of the jungle still evident in their grace of movement, but Georgy had taken them that extra distance and transformed them from Vivienne's furry familiars into abstract expressions of fluidity, a subtle mix of light and shade. She was enchanted.

"You really are incredible," she said, giving Georgy a hug. "Amazingly talented. You must think about taking this sort of thing seriously instead of just doing magazine spreads. People will pay good money to have their animals immortalized—their children too. Loads of my friends would leap at the chance to have family portraits as good as these."

Georgy pulled a face. "I'm allergic to kids," she said.

"Then stick with animals. Here, I'll get my address book and let's work through it to see where we can begin. Once you've started making your mark with the smaller stuff, there are whole worlds we can conquer."

"We?"

"I'm in this too. I need something to fill up my time and I've always been good at organization. I'll do the business side—make the appointments, keep the books, that sort of thing—leaving you to be creative full-time. What do you say?"

Georgy was totally silenced.

"What about my career?" she protested, weakly, after a pause. "All those assignments I already have lined up?"

"Work through them, then just don't take on any more. There are much more challenging things ahead of you, believe me. You ain't even started yet. I've been talking to some of my fund-raising chums and they've all got ideas of how we can harness such talent. If you stop and think about the vast amounts of money flowing through all the major charities, you'll get an idea of what I'm talking about. Just one exclusive contract to one of the main fund-raising organizations should set you up nicely for quite a long time. And think of the good you'd be doing. I'm talking to the World Wide Fund for Nature next week, just for starters."

"Mind if I sit down?" said Georgy, with mock faintness. But she was genuinely stirred by Vivienne's generosity and kindness. It was years since she had been the focus of so much attention; it felt good. And the animal connection was really quite spooky, for that was how it had all begun, the year her father dragged her off to Australia when she was five years old and bought her her first camera, just to keep her occupied.

"Mum was having Risa," she explained to Vivienne, "and I guess I was getting under her feet. Anyway, Dad had to fly to Sydney to give evidence in a murder case and, on an impulse, took me along. In those days, he was always doing that sort of thing."

Her childhood had been fun. She looked back on it with a degree of regret.

"It was really exciting, the first time I'd ever been away from my mother for any length of time, and they bought me a whole lot of new clothes for the trip, practically a trousseau. I even had child-sized matching Vuitton luggage, can you imagine?"

In those days she had really been cute and the constant focus of both parents' indulgent attention. There were pictures in the family album of how she'd looked then, a right little madam if the truth be told, dolled up in her miniature furs and pint-sized versions of her mother's gowns, with huge bows in her hair and even a doll identically dressed.

"We flew to San Francisco, where Dad had some business, then on to Hawaii for a couple of days' vacation, just me and him alone together. Really great. I don't remember a lot about it apart from the hotel, which was grand and luxurious, and he let me come down for dinner, just like a grown-up. We had a table right next to the dance floor so's I could watch the floor show, and he bought me a white rabbit evening cape, which I wore with white knee socks and black Mary-Janes. I felt like a film star."

Georgy stopped. He'd always been big on the flamboyant present, her dad. She thought of her Christmas sable and sighed. Where had it all gone, the happy childhood days before the intrusion of Risa and Lois and all those other women? And now Ariel.

"In Sydney Dad was busy all day with some huge, lurid murder hearing that was all over the papers. I remember being mobbed when we stepped out of the cab outside the hotel, and all those flash bulbs crowding round us. Pretty scary when you're just a kid. He left me in the charge of a nurse in the hotel during the court proceedings."

Dorabella wheeled in coffee and Vivienne poured.

"Once she even took me home with her because her kids were having a birthday party. There were balloons and a cake with an engine on it, even a miniature pony to ride. It was really neat. We didn't get things like that back home, least not in our apartment because my mother had allergies and thought animals were unhygienic."

Isabella arrived on her knee and nuzzled her velvet nose against Georgy's chin. Georgy stroked her abstractedly. Looking back so far into the past was unsettling; Vivienne could tell she was beginning to hurt.

"Finally the case was over and Dad took me off to the outback as a treat. That's the bit I remember best. Those great wide-open spaces and the animals—kangaroos, wallabies, and those enormous birds, all hoofing around in the scrub. And that's when Dad gave me my first camera, a push-button Brownie, entirely foolproof." She stopped and thought awhile.

"Guess that's where it really started," she said. "I've always loved animals. I just never realized it till now."

Vivienne rose to her feet and lifted Isabella out of Georgy's arms and onto the sofa.

"Follow!" she commanded and led the way upstairs to a room in a part of the house Georgy had never before penetrated. With a flourish, Vivienne flung wide the door and ushered her inside.

"Take a look," she commanded, standing back.

What Georgy saw was the studio she had dreamed of—high ceiling, varnished floorboards polished to a satin smoothness, the lot—and light, great quantities of it, pouring through giant windows fringed by blue and cream. One wall was fitted with walk-in closets; otherwise the room was bare.

"Do with it what you like," said Vivienne. "A complete refit if that's what suits you."

Georgy turned to her, eyes bright with emotion.

"Thank you," she said simply, and Vivienne enfolded her in her arms.

"Welcome," was all she said, "to your new studio and our new partnership. Nugent and Kirsch—or would you prefer it the other way around?"

And, right on cue, the door knocker banged again.

"And here's our first customer," said Vivienne, turning to greet a flushed Phoebe, rushing up the stairs as if she were late for class.

"Meet Phoebe Harvey, a fellow American," said Vivienne, and Georgy was instantly drawn to the pretty, dark-haired woman with a smile like an angel.

Vivienne outlined again all she had just told Georgy, and Phoebe rummaged in her shoulder bag and triumphantly flourished her own card. *Cancer Research,* it said.

"We've been fighting this major battle to save the Royal Marsden Hospital," she explained, "and that has given us the impetus to move on to bigger, more ambitious projects. When Vivienne first mentioned you, I instantly saw how we could use you. How would you feel about being our official photographer on, say, a year's initial contract? I am positive that, between the three of us, we can really get things moving and achieve miracles for our cause."

Georgy didn't need convincing.

"Lead me to it," was all she said, still dazzled by the dimensions of this wonderful, empty room.

Chapter Thirty-nine

Now that she had quit her job, Sally didn't have a lot to occupy her time, so she took to dropping in on Eleanor, to cheer the old girl up and see how she was coping. A strange bond had developed between these two. They were nearly fifty years apart in age, yet shared the same indomitable spirit; full of guts and fire, adventurers both. Sally would have liked Eleanor as a gran and she knew Eleanor had a soft spot for her too, though she was usually careful not to let it show.

She found Eleanor seated at the piano, browsing through a pile of musty-smelling photo albums. A frumpy cleaning lady in a flowered pinafore let her in, then went off muttering, back to her hoovering.

"They're not what they were," said Eleanor, sighing, waving her hands theatrically in an attempt to disperse the smoke that trailed from the fag in the woman's slatternly mouth. "In the old days we always kept two maids and at the Embassy we also had a butler and a chauffeur, of course."

She graciously allowed Sally to peck her cheek, then went on turning the pages with a gnarled, blue-veined hand. Sally peeked over her shoulder.

"This is me as Lucia di Lammermoor," said Eleanor, "nineteen fifty-three in Milan."

She was thinner then but every bit as stately, and totally recognizable with her soaring raven's-wing eyebrows and lavishly piled-up hair. Today she was formally dressed in dusky eau-de-Nil lace with ropes and ropes of yellowish seed pearls wound round her sagging throat. On the cloth covering the piano was a glass of sticky-looking yellowish liquid from which she took the occasional sip. Sally glanced at the clock. It was still only eleven twenty-five but if it kept the old girl going, who was to say she shouldn't?

"Anything I can do to help?" she asked. "I'm not a lot of use on the cookery front but I'm a whizz with a duster."

Eleanor looked abstracted and fiddled with her pearls.

"What, dear? Oh, no thank you. Mrs. Whatsit does what she can though it's never quite enough and she does complain so. But there's only me left to bother about now, so who cares how the place looks?"

"Now, now," said Sally firmly, putting an arm round the slumped shoulders and giving her a squeeze. "That's no way to talk. You should get into your glad rags and go out on the town. What say we shake a leg together like we did that time before? Streisand's coming to town in a week or so, for the first time in ten years. I could try and get tickets if you like."

She was, as usual, broke but that had never been known to stop her. And the old lady must be loaded, whatever she might say. But today the vital spark appeared to be missing; Eleanor simply wasn't up to it. She clearly hadn't a clue who Streisand was so Sally reluctantly let it drop. Another time, maybe, when some of the old joie de vivre had returned. The tickets cost a bomb but there was still time. It was a shame to watch the old trouper crumbling slowly into self-pity.

"Tell me more about Catherine's death," said Sally cautiously. She was treading on thin ice but she needed to know. For a moment it appeared as if Eleanor had not heard her, then the old head came up slowly, chin in the air, defiant.

"She's dead, that's all," she said simply. Then, more softly, "She always was a thoughtless girl."

Whatever else the old woman might or might not know, she was clearly not telling, which was fine as far as Sally was concerned. What was done was done; nothing now could bring Catherine back. And she couldn't throw off the memory of Beth's accusing questions or Duncan's searching eyes boring straight into her soul. Let the truth about what actually did happen that night remain buried. If Eleanor was prepared to leave it like that, so was Sally. Addison Harvey had been with her at the last; let him carry the load. It was, after all, his job and therefore his responsibility.

Sally had to go. She had a lunch date. Vivienne was treating them all to San Lorenzo for some sort of celebration, though she hadn't said what, and Sally was already running late. She had always wanted to see inside that trendy, fashionable restaurant, haunt, they said, of many celebrities including the Princess of Wales.

"I gotta go," she said, "but I'll be back soon. Is there anything you want before I pop off?"

"No, dear. I've all I need. These photographs and my memories. When you get to my age, you know . . ."

Sally gave a cheeky grin and mimed playing the violin. She left Eleanor sighing to herself like the Mock Turtle and skipped into the sunny street. Outside the air seemed that much cleaner and fresher after the airless fug of Albert Hall Mansions, and she felt privileged to be alive. There was nothing like a spot of death to make a gal feel great. She walked the short distance to Beauchamp Place, zigzagging through the wide, tree-lined streets of Kensington, and reflecting, not for the first time, that summer was approaching and she still hadn't made any firm plans for moving on. Maybe she would, after all, hang on here for a while to see how things panned out. With Catherine dead, Eleanor was going to need a friend more than ever. And she still couldn't get the thought of Duncan out of her head.

They were all there ahead of her, sitting at Vivienne's favorite corner table. The restaurant was three-quarters full but even to Sally, there for the first time, it was evident that Vivienne was a regular and valued customer. Vivienne waved and Sally threaded her way toward them, recognizing in passing Albert Finney and Lord Snowdon at different tables.

"G'day," she said, sitting down. "Sorry I'm late."

Vivienne was as sleek and immaculate as always, in a blazer and a white silk stock tied in a pussycat bow, while Georgy wore jodhpurs and a Ralph Lauren tailored jacket with her hair tied severely back to reveal enormous tortoiseshell earrings. She scrubbed up well, thought Sally, accustomed to the American girl's working uniform of T-shirt and dungarees.

Beth wore something shapeless and woolly that made her look huge, but in a misty grayish blue that set off her wonderful skin and brought out her wide gray eyes. You had to hand it to her, the overall effect was pretty damned effective. Beth was always breaking the rules yet somehow got away with it.

"How're ya doin'?" asked Sally, accepting a menu from the waiter. The morning sunlight had given her cheeks a slight flush and raised a light dusting of freckles across the bridge of her nose.

Sally was a natural, thought Beth. Dressed like a rather fetching ragbag yet always looking effective in some indefinable way. After they had all ordered, and while the wine and mineral water were being poured, Vivienne tapped her glass for silence and called for a toast.

"Here's to Georgy and me and our new venture," she said, and they all squealed in amazement and clamored for details. Small wonder Vivienne looked so good, all lit up inside, which was unusual.

Georgy looked a touch embarrassed.

"It's all her idea," she explained awkwardly, "and it may not work. She's being amazingly generous with her house. And her time."

"Nonsense!" said Vivienne briskly, waving her glass. "You've no idea what you're doing for me, giving my life a whole new sense of purpose.

"Georgy and I," she explained, "are setting up in business together. To begin with, we are going to provide portraits of pets and children for people of discerning taste with expansive pockets; after that, who knows. We have all sorts of plans for conquering the world and taking on the mighty business of international charities, beginning with Cancer Research and leading on to who knows what."

"There's Jerry Hall just come in," said Beth, nudging her. "Pop over and give her your card, if you have one. She's got those Jagger kids, plus the loot to pay your no doubt exorbitant fees. I'm sure she'd be delighted. And then you'll have to track down Paula Yates."

"I've never actually done portrait photography," admitted Georgy. "She's forcing me into it. Help!"

"It's a pity Catherine's not still with us," said Sally. "She could have stuck a poster up in the waiting room. Snared all those Kensington ladies with their pampered pets."

"Great idea!" said Beth, beaming. "I'll talk to Duncan and see what he says. It's a lovely concept and I wish you both loads of luck. We small business persons have to stick together, so do feel free to pick my brains if ever you need to. I've survived twelve years so I must be doing something right. They say if you can make it for seven, you're more or less home and dry."

She thought for a second. "Hey, why not do Imogen? That's a great idea. They grow so quickly at this age and I'd love to have a permanent record of her. She's not exactly an animal but close. Certainly as rowdy. I'll speak to Gus."

Now she was talking; maybe he'd come to the sitting. Georgy visibly brightened. It had all seemed rather absurd at first, when Vivienne first broached the idea, but now it was beginning to take shape and these women, her friends, were certainly not scoffing.

"I've already made one connection," said Vivienne, beaming. "A friend has put me in touch with the World Wide Fund for Nature, formerly the World Wildlife Fund, and they are interested in seeing some of Georgy's work with a view to perhaps using her in some of their propaganda campaigns."

Georgy looked stunned. This woman was too much.

"The cat pictures, I thought," said Vivienne to Georgy. "Those are a natural."

"What does Oliver have to say about all this?" inquired Sally, and Beth was fascinated to see Vivienne's face harden and her eyes lose some of their sparkle.

"He doesn't actually know yet. After all, it's my house too and he's hardly ever home."

Interesting, thought Beth. *Obviously things haven't exactly improved.*

The food arrived and they ate. Tucking into her lobster pasta, Georgy thought she had never been happier. Viv was a dear, yet who would possibly have thought it a few weeks ago? She remembered the chilly, supercilious hospital patient who didn't want to know them, and the peremptory brush-off in Harrods. Now Vivienne was revealing her real self; rich maybe but sensitive as well as beautiful, with feelings as delicate and easily bruised as her own. And not as well off as the world might perceive; childless and rudderless in that great barn of a house, married to a womanizing bastard who clearly didn't appreciate her worth.

She glanced across at Beth, sitting serenely chatting to Sally and spearing ravioli with an expert fork. Georgy still didn't know the details but she had her suspicions about Beth and Oliver. A bit of hanky-panky going on there, if she read it correctly; she wondered if Vivienne had any suspicion of the viper she was nurturing so generously in her bosom? Should she, she agonized, drop her a hint, now that they were to be partners and were fast becoming friends? Probably not. Loyalty was all very well but it worked two ways. Georgy was not an expert on female friendship but she was beginning to learn. And, to give her credit, most of what she had learned she owed to Beth.

At twenty to four they were still there drinking and the fourth bottle of Pouilly-Fuissé was being uncorked.

"To Catherine!" said Beth suddenly, on a more sober note, and they raised their glasses in silence.

They were all in tremendous form by now but the management didn't seem at all concerned. *That's what money and clout can do,* thought Sally tipsily, and Beth reached out a restraining hand to prevent her chair from toppling backward. Albert Finney and Snowdon were long since gone, and so was Jerry Hall, but two thin young things in huge dark glasses, who looked tantalizingly familiar, had arrived in the last half-hour and were canoodling in the corner, so it was obviously all right for them to linger on.

Vivienne was glowing and Georgy had slipped the band from her hair, so that it flowed over her shoulders like Botticelli's Venus. Beth had left the table twice to make discreet phone calls but seemed at ease about leaving her business to run itself.

"Deirdre can cope," she explained. "In fact, it does her good to have some responsibility for a change."

The waiter topped up their glasses and Beth proposed a second toast.

"To friendship!"

"Friendship!"

Georgy still hadn't told them her real news, so now she did. Looking prettier than they had ever known her, with flushed cheeks and tumbling curls, she made the announcement she had been hanging on to for so long.

"Guess what, my dad's going to be here next week! And I'd love for you all to meet him, if there's time."

He'd be so pleased to find she was settling in well, and all these women, in their separate ways, would impress

him. Even Eleanor, if she could persuade her out one night.
Fancy Dad meeting a singer of that standing; that would really knock him for the count. He loved the opera, though rarely found time to indulge himself.

"It's on then?" said Beth with a warm smile. "That's really terrific."

She was ashamed to realize that Catherine's death had driven this important occasion clean out of her mind.

"Now this guy," she said, turning to the others, "we simply have to meet. I read all about him in *Newsweek* the other day and he really does sound like something else."

Georgy squirmed with pleasure while Sally studied her with curiosity. How odd folks were, to be sure. All this excitement about a parent, and an elderly geezer at that, if what she remembered from the hospital were true. White hair and a stern expression; his face had lingered in her memory since she saw his photograph, like some half-submerged memory. And he wasn't even married to her mother anymore, so why was Georgy wetting her pants at the prospect of seeing him?

"He's staying at Claridge's," said Georgy, "though I'm not quite sure how long for, but I do want him to meet my friends, so I hope you'll all be free." She beamed at Vivienne, who patted her hand.

"And Viv says we can do it in the studio." She laughed. "Well, it won't really be a studio by then but I do want him to see where I'm gonna be working."

Beth found it quite touching. In reality, Georgy was all vulnerability, with the softest underbelly imaginable. What a pity she didn't let it show more often.

"If you need help with the canapés," she said impulsively, "you know you can count on me."

But Vivienne wouldn't hear of it. This was her protégée and her party.

"Dorabella would never allow it," she said firmly, widening her brilliant eyes in horror.

"Let's hear more about your dad," persisted Sally. She

now had his face fixed clearly in her mind, as handsome as hell. "What does he do?"

"Psychologist," said Georgy proudly. "One of the best. He's always on the go, all over the world, which is why none of us ever gets to see him anymore. Even my step-mother, Sylvia, says she wishes she'd married an astronaut."

"Does he specialize?" asked Vivienne politely, picking up the bill and signaling for a pen.

She was having the best time ever, slightly tipsy in her favorite restaurant, celebrating new beginnings with her closest friends. Yes, her friends. Against all odds they had bonded, this disparate gang, and Vivienne felt life had taken on a whole new meaning. As far as Oliver was concerned, he'd blown it the other night; from this point on, they'd go their separate ways. She had a suspicion he'd been seeing someone else but suddenly that no longer mattered. Let him do as he damn well liked. She certainly intended to.

Georgy was talking and Vivienne hadn't caught a word she'd said.

"I'm sorry, *ma chère*," she said, passing the plate with her check back to the waiter, "what did you say he does, your father?"

"Oh, didn't I mention? He's an expert in criminal psychology. I suppose you might say he specializes in psychopaths."

Chapter Forty

Georgy wanted to tell Gus about her studio and see if she could persuade him to meet her father. Karl answered the phone. Gus was out. She tried again later but he was still not home so, on an impulse, she hopped on a bus to King's Cross and trudged up the Caledonian Road to Ripplevale Grove. It was ten past six; he was bound to be home soon. Karl opened the door in T-shirt and jeans and the powerful smell of cooking wafted past him from the rear of the house. When he saw Georgy on the doorstep his handsome features twisted into a snarl and he moved as if to close the door in her face.

"He's not here," he said.

"I'll wait."

"I don't know when he'll be back."

"Soon, I'd guess. You're getting his meal."

She virtually pushed past him and, ignoring the sullen looks, walked boldly down the hall and into the spacious drawing room. There was no chance Karl would offer her a drink or anything but she felt she'd scored a tiny victory against the bully even by getting this far. With an air of calm she was far from feeling, she browsed casually through the pile of expensive art books on the minimalist glass table, affecting to be unaware of him watching her.

She settled for a massive volume of Leonardo's drawings, which she then lugged to the window in order to be able to study it in proper light. For a while Karl hovered, uncertain what to do, then, with a muttered German oath, headed back to the kitchen.

Georgy's heart was beating fast and her palms were damp. Though she would never show it, she found Karl really quite scary; there was something dark and threatening about him, even when Gus was around. He was the sort of man who really hated women and made little attempt to disguise it. Physically, too, he was quite frightening, with his smooth, well-developed dancer's muscles. He clearly kept himself in peak condition. She knew he belonged to a gym where he worked out regularly and there was a rowing machine in one of the bedrooms which she had spotted while snooping on an earlier visit.

To her relief, it was not too long before she heard the steady thrumming of a taxi engine outside and light footsteps hurrying along the path. She was in time to see Gus, chic in well-cut jeans and a black leather bomber jacket, bending his silver head as he fumbled for his keys. She hurried to meet him but Karl had got there first, so she stayed in the room and hovered behind the half-open door. She could hear rapid conversation in lowered voices, punctuated by a number of stabbing interjections that sounded like Teutonic curses. She went quickly back to the window and her book.

After a pause, Gus swept in, jacket removed to display a white cashmere polo neck, a bottle of something chilled in his hand.

"Georgy Kirsch!" he exclaimed, kissing her cheeks three times. "What a marvelous surprise."

Georgy carefully replaced her book while Gus searched for glasses on the drinks table. Karl was clearly not intending to join them; she could hear him in the kitchen at the rear, angrily banging about. When she was with Gus, everything in Georgy's world made sense. He was sympathetic and attentive and paid her the compliment of always giving her one hundred percent of his concentration. Gus made her feel clever, even pretty, and, better still, important. She laughed more when she was with him and all the time fell deeper and deeper in love.

He was enthusiastic about the studio.

"Let me help," he said, opening the bottle. "I have no doubt *la belle* Vivienne has the most exquisite taste but it might be fun to create a really contemporary setting for your work. How about a couple of Hans Wegner chairs to throw around? I'm pretty certain we've still got some stashed in the attic, left over from the last time we re-vamped the decor. And we must make sure you get the lighting exactly right, though who am I to be lecturing an expert!"

Georgy preened. She told him about the partnership and Vivienne's ambition to make her into the best animal por-trait photographer in London. Gus was far too well man-nered to let it show if he felt a twinge of dismay, but his enthusiasm when she went on to tell him about Cancer Research and the World Wide Fund for Nature was entirely unfeigned.

"Now you're talking," he said. "Saving whales and dis-suading rich bitches from flaunting their furs is really worthwhile, not to mention what it should do to your repu-tation as a quality photographer."

Karl stuck his head round the door to tell Gus that the stroganoff was almost ready, and naturally Gus invited her to join them. Georgy, however, knew her limits.

"I have to go," she said regretfully. "I have a dinner date on the other side of town."

But she did tell him about her father's impending visit and that Vivienne was hosting a small drinks party in his honor, to which she hoped Gus would come.

"Such a distinguished man," said Gus, after he had checked his diary. "These days you can't pick up a paper without seeing his name."

He said he'd come if he could and Georgy went off in a warm glow of happiness. It wasn't a lot but it was something. Despite what he'd said to her that afternoon on the edge of the canal, she still had hope. She felt certain even her father would approve of Gus.

Her hopes were dashed, however, later that night when Emmanuel called from Amsterdam just as she was getting into bed.

"Sorry, sweets," he said. "I'm desolate but I have to fly right back to LA because they need me in court the day after tomorrow. So I'm afraid I'm gonna have to take a rain check on London for a while."

She was shattered. It had been so long and she had so much wanted to see him, to show him her work and introduce him to her friends. She'd even fixed tickets for the ballet and arranged to get her hair thinned and tinted. It wasn't fair. But then it never had been.

"Are you still there?" inquired her father, who knew his daughter well. "Look, how's about popping out and buying yourself something you really want on my Amex card."

But this time it wasn't going to work. She was grown-up now and could no longer be fobbed off with toys and trinkets in place of love.

"There's nothing I need," she said stiffly, twisting the phone wire tightly round her fingers and chewing a strand of her hair. And, for once, it was she who ended the call.

One of these days, thought Emmanuel regretfully, he'd really have to take a break in London, maybe even bring along Sylvia and the kid, and try to catch up with this daughter of his who so much resembled him in everything but charm.

It was a shame about the party but Vivienne suggested they do it anyhow but shift the date to a Sunday morning and turn it into a working party so that everyone could contribute to the transformation of nursery into studio. She was pretty certain Oliver would be away—she hardly ever saw him these days—so they had a clear day for scraping and painting and changing the rather twee drapes into something a little more sophisticated. She had wanted to call in a decorator but Georgy wouldn't hear of it.

"This is business, remember," she said sternly. "You've been marvelously generous already but if it's going to work on a professional level and not just as a hobby, it's got to be self-supporting right from the start."

Sunday morning was bright and sunny and The Boltons resounded with the pealing of church bells. It could have been part of the Riviera, with its immaculate white villas and a riot of trees in full blossom. You certainly got what you paid for, thought Beth, as she parked beside the magnolia. She hauled a basket of homemade goodies from the backseat, her contribution to the picnic, and gave it to Imogen to hold while she locked up. Or did she mean you paid for what you got?

There was a sharp blast from a horn directly behind her and she turned in time to see her ex-husband leap nimbly off his motorbike. Imogen dumped the basket and rushed to give him a hug. The joy about Gus was that he was Peter Pan incarnate, as lithe and boyish now as when they'd first met at RADA. He was pushing forty yet showed no signs of it. Only the silver hair added a note of gravitas, but that was distinctly a plus.

"No Karl?" she said as they kissed. She had nothing tangible against the taciturn German, just preferred it when he wasn't there. And at least it meant they'd get the best of Georgy.

"Sulking at home," said Gus cheerfully. "I told him that if he was going to behave like a child, he could stay in and turn out his room. Either that or move out altogether. I can't be doing anymore with all his tantrums. Life is simply too short."

What a waste, thought Beth, not for the first time, as he hugged her. *Such a lovely man, throwing away his life on someone like that.* Then she saw the dusty bonnet of Duncan's black Range Rover, parked on the corner, and her heart gave a little hop and a skip of joy.

As a concession to the working party, Vivienne wore designer dungarees but nonetheless managed to look a million dollars. How she had improved, thought Beth, as they kissy-kissed in the hall. In just a few months her whole personality seemed to have altered and she was revealing a zest that had not been apparent before.

"Everyone's here," said Vivienne gaily, taking the basket through to the kitchen. "Sally's up a ladder, painting hard, and Duncan's giving her stalwart backup by opening beers."

"Then we'd best get our skates on," said Gus. "Lay on, Macduff!"

These are my friends, thought Georgy, as they lolled around over a late lunch devouring the contents of Beth's basket, backed up by Dorabella's huge salad and washed down with white wine and chilled lager. The windows were open wide to let in the sunshine and what had been a rather sterile nursery was now dramatically transformed by clean white paint and a row of new shelves in plain varnished pine, erected with professional skill by Gus and Duncan. Imogen had lent her portable cassette player, just to keep them on their toes she said, and they had scraped and varnished and rollered their way through the morning to a background of Meat Loaf and the Pogues.

Across the road the bell was already announcing Evensong. Beth glanced at Imogen—surely not that late already—and then at Gus and mumbled something about supper. Duncan said he had evening surgery and must be on his way. He offered Sally a lift, then mouthed a kiss at Beth and promised to catch up with her later.

Beth wanted to help clear up.

"Don't be absurd," said Vivienne. "After all you've done already, are you crazy?"

She was as thrilled as Georgy with the room's new look,

every trace of her unfulfilled dream obliterated by a sparkling new beginning.

"Don't forget your basket," she called but Beth told her to hang on to it.

"There's heaps left," she said, "which I certainly don't need. Give it to the creative one, the poor little starving artist who never gets time to eat."

Beth and Imogen finally departed, leaving just Vivienne and Georgy to clear up, but they didn't care. As they washed paint rollers and swept floors in the haze of early-evening sun, they laughed and chatted and reveled in their new adventure. Everyone had worked so hard and Georgy was aching all over but when they had finally finished and she said good-bye, she still felt quite wonderful, on a high of anticipation about the future.

She grabbed a cab and threw herself into it, picnic basket in hand. It was a little after ten and she reckoned she'd earned an early night.

The house was dark but she could see by the streetlamp where to stick her key. She had grown fairly lax about using all those locks and figured, in a city as safe as this, one was sufficient. That was how much she was acclimatizing; imagine even contemplating that in New York! Her single concession to security was to leave a light burning when she was likely to be back late, but this morning she had set off early so a light would have been self-defeating. Besides, the house was adequately protected and there was nothing worth stealing, apart from her cameras, which she normally lugged around with her anyway.

She reached for the switch but nothing happened. Which meant the bulb must have gone and, right now, she couldn't recall where the Hunters kept their spares. So she fumbled her way like a blind person along the hall to the top of the basement stairs and tried that switch instead. Nothing. The house remained in darkness. A fuse must have blown, which was a nuisance but not the end of the world. And at least the kitchen had gas.

Still clutching her basket, she felt her way carefully down the stairs, glad now of the slightly twee guiding rope which at least stopped her breaking her neck in the impenetrable darkness. She didn't even bother with the bottom switch; just shoved open the kitchen door and went in. Dim light from the garden restored her bearings and she was just feeling for the kitchen switch when there was a sudden whoosh of movement from behind and something hit her very hard in the middle of her back, knocking her to the floor.

Georgy lay there, stunned, as two more blows caught her in fast succession, in the kidneys and again in the back. *Ah, come on,* she thought wearily, *at this time of night this is more than a joke.* It was only when she tasted blood that she knew she had been stabbed.

And passed out.

Part
Five

Chapter Forty-one

Emmanuel Kirsch was even more handsome than his photos admitted. He rose and offered Beth his hand as she was shown into Georgy's room. He was immaculately groomed and smelled of lemon aftershave but his eyes were bloodshot from fatigue and distress, and her heart went out to him. Absentee father he might be but this he did not deserve. She liked him immediately; he was her kind of man. Strong but humane, driven but centered. No wonder poor Georgy was so fucked up. With this man as her role model, what chance had she ever had?

Poor Georgy indeed. Her bony figure lay supine under the sheet, as flat and defeated as a corpse. *We have been here before,* thought Beth, *only last time it was only her appendix.* Back in St. Anthony's, this time in a private room, not six months since they had all first met, yet nothing appeared to have changed. The corridors still reeked of a subtle mix of cabbage and medication, the lifts were slow and unreliable, and Beth found herself greeting several of the nurses as she headed for the third floor.

Emmanuel pulled out a chair for Beth, then resumed his own at the bedside. He wanted to hold the thin little hand but an intravenous drip prevented that, so he had to make do with just stroking her forehead. Georgy's pulse was barely visible but a heart monitor attached to her chest with suction pads recorded a beat that was shallow but steady. She was holding her own, but only just. It was a miracle, they said, that she had survived at all.

Beth had brought flowers, blue irises mixed with white stephanotis, which she laid now on the vacant chair with a feeling of hopelessness. What was the point if the patient was barely conscious? The spirit of cheerful optimism that had pervaded Florence Ward in what now seemed like the good old days was missing entirely from this bleak, cell-like room. *How precious life is and how quickly we forget,* thought Beth.

Sixteen times he had stabbed her. How could anyone suffer an attack like that and still survive? Particularly someone as slight and undernourished as Georgy. And what sort of an animal carried that much hate in his heart?

"Do they know what happened?" asked Beth in a low voice, since Emmanuel didn't appear inclined to speak.

He grunted.

"It's not clear. Seems she came home late, let herself in in the usual way, and someone jumped her at the foot of the stairs as she walked into the kitchen. Got her from behind, the coward, so she won't be able to identify him even if she does come around . . ." His voice faltered and broke and he blew his nose hard.

"Besides, it was dark. The light bulbs had all been removed."

"How very odd."

Beth longed to be able to touch him but resisted. They were strangers and she dared not intrude on his terrible suffering. With a visible effort he pulled himself together and went back to gently stroking his daughter's delicate head.

"How did he get in? Do they know?"

That house was pretty secure, as she recalled, with its spyhole and row of Banham locks. She also knew there were burglar locks on all the windows as well as an alarm.

She had always kidded Georgy about the paranoia of New Yorkers. How wrong could you get?

We don't get crime like that in London, she remembered teasing Georgy. *Certainly not in a respectable yuppie area like Fulham. What's wrong with your friends that they're so nervous? Even where I live you can leave your windows open at night, and we're just around the corner from Little Africa.*

How futile it all was, how depressing. Beth felt like weeping but took a firm grip on herself. No point in adding to the general gloom; Emmanuel Kirsch needed all the support he could get, and, besides, she was not the sort to buckle in a crisis. And she had meant what she said, more or less. In all the years she had lived in London, she had always felt totally safe and relaxed about walking the streets at any time of the day or night. Beth was very much a city animal. Perversely, it was the countryside that made her nervous. She even allowed Imogen to walk home alone at certain times, provided she was careful and didn't take any foolish risks.

Paranoia breeds aggression, she had told her. *If you look a barking dog straight in the eye and show you are not afraid, it won't bite you.* Street-smart, that was what Imogen was learning to be, but what was the use of all that wisdom when you found yourself confronted by a maniac with a knife? Or, as in Georgy's case, not even confronted: the monster had caught her unawares from behind. What sort of a coward could behave like that?

"There's no sign of a forced entry," said Emmanuel. "Whoever it was apparently had a key. I've not been over there yet but the police seem to be doing their job. There was no damage, nothing appears to have been stolen, and the only abnormality was the removal of the bulbs."

"Then it was premeditated."

"So it would appear."

Now who would want to harm poor old Georgy? True, with her uncertain temper and mercurial mood swings, she was not always the easiest of companions, but that surely was no reason to want to kill her. The fact that she was virtually a stranger in this town reduced considerably the list of likely suspects. Presumably the police were investigating every lead, but goodness knows where they would even start.

"Maybe it was a case of mistaken identity," said Beth. "Someone, perhaps, with a grudge against Josh Hunter? He's constantly on the move, traveling the world in the course of his work. Who knows what he gets up to, we've not even met him. Or maybe it was just a lunatic on the loose who picked on Georgy at random."

There was nothing she could say that made any real sense; she just couldn't bear to look into this man's face and see his suffering. They both fell silent and watched Georgy breathe while Beth racked her brains for anything at all that might help. As it was, she was only here on sufferance. The police had called and requested her presence. Outside in the corridor sat a uniformed officer. Pretty soon they would doubtless be asking her questions. If only she could come up with anything at all that might help.

It was almost by accident that Georgy had survived at all. Her attacker had left in a hurry and mistakenly activated the burglar alarm which had, eventually, alerted an irritated neighbor. They had found Georgy in a pool of blood on the kitchen floor. Had it not been for that one error, she would most certainly have bled to death. As it was, they got her to hospital just in time for a massive transfusion, and even now it was touch and go that she would ever regain consciousness.

"So he planned it meticulously, then boobed at the last minute."

It was ghastly, quite beyond belief; something out of the newspapers, not real, everyday life. Beth found herself growing quite faint with shock and put her head in her hands to assuage the blood thumping at her temples. A strong, warm hand took hold of her arm, and when he spoke, the deep voice had softened.

"Go lie down," he said. "I'm sure they can find you a bed somewhere in a place like this. You've had a terrible shock and it's bound to catch up with you. You've been a good friend, I know that. I won't forget it."

Beth took great gulps of air, then slowly raised her head. Her face was streaming, her neck and hands felt clammy, and there was an urgent ache in the pit of her stomach.

"It's okay," she said. "I'm fine. Don't go bothering about me when you've got Georgy lying here in this state."

Then: "How did they know to call me?" So many questions.

"Easy," said Emmanuel. "There's a pad beside the phone with just a few personal numbers on it. Yours was one. The police are very thorough."

The next visitor through the door was Gus, pale and unshaven and looking distinctly under the weather. Beth gave a great sigh of relief and launched herself into the safety of his arms. There were occasions when husbands had their uses, even discarded ones. She introduced him to Emmanuel and the two men shook hands gravely. Then, seeing the strain and fatigue on Beth's face, Gus suggested she go home and lie down.

"I'll just check with the policeman outside," he said. "But I can't see why he should mind. You're not exactly on the wanted list, I would think, and they know how to find you if they need you. Run along home to the infant and I'll take over here. I promise I'll call you if there's any change."

Beth glanced at Emmanuel for approval and he nodded and patted her shoulder.

"Go. There's nothing you can do. It was good of you to come."

But she didn't go home, she drove straight to the surgery, and when he saw the look on her face, Duncan made his excuses and closed up shop. He led her into the seclusion of the X-ray room and took her in his arms.

"What's up? You look terrible."

"Thanks a bunch."

Leaning her head against his chest and inhaling the comforting nursery smells of starched linen and good clean soap, she told him the grim news. Here with Duncan, she began to feel human again. Outside she could hear an insistent phone but he let it ring. Vanessa had knocked off early, as she did so often, but no matter how serious Duncan was about his work, it seemed Beth took priority. She was grateful. She had known him hardly any time at all but now she never wanted to leave the shelter of his arms. Morning surgery was over at one so he took her around the corner to the pub.

"Who could possibly do a thing like that?" she asked him over a beer. "And why? Georgy can be a pain at times but she's basically harmless. Besides, you don't try to kill someone just because they irritate you."

"Unless you're a raving lunatic."

She started to cry, helplessly, ashamed at her own vulnerability. Duncan put an arm around her and waited till she had control of herself again.

"The Catherine thing was quite bad enough, but this is immeasurably worse. What's going on, what's happening to all our friends? We seem to have strayed into some sort of ghastly B movie. I can't bear it."

The blue of Duncan's eyes matched his denim shirt—but this was not the time to be thinking frivolous thoughts.

"We were all together on Sunday," he said thoughtfully. "Then we all left separately except for Georgy. And that was the night it happened. Perhaps someone followed her home."

"I'll talk to Viv," said Beth. "See what time she left and how she traveled. Anything like that might help, though no doubt the police have already thought of it.

"I think I'll drop over and see her," she said on reflection. "Just in case she hasn't heard."

Normally nothing in the world could prevail upon Beth to visit Oliver's house unannounced but this was different; this was an emergency. And, knowing how strongly Vivienne had taken to Georgy, it was likely to be extra dreadful news for her.

Vivienne did know and had taken to her room in shock. Dorabella let Beth in and showed her upstairs to the drawing room where, after a brief wait, Vivienne joined her, ghostly pale, wearing only a plain toweling wrap.

"I still can't take it in," she said, pouring them each a hefty drink. "It's too terrible for words. Who could have done it?"

"And why?" said Beth.

"A burglar, no doubt. High on drugs and desperate enough to try anything for a fix."

"Maybe. But I'm positive the police will sort it out," said Beth. "Try not to worry. Georgy will recover, you'll see. She's a tough little thing and fit as a flea. Look at all that heavy equipment she lugs around and the hours she spends, outside in all weathers, just doing her job."

But Vivienne would not be comforted. What was it about her life these days that everything she touched seemed headed for disaster? She went back upstairs to cry, aware she was wallowing in self-pity but for once unable to stop herself. And, come to that, where was Oliver just when she needed him most?

The close was blocked by a couple of squad cars so Beth had to park outside a neighbor's house. As she pushed aside the wicket gate, she saw that her front door was open, and Imogen came crying from the house and flung herself into her mother's arms.

"What on earth's going on?" asked Beth, soothing Imogen and looking up at two solemn policemen standing in her doorway.

"Mrs. Hardy?" asked one of them, proffering his ID. "I'm afraid we are going to have to ask you to accompany us to the station."

"Mum, Mum," shrieked Imogen in panic. "They're arresting you!"

"Nonsense," said Beth, smiling conspiratorially at the officers, who did not react. "You've been watching too much TV. I'll just ring Jane and have her pick you up, then we'll be off. Though it would be a great deal easier if we could do it here," she added. "There's not a lot I can tell you, I'm afraid."

The more senior of the policemen led her into the house, out of earshot of her sobbing daughter. In the kitchen another two men were hard at work, going minutely through her things with rubber-gloved fingers and dusting some of her kitchen equipment with what looked suspiciously like fingerprint powder.

"Now hang on a moment . . ." For the first time, Beth was alarmed.

"I'm afraid, Mrs. Hardy, that we're going to have to take you in." It did sound like a corny line from a police soap but he wasn't joking.

"You see," he said, licking his pencil just like they did on the telly, and opening up his notebook, "the knife that was used to attack Miss Kirsch came from this kitchen."

"What?"

Beth's eyes flew to the knife block on the dresser but now its contents were spread across the table, neatly in order of size. And indeed, her largest Sabatier steel, the one she used for jointing poultry, was missing.

"When did you last see it?" asked the policeman.

"Don't know," said Beth, suddenly speechless. "Oh, sometime last week, I suppose, when I had them all out to give them a good sharpening."

Chapter Forty-two

All hell broke loose when they heard the news, and Beth's entire cavalry came riding to her rescue. *That's the great thing about friends,* she thought with quiet satisfaction, when she saw them all standing there. *They do come through when a girl's in trouble.* Gus, as was fitting for an ex-husband, escorted her from the clink. Duncan, the newest contender, stepped forward and took her in his arms in a display of solidarity, and even Richard Brooke and his cronies were there, standing grinning beside his ancient Jaguar, thoroughly enjoying the lunacy of the moment while also keeping a wary eye out for Beth.

To Beth's utter amazement, even Oliver turned up, looking as he obviously felt, like a spare prick at a wedding, embarrassed and out of place, fiddling with his car keys and wishing he could be anywhere else but here.

"Vivienne sent me," he explained, almost apologetically. "She thought there might be something I could do."

With his money, influence, and power, he meant; that was not lost on Beth. He glared past her at Duncan, who was standing serenely by, not in any sort of hurry, content simply to wait. Beth saw the direction of the glare and smiled.

"Not a thing, thanks," she said softly, reaching up to

touch his cheek. "You're a dear to have come but there was really no need. Look at me, safe and sound, out on bail and planning to prove my innocence."

She glanced around. Even Sally had come, bless her heart, and was sitting with Imogen in the back of Duncan's Land Rover, waving like a thing demented, clearly enjoying every minute of it. As well she might; this was very much Sally's sort of scene and the sheer absurdity was bound to appeal to her zany sense of humor.

"Well, if you're sure," said Oliver darkly, suspecting he was being made an ass of and resenting it.

"Quite sure," said Beth firmly. "Lots of love to Viv and tell her I'll be around later to fill her in on all the gory details."

That was more or less the final straw. Looking as if he would like to disembowel her on the spot, Oliver took his leave, nodding curtly to the curious hordes and driving off noisily in his Mercedes.

"Pompous prat!" remarked Gus cheerfully, then gave Beth another hug and released her to Duncan. Gus was a gentleman. He knew instinctively when it was time to make an elegant departure; another excellent reason for loving him so much.

It was balm to Beth's ears to hear they had picked up Karl as well and that he was still languishing in St. Pancras police station, the subject of further questioning.

"But why?"

"His own fault entirely," said Gus serenely. "It's that bolshie manner, I've always told him it'll land him in trouble in the end. A few hours in the cooler will do him no harm at all and may make him more respectful in the future, particularly where authority is concerned. Actually, I was going to tell you—I've given him the boot."

Beth was astonished. And he seemed so calm and matter-of-fact about it, too. Wait till Georgy heard . . . Then she remembered.

"Why, what happened?"

"Oh, we'd been heading toward nowhere fast. It was long overdue. In some ways he's a dear fellow but he does have the most amazingly murderous temper. We had a bit of a tiff after the lovely day at Vivienne's, and he ended up doing some damage around the house, which is something I really won't tolerate."

He flashed his boyish grin. It was clear he wasn't in the least concerned.

"Broke some of the downstairs windows by hurling beer bottles at them," he said. "Well, that was it. I told him he had to go. So off he went, roaring into the night, full of venom, looking for a fight. The next thing I heard was they'd got him in the cooler and won't even let him out on bail. Not till they've checked his movements last night."

Beth was amazed at his coolness. But why should the police pick on Karl? Surely his connection with Georgy was tenuous in the extreme, even if he did have a lethal temper? The police were certainly thorough. Gus explained.

"Karl has always loathed the very idea of Georgy; just seeing her brings him out in hives. Sees her as some sort of a threat or something lunatic like that. He avoids her whenever he can, and when he can't, showers her in poisonous bile which he simply can't control. You know how these things go. And they get noticed, you'd better believe it, particularly in a small, incestuous world like the theater, which thrives on gossip and sexual innuendo."

He laughed. "They're pretty bloody thorough in the Met, I can tell you. They nose around and uncover all kinds of things. I know it's upsetting, but at least they're doing their job. And I suppose it means if anything awful happened to any of us, we'd get the same protection. Let's hope. Unless, of course, you happen to be queer."

Unless, of course, you happen to be guilty.

They had cross-examined her for several hours, taken detailed statements over and over again, about her knives, their different uses, their locality, and who had access to them.

"It was probably Dreardre wot done it," said Sally darkly. "She always did remind me of Norman Bates's mother."

They all laughed.

But it wasn't really funny. They asked questions about Beth's relationship with Georgy; how long they'd known each other, how often they met, whether they ever quarreled, stuff like that. Superficially, she seemed to be in the clear. After leaving Vivienne's house, in front of a whole gang of witnesses, she had taken Imogen home and not left the house again that night. Imogen could swear to that; except that for most of the time she had been tucked up fast asleep in bed.

"It'll never stand up in court," mumbled a policeman, but it would have to do, at least for now, so they let her go. On condition she didn't leave the country, or even town, without first reporting to the local police station. Fair enough. Beth had no plans for going anywhere and was as anxious as the next person to identify Georgy's attacker.

Whoever that might be. Beth's money would be on a casual intruder but the police were pretty positive that whoever it was had a key. There might, of course, be loads of duplicate keys floating around but until the police could contact Josh Hunter, they wouldn't know for sure. And to complicate things still further, Josh was off on a photo call in China and not expected back for a couple of weeks, while his wife was reportedly somewhere in the Midwest, visiting her folks.

Yet why would a casual criminal risk entering an empty house, lying in wait for its occupant, a total stranger, all but kill her, and then leave empty-handed? It made no sense unless she had disturbed him in the act, in which case how did the downstairs light bulbs come to be missing? Very Ruth Rendell, thought Beth, the crime novel addict. Perhaps he was a light-bulb thief. She was about to share that hilarious thought with the others—then remembered poor little crumpled Georgy, lying so sick in hospital, and thought better of it.

"Probably it was just a drug-crazed down-and-out," she told Duncan as she lay that night on the sofa in his arms. "And Georgy was a random target. Maybe her friends are careless about who they let into their house. It's easy to get a duplicate key cut."

"Unlikely," said Duncan into her hair. "Those are Banham locks and you practically have to swear on your grandmother's grave before you can get a copy made. That's what makes them special. They are supposed to be foolproof."

The last thing he wanted to do was alarm her, particularly after all she'd been through already, but Duncan was pretty concerned, and not just about Georgy. First Catherine, now this—possibly just a macabre coincidence but until he was sure, he wasn't going to take any chances. Beth was the best thing that had happened to him in years; with him her safety came first.

Vivienne locked the door of the brand-new studio and stowed the key in her dressing table drawer. After all the hard work they had done on its refurbishment, she couldn't bear the thought of Oliver bursting in and making a mockery of her dreams. She felt weak and unwell and absolutely drained of emotion. She hated to be selfish but it was hard to have to lay aside a vision that had been gathering momentum for so many weeks. Meeting Georgy had changed her life and opened whole new vistas to her. After years of sterile inactivity, squandering money because she was lonely and bored, she had seen the chance of making something worthwhile of her life and maybe doing a little good as well. Now Georgy was gone and the dream was dead. Even if she were to recover, the chances were that the dominant father would snatch her back home to the States where he could keep his eye on her in future.

And she missed her. With a wrench, Vivienne realized

that the younger woman was fast becoming the daughter she had never had. No Georgy meant no studio. It was that simple. Today was the day Vivienne had planned to start work, phoning around and drumming up business; setting up appointments for her talented new partner. Listlessly she reached for the telephone and booked instead an appointment for a wash and blow-dry with Jean Paul. A visit to the beauty parlor was the drug she always turned to whenever the going started to get tough. It was an automatic reflex action. She knew she could always depend on Jean Paul for a mind-caress and a sympathetic ear. Lately, she had been just too busy to care if her ends needed trimming or her roots coloring but the sudden loss of Georgy gave her an overwhelming need for a dose of tender loving care. Even though she knew she would have to pay for it through the nose.

The salon, as usual, was a whirl of activity but Jean Paul, eager as a lover, rushed to kiss her when she came through the plate-glass door. He helped her out of her jacket, lavishly admired her understated Gucci dress, then ran sensuous fingers through her hair.

"Très bon," he murmured. "Just a little bit of color I think, to lighten your spirits, *n'est-ce-pas?"*

He examined her shrewdly through narrowed Gallic eyes and instantly divined the weight of angst in her soul.

"Madame is a little sad today, I think? Here!" He snapped his fingers at a junior with kohl-rimmed eyes and hair like a stiff bleached bottlebrush. "Get madame gowned and washed, then bring her a magazine to read and some herbal tea. Passionflower today, I think. Madame looks as if she needs a little soothing."

He took her hand and kissed it reverently.

"I won't be too long, *chérie.* I have just one lady to attend to and another to brush out, and then I'm all yours."

The patter was corny but it never failed. Even though Jean Paul hailed from Hackney, not Paris, she didn't care; it was all part of the illusion he created in this elegant, womblike place, the feel-good factor that kept his clients happy and made them his devoted slaves.

The girl brought her *Vogue* and *Marie Claire* but today Vivienne was feeling sorry for herself and could do no more than flick halfheartedly through the glossy pages. The clothes, the jewelry, the beauty treatments, the furs; more meaningless trappings of a life she no longer relished. She glanced around the luxurious pink and silver salon, at women she saw regularly yet still scarcely knew, whiling away their own empty hours the way she had done for so many years; a pointless succession of hairdos, facials, manicures, whatever, in a vain attempt to keep the years at bay and hold on to the attention of the wealthy husbands who paid their bills. And who, in the end, always strayed.

"Mon Dieu! Quel visage!"

Jean Paul had appeared behind her with panther tread and caught the expression of utter desolation on her face. His tapering, prehensile fingers massaged her neck, kneading the knots until the tension fell away and a soft smile returned to her face. She looked at him with warmth. Expensive he might be but, bless him, he certainly knew how to hit the spot.

"Better, *ma chère*?" he purred in her ear, almost as if he really cared. It was this persuasive charm that earned him his captain of industry salary and an appointments book fuller than Princess Di's; his facility to charm and soothe, rather than any fancy fingerwork with the scissors.

He set about combing, clipping, and threading her hair onto tiny squares of silver foil, all the time giving her one hundred percent of his attention, the fake French accent edging more toward East London as he grew careless. A chubby manicurist, wrapped in a cerise overall, drew up like a tug alongside Vivienne, with her wicker basket of polishes and tools, and set to work on the flawless nails. Sometimes she had her toes done too but today she had neither the energy nor the interest. Who was there, after all, to see them anymore? Oliver had hardly been home since the night he virtually raped her but, in light of what had happened to Georgy, she realized she simply no longer cared.

Jean Paul was practically on his knees now, weaving and dancing around her with his smooth talk and his silver paper, and all of a sudden Vivienne failed to find it cute. It was a wicked waste of money to be pampered like this for no reason at all, while her friend was lying broken in the hospital, possibly dying. With a jerk of sudden revulsion, she told him sharply to get a move on as she had just remembered an important appointment on the other side of town.

Georgy might be out of it but Vivienne was barely in her prime, with the rest of her life still ahead of her. She would go ahead with the studio as planned, in the expectation that Georgy would recover; that was the very least she could do. And if that didn't work, she'd think of something else. She'd had one great idea already, so why not more? She would call Phoebe and arrange a meeting to see what the two of them could dream up together. They would start a mutual support group to prop each other up while their husbands were occupied elsewhere.

She told the manicurist to leave her nails unpainted, slipped her a heavy tip to make up for any offense, and strode off into Bond Street, a changed woman with a heart unexpectedly lightened.

Chapter Forty-three

Vanessa opened the door to show out an elderly lady with a similarly decrepit dog, and glanced back up the mews. The girl was still there. Sitting in the sun, wearing a floppy denim hat over her streaming hair, humming to herself and smiling. She had been there for the past two hours and showed no signs of ever moving on. For some reason, this irritated Vanessa profoundly. She looked exactly like a six-ties' flower child; if there had been any daisies handy, she would have been weaving them into a chain. Vanessa closed the door and sniffed. Today's layabout generation, each as feckless as the next. She was only thirty-four her-self but motherhood had made her middle-aged. She just could not bear to see anyone else enjoying themselves.

At noon there was a gap between patients so Duncan emerged into the mews for a breather.

"G'day!" said Sally, slithering off her perch and walking barefoot across the cobbles to greet him.

"You shouldn't do that," said Duncan automatically. "With all the dogs there are around here, you never know what you might pick up."

"Chance would be a fine thing." Her white teeth gleamed and her tongue licked lips as ripe and firm as the flesh of a peach. There was no escaping her innuendo and, in spite of himself, Duncan found that he was smiling. Sally was a bit over the top but beguiling nonetheless.

"So what brings you here?" He was not to know she had been loitering there all morning just to catch a glimpse of him.

Vanessa knew, though, as he led her back into the waiting room. With a slightly pursed mouth, she clattered away at her keyboard, rejecting Sally's friendly overtures. *Stupid cow,* thought Sally. *She's hardly older than me but just look at her.* What was it about this man that he chose to surround himself with dried-up old prunes with sex appeal in inverse proportion to his own? First Catherine, now this one, already on the slippery slope to spinsterhood despite the shiny new ring on her finger. She was not to know it was Duncan's deliberate policy. Women with nothing much else to offer were, he found, inclined to be better workers. It might be sexist but it was the truth. He had enough on his hands already, with the ailing animals and their often very silly owners, without cultivating trouble on his own doorstep too.

"So what gives?" He propped his tall frame against the doorpost and looked down at her with a lazy grin.

Sally said the first thing that came into her head, which was not at all her usual style. Normally she was cool-headed, but not today. She had waited so long for just this moment, yet now found herself strangely tongue-tied.

"Actually, I need a job. I thought maybe there'd be something going here."

She stared at Vanessa in cool defiance but Vanessa had her own surprise up her sleeve. Just as Duncan was spreading his hands in apology, about to fob Sally off, her voice piped up from behind the computer.

"Actually, I was rather hoping for some time off next week," she said. "My parents are coming to stay and I'd like to take them around a bit. With the baby, of course."

Her smug smile was spoiled by the lipstick smudged on her teeth, but Sally felt like kissing her. She turned to

Duncan with a smile so radiant, there was no way he could possibly refuse her.

"Have you done this sort of work before?" he asked doubtfully, his eyes beseeching Vanessa to get him out of it, cursing her for speaking up without first consulting him. But his plea fell on deaf ears; Vanessa could be relied upon to put her own interests first.

"I've worked in an office and I know how to file," said Sally easily.

"Then you should have no problem here," said Vanessa. "Stick around and I'll show you the ropes. It's all perfectly straightforward."

"Actually," Duncan heard her say confidentially as he closed the surgery door, "you'll be doing me a favor."

Sally was still there when he emerged again at twenty past one, with a cricked neck and a thirst on him like a bushfire. She was hovering in the doorway with her hat back on her head so he could see nothing for it but to ask her to join him for a drink. Might as well be friendly.

"To cement our working relationship," he said dryly, and she fell into step beside him, still beaming that radiant smile.

"I'll be back at two," he told Vanessa firmly and was startled to see that even she was smiling now. This girl could obviously charm the pants off anyone who came within radiation distance, so he'd really have to watch it. Well, they'd be working cheek by jowl for at least a week, so now was the time to get to know her better. Also, there was something tugging at the furthermost corner of his mind, something Beth had said, that he'd quite like to get straight with her now—if only, for the life of him, he could remember what it was.

Sally looked a bit scruffy but her clothes were clean and she managed always to turn up on time and smile continually, which was a major plus after some of the moaning minnies he'd had to put up with in the past. And although

her recordkeeping left much to be desired, she was quite
brilliant with the animals and their owners, who fell under
the spell of her luminous charm in seconds. After
Catherine, with her lingering *tristesse,* and Vanessa, with
that little pinched mouth, this was indeed a welcome
change. This girl had the spirit and enthusiasm to be a real
asset if she stuck at it. If Vanessa wasn't careful, she'd
likely be finding herself out of a job.

Yet there was still something about Sally that Duncan
didn't entirely trust. It might have been the raw sexuality
and the reflective way she looked him up and down whenever he appeared in the doorway, the way a sailor just back
from a long stint at sea looks at a tart. It was so deliberate,
it was actually quite funny, but Duncan, though certainly
not a prude, was not particularly amused. This was his
patch and he took his vocation seriously. Also, she was
Beth's friend and should not be acting this way, certainly
not around him. She wore a uniform of jeans and a skimpy
T-shirt, nothing else, and all she had to offer was on full
view to the world. He found this disconcerting, as any red-
blooded male was bound to, but what could he do? She was
only going to be here for a week and she was doing him a
favor. If she stayed on longer, he might suggest she wore an
overall; meantime the dowagers would just have to lump it
if the sight of those glorious breasts offended them.

Beth took it like a lamb, but that was Beth all over.
Duncan had been nervous about telling her but Sally got
her twopennyworth in first so he was glad he'd had the
foresight to mention it, if only to prove he had nothing to
hide. Sally was there already when Duncan walked in, ensconced in her usual place in Beth's kitchen and apparently
just through telling Beth about her brilliant new job.

"That's wonderful, sweetie," said Beth, flinging her arms
round his neck and rubbing her nose in his beard. "But how
did all this come about? Don't tell me you two have been
meeting behind my back?"

"We bumped into each other in the pub," said Sally

cheerfully, winking at Duncan and putting him instantly on his guard. "And since old Sourpuss had just asked for time off, nothing seemed simpler than for me to step into the breach. Right, Duncan?"

He was annoyed but tried to hide it. He had been right not to trust her, he sensed she was basically bad news, but as far as Beth was concerned the sun shone out of her backside. That was something he'd have to watch.

"Hurry up and get sorted out," he said, making a show of kissing Beth's neck. "I was planning to take you out for a change."

"But Sal's here," objected Beth. "How's about we all stay in and I'll throw together some spaghetti or something?"

"You're always doing that." Now his anger was beginning to rise and he had to take a firm grip on himself. Beth noticed nothing but he saw Sally watching him shrewdly and knew she had his measure.

"You guys go," she said. "And I'll stay here and wait for Imogen. I love that kid," she explained to Duncan. "She's everything I ever want in a child, when I finally get around to doing it myself. Though it has to be a girl. I can't stand boys."

"What do you mean, you can't stand boys?" said Beth, in amusement. "I rather got the impression you were addicted to them."

"Not small ones, with runny noses and scabby knees. Ugh! Can't bear them, won't have them near me. They bring me out in a rash!"

They both screamed with laughter while Duncan felt dismay. The kid; he'd forgotten. Now he really was in the doghouse. Sally was smiling but he wanted to slap her around the face.

"Spaghetti sounds just the job," he said lamely, taking Beth in his arms again and hugging her to him. She felt so good, this lovely lady; so warm, so comfortable. He couldn't get enough of her.

"Spaghetti for four coming up!" said Beth gaily, shaking loose. "You set the table, Sal, while I fix the sauce. How does everyone feel about anchovies?"

"I'll just pop round the corner for a couple of bottles of Valpolicella," said Duncan, knowing when he was beaten.

He still couldn't figure out the thing that was elusively nagging in the corner of his brain, irritatingly just out of sight.

It was Friday evening, Sally's last in the practice, and still she lingered. The last patient was long since gone and Duncan was puttering around in the surgery, reduced to re-arranging the drugs cupboard and wishing she would go home so that he could lock up. He was reluctant to leave with her as he wanted to avoid that crucial parting exchange that would result, almost certainly, in either a drink or the promise of future work. Which he was not prepared to give.

She wandered into the surgery now, barefoot, and heaved herself up on the examination table where she sat with legs apart, watching him.

"Do you always work this late? What is it, don't you have a home to go to?" She was mocking him; he felt her eyes burning into the back of his neck.

He muttered something from the depths of the cupboard and told her not to bother to wait.

"I'm in no hurry," was all she said.

Finally he'd finished and could delay things no longer. Besides, his back was killing him. He straightened up, closed the cupboard door, and locked it, slipping the key back on to his keyring and into his inner pocket. Where drugs were concerned, you simply couldn't be too careful. He turned to face her and, as he did so, she took hold of the lapels of his starched white coat and drew him slowly toward her, all the time holding his gaze with her luminous, aquamarine eyes.

Duncan hesitated but only for a moment. She was so

close he could smell the honey of her hair and he was, after all, just a man, with the same basic appetites as the next guy. He laid his hands on her shoulders and felt the heat of her skin through her skimpy T-shirt and those impressive breasts pressed up hard against his shirt. She was pushing the coat from his shoulders and he bent his head and kissed her firmly on the mouth, feeling it open to draw him in, her tongue soft and sinuous against his own.

But then he straightened and pushed her gently away, seeing the rage and incomprehension flare in her eyes, knowing that in one false move he had made himself an enemy.

"Sorry, sweetie," he said, shaking his broad shoulders back into his white coat. "But I don't believe in mixing business with pleasure."

"Aw, come on!" She couldn't believe he was serious, already had her T-shirt halfway over her head.

Duncan switched off the lights in the surgery and went on outside to the deserted waiting room. He had never been in a situation like this, where it was being offered to him on a plate and he found he had lost his taste for it. But these days the image of Beth was uppermost in his mind and he knew he'd never be able to live with his conscience if he trifled any further with this delectable little whore. But how was he going to get rid of her tactfully, without damaging her feelings any more?

And then Duncan heard a sound he had never imagined he would welcome, the crunch of tires on the cobbles outside, announcing the arrival of the cavalry.

"Coo-ee, anyone home?" called Serena, as she barged on in through the door without waiting for a reply. She was wearing pearls and a little black number and her hair hung straight and shiny over her shoulders. She was fresh back from the Maldives so her impeccable tan was classily authentic and she looked at Sally as if she were dirt as she followed Duncan, barefoot, from the darkened surgery, jerking her T-shirt back into place.

"Working late?" she sneered before she could stop herself, trembling on the verge of bursting into tears. Duncan drew her into his arms, with more enthusiasm than he felt, and kissed her full on the lips.

"Just locking up, my love," he said cheerfully. "If you wait a sec, I'll be right with you."

Serena's astonishment showed but at least it put a stop to the tears; she glanced back at Sally, who was flamboyantly brushing her hair, with a look of pure triumph.

"I'm on my way to the Philipsons," she said, slightly mollified. "They're having a drinks do and I thought you might like to come."

"Terrific." Duncan took off his white coat and tossed it into the corner. As usual, he was dressed head to foot in denim but it didn't stop him looking like a million dollars.

"Am I too casual?"

She shook her head. Just looking at this man rendered her speechless; she knew he would have the same effect on her friends and longed to show him off.

Duncan waited while Sally, with a bad grace, slid her grubby feet back into her thongs, grabbed the canvas bag in which she toted her possessions, and crammed her denim hat onto her springy hair.

"Can we drop you anywhere?" Duncan asked as he locked the door but Sally, as she pushed on past him, was far too choked to speak.

Much later, after he had endured an hour or two of inconsequential banter on a penthouse terrace with views across the Thames, Duncan excused himself from Serena's boisterous friends, who were set on going clubbing in the West End, by pleading middle age and an early start in the morning. He let her down as gently as he could, seeing how close to tears she was again, kissed her paternally on the forehead, and promised to ring sometime soon when maybe they could grab a movie or something. He knew it was unlikely he ever would. These lightweight girls just weren't worth the strain on his nerves.

He took a taxi back to the surgery, where he picked up the Land Rover, then meandered on down to the Fulham Road for a late-night cognac before turning in. All he wanted in the world was Beth; both today's amatory encounters had simply served to focus his thoughts and underline how very much he loved her. He cursed himself for wasting so much time and knew that if he lost her, it would only be his own damned fault. Tonight was really too late for an impulsive visit to the house in Ladbroke Grove that was fast becoming the center of his universe but he swore to himself he would do something positive first thing in the morning. Besides, he needed all his wits about him for the important decision he was on the brink of making.

He drove back home to Putney deep in thought. A short, sharp shower, some food, and a few hours' kip should set him up. Tomorrow would decide his fate—for the rest of his life he hoped, the way he was feeling now. He had wandered around the world too long, in some sort of time-warp soft-shoe shuffle. The fact that the feel of Sally's firm young breasts had faintly repelled him was telling him something he could not ignore. He was no longer the wild young man he used to be; it was time to abandon his macho attitude toward life in general and women in particular, to think about putting down roots and taking things a tad more seriously. In an odd way, he was grateful to Sally—Sally and Serena. When you felt you were losing your appetite, it was surely time to quit.

The message light on his answering machine was blinking so he flicked it on and played back the tape while he poured himself another cognac. The voice from Western Australia sounded cautious and ill at ease at making a long-distance call and it was difficult to hear what it was saying through the static on the line. But eventually he got the picture. It was his parents' nearest neighbor in Perth and she sounded fairly distraught. His father had had a coronary and been rushed to the hospital.

"I'd come quickly if I were you," she said.

Chapter Forty-four

When Georgy eventually opened her eyes, she thought she must have died and gone to heaven. The one face she loved most in the world, her father's, was hovering over her with eyes filled with concern and love, and furthermore he was weeping. She closed her eyes again and tried to throw off the dream but gentle fingers were caressing her cheek and a deep, familiar voice whispered endearments with a catch in the throat that made her want to cry too.

"Daddy?"

"My darling."

So it was true. He was really there.

Strong fingers enfolded hers but she found she could not move her arms to embrace him because of the tube in her wrist and what felt like a lead waistcoat around her ribs which restrained her as effectively as a straitjacket. Also, it hurt, monumentally, whenever she tried to move.

"Daddy?"

"Sweetheart, I'm here." Lips touched the back of her hand and she felt something suspiciously like a tear.

"What's going on? Where am I?"

"Take it easy, my love, you're quite safe now."

"But what happened?"

Emmanuel Kirsch, rubbing his sleeve across his eyes, let

go of her hand and rose to his feet, shrugging his shoulders helplessly to the two uniformed policemen waiting discreetly at the foot of the bed. One of them, the more senior, nodded his head and touched Emmanuel's shoulder, indicating he should continue.

"There was an accident, sweetheart, and you were hurt. Don't you remember?"

She didn't. She lay there, immobile, and ran her confused mind over her jagged memory. An accident. All she knew was she hurt like hell, it seemed all over, and Daddy was here, holding her hand and actually crying. That was all that mattered right now.

It's a gag, right? A—what do you call it?—April Fool? Any minute now some joker is going to leap around that door and holler, Gotcha!

Her fingers tightened over her father's. He hadn't gone away.

"Daddy," she said, in a whisper this time.

"My darling."

"Please take me home."

He did, too. Yes, there were questions she couldn't quite understand, let alone answer, and strange uniformed figures looming over her and then receding, and Beth—she could swear it was Beth—kissing her cheek and talking in a low, concerned murmur, and then a lot of noises and movements with Georgy drifting in and out of consciousness until finally they were in an ambulance and driving away to safety, Daddy still with her, still holding her hand.

"I'm so sorry," she tried to say a number of times, but it seemed he couldn't understand, so she waited awhile and then tried again.

"Sorry for what?" he whispered, smothering her face with careful kisses and trying hard to control his tears. "It's I who should apologize, I ought to have been there. All these years, while you were growing up . . . And to think. I might have lost you . . ."

And then she was comforting him, which was a novel idea but a delicious thought, if only she could work out why he was so upset.

The plane was a bit of a performance but there were nurses to give her injections and take care of her, just as if she were still safely in the hospital. She was dimly aware that there seemed to be no other passengers but someone explained it was an air ambulance, so she really was flying in style. Thank God for Dad and his money.

"Oh, Lord," she thought as the drowsiness took over, "did I remember to pack my Burberry? And my passport? And what about presents for the family? They always expect presents. And what about getting my legs waxed? It's summer already and Ma will go on about it."

Then she had the most worrying thought of all.

Myra—give me strength. And won't there be one helluva row when she sees me like this with Daddy.

She slipped off into a gentle, drug-induced doze.

Emmanuel Kirsch sat in the air ambulance and worried about his daughter. He was only just beginning to recover from the shock of hearing that she might be dying and blessed his stars they had reached him in time, on a stopover in New York before he'd reached home. He turned his head to look at her now, sleeping peacefully nearby, bound up like a papoose in red hospital blankets, as small and defenseless as the child he had once worshiped but had lately neglected so shamefully.

Well, this time round he was going to make up for all that. Sylvia was right when she said he was too obsessive; it was a miracle that this latest marriage had survived at all considering his track record and how little time they actually managed to get together. He owed it all to Sylvia. She was a wonderful, caring woman of unfathomable strength and staying power who had curtailed her own high-flying career with scarcely a murmur because, she told him, she had her priorities right and wanted only to make this relationship work. And, of course, now there was Ariel to consider too.

At the thought of his son, a tender smile crossed Emmanuel's careworn face. Whoever would have thought that, this late in life, he would finally be given the son he had always longed for? Ariel had brought new meaning to his life and in his presence Emmanuel felt quite humble. He had always considered himself an exemplary paterfamilias, but raising girls was not the same as having a small replica of himself to follow in his footsteps. It might be an unpopular view in these days of political correctness, but Emmanuel Kirsch was an old-fashioned man and proud of it. That was how he felt.

Once he had felt that way about Georgy, had smothered her with love and admiration, and lugged her around with him whenever he could. But then things had radically changed. He had abandoned her mother and left his first family to cope without him. His Little Princess had been tossed to one side, when she was not much older than Ariel was now. Guilt filled him; he knew how badly he had behaved and also how it had affected his daughter. She had every right to feel bitter and deserted; the question was, would she ever be able to forgive him? He swore he would do everything within his power to try to make things up to her. He could only thank the Lord he had been granted a second chance.

Sixteen times she had been stabbed; who could possibly have hated her that much? Though they had permitted him to take her away, the case was by no means closed and the really sickening part was that the police appeared to have practically no firm leads at all. Emmanuel sat back and, for the hundredth time, ran his incisive mind over the list of possible suspects.

The cook first, the one whose knife had been used in the attack. The odds against it being her were gigantic. Quite apart from her open, friendly personality and her obvious fondness for his daughter, there was surely no way she would be so stupid as to use her own weapon and then leave it carelessly at the scene of the crime? But Emmanuel Kirsch was accustomed to keeping an open mind. In his profession he knew not to jump to any conclusion until he had hard evidence to back it up.

Then there was the odd coincidence of the death of Catherine Palmer, one of the women who had shared Georgy's hospital ward when she burst her appendix. Almost certainly just that, coincidence, yet still worth looking into. Sick people have a tendency to die and one out of five was not such a terrible statistic, yet a death and a near-death in the space of just a few weeks, among five random patients in the same small ward, seemed unlikely. Even the slightly dozy London police had picked up on that and were interviewing all three surviving patients to see if they could establish any connection.

Next there was the doctor, Addison Harvey. Great reputation in the States as a leading surgeon—Emmanuel had already had him checked out back home. No slouch in England either, come to that; strongly tipped, so he had heard, to be the next personal gynecologist to the Queen. And that must still mean something in this funny little off-shore island. Harvey had been out of town during Emmanuel's brief visit but he meant to catch up with him once Georgy was safely sorted.

He was determined to find out more, too, about Catherine Palmer's death. It was not Emmanuel's way to intrude upon private grief, but as long as the question of her overdose remained unresolved, other people had to be suspect and Addison Harvey must come at the top of that list. It was a bit of a cliché to suspect the doctor. Yet who more than he had the knowledge and expertise to have carried out both crimes?

Emmanuel took out a Havana cigar, looked at it longingly, then glanced across at his sleeping daughter and thought better of it. These past few days had been particularly grueling, and he had to be in court in San Diego in two days' time. First, and most important, there was his daughter to take care of. He would do anything within his power to protect her and hunt down her attacker, no matter what it might cost him in time and money. Once he was clear of the case in San Diego, he meant to head straight back to London to do some sleuthing. Strictly speaking, this was the province of the British police but no one hurt a child of Emmanuel Kirsch and got away with it.

Looking at what evidence he had so far, he would put his safe money on the German *faygeleh* who seemed so full of pent-up poison and an inborn hatred of the female sex. He had had the inclination, the opportunity, and the motivation, particularly since his erstwhile lover, whom Georgy seemed so stuck on, had apparently recently booted him out. What Georgy, with her healthy appetite for life, could ever have seen in that guy was beyond her father's comprehension. He blamed himself for having deserted her so badly during the crucial, formative years of her adolescence. Once again, he hoped it was not too late to make amends.

Karl was still in police custody and had, it turned out, a record of violence from his teenage years in Berlin when he was an active member of the neo-Nazi party. Emmanuel recoiled with distaste, yet had to be fair and try to retain his clear-sightedness. How could Karl have got hold of the knife without Beth knowing? Even though she appeared to live a lax and careless life—*with a young daughter, yet; what sort of an example was that?*—surely not even in her bohemian circles would she be on such cozy terms with the lover of her former husband?

Next there was the veterinarian, who seemed, on brief acquaintance, a decent enough fellow, yet, when it came down to it, what exactly did they know about him? It was clear to see he was fairly smitten with Beth but Catherine was the one who had known him best, and she was dead. Why was he paying so much attention to the mother? Was it just that he was a decent guy or could there be a hidden agenda? Might his apparent solace mask a motive altogether more sinister?

Then there was Oliver Nugent, suave, smooth-talking husband of the rich bitch who seemed to be attempting some sort of takeover bid for Georgy's career. Emmanuel had not managed to meet Vivienne more than fleetingly, because she was so upset, but the husband had taken her place at the hospital and he'd managed to have a word with him. Coming to no satisfactory conclusion. Oliver was certainly clever and ruthless, successful too, but where exactly did he slot into the general scheme of things, regarding Georgy's life? He was the sort of Englishman Emmanuel distrusted on sight. The sort, he was afraid, Georgy would find all too appealing.

Last on the list came the couple who owned the house, friends—so he understood—from New York. The police had not yet succeeded in tracing the Hunters but were keen to do so if only to account for the key that had actually unlocked the door. It might all turn out to have been an unfortunate accident but until Josh Hunter could be located, his name had to remain on the list.

In all, quite a conundrum, but meat and drink to Emmanuel Kirsch. In any other circumstances he might have relished the challenge, but this was his child's attacker he was seeking; this one he had to catch. He slipped off his shoes, eased his feet into his monogrammed slippers, and prepared to sleep.

Georgy did not wake until the plane had touched down and the orderlies came to maneuver her stretcher onto a trolley, to be carried down the stairway like a coffin. As bright sunshine hurt her sensitive eyes, and since she couldn't reach her sunspecs as her arms were still strapped down, she sprang awake and started worrying all over again. She felt terrible after the flight, a mass of throbbing aches and pains, and longed to relieve herself if only she knew how.

The thought of seeing her mother again filled her with dread. She just wasn't strong enough to cope with all that now, the fuss, the excitement, the tears; all that suffocating love that had caused her to run away in the first place.

They pushed the trolley across the tarmac, with Emmanuel walking beside her, holding her hand, then into the international terminal and straight through Customs, ahead of the other passengers. *This is the way to travel,* thought Georgy. *In the future I'll always be sure to do it on a stretcher.* Then there were people milling all round her and making way to let her through—and all of a sudden, a familiar smiling face looking down at her and kissing her gently in a haze of delicate citron-flavored perfume. Sylvia.

"Georgy, my darling, are you all right?" She knelt on the ground in her sharply pressed white pants in order to talk to her properly, real concern on her lovely face. Georgy was touched but her strength was fading; all she wanted was to sleep.

"Where are we?" she whispered, confused, expecting Myra to materialize at any minute and provoke another of those ugly scenes. Myra and Sylvia in the same airport, what did her father think he was up to? Even the same city was not large enough to accommodate two such forceful ladies.

"Los Angeles," said Sylvia gently. "I've got the Cadillac outside and we're taking you home to Newport Beach for a spot of rest and recuperation until you are well enough to make your own decisions."

California—no wonder the air was so balmy, the sun so warm. How they had managed to fix it with Myra, Georgy could not imagine, but right now that was the least of her concerns. A wonderful feeling of calm swept over her as she allowed Sylvia to take control and wheel her out to the waiting limousine.

She awoke next morning in a large, airy room, with th windows flung open to let in the warm air, filmy whit tains fluttering in the breeze. From where she lav up on a lavish pile of pillows in the great canopied bed, Georgy could see a wide vista of manicured lawns and well-tended flowerbeds sloping down to a small orchard of orange and peach trees. As she stirred slightly and attempted to sit up, Sylvia leapt from the easy chair by the window where she was quietly doing needlepoint.

"You're awake! How do you feel?"

Georgy moved cautiously and considered.

"Well, I guess I've felt better."

She smiled and, not for the first time, her stepmother reflected how much more attractive she was when her face was not all scrunched up with some resentment or other.

"Do you need a bedpan or can you make it to the bathroom?"

Pure tact; as different from Myra as it was possible to be. Georgy felt her fighting spirit beginning to rally. A door on the right led to a pretty, sun-filled bathroom, done up completely in red and green Spanish tiles, with a thick Mexican rug on the floor. Georgy considered.

"Why not start as I mean to go on," she said determinedly. "Give me a hand and let's see if I can make it."

Later, when she had sorted herself out, she asked, "Where's Dad?"

"Off in San Diego, giving evidence in a double homicide trial." Where else?

"So why can't he have a nine-to-five job, with full vacations and a pension, like everyone else's dad?"

Sylvia laughed. They were so much alike, these two.

"Search me, babe, but he wouldn't be your father if ever he decided to settle for second best."

She returned to her needlepoint in the window. They had all the time in the world; for the first time she looked forward to getting to know better this spiky young woman who was so much like her father.

A small figure filled the doorway and Georgy looked up, startled.

"Oh, there you are," said Sylvia. "I wondered where

you'd got to. Come on in, Ariel, and meet Georgy, your big sister."

And she smiled as she watched the two like spirits start to take their first steps in the long process of bonding.

Chapter Forty-five

Sally was giving Beth a treat; at least, Sally had organized it, Beth was paying. Beth was down and missing Duncan so Sally had turned up trumps—just as she always did, bless her—and persuaded Beth to take a break for the day and come with her to the Sanctuary in Covent Garden. Beth did not take a lot of persuading. Just lately work had become a bit of a drag; she was glad of any excuse to put up the shutters.

"But how can you afford it?" she asked worriedly, and in answer, Sally unzipped one of the pockets in her denim jacket and waved a bunch of fivers in her face. Beth was startled.

"I thought you were out of work?"

"I've been doing shifts at McDonald's."

"You who can't cook."

"No need to. All I do is clear tables and sweep up. I'm an expert at that, as you know."

"And as many of those disgusting, cholesterol-filled hamburgers as you can eat, I suppose."

"Don't knock it."

Beth laughed. Sally never failed to be a tonic. She was feeling considerably brighter already.

"Keep your money," she said, shoving it back into

Sally's pocket. "You can't afford to buy me treats, not till you're on your feet again and working. It's the thought that counts and you are a dear to have suggested it. But let me do this, I insist. You can treat me when you've found a proper job or caught yourself a rich husband."

"Have you heard from him?" asked Sally on the Tube. Parking in central London was such a drag these days, so they had elected to leave the car behind.

"Just once, a quick call to tell me he'd got there and to leave the number in case of emergencies. His dad is really pretty poorly so he's planning to stick around with his mother for a while and see how things shape up."

"What about the practice? Who's looking after all those lovely animals?"

"He managed to get a replacement in, another transitory Aussie, would you believe, and I suppose Vanessa's coping with the rest. Maybe you should offer your services again. Shall I ask him next time he calls if he wants you to help out?"

"If you like."

That was Beth, generous to the nth degree. Sometimes Sally couldn't believe she was real, but she wasn't knocking it. They journeyed on to Leicester Square in companionable silence.

The Sanctuary in Floral Street is a health club where women go to be pampered and cosseted. For the cost of a fairly hefty entrance fee, you can stay there all day, just lazing about, having different beauty treatments, generally unwinding. It felt like a mini holiday; exactly what Beth had needed for a long time. They both had a swim and a full body massage, booked pedicures for the afternoon, then wrapped themselves in towels and went downstairs to the Jacuzzi.

No one else was using it so they sat facing each other among the bubbling jets, looking up at the lovely vaulted ceiling that gave the converted warehouse the feel of an authentic Roman villa. Sally's hair was pinned high on top of her head, with long strands escaping and floating round her face like fronds of seaweed, while Beth's short curls were plastered to her head giving her a look like a profile off an ancient Greek coin.

"This is certainly the life," said Sally, lying back and spreading her arms and legs. "One day I want a holiday in a health farm so I can do this sort of thing for days on end."

"You don't need it," said Beth ruefully, admiring her friend's flat stomach and spectacular curves through the churning water. "That's for middle-aged fatties, like me."

She looked down at her own ample stomach, curving comfortably above strong thighs and shapely legs. From the hips down she was still in great shape; her problem area had always been around her middle. Mostly it didn't bother her—these days clothes were cut to disguise a bit of a spread—but in these intimate circumstances it wasn't possible not to compare her body with that of the younger woman.

Sally was looking too.

"So that's your scar." She examined the neat, curved line, like the blade of a scimitar, that faintly intersected Beth's pubic hair. Already, after just a few months, it was scarcely visible and certainly not unsightly. Marvelous what they could achieve these days with surgery. Beth looked at Sally's lean, flat belly, fully exposed as she lay spread out in the water, and saw not a trace of anything.

"So what did they do to you then?" she asked curiously. "Those doctors?" Now she came to think of it, Sally had never actually said. "Something internal," was all she had muttered when they first discussed it, but that surely was true of all of them in the gynecological ward.

Sally's eyes were as clear and translucent as the water and gave away nothing.

"Come on, Sal. You can tell me. It's all girls together here and, besides, we're mates. I thought you were having surgery like the rest of us?"

"It was exploratory," said Sally, after a short pause. "They managed to fix it from inside."

"But whatever it was, they did fix it?"

"Oh, yes." Sally flashed her famous smile. "I'm fit as a fiddle and as good as new. Can't you see?"

And that was obviously all she was prepared to say, which was slightly odd in someone normally so open and direct. Beth didn't press it. Sally was entitled to her privacy and if she didn't fancy talking about it, that was her own business. She hoped there was nothing sinister about this silence though; it would be too awful if Sally had a health worry she felt she couldn't discuss. It didn't bear thinking about, Beth loved her far too much for that.

They dried off, then lay for a while on the sunbeds, working up a becoming glow before they went down for lunch. Amid an exotic scenery of ornamental fishpools and real live parrots in trees, they sat on stools at the health food bar and drank enormous cocktails made from freshly squeezed vegetable juice. Not a drop of alcohol in sight, but what the hell, it was only for one day.

"I suppose it's good for the soul," sighed Beth. "Not to mention the liver."

"This place reminds me of Viv's conservatory," said Sally. "She needs a couple of parrots to set it off. What do you suppose she will do, now that Georgy's bitten the dust?"

"Don't know. Can't imagine. It's a pity really. She seemed such a sad sack when we first got to know her and it looked like Georgy was about to bring new life into her static existence."

"Jesus!" said Sally. "Some sort of static! I could be very content, thank you, with a house like that and all that loot. Not to mention that husband!"

"You'd be content anywhere," said Beth, ignoring the barb. "You're that sort of person. You must have been an angel in an earlier life."

Sally laughed and her eyes crinkled up. Draped in her

towel, with her hair pinned up, she looked even more fetching than usual, like a beautiful French courtesan waiting for her lover. Yet, oddly enough, she never seemed to have a real boyfriend, at least not one that stayed around. Sometimes Beth worried about her but she didn't want to spoil the mood by bringing up all that again. Things were going so well with Duncan, despite his absence, that she wanted Sally to share her happiness. Indeed, she would like to spread it around as much as possible; Beth had that sort of a nature.

Which brought her back to the subject of Vivienne and Georgy.

"It's a real shame if Georgy's accident keeps Viv from getting her act together," she said. "She was right on the brink of something really good, what with her interest in the World Wide Fund for Nature and all. It seems she just needed a jolt to get her going and now it looks like all being spoiled. I think she'd do terrifically well as an organizer, given something that would really challenge her."

"And she couldn't do it alone?"

"Well, hardly. Not without Georgy to focus things and take the photographs. Viv may have money but she doesn't have confidence."

"Maybe Georgy will be back." But right now, that didn't seem awfully likely.

They thought about Georgy and the frightful attack.

"What do you really think happened?" asked Sally. "You don't suppose it was a bit of rough trade who got out of hand?"

"Sally!" Beth was shocked. Even the police hadn't come up with that theory, at least as far as she knew; certainly not in front of Georgy's father.

Sally shrugged. "These things do happen. I knew a bloke once who got strangled on a casual date, and he wasn't even gay. At least, not officially."

"Come on, Georgy's not like that."

"You never know."

Sally was smiling. Beth looked at her cautiously. She

was the sunniest, cheeriest person in the world, yet just occasionally, at unexpected moments like this, something slipped and a dark side surfaced. What a strange little person she was, and what a time she must have had these past years, constantly on the road and having to fend for herself. Beth longed to know more about her earlier life but was wise enough not to pursue the subject. The more you listened, the more you learned; she'd always known that. It was frustrating, but maybe one of these days Sally would learn to trust her.

"Come on," she said, draining her glass. "That carrot juice was something else, but now I've got to get into that pool. Race you!"

Duncan hung up with increasing exasperation. She still wasn't home and he had rung four times, so where on earth could she have got to? He hated to feel possessive but he was really missing her and badly needed to hear her voice. It was seven o'clock in the morning in Perth and he'd been up all night at the hospital, pacing a sterile corridor hour after hour, waiting for a verdict on his father's chances and thinking obsessively about Beth.

Just lately, everything in his ordered life seemed to have spun into a downward spiral; first Catherine, then Georgy, now Dad. Meeting Beth had been the one bright beacon in these weeks of catastrophe, but now he couldn't reach her and that made him tense. It was a feeling entirely alien to Duncan's normally easygoing nature. He had never felt like this before; it simply wasn't his style.

He never had got round to having that meaningful conversation with her, and that was what he regretted most. All they had was a hurried conversation over the telephone from the airport and since then he'd been so occupied with the worry of his father's health that he hadn't done more than make one brief call to give her a contact number, should she need one. And now he couldn't reach her and it rattled him.

He kept on thinking about Sally and their aborted encounter in the surgery. She was, on the surface, a good enough sport but there was something about her he still couldn't trust, nor could he shake off the memory of the look in her eyes when he thwarted her attempt at seduction. It drove him mad to think of her now, back there close to Beth, telling her God knows what, with her confidential manner and that winning smile.

Time was hanging heavily on Duncan's hands, away from his real life, confined to this dull backwater for an indefinite period which could well drag on for weeks or even months. He loved his parents and was glad he had got there in time to hold the old man's hand, to comfort his mother and talk to the doctors on her behalf. Having come so far, he knew he must stick around, at least until his father's future was more settled. Duncan was an only child who had been traveling since he first quit college and took off to Europe to see the world before he settled down. That period had extended until here he was, a middle-aged man, based in London with a thriving veterinary practice but without any proper roots.

His mother was longing to hear his intimate secrets, he could see it in her eyes, but there was really nothing he could tell her, even if that had been his style. So he went off in search of his misspent youth and found it, alarmingly unchanged, down at the local bar where some of his boyhood cronies still hung out. It was amazing. After the hectic pace of Chicago and London, life in Perth jogged along at a far slower rate, a good thirty years behind what he had become used to.

It was fun for a while, catching up on their lives, talking about old times, but he was already beginning to chafe. Of his inner circle from adolescence, three out of four remained in town; a banker, a lawyer, and a golf professional. The fourth one, Paul, had astounded them all by taking holy orders right after he graduated and was now a hospital chaplain in Parramatta, a suburb of Sydney.

"You ought to look him up, mate," said Greg. "Hasn't changed a bit. Still the same randy old bugger."

"Why did he do it? Rather extreme behavior, even for Paul," said Duncan, remembering with a touch of regret his closest pal among the group, the jokes they had shared, the girls they had chased, the pints they had consumed.

"Got the call, or so he claims. Personally I think it was just an excuse not to have to marry that dork who was always hanging around."

"You mean Giselle?"

"The very same!"

They roared.

"Man, was she some dog!"

Duncan realized he was homesick—for the traffic, pollution, overpopulation, and political unfairness of London, a city he had once found so oppressive. He longed for soft summer rain, the sight of a red double-decker, warm beer, and Capital Radio, with its cheerful reports of traffic snarl-ups and signal failure on the Tube. Right now he was missing the end of Wimbledon, the cricket at Lord's, and Shakespeare in the Park. He loved his family, was happy to catch up with his old mates and to sleep in his boyhood bedroom again, where his sports trophies and framed diplomas still held pride of place. But he also saw there was no longer room for him here. Life had moved on.

Most of all, he longed for Beth, who dominated his every waking moment. Being this far away only helped to accentuate just how heavily he'd fallen and, like measles, when it hit you this late, it was that much more devastating to the system. If only he'd found the time to tell her how he felt. He had held off deliberately for far too long from a strange, misplaced delicacy and a basic fear that he was still not ready to make a firm commitment. Now, through a quirk of timing, he might have succeeded in wrecking everything. Women like Beth weren't exactly thick on the ground and she already had a whole bunch of admirers; witness her triumphant rescue from police custody.

And what was also nagging in his mind was the fact that she might not need him at all. She had her child, her business, her friends, and her freedom. In Duncan's mind, a recipe for total happiness with no strings attached. She was financially independent, surrounded by love, her health was good, and she was happy. The only thing she lacked, as far as he could see, was the thing he was now prepared to offer her. A great, abiding love, in sickness and in health. And he'd managed to screw up his timing.

If only she'd answer that damned phone. He dialed again and again got the machine, with Beth's cheerful voice inviting him to leave a message and she'd get back to him as soon as she could. Where on earth could she be? He banged down the receiver in total frustration and went back to pacing the bleak corridors.

Duncan was starting to panic. It was, he knew, entirely irrational, but a terrible premonition was beginning to take hold of him. From just around the corner of his memory.

Chapter Forty-six

Georgy was getting better by the minute, stretched out by the pool all morning, then moving onto the terrace as the sun grew too hot to bear. Sylvia waited on her personally, making her fresh coffee whenever she needed it, bringing her peaches from the orchard with the dew still on them.

"You're spoiling me," said Georgy, stretched out like a cat. "But I'm not complaining."

She was really enjoying this sybaritic existence and her wounds were beginning to heal, even though she still needed painkillers at night. But not too many; memories of Catherine made her cautious. Georgy was determined to beat this thing as far as possible through her own resources. She was nothing if not a fighter, always had been.

She still had nightmares about it but that, she reckoned, was healthy. All she could recall was that hesitant walk down the pitch-dark stairs, holding on to the rope, then the flood of moonlight through the half-open kitchen door, followed by the awareness of someone just behind her and the awful impact. That was always the moment she woke up sweating, but even when it was a waking dream, there was no further light she could throw on it. All she knew was that someone had been hiding behind that door, someone who hated her enough to want to kill her. Not a comforting thought, especially since she hadn't a notion who it might possibly have been.

The joy of her days in this Californian paradise was getting to know her small half-brother, Ariel. He was the most enchanting child she had ever encountered, loads more fun than her sisters, Risa or Lois, had ever been, and she could not get enough of him. He was funny and zany and wise beyond his years, yet surprisingly unspoiled. Sylvia worried he might be sapping too much of Georgy's strength.

"Don't let him be a pest," she said, whenever she found them together, heads bent over the computer or some book, or playing a game of Scrabble which Ariel nearly always won.

"No chance of that," said Georgy placidly. "I'll shove him in the pool if he steps out of line—and don't think I won't, brat!"

She wished she had a camera with her so that she could take some really good pictures before he lost his childish radiance and developed into an adolescent lout. He'd have to come to London, she decided, so she could show him off to her friends. And maybe one day, when he was old enough, he'd get the photography bug too, even join her in the business. Kirsch, Kirsch, and Nugent perhaps; it felt good. And that was when she realized the trauma was slowly beginning to recede, that she was thinking about the future again—looking forward to returning to London and Vivienne's dream.

"I guess I knew it would come to that someday," said Sylvia with a sigh. To her own extreme surprise, she was really enjoying this sojourn with her stepdaughter and knew she was going to miss her when she'd gone. This sun-soaked paradise was all very well but Georgy's returning energy reminded Sylvia of what she had sacrificed for love.

"It's my life," said Georgy. "It's where my work and all my friends are, my home."

For the first time she talked about Gus and Sylvia listened intently, eyes fixed on her delicate stitchwork, giving

Georgy her full attention. Stretched out like this, miles away, Georgy began to see the whole thing in perspective; how hopeless it had been from the start, how ridiculous. How pathetic, really, to have worn her heart on her sleeve so long for a man who could never care for her. Not in any way that really counted.

"He's just the most perfect man I've ever met," she explained, feeling gauche and foolish at betraying so much of her secret longings, yet able for the first time to open up to an older woman, which felt good. This was something else she owed to Beth; learning to trust and share her feelings.

"Why do you think that is?" asked Sylvia.

"Don't really know."

Georgy lay back on her recliner and stared across the pool at the distant orange grove. "I guess maybe I was looking for . . . a father?"

The realization came swiftly and knocked the breath out of her. She turned to stare at her stepmother in shocked horror but Sylvia was smiling gently and nodding her head.

"I know how you feel," she said quietly. "I've been down that road myself."

"Really!" Georgy was astonished. One of the things she admired in Sylvia was her composure, the impression she gave of always being able to cope.

"Why do you suppose it took me so long to settle down? It took a real man, your father, to wake the sleeping princess from her dream. Love at arm's length can be so much . . . tidier. Altogether less threatening, don't you agree?"

She put down her cushion cover and slipped away to make tea, leaving Georgy to ponder this startling revelation.

Vivienne Nugent was waiting for him when he came through Customs. She was easy to spot, standing slightly apart from the rest of the waiting crowd, distinctively elegant in her ice-blue linen suit, set off by a discreet emerald pin. He was surprised to see her, touched too, and pushed his way through the other, slower passengers to grasp her firmly by both hands.

"Good of you to meet me," he said gruffly, taking her by the elbow and steering her skillfully through the crowd to the lift to the car park. He had remembered her as a beauty but had forgotten how chic and classy she was as well. Emmanuel Kirsch had always had an eye for a striking woman and this one definitely fulfilled all his criteria. Though he was not entirely sure if she had a sense of humor.

"It was the least I could do," she explained as they stepped out on the third level and she led the way to her Mercedes coupe. "I want to hear all about Georgy and what I can do to help you while you're here."

Later, over tea at Claridge's, he told her more about his mission. Georgy was finally on the mend, he was pleased to report, so now he could focus all his energy on the next most important issue, tracking down the perpetrator of the terrible crime that had very nearly cost her her life. The police knew of his visit to London but he could tell from their rather guarded responses to his calls and faxes that they did not want him meddling in the case and resented the implication that they were not doing their job effectively. He smiled and squeezed more lemon into his cup.

"They think I should butt out, but what am I to do? For chrissake, I'm a criminal psychologist by profession and this is my daughter's life."

Vivienne sat bolt upright, poised on the edge of the sofa, gazing at him with bright eyes and a willing smile, showing a becoming extent of leg and all the alertness of a well-groomed fox terrier. As Tonto to his Lone Ranger she might seem an unlikely choice, but she'd do. In fact, he was rather looking forward to working with her.

Vivienne was impressed by Emmanuel's methodical mind. He had already done a considerable amount of thinking about the case and produced a yellow legal pad covered with notes in his small, precise handwriting. He handed Vivienne a list of all Georgy's known contacts in London and together they scrutinized and updated it.

"You can forget about Duncan Ross, the vet," she said. "He's away in Australia and, besides, she hardly knew him. Apart from Beth, I'm the one who knows him best, but Georgy didn't meet him till Catherine's funeral, and then only fleetingly."

"That's just my point," said Emmanuel grimly. "If he was at the funeral, he was acquainted with Catherine and there is still the outside chance that the two cases may be connected."

"She worked for him," said Vivienne. "She was his receptionist."

Emmanuel raised one eyebrow and made a note, nodding slowly to himself.

"There you are, you see. Possibly implicated in her death. You can't rule anyone out until you have firm evidence that they are in the clear. How long did she know him?"

"I'm not quite sure, her mother would know. Certainly a year or so, since I've been going there. He was very good to her, particularly at the end. And he still keeps an eye on the mother, which is entirely beyond the call of duty."

"When did he last see Catherine, do you know?"

"Shortly before she died, according to Sally."

Emmanuel nodded again, lips pursed, and made another annotation beside Duncan's name. Vivienne peered at the list and was startled to see her husband's name as well as her own.

"I can understand how I might be a suspect," she said, "but why Oliver? What's he got to do with it?"

"No offense," said Emmanuel, "but this list has to be comprehensive to be at all effective. You could be implicated because you were investing money in Georgy's career—for which, incidentally, I am profoundly grateful—and money is always a potential cause of discord."

"But Oliver? He scarcely knows her and has nothing at all to do with our proposed partnership. I am financially independent of him, I am happy to say."

And she was. She had never really thought about it that way before; it was a pleasing revelation.

"He's still your husband and therefore potentially suspect. Whoever attacked my daughter did it with such savage force, it is more likely to have been a man than a woman." He looked at her with a slightly flirtatious smile. "With all respect, with your delicate wrists I doubt you could wield a weapon with such force."

"Well, that's something," said Vivienne faintly, remembering with sudden apprehension Oliver's unexpected savagery during their last sexual encounter. For a moment she began to wish she had not become involved in this inquiry, then remembered poor Georgy and hardened her resolution. Whatever the outcome, no matter what skeletons might be unearthed, there could be no going back. The sooner it was resolved, the sooner they could stop suspecting each other and get on with their lives. Though it was a truly sobering thought that one of them might be guilty. Vivienne hadn't really faced up to that before, preferring to believe in the casual intruder theory.

"Beth Hardy the police have already dealt with," said Emmanuel, flicking through his pages of notes. "Although she seems to be a suspect—she is the owner of the weapon—I doubt she'd be so stupid as to use her own knife and leave it carelessly at the scene of the crime. And," he went on reading, "her daughter has vouched for her presence at home at the time of the crime. Though, of course, that evidence would not stand up in court.

"Her husband, however, Gus Hardy. He knows Georgy well, I understand, and must therefore still come under suspicion."

It seemed unlikely, though. Vivienne thought of Gus with

his immaculate manners and easy charm and the detached kindness he had always shown to Georgy who could, she knew, at times be a pest. But Karl was a different kettle of fish entirely, all the more so since the police had discovered he had two previous convictions in Germany for aggravated assault. Luckily, he was locked up and out of harm's way for the time being.

"Tell you what," Vivienne said, brightening. "Why don't I make things simpler for you and invite the lot of them to dinner?"

"Would they come?"

"Yes, I rather believe they might. All except Karl, of course, but he's not in a position to go anywhere at present. They all cared about Georgy and were shocked by her attack, and each, presumably, has a stake in clearing things up. Let's give it a try and see what happens."

Vivienne fixed her dinner party for Friday night and rang round to see if she could corral all the names on her list. To her surprise, each one accepted, which was, she felt, a tribute to Georgy, tinged perhaps with curiosity. Even Oliver graciously agreed to stay home for once that night. Lately he'd seemed less busy in the evenings; she did not want to think about why.

"The vet can't make it since he's still away, but the doctor will be there," she reported. "That makes eight in all, with Phoebe, his wife. Beth and Gus, Oliver and me, yourself—oh, and Sally, of course. I thought about including poor Lady Palmer but really don't think she'd want to come. And she cannot possibly be relevant."

"Anyone with a connection to Georgy is relevant," said Emmanuel, studying his notes again. "Who's Sally?"

"Sally Brown." Vivienne was surprised. "Didn't you meet her?"

"Not yet. Where does she fit in?"

"She was one of the group in hospital. Nice girl, a New

Zealander. Does occasional bar work, only passing through. Good friend of Beth."

Emmanuel made a note. "How does she get on with Georgy?"

"All right, I think. Certainly it would seem so whenever we get together. She was marvelous when we did up the studio, wielded her paint roller like a professional. You must talk to her; you'll like her. And she was a brick while Catherine was dying. Always round there, rallying her spirits. Still goes to see the mother, so I understand."

Tonight Vivienne served dinner formally in the dining room and Beth was struck how elegant the room looked by candlelight, set with its full panoply of Georgian silver and monogrammed crystal. *It's me she should be sponsoring,* she thought. *Think of the dinners we could organize in a room like this!* She had braced herself for the confrontation with Oliver but he greeted her with perfect cordiality and did not betray, by so much as a flicker, that she was anything more than a casual acquaintance of his wife. He took the head of the table, as master of the house, while Emmanuel was given the seat of honor at the far end.

All eyes were upon him as he unfolded his linen napkin and glanced around the table. They were an attractive bunch, these friends of his daughter; the handsome, affluent hosts, the smiling cook with her faintly camp husband, who turned out, on closer acquaintance to be a charmer of the first order, and the doctor's wife, a smiling, dark-haired beauty with no connection whatsoever to either of the victims but simply there as an adjunct to her husband. She apologized for that. The doctor himself had rung from the hospital to say he had been delayed but would get there as soon as he could. The eighth chair remained empty.

"Where's Sally?" asked Beth.

Everyone looked at each other.

"I don't know," said Vivienne. "She definitely said she was coming. I assumed she'd turn up with you."

"I haven't spoken to her for several days. I wonder where she is? It's not like her to be rude—or, indeed, late."

"Probably found herself a new boyfriend," said Oliver. From the little he'd seen of her, that one seemed a right little raver. He was disappointed she hadn't turned up; he'd been looking forward to having a closer look at those truly delectable breasts and the faintly lascivious smile with its hint of a promise. Also, he had space in his life these days for a little sexual excitement. He tried hard not to look at Beth and felt his mood beginning to darken.

"Please eat," said Vivienne cordially. "I'm sure she'll be here soon and there's no point in ruining the food."

Emmanuel looked round at the assembled company and raised his crystal goblet in a toast.

"*L'chayim,*" he said. "And destruction to our enemies. Let's hope this is the end of the carnage."

Chapter Forty-seven

Seen close to, the Duomo was even more awesome than she had expected, despite the narrow dark streets leading up to it, filled to bursting on this stifling summer's day with tourists and Florentines going about their business. She stepped out of the tour bus and stood bewildered, gazing about her in the strong Italian sun, unused to so much bustle and life, practically overwhelmed.

"Care for a coffee? I think we have time." The priest from Ohio stood smiling down at her, indicating one of the crowded street cafés nearby, but she shook her head. She had come all these miles to see the cathedral and had no intention of loitering now.

"No thank you, Father. There's still so much to see."

Modesty prevented her from telling him she was hot and craved only the coolness of the vast Renaissance interior, away from the heat of the bus and the proximity of too many chattering companions. Not for the first time, she regretted the thick stockings she was bound by convention to wear but when she stepped through the mighty carved doors and stood beneath Brunelleschi's imposing dome, all mundane thoughts fled and she gloried only in the presence of her God.

The priest from Ohio had found another companion and

she was relieved not to have his hornetlike presence constantly buzzing in her ear. It seemed uncharitable but this was a vacation, one she had dreamed of and saved for over a great many years. As it was, only the charity of her sisters had enabled her to come at all. She was determined to make the most of it and waste no time. She had been correct. It was wonderfully cool in the dark interior and even the tourists no longer troubled her. The Duomo was built to such lavish proportions, the crowds outside dwindled to a mere trickle within.

There was no time to ascend to the dome, and besides she had no head for heights. Instead, once she had admired the relief of *The Assumption of the Madonna* and the various carved monuments that surrounded her, she made her way through the echoing space and stood before the high altar where she murmured a few silent words to her Lord, with her again for the first time in months. Then she crossed the nave and descended a short flight of stone steps to the crypt, to view the Roman remains.

Soft footsteps descended behind her and she hoped it was not her friend from Ohio. Oh well, she supposed it could not be helped. She was at one with her God again, which was all that mattered, really the purpose of the whole trip. Now she could afford to show a little Christian compassion for others.

As she stooped to read the inscription on Brunelleschi's tomb, the blow that caught her across the back of her neck was as light and swift as a caress, severing her spinal cord instantly so that she made no sound. It was a good twenty minutes before an Italian guide found her, crumpled as if in prayer, and summoned the guards.

Chapter Forty-eight

You're all right!" said Duncan, when he finally got through. "Thank God for that."

Beth was puzzled. "Why on earth would I not be?"

"It's crazy, I know, but I do worry about you when I'm not there to keep an eye on you."

Beth smiled. How adorable this man was, to be sure, and how wonderful to hear his voice again, sounding distant and strained but still full of the warmth and passion she was growing so much to rely on. He had been gone too long. She found it hard now to conjure up his face, and that was bad.

"How are things, and when are you coming back?"

"Not yet awhile, I'm afraid. Dad's still not out of danger and in a day or so we'll be getting the results of his tests and will know the worst. The very second I've sorted things out at this end and am sure my mother can cope, I'll be on the next plane home, don't you worry."

Home, he had said. That was encouraging. Beth had feared this sudden return to his roots might unsettle Duncan and set him off on the road again, for she knew he was, at heart, a wanderer. Rather like Sal, now she came to think of it. Maybe it was something to do with the way these Antipodeans were raised.

"Miss you."

"Me too. More than you will ever know."

After he had rung off, Beth went on sitting there in the dark, hugging herself with sheer joy at hearing his voice again, aching with the desire to see him and touch him too. He had been gone far too long; summer was almost through. Friday was the start of the August Bank Holiday weekend, the last three-day break before Christmas, and this year she would be spending it alone. It seemed the whole of London was deserting her, not that she really minded.

Gus was taking Imogen to visit his parents in Jersey. She loved seeing her grandparents and the break would do her good. He'd suggested Beth tag along too but she had declined. No point in giving the old folks false hopes and, besides, she rather relished the luxury of having the house to herself for once.

"Come with us to Cornwall, why don't you?" said Jane. "I know it's not the most exciting place in the world but it's good at this time of year and this weekend it will just be us and the boys, no hordes of visitors and endless entertaining."

Beth was seriously tempted. Jane was her best and longest-standing friend in the world and she loved the wind-blown granite cottage set on a high point overlooking the sea near Polperro. She thought of the walks they could have and the long intimate conversations. But she resisted. All she really wanted these days was Duncan, and until he returned, she couldn't really concentrate. She'd just as soon be alone. She tried to explain this to Jane, who was a good enough friend to understand.

"Just promise you'll ring if you start to go spare," she said. "You'll miss the drive down but we can always pick you up off the train."

"No, really," said Beth. "It's a lovely idea, but I think this time I'd rather stay home and tidy my cupboards."

They left it like that. The great thing about friendship was that she knew she was always free to change her mind.

Duncan sat in his mother's front parlor and tried hard to dispel the feeling of gathering menace that lately seemed to be with him most of the time. What was it that was haunting the back of his brain and wouldn't go away? He tried to be reasonable and figure it out in a rational way. He was normally a man of sound common sense, not given to hysteria or flights of premonition, so why did he have this doom-filled feeling that Beth was in danger while he wasn't there to protect her? *Maybe this is what love is about,* said a voice in his head, but he felt it was more than that.

The window was framed by macramé ropes, each one a different length and supporting an earthenware pot with a spider plant in it, beyond which a sea of grass stretched down to an electrified fence, bordering a vast meadow where sheep were grazing. It was a pleasant enough scene but not inspiring; a few days of undiluted pastoral peace and Duncan was itching to get moving again, back to pollution and life in the fast lane.

Across the room his mother sat in a high-backed chair, studying the local paper. She was a big woman, from whom Duncan had inherited his height, with strong shoulders accustomed to hard work and a square, sensible face from which all traces of youthful prettiness had long since been eroded. Now that her husband was off the critical list and beginning to make progress, some of the lines round her mouth had softened slightly. Duncan glanced at her with affection and wished she could learn to show a little more emotion.

He longed to be able to tell her about Beth but it was altogether too soon. He had also inherited caution from his mother and believed in keeping his feelings to himself until he was absolutely sure of them. He hated the notion, after so many disappointments in her life already, of raising her hopes about his future only to have them dashed again. She would love him to settle down and live what she would consider a more normal life, but she'd never, ever pressure him. He was grateful for that.

Her hair, like his, was thick, wiry, and mole-colored, heavily streaked with a distinguished gray, and the eyes behind the severe pince-nez were a clear, gentian blue like his own. A feeling of love swept over him and he went to stand beside her and read the headlines over her shoulder. She glanced up and smiled, but went on reading.

"Something's troubling you," she said after a while. "Do you want to talk about it, son?"

"There's really not a lot to say." He paced the old-fashioned room, with its framed samplers and crocheted table mats, and wondered if he was finally going off his head. It was the impotence of his situation that was really bugging him. But then he thought, if he couldn't trust his own mother, who else was he going to talk to? Especially in this godforsaken backwater where what was going on in London seemed light-years away. He took the paper gently out of her hands, pulled up another hard chair, and settled down to tell her all about his darkest fears.

Vivienne took the call and was surprised to hear the familiar Australian twang.

"Duncan? Is that really you? Back already?"

He told her he was still on the other side of the world, and then what he wanted her to do. Discreetly, he said, and as soon as possible. Instinct told him they hadn't much time.

"And whatever you do, don't tell Beth," he instructed, before he rang off.

"Why not?" Vivienne was perplexed. Life was getting stranger and more fraught by the minute; just lately she had begun to fear she was losing her grip.

"Just don't. I'll explain next time we meet. My love to the pussies and I hope to see you soon. And tell him he can call me here any time of the day or night. I mean that literally."

That urgent. Vivienne's fear grew.

"It was a strange case," said Addison ruminatively, as he watched the umpire declare the third ball of the second over a wide. It was the second day of the test match and Pakistan had bagged seven English wickets.

"In fact," he said, "one of the strangest I have ever come across. I remember discussing it at the time with my students."

He was wearing a cream lightweight suit with his red and gold MCC tie, and they were sitting in the members' stand at Lords in a pale, tentative August sunshine. They had just finished lunch. Oliver, in blazer and dark gray slacks with a knife-edged crease, his own concession to casual wear, stretched and glanced surreptitiously at his watch. He had urgent bank business he ought to be attending to and should not linger here too long. But it was very enticing on a day like this and he always found Addison good company.

"Go on," he prompted. He was really doing this for Beth, not Vivienne, even though his wife had been the bearer of the message. He could not, for the life of him, understand the urgency but the vet had spelled it out loud and clear and conveyed his alarm to Vivienne.

Addison sighed and stroked a weary hand over his graying hair. Since Catherine's death, he had become a mass of nerves and this latest inquiry seemed too horribly close to be coincidental. But Oliver was waiting; he could not stall him any longer. Perhaps if he answered this one, apparently innocuous, question, he would finally get them off his back.

"There was nothing clinically wrong with her," he said. "She was young, fit, and in the peak of good health, so I was surprised to see her on my initial ward round. She had come in via Casualty, with a cut hand or something like that, and had managed to inveigle the casualty officer into admitting her as an in-patient while she was actually on the premises. Slightly out of order, I know, but sometimes rules are made to be bent and at the beginning of the year the hospital is inclined to be quiet. Also, considering her age, there was really nothing against it, so we went ahead and did it, partly—I confess—in a spirit of experimentation."

"And it was a success?"

"Completely. As far as you can be sure of anything at that stage."

There was a pause while both men concentrated on the bowling. This Pakistani chappie was staggeringly good; England would really have to pull their socks up if they were to avoid another ignominious defeat. A brilliant googly and there went the middle stump. Eight wickets. As a disgruntled Atherton walked off the ground to a smattering of applause, Oliver turned his attention back to the discussion in hand.

"What exactly did you do?" he asked. "I realize it's against the Hippocratic oath and all that but I gather it's fairly vital that you tell me. You can trust me to be discreet, old chap."

Addison paused, weighing up his conscience against his common sense. What the hell; he was in it deep enough already and Oliver was a good bloke and an English gentleman, when all was said and done.

"We reconnected her tubes," he said. "After a sterilization when she was still a child."

"Good God! Is that normal? Why on earth was it done?"

"Not normal at all, that's entirely the point. Never seen it before in my life, as a matter of fact. But she's over the age of consent, mentally sound, and it was what she wanted. So good luck to her. Whether she will be able to conceive in a normal way remains to be seen but she's been discharged so it's out of my hands now."

"But how come it was done at all? Sounds barbaric to me." Knowing how much his own wife longed for a child, it seemed incredible to Oliver that such an operation could be undertaken so lightly. Vivienne would be seriously upset if she ever found out; it seemed such a criminal waste.

"Search me, old boy. That's exactly the question I asked at the time. But I couldn't get hold of any background information. All I know from her medical records is that it was done in a private clinic in Gladesville, which is a suburb of Sydney. We had to get that one referral before we could go ahead but the case is shrouded in secrecy and the clinic refused point-blank to be more specific. As it was, I had to pull some strings and fall back on the Old Boy network without letting the patient know. Sometimes it happens that way, it has to be done. The file was marked Confidential, they said. Odd, don't you think?"

"Indeed." Oliver glanced at his watch again; it was time he was off. He thanked Addison for lunch and the couple of hours of cricket and took his leave. Got to get back to the bank for a four-thirty meeting, but before that there was a call he had to place. To Australia.

The news in Perth was encouraging; Duncan's father was off the danger list and likely to make a full recovery. A pacemaker was called for but these days that was a relatively straightforward procedure. Duncan decided to wait till the minor operation had been successfully performed and then make tracks, long overdue, for London.

In the meantime, he was mesmerized by what Oliver had told him. A sterilization reversed; it made no sense, certainly not for someone of Sally's age. But who would sterilize a child, and for what reason? He was damned well determined to find out more. With Dad on the mend and Mother so much calmer, Duncan had time on his hands and meant to put it to good use. There were certain subjects, even in these enlightened times, that he simply could not discuss with his mother but she had got the gist of his concern and was as curious as he as to the outcome. Gladesville, he now recalled, was not a million miles from

Parramatta, the suburb where Paul, his erstwhile best friend, was now a hospital chaplain.

"I think I'll hop on a plane," Duncan told his mother, "and go look him up for a couple of days."

"You do that," she said, sorting the ironing. "You get along and see your friend and don't you go worrying about your dad and me. You're a good son and you were here when I needed you. Reckon I can manage once he's home from the hospital."

There was something on his mind, she knew; more than he was telling her. Best if he could sort it out while he was still here. Besides, with all this waiting around, he only got under her feet. She smiled as she folded the sheets. He was worse than his dad.

Chapter Forty-nine

Sally never did show up the night of Vivienne's dinner party, but two days later she telephoned to apologize for her absence. It turned out she had dropped by to see how Eleanor Palmer was faring and found the old lady in a very distressed state and a little the worse for drink. By the time Sally had sorted her out, made her a pot of black coffee and persuaded her to drink it, then sat with her until she had calmed down, the dinner had completely slipped her mind. She was truly sorry and hoped she hadn't messed things up too much.

"What was Georgy's old man like?" she wanted to know.

"Absolutely charming," said Vivienne, a touch abrasively. Sally's facile excuses cut little ice with her. *Manners maketh man,* as her old nanny was wont to say; Sally had definitely dropped several points through her casual behavior.

"But you're bound to get a chance to make your own assessment," said Vivienne, "since he is still in town and wants to meet all Georgy's close associates before he leaves."

Vivienne had wanted to tell Emmanuel what Oliver had found out from Addison but Oliver said she had better not. When all was said and done, it would be transgressing medical etiquette and, until they had some reason to believe it was truly germane to the case, it was best to honor Addison's confidence and remain mum. It worried Vivienne but she could see his point. There was no reason to suppose that Sally had anything whatever to do with Georgy's accident, so why drag the poor girl into things unnecessarily? It would only muddy the waters and add to the general complicatedness of things. It was just curious that Duncan was so interested in her medical past.

Father Paul Costello lived in a spacious flat in the top half of an old converted house overlooking the water in Parramatta. To reach it, you had to walk up a wide staircase made of ornately carved oak, with ecclesiastical stained-glass windows even though the house was not actually built on sanctified ground.

"It's just like living in a church," said Duncan in delight, dropping his flight bag on the floor and looking around in appreciation. Except that, at this level, the rooms were wide and airy, with white canvas blinds rolled up to reveal a stunning outlook of sunlight striking on the choppy surface of the river. The two men embraced then Duncan perched himself on the windowsill while Paul, in his shirtsleeves, rummaged in the fridge for a couple of beers.

One of the great things about friendship, Duncan reflected, was that you could jump straight back into it even after a distance of something like fifteen years. Paul's hair had receded and he had thickened round the waist but it was already clear that he was, in essence, still the same exuberant guy Duncan had hung around with in the bars of Perth when they had so much growing up still to do and their mark to make on the world.

"So how's it going, cobber?" asked the priest, handing him a chilled can of Foster's and flipping the lid of his own.

"Not so bad. How's yourself? Ever make it to London these days?"

"No chance. Church funds wouldn't rise to it."

Duncan laughed. "It might sound irreverent but I still can't get my head around you being a priest."

Paul smiled, a trifle awkwardly. "It's just one of those things that happens in life. Blame my Auntie Alice, she always said I'd come to no good. Let's face it, I could have swung either way—drink and the devil or this—but as it happened, God won. Hasn't changed me, I think you'll find. Not where it counts."

"Are you happy?"

"As Larry. And you?"

"Can't complain."

That established, they spent some time catching up on old times, old friends, old places, and then Duncan washed up and changed his shirt and the padre took him out for a Thai meal.

"Do us a favor, old sport," said Duncan later, over more cold beers in a waterside bar. "There's something I need to find out and you're the only person I know in this place with the sort of connections that might open doors."

"You mean God?"

"I mean Establishment."

"Go ahead, shoot."

It wasn't an easy one to explain, especially to a man of the cloth and one he hadn't spoken to for a decade and a half, but Duncan did his best. And found, to his delight, that he had a ready listener with an alert mind and a sympathetic ear.

"It's not really any of my business," Duncan confessed. "I just feel I have to find out the truth before something else catastrophic happens."

Paul cocked an ear, ever alert where something more than altruism was involved. He listened to Duncan's story, then sat very still and stroked his chin while he reflected.

"Let me get this straight," he said eventually. "What you are looking for is a private clinic in Gladesville, where, some fifteen years ago—while you and I were still bumming around in Perth—an operation, perhaps illicit, was carried out on an underage girl?"

Duncan nodded.

"And you really believe that, even if we can find it, they'll be willing to let you look at their confidential records? Records they wouldn't even disclose to a distinguished London gynecologist at a major hospital? You, a Pommie vet from the other side of the world and, as far as I can make out, with no direct connection whatsoever to the patient?"

Put like that it did sound a trifle ludicrous. Ruefully, Duncan nodded—only to reel back in surprise when his spiritual friend burst into a cackle of merriment and punched him matily in the biceps.

"Knock that back," he said briskly, "and follow me."

"Where are we going?" asked Duncan, grabbing his jacket.

"On a family visit. To see my Auntie Alice, where else?"

Emmanuel was getting nowhere and beginning to admit defeat, though he really hated to do so. He had studied the cast of characters Vivienne had drummed up for the dinner party but had come to no firm conclusions about any of them, except for a renewed conviction that Beth was innocent. She was far too straightforward and up-front to have done it, not to mention too smart to risk leaving the weapon around for the police to find. And what possibly could be her motive? She seemed genuinely fond of Georgy and anxious for her welfare, which was why she was so keen to give the police the fullest possible cooperation.

The police had suggested jealousy as a possible motive, since Georgy was so caught up with chasing the ex-husband, but that, to Georgy's father, was patently absurd. It was clear that any residual affection between the Hardys, who certainly made a handsome couple, had more of a sibling quality these days and was in no way sexual. Besides, he had also picked up on the vibes between Beth and the smarmy husband of Emmanuel's new friend, Vivienne. He was pretty certain something was going on there, even though Vivienne appeared entirely oblivious to it. He was sorry about that; he liked Beth's openness and apparent honesty and was surprised she would indulge in anything underhanded. He would have preferred to be able to think better of her, but that was Emmanuel's professional specialization—the unpredictability of people.

The number one suspect, as far as the police were concerned, continued to be Karl, Gus Hardy's former lover, but Emmanuel was not convinced. He had not had a chance to meet the German yet, as the police had him back in custody but his personality profile did not match up to the likely perpetrator of such a savage crime. He might be hostile and uncommunicative, packed tight with anger and a frightening pent-up aggression, but that did not automatically make him a murderer, even though the police had unearthed a history of thuggery back home in Berlin, before he emigrated to New York.

He might well be the victim of jealousy, for it was not impossible that he held Georgy responsible for the bust-up of his relationship with Gus, and it was also possible that he might have tried frightening her in order to scare her off. But Emmanuel was pretty certain he would not go so far as to hurt her, certainly not in any premeditated or studiedly vicious way. Push her downstairs, maybe, or even into the path of an express train, but cold-blooded butchery like the attack on Georgy was the work of a different type of warped mind, something far more sinister. Only a psychopath could have acted like that, leaving apparently no trace. And on that particular subject Emmanuel Kirsch was an expert.

It was ten o'clock and the cypress trees surrounding the stone doorway were densely black and seemed to be crowding inward. Duncan recalled his boyhood nervousness of the dark and waited for an owl to add to the ghostly feeling.

"Where are we going?" he whispered, as if he were still ten years old, but Paul merely wagged a finger at him and told him to wait and see.

The door itself was made of heavy, weathered oak, studded and bolted in black cast iron, and the bellpull was right out of a Hammer Horror movie, setting off an antique jangling from somewhere deep within. Duncan was intrigued and beginning to enjoy this; trust his old mate Paul to show him an unusual time. There was a sudden click and a pale face appeared at a grill beside the door which Duncan had not noticed, and waited wordlessly for Paul to explain his business. But speech turned out not to be necessary. Paul simply made the sign of the cross, the grill was sharply closed, and they heard the sound of bolts being withdrawn on the other side of the door.

"Enter," said Paul cheerfully, leading the way, and Duncan stepped into the dimly lit hallway with a vaulted ceiling and white walls on which were hung some of the most exquisite examples of High Renaissance art he had seen outside a national gallery. Behind him, he heard the jarring sound of the bolts being slid back into place.

"Pardon the theatricals," hissed Paul, in a loud whisper, "but several years ago there was a spot of bother here, since when they have acted as if they were a cover-up for Fort Knox."

"What sort of bother?"

"I'll tell you later."

The ghostly presence who had admitted them stood holding the door and Duncan realized, with a start, that it was not the janitor he had expected but a little old lady clad from head to foot in gray, with a white wimpled headdress concealing all but her small face. A nun.

"Welcome to the Convent of the Holy Child," said Paul.

Sister Annunciata listened to Duncan's request with patient

thoughtfulness and Duncan was rocketed backward to childhood when, as Paul's Auntie Alice, she had so often swatted his backside for bad behavior.

"I know it's a tall order," he ended lamely, "and forgive me for trespassing on your time like this. It's just that I have this intuition that all is not as it should be, and Paul thought you might be able to help."

She stared into space, ignoring him, her plump fingers fiddling with her rosary beads, then suddenly the far from ascetic face broke into a familiar broad grin and she leaned across and touched his hand.

"Leave it with me, mate," she said with a wink just like Paul's. "This is far too intriguing not to follow up."

Deirdre was taking her family to the Isle of Wight for the holidays, though not exactly looking forward to it.

"It's bound to rain," she said gloomily, tying her apron around her ample waist and preparing to cut up the bread for the quails eggs en croutade.

"Nonsense," said Beth briskly, poaching tiny eggs and leaving each one to drain. "The sun always shines in that part of the country, I had holidays there as a kid. I remember it as being like *Monsieur Hulot's Holiday*, all sandy beaches and Punch and Judy shows, with sandy shoes and shrimping nets left in the hall to dry."

"And gruesome boardinghouse meals—ham salad with Heinz salad cream and sliced white bread, and one egg each for breakfast," grunted Deirdre. "And out of your rooms by ten so the maid can tidy up and nothing to do with the kids on a wet afternoon."

Beth laughed. Deirdre's pessimism never failed to cheer her.

"Try looking on the bright side," she said comfortingly, "there's probably a fossil museum or something elevating like that. And there's bound to be bingo, if not a cinema. And just think of all the knitting you'll be able to do."

Listening to Deirdre—day in, day out—a person might

think she did not have a happy home life but actually the opposite was true. Deirdre was very content with her equable draftsman husband, Jack, and adored her four noisy children. She just liked to put it about that life was all a bit too much for her. Beth was well inured to her moanings; she made an excellent sideshow where Beth's friends were concerned.

"The day Deirdre actually gets a kick out of something," said Beth, "I shall know things are seriously wrong."

August was a good month for Deirdre to take her annual holiday since business was always at its slowest then, and the occasional booking that did come up Beth was perfectly capable of handling on her own.

"I can always rope in Sally if needs be," she said, since Deirdre also liked to worry about leaving Beth to cope.

Now she came to think of it, Sally would probably welcome some work, since she was nearly always broke. Summer was the season to start bottling and preserving for winter, while everything was at its lushest and business was slow. They could have a lot of fun together, trawling the street markets and generally stocking up. Sally was always brilliant company, prepared to pitch in and help, but Beth was determined she should only do so this time on a proper business footing. She did not approve of using people, not even old Sal who was virtually one of the family.

She made a note to talk to her about it next time they spoke.

Chapter Fifty

The Mother Superior came straight to the point. Father Costello and Sister Annunciata had done their work well and when Duncan finally came face-to-face with her in her stark, businesslike office, she knew exactly why he was there.

"Your request, Mr. Ross, is a most unusual one," she said, "and under normal circumstances I would not be empowered to help you."

Far from the sumptuous surroundings of Sister Annunciata's closed order, St. Margaret's, Gladesville, had more the demeanor of a prison, which in many ways, of course, it was.

"However," she continued, "Father Costello has convinced me, so, subject to the usual constrictions of absolute discretion, I have the file you are asking for here for you to view."

From the woven leather girdle round her waist, she selected a key, unlocked her desk drawer, and extracted a plain green file marked "Strictly Confidential," which she laid out on the mahogany desk in front of him.

"And now I must go and attend to Vespers. You have exactly one hour in which to examine it."

As she rose and glided across the room, Duncan stood to

attention and almost felt he should bow. She was a severe-looking woman but humane; that was reflected in the calm, wise eyes beneath her starched white wimple. He really appreciated this concession and was determined not to betray her trust unless it should turn out to be crucial, literally a matter of life and death.

Sally O'Leary was just sixteen when she made her first break for freedom. Week after week she had stood at the convent window, gazing down into the courtyard, watching the other girls greet their families and friends and be whisked away at weekends for special events and quality visiting time. But never Sally. No one at all came to visit her these days, other than sanctimonious welfare workers and the occasional psychiatric busybody, asking eternal questions, forever attempting to probe into her mind. It was years since her father had bothered to make the trip into the city, while the rest of the world appeared to have abandoned her completely.

It was early October and the fine spring sunshine filtered between the bars on the window, bringing with it the scent of rising sap, reminding her that life was out there for the tasting and rapidly passing her by. That particular weekend she was on kitchen duty and it was the work of only minutes to throw together a handful of things she might need, stow them, wrapped in a plastic bin liner, at the bottom of one of the vast aluminum garbage containers, then carry the whole thing out to the dustcart and climb aboard. It proved that easy. Maybe they thought nuns and their charges lacked sophistication or, more likely, they had simply lost interest. But by late afternoon, Sally found herself, beneath a mountain of sour-smelling vegetable waste and other things far worse, rumbling across the courtyard, out through the iron gates, and into the world outside.

In fifteen minutes she was free, dodging like the kid she still was through the back streets of Sydney, looking for a public lavatory where she could wash and comb some of the stinking refuse out of her hair and swap her telltale convent uniform for the jeans and T-shirt she had had the foresight to bring along with her.

She had no money but that did not deter her. Just walking the streets like a regular person, inhaling the freshness of the air, looking in shop windows, and generally hanging out, filled her with such excitement, she hadn't a thought about how on earth she was going to survive. Something was bound to turn up, something always did. Caution, however, told her to get the hell out of Gladesville as fast as possible before they noticed her absence and the balloon went up. The first truck she hailed, full of sheep crammed into wooden pens, stopped for her and the taciturn driver, asking no questions, carried her as far as Wagga Wagga, where she told him her uncle lived. Then she was on her own again but no longer in a hurry.

Just being away from those harsh stone walls was enough for Sally. She was hungry and tired but full of optimism. Her whole life lay in front of her and no one was ever going to stand in her way again. She had made that clear enough to her family even though she had had to pay the price for it. Let the rest of the world take notice and watch out.

They were sailors on leave, headed for Adelaide, and they spotted her hanging about in the bus station as they hauled down their kitbags and prepared to look for cheap accommodation for the night.

"Take a look at that sheila," said Jerry, pointing.

"Looks lost to me," said Barney. "Let's go get her."

She was bright and extremely pretty and told them she was on her way to Adelaide too, to take up a waitressing job, so they said she could tag along. While Sally sat guarding the kitbags, the boys found a room in a run-down hotel and smuggled her in while the desk clerk had his back turned. They had money for beer and cigarettes and they bought her a hamburger and showed her the sights of

Wagga Wagga, such as they were, before turning in in the early hours, by which time Sally was pretty near dead on her feet.

The three of them shared a bed that night and Sally did not get much sleep but certainly earned her keep, to the delight of the sailors. The sheets were stained and the bed full of bugs and the noise from the streets never abated all night, but to convent-bred Sally it seemed as luxurious as the Ritz. When they left in the morning they took her with them, rewarding her with a bus ticket all the way through to the end of the line.

Jerry was short, stocky, and heavily tattooed but Barney was the one Sally fancied. He was thin and willowy with smoky, romantic eyes and hair cut in a Frank Sinatra sleeked-back style. They had been at sea for months and were lusty and oversexed but Sally gave as good as she got and astounded them both with her sexual inventiveness.

"I don't believe you're a convent girl."

"No kidding."

"How long you been there?"

"All my life."

"So where did you learn to fuck like this?"

"Just naturally talented, I guess."

"How old are you?"

"Twenty-one."

But she was sixteen. And when they got off the bus in Adelaide and found the cops waiting, Jerry and Barney were instantly arrested while Sally was taken straight back to the convent, to be locked in solitary confinement while the nuns discussed what to do for the best.

The Mother Superior glided back into the room just as he was reading the bit about the clinic. Gladesville Clinic, privately owned, run by the nuns for the serious young offenders under their care. Duncan was aghast.

"I can't believe they did that to her," he said, stricken.

She stood, a column of righteousness, in the corner of the

room, tall and imposing, a jeweled ivory cross on a chain round her neck.

"It was the only way," she said. "She was young, she was promiscuous, she was beyond control. We are not talking about a normal child, you understand, but a deranged animal without a modicum of sense or conscience. She was growing up and there was no telling what she might get up to next; we couldn't afford to take the risk. She was, after all, under our care. Think of the scandal had there been issue from her misdemeanor."

"She was a child. How could her parents allow such a thing?"

"She had no parents," said the Mother Superior with finality, holding out her hand for the file and making it clear that all favors were now at an end.

But Duncan was still reading. One further detail had caught his eye, leaping up at him off the page, almost too incredible to take in. He stopped and read it again. Among the documents relating to the patient, Sally O'Leary, and her brief hospitalization was a statement taken at the time of the operation and witnessed by the medical staff in attendance. There on the page, in the clear spidery writing he recognized so well, was the signature "Catherine Palmer."

He glanced again at the date on the file. October 1979, fifteen years ago, the time straight after Catherine's breakdown, when she ran away to Australia to forget. But how could it be that in all those months—from their first meeting in St. Anthony's in January to Catherine's death in May—neither Catherine nor Sally had ever mentioned that they had encountered each other before? And what weird act of providence had contrived to throw them together again fifteen years and half a world away? There were more questions now unanswered than there had been before but the Mother Superior was coughing discreetly and looking at her tiny fob watch.

Emmanuel had to go. Something had come up in

California, a court hearing he could not afford to miss, so he said reluctant farewells in London but promised he would be back.

"Just as long as this case remains open," he told the police, "I shall be breathing down your necks. Don't ever forget that."

"I'm gonna miss you," he said to Vivienne on the way to the airport. "Even in these particularly harrowing circumstances, I have to admit I've rather enjoyed these past few weeks, thanks entirely to you."

For all her upper-class mannerisms, she was, he had discovered, one gutsy lady, shamefully neglected by that shmuck of a husband. There was a time when Emmanuel might have been tempted to stray but these days, he reminded himself, he was faithful to his wife. But Vivienne had proved a delightful and helpful companion; they'd certainly stay in touch, especially since he was sure she was going to make things work for Georgy.

The police had made minimal inroads into the case and looked like they were losing their enthusiasm as the weeks ticked by. They had managed to locate Josh Hunter eventually and he had assured them there were only two house keys in Georgy's possession, one of which she still had on her keyring. The other, the spare, had lived on a nail on the cork board in the kitchen but was now missing.

"That's one hell of a stupid place to hide a key," grumbled Emmanuel, but the damage was done and at least it proved that the intruder must have been in the house before and known it was there. Not that that got them very much further in this particular maze.

Vivienne was going to miss Emmanuel, too. He was the sort of man she found most stimulating, worldly and mature and appreciative of all she had to offer. A total contrast to her absentee husband.

"Is Georgy ever likely to return to London, do you think?" she asked wistfully. She hesitated to come between father and daughter but the need was there and she was learning to recognize it. He laughed and patted her knee.

"What do *you* think? You know my daughter," he said. "Can you seriously see anyone stopping her once she's up and about again? I'd buy her her own studio in Los Angeles if I thought she'd take it, and give her all the help she needed to set it up, but that's not what Georgy's all about, whatever she may think. She's truly her own person, even though she may think she's hard done by. She's determined to make a go of this photography racket and I reckon I will. I hate to think of her back here with that lunatic still at large, but I know I can trust you to take care of her for me."

Which he most certainly could. Tears swam into Vivienne's eyes at his generosity and she rapidly blinked them away as she felt her dreams come flooding back. They would announce the partnership as planned and as soon as Georgy returned and felt up to it, they'd throw a huge launch party. Beth could do the catering. As soon as she'd seen Emmanuel off at the airport, Vivienne was going straight back home to set the wheels turning. By the time Georgy did make it back to London, she would find she was already on the way to being famous.

The World Wide Fund for Nature were delighted to hear from Vivienne and suggested she come to visit them in Switzerland straight away. Oliver had agreed she could make a regular donation to their funds but, more to the point, they were interested in her publicity ideas and the photographs Georgy had taken of her cats. With skills like that, this was only the beginning. Already there were plans brewing for worldwide advertising campaigns with a powerful, controversial thrust, and there was a strong chance she and Georgy could get involved right now, at the planning stage. And at the same time, Phoebe reported that Cancer Research were equally impressed. She had done a great job in selling Georgy to them as an idea but it was her own talent that would consolidate the deal. This could well be the double breakthrough most creative people wait whole lifetimes to achieve.

Vivienne rang to say good-bye to Beth before she boarded the plane to Geneva. She sounded forceful and energetic, happier than she had done in ages, and she confessed she hadn't had a drink for two weeks. Beth was pleased. She was growing cautiously fond of Vivienne and wanted things to work out for her, at the very least to compensate for that dreadful marriage.

Not that she still felt any guilt. Apart from that one time, the dinner in honor of Georgy's father, she had had no contact at all with Oliver, even though he still bombarded her with calls. These days, every waking moment was fully occupied with dreams of Duncan. She guessed from things Viv said that Oliver was probably playing away again, but it was no longer any concern of hers.

"I shall be all alone in London next week," Beth told her. "Deirdre's on holiday, Jane's in the country, even Imogen's off on a spree with her dad. Thank goodness I'll still have Sally to keep me company. Where on earth would I be if it wasn't for her?"

Chapter Fifty-one

My goodness," said Duncan's mother in wonder, "how that does take me back, to be sure. How well I remember that story, it was blazoned all over our papers for months on end, the most shocking case that had hit this part of the world, I reckon, probably since the convicts first turned up in Botany Bay."

Dad was home from the hospital at last, putting his feet up in the parlor, and Duncan and his mother were sitting under the trees, enjoying the end of another perfect early spring day. Soon, very soon, he'd be able to leave. He longed only for London and Beth.

"So how come I don't remember it?"

"It must have been about the time you left on the hippy trail. That was it. The summer of seventy-nine, just after you passed your finals and set off on the road. Though I'm surprised you didn't hear about it, even so."

"They're not so hot on that sort of thing in Kathmandu. But go on."

"Sally O'Leary—yes, that was her name. I remember her as if it were only yesterday. Pretty little thing she was, bewitchingly so. Just think of it. Younger even than Maud next door's granddaughter. Very nearly got away with it too."

She paused, remembering, her fine eyes creased in horror.

"Funny," said Duncan, "I always thought she was a New Zealander. That's what she's told us. Though I have to admit, her accent was never quite right."

"Not a bit of it. Came from Wagga Wagga, she did, where her father was a farmer."

He remembered the time he had challenged her, the day he met her at Eleanor Palmer's flat. She must have flatly lied to him; now he was beginning to understand why. He ought to have smelled a rat way back then; well, in a way he had, but had dismissed it. That was one of the things lurking around the edges of his memory, just out of sight. He wondered what other lies she had told.

"And then she hit the headlines again, when she escaped from the remand home where they were holding her. Slipped out one day and hitchhiked across Australia with a bunch of randy sailors, partying all the way. It was all over the papers, as you might imagine, there were even questions raised in parliament about safety in prisons and high-risk prisoners. What exactly happened to her? You're not telling me she's out again? A thoroughly bad lot she was. Ought to have been destroyed, if you want my opinion, before she could do any more damage."

"Mum!" said Duncan in surprise. It was not like his calm, rocklike mother to show such emotion or so reactionary an opinion.

"Come on, Mum," he went on in exasperation as she sat in silence, ruminating on the remembered story. "Spit it out. Tell me what exactly she did, don't keep me hanging on."

She was as bad as the nuns and clearly enjoying herself, driving him mad with exasperation. She was no fool, his mother, but it was good to see she had regained her sense of humor. He grinned. They were all the same, women. His longing for Beth grew more urgent by the minute.

"If you want the full gory details, son, you go on down to the newspaper library and look it up for yourself. It was some years ago now and I'd likely get the details wrong. Don't want to risk spoiling it for you, do I?"

She laughed and closed her eyes for a moment or two, relishing the feel of sunshine on her weathered skin and the new peace in her heart now that she knew her man was safe.

It had taken him a lot of deliberation, but Sam had reached a momentous decision and tonight was to be the night. He couldn't wait to get home. It was another two hours before the markets closed but his mind was no longer on his work as he made his calls and placed his orders, all the time thinking of opalescent eyes and skin as delectable as a ripened peach.

He was terribly scared of rejection but dared not risk delaying things any longer for fear he might lose her altogether. It seemed impossible but this weekend was August Bank Holiday again, a whole year since that magical night when she'd first climbed into his bed. The others thought he was daft, he knew it, but that did not deter him. There were other men in Sally's life—he wasn't a fool and had few illusions about her—but as far as he was aware there was no serious competition. Even that black fellow seemed to have vanished since she walked out on her job in the pub.

Dave was returning to Wellington in just a few weeks, while Jeremy was practically engaged; if Sam didn't act soon he might miss his moment altogether and then the whole ménage would break up and go their separate ways. As it was, Sally was liable to walk at any minute. She was unpredictable and had never pretended to be more than just passing through. Then he would certainly lose her forever, whereas now he felt he was still in there with a chance. Timing was the crucial thing, or so his mother always told him.

He noticed Sally had been restless of late, working shifts at McDonald's but not enjoying it, staying home at nights in order to save money, which was absolutely not her style, and talking vaguely about moving on to Florence or Rome or even Athens for the winter.

He couldn't get away till almost seven so that it was a quarter to eight by the time he emerged from the Tube and set off up the Earls Court Road toward home and his Big Decision. He stopped off at the off-license for a bottle of champagne, then went back and made it two in case the others came home and it turned out there was something to celebrate. The holiday exodus was already well under way and the traffic was unusually thin. It was amazing the way the Brits liked to skive, especially in light of their falling pound and generally shaky economy, but Sam liked it here and had developed quite a fondness for the Old Country, for all its faults.

If she accepted him, he wondered if she would agree to them staying here, at least for a year or two until they decided to put down permanent roots and start a family. He knew Sally wanted babies—girls not boys she always said, though she never explained why—so they ought not leave it too long, since she was already over thirty. She'd make a wonderful mum, would Sal, and he couldn't wait to take her home and show her off to the family.

It was really odd that after all his travels, he should end up falling for another Kiwi, as far away from home as he could possibly be. Fate, that was what it must be. Up till now he hadn't believed in all that astrology tosh but there was no denying the facts. Wait till he saw his father's face when he brought home this little beauty!

He crossed the Cromwell Road and walked on up past the church. The evening was golden but with the faintest nip of autumn already in the air. The time felt right for new beginnings; the future beckoned. The house looked shabby and already half-deserted as he climbed the steps and turned his key in the lock. Time to move on in more senses than one; whatever happened, he was through with communal living.

A small house in Chiswick, to begin with, might be nice, or even a flat in the Barbican.

"Hi there, anyone home?"

The downstairs was deserted; all the doors had been left wide open so he could see right through. There were plates in the sink, crumbs on the table, and someone had left the milk out to curdle. That would be Sally; she was a regular slut in the kitchen. Sam put it back in the fridge, along with his champagne, and went on up to his room to change, his heart still pumping with pent-up adrenaline.

Jeremy's door was tight shut, with no sound issuing from within, while Dave's was open and showed signs of a rapid departure. That was right, Sam remembered. He was spending the weekend in Edinburgh with friends and not planning to be back till Tuesday. For once Sally's door was closed, so Sam left her undisturbed while he took a quick shower and shave.

"Sal? Are you in there?"

There was total silence. He tapped again.

"Sal?"

He strained to hear the sounds of occupation but there was nothing. Maybe she was napping. He tried the handle and the door swung open.

The room was empty, emptier than he had ever seen it before. The bed had been stripped and the blankets removed so that only the pillows, in their dingy striped ticking, remained on the bed. The door to the wardrobe hung open and so did all the drawers of the tallboy. Empty, the lot of them. Even her clock and radio had gone from the bedside table, and only a dying avocado plant remained to remind him that the room had once been occupied. That and the Maxwell House tin which was crammed full of used tissues and dirty cotton wool.

Sam was stunned. He raced downstairs to the kitchen, hoping she'd left a note, but of course there was nothing. The fridge, now he came to look properly, was empty too, stripped of most of the things he had bought last night, in his big Sainsbury's stock-up for the long weekend.

She had gone. There was no doubt about it. He glanced round the living room door, still searching for a note or something, to be confronted by a gaping blank where the television once stood. It was also the end of the month, he realized, and she owed them a quarter's rent.

Duncan was waiting on the doorstep of *The West Australian* first thing next morning, his authorization to use their library in his hand. Another old school friend, Barry, had done the honors. One thing about returning to your roots, it was a hell of a lot easier to pull favors on the old pals' network.

He quickly located the appropriate file and settled down to read. And there it all was, spread sickeningly across the front pages—headline after headline screaming the details of the child murderer who had escaped, only to be recaptured by the police after a weekend's rampage involving a pair of sailors. And there, indeed, was Sally Brown, sixteen years old but still recognizable in her stark convent uniform with the honeyed hair cut short and severe. He drew a sharp breath. Until this moment it hadn't seemed possible, but here was irrefutable evidence. He had been right to have qualms; even in handcuffs, surrounded by mean-faced cops, the expression was the same, the seraphic smile with the fuck-you look in the eyes he recognized only too well.

Richard Brooke rang as Beth was unpacking the groceries. Early-evening sunlight slanted across the kitchen table and Bruch's violin concerto was playing on the stereo. Beth wore a long T-shirt over leggings and wonderful thonged sandals she had picked up for a song last year in Tuscany. She felt terrific. It was the start of a holiday weekend and, for once in her life, she had nothing in the world to hurry for.

"Hi, sweetie, how's it going?" she said, sorting chickpeas

and sun-dried tomatoes and coconut milk ready for stacking on the appropriate shelves. Organized, was Beth, at least where her cooking was concerned. She nibbled at a piece of Brie and debated whether the phone wire would stretch as far as the fridge, so that she could pour herself a drink while she gossiped.

"I'm off to the south of France," he told her.

"For how long?"

"Forever. It was your idea."

"Hang on while I get myself a drink," she said. "I certainly need it after that!"

It was all her fault, he told her, for putting the idea into his head in the first place, and now everything was fixed. The studio was sold, along with most of his paintings, and he was off to Perpignan at the crack of dawn to become a tax exile and live a rural life.

"Perpignan's not exactly away from it all," protested Beth, her heart sinking at the prospect of no longer having him within easy reach.

"Come with me!" he said, as he'd said before, and she knew he really meant it.

"Sweetie, I'd love to but I've other things to do," she replied, sipping her wine. Richard was charming and talented and kind but his treacle-colored eyes were not the eyes she yearned for.

"You beast," she said, "fancy leaving without a proper good-bye. I would have given you a party or, at the very least, a farewell dinner."

"I know you would," he laughed. "That's why I didn't tell you. You're altogether too generous, lady, and I insist you spend whole summers with me once I'm settled, so that I can repay some of your hospitality."

She would, she said, and wished him loads of luck.

"Be sure to ring," she said, "as soon as you're connected so that we can keep up the gossip."

Imagine, Beth thought to herself, as she went on stashing the food, *that's the last of my inner circle left town for this long weekend. Apart, of course, from Sally. And I wonder what's happened to her.*

Duncan still sat at the library table, his head in his hands, unable to believe what he had just been reading. All the papers carried details of the notorious jailbreak, and the unrepentant young sinner who had raved her way across half a continent before being caught and returned to the nuns to finish her sentence. What they did not reveal was the severity of her punishment, details of which were concealed in the file locked in the drawer of the Mother Superior. To some extent he could see her point; the girl was a reprobate and entirely beyond control. But such an act seemed excessive, even for a murderer, and a serial one at that.

The crime itself, the part his mother had flatly refused to discuss, was also here in all its lurid details. It preceded the escape by six years and covered acres of newsprint. Duncan was sickened but quite unable to stop; on and on he read in fascinated horror when all the time he should have been scrambling for a phone.

This was the story he read: a ten-year-old girl, Sally O'Leary, had murdered her two young brothers on the family farm outside Wagga Wagga by sticking them ritually to death in an outhouse where her father had earlier been slaughtering pigs. She had then calmly returned home, in the middle of the afternoon, while her father and his men were tractoring a distant field, and murdered her mother too. She had hit her over the head with a brick tied up in a stocking, then finished her off, as she lay wounded on the floor, by tipping a cauldron of scalding jam over her. She was still there in the kitchen, laughing and calmly eating a piece of bread and jam, just as if nothing had happened, when a neighbor dropped by.

Duncan felt totally nauseated and had to go outside for a while to walk in the courtyard in the fresh morning air until the faint dizziness had passed. Could this be their Sally, this monstrous child? It seemed beyond belief but the photographs were there to prove it. Small wonder she had changed her name, even though by now she had served her sentence and was legitimately free.

There was more. She was underage but still went on trial, the family lawyers putting up a defense of unfitness to plead due to insanity. But the town officials, appalled by the crime and the bad publicity it engendered, had done something unprecedented and hired themselves the best criminal psychologist they could find to come in and examine the patient. They had done it, it transpired, with the full consent of her shattered father.

He was expensive, he was American, but he had done an excellent job. After weeks of intensive interviews and tests he had come to a terrible conclusion, based on his years of expertise in the field of criminal pathology. There was no question of insanity or of her mind being temporarily unbalanced. There was no evidence she was anything but sane. She was guilty, he said, of the most heinous crimes he had ever encountered and, furthermore, she showed not an ounce of remorse. It had taken the judge and jury only a few hours to agree on a unanimous verdict.

"Guilty!" they had thundered, and Sally O'Leary had been sent down for the longest period on record for a child.

"The most savage crime I have ever encountered," the criminal psychologist was quoted as saying after the trial. "Just once in a hundred years a child is born that is pure evil; perfectly sane but without conscience or soul. Sally O'Leary is just such a one and ought rightly to be destroyed before she can do further harm."

There he stood, outside the courthouse, surrounded by reporters and cameramen, holding in his arms his own small daughter for the sake of the world's press. Emmanuel Kirsch, handsomer then even than now, with hair raven black—and Georgy, cute as a button in a red pixie hood trimmed with white fur, just five years old.

"My God," said Duncan, coming at last to his senses. "I have to warn Beth!"

Chapter Fifty-two

Philomena Jenkins, glistening with goodwill and with a smile as wide as her hips, progressed along All Saints Road at the stately rate of three conversations for each ten houses, slapping palms, calling out greetings, letting the world know she was finally returned from Bridgetown, having successfully birthed her latest grandchild, her eighth.

"Yo there, Philomena," they greeted her, with smiles as wide as hers. "You back then?"

"You be sure of that," she beamed, gold tooth flashing. "Another fine boychild for my Josephine, an' now she can raise it alone, along with the rest."

"So you didn't linger for the fine hot winter?"

"You'm crazy, man. I be back for Caan-ival. Can't have Caan-ival without Philomena. Wouldn't be proper, now."

And cackling with pure happiness she continued to patrol her route, her janitor's keys jangling from the rope she used as a makeshift belt, comfortable straw sandals flipflopping from her feet. Three months she'd been gone and not even the company of all those children and their own children had stopped her pining just a little. For Philomena was happy to turn her back on the sunshine and golden sand of the island of her birth to return to the rain-soaked streets of London, the London she now called her own.

She stopped outside a gaunt house with peeling paint and selected a key as she slowly mounted the steps.

"Lawdy me," she breathed as she stepped into the musty, rubbish-strewn hallway and inhaled the familiar scents of faded pee and stale cat. "Can't leave them to cope alone for a minute," she muttered, clumping heavily up the stairs toward the first of her tenants' flats.

The stench on the first landing was considerably stronger, exuding from the floor above where that nice young drummer had lived for two years and never given her an ounce of trouble. Off on the road, they had told her; touring Ireland with a reggae band and probably left his fridge full and unplugged, in that switched-off way creative people had. Philomena shook her head as she sorted through her keys. She was well used to cleaning up around her boys; after the number of children she had raised it was purely second nature.

Joe's door unlocked with one turn of the key, which was odd considering how highly he valued his drum kit. She pushed open the door and went inside, squinting into the dimness because a bedspread had been pinned across the window, cutting out most of the light. At first she thought the room was empty. There were glasses on the table and a full ashtray, and a strong sweetness on the air as if he had lately been burning joss sticks.

Then she saw the mass on the mattress which she took at first for a tangle of old clothes but which slowly assumed the form of a man, lying—arms flung wide—staring sightlessly at the ceiling. Philomena sighed as she stared down into the gasping face of her favorite streetboy. With his eyes rolled back, displaying the whites, he looked as though he were grinning.

Until she saw that beneath the buzzing dark mass, his throat had been skillfully slashed from ear to ear.

Chapter Fifty-three

The Carnival, of course. She had quite forgotten. The muffled beat of distant drums that greeted Beth's ears as she stood at her open window was simply the sound of all those West Indian neighbors warming up for the biggest steel band event of the year. For once it looked like they were getting the weather for it, too. It was nine o'clock but the sun was already high and the sky a wonderful Wedgwood blue with not a hint of a cloud in sight.

Beth unlocked the kitchen door which led into the garden and propped it open with a brick to let the warm air circulate. Then she made herself a pot of coffee, picking up the newspapers from the mat, and carried them into the living room to indulge herself in a solitary breakfast. Though she lived in a constant frenzy, surrounded by other people, being alone was still a private luxury, a rare and exquisite pleasure to be savored slowly. Two more empty days stretched ahead of her, with nothing whatever to hurry for, no commitments of any kind except to pamper herself a little and unwind.

She stretched out her suntanned feet and noticed the varnish was chipped. She would finish her breakfast, have a laze in the tub, then make that batch of crabapple jelly and get it out of the way. After that, and a midmorning Bloody

Mary in the garden, she would fix a light lunch and watch the omnibus edition of *EastEnders*. Then she'd have a nap, give herself a thorough pedicure, and perhaps stroll up the road and join in the Carnival festivities for a while. Delicious. This was life as she loved to live it—occasionally. Beth's greatest privilege was that she was never lonely; indeed not often enough alone. She knew she was lucky. Weekends alone through necessity must be a different matter entirely.

She had gone a bit wild in the market yesterday and bought up all the crabapples they had, but she loved the consistency of the clear, sparkling jelly and could always give away any jars she did not need; they made useful and attractive Christmas presents. She poured the apples into two huge plastic mixing bowls, put a Barbara Cook CD on the hi-fi, and set to work to pick them over while a cauldron of water heated slowly on the Aga. This was the sort of mindless labor she found therapeutic, normally undertaken by Deirdre.

She smiled as she thought of Deirdre and her squabbling kids on the Isle of Wight; at least they were getting a bit of fine weather, which meant they would not be cooped up inside. Imogen too. Jersey at this time of year was always great and Gus the best possible company anyone, young or old, could ask for. It was odd not to have the child around for once, constantly asking questions and getting in her way, but something she would have to get used to as Imogen grew older and headed more into a life of her own. As it was, she had borrowed one of her mother's silk shirts and Beth had even caught her rooting around in her tights drawer, about to filch a pair of her best ten deniers.

"You won't need tights in Jersey, certainly not in this weather."

"Mu-um." The eternal cry.

"Well, at least take something a bit more substantial. Those fine ones won't last you a second, the way you go through them."

They had compromised on Lycra with a satin finish and Imogen left, well pleased. Kids. She'd certainly miss her when she finally flew the nest.

If only Duncan were here, what paradise it would be to have him all to herself for once. She smiled as she thought about him and, right on cue, Barbara Cook swung into "I'm in the Mood for Love." She wondered when he'd be back, whether he'd think to call her over the holiday weekend if he knew she were here alone—she couldn't remember what she had told him. Outside, the reggae music was growing louder, with the urgent beat she always found so stirring, and soon the decorated floats would be on the move. She must get down there in time to see them properly this year.

The telephone rang. It was Sally, the first time she had checked in for several days.

"Sweetie!" said Beth in delight. "Where *are* you? I've been so worried, you seemed to have dropped off the face of the earth."

Sally explained she had been moving house. It was a sudden decision, as usual done on the spur of the moment, but she'd save the details until they met. No, she wasn't doing a thing this weekend, now that she'd sorted herself out more or less, and yes, lunch was a great idea.

Terrific, thought Beth, speeding up the fruit-picking process. Sally was exactly the extra something she needed to spice up the weekend. They could have a salad in the garden, then mosey on over to the Carnival together, which would be far more fun than doing it alone. *How my resolutions crumble,* she thought. But that was the joy of the single life, flexibility, and Sally was, after all, one of her dearest friends.

Duncan got through at last, to his infinite relief. Connections from Western Australia were not always as instant as they might be and there had been some trouble on the line which had kept him trying on and off for several hours. It was ten o'clock at night in Perth, which meant noon in London. She was bound to be home on a

Sunday morning and, in a way, the delay was good since he didn't want to scare her unduly. Just alert her to be on her guard.

Beth was overjoyed to hear his voice and ran to turn down the volume of the music. The fruit and cloves were simmering gently and could be left alone for a while, certainly as long as she chatted to Duncan.

He began carefully, protective of her feelings, and told her first the good news about his father: that the pacemaker had gone in safely, which meant he would soon be making tracks for home.

"That's wonderful!" cried Beth, a touch teary at the sheer relief of hearing his voice. "I just can't wait, it's been so long."

"I know."

He could picture her there in her kitchen, probably with something simmering on the stove, brown and healthy and reliable, so infinitely dear. He ached to be there with her, to hold her in his arms and breathe the fragrance of her healthy skin. After that, he meant to make sure they were never, ever apart again; he had wasted too much time as it was. But he still had other things to tell her; it was time he got to the point.

"Beth," he said slowly, "listen to me. There is something you need to know but I don't want to rattle you unduly."

"Oh dear, that does sound serious," said Beth gaily. And then, distinctly, he heard her doorbell ring.

"Hang on, that's the door. It's only Sal. Wait while I let her in."

Sally stood on the doormat in her familiar garb of check shirt and jeans, her arms full of lilies which she handed to Beth with a radiant smile. They kissed.

"Lovie, how marvelous! It's great to see you. Quick follow me through. Duncan's on the line and he's about to tell me something terribly important."

She sprinted on bare feet back into the kitchen but when

she picked up the dangling receiver, she found they were no longer connected.

"You just caught me."

Oliver was literally out of the door, suitbag in hand, when he heard the phone and went back in to answer it. With Vivienne gone for the whole three days, he was taking advantage of her absence for a little unscheduled dallying with his latest inamorata in Henley. Duncan sounded tense and urgent so he cut the cackle and listened. It only took a couple of minutes and Oliver was set to go.

"Leave it to me, old boy," he said, relishing a drama. "And give me a number where I can call you back."

It couldn't possibly be as dangerous as Duncan was suggesting but he'd check it out anyhow. The vet seemed a sane enough fellow, even if he was overendowed with whatever it took to pull all these birds, and it surely wasn't like him to panic. Oliver could easily detour to Ladbroke Grove on his way to the motorway and still be in Henley in time for lunch. Besides, it gave him the perfect excuse to look Beth up again, which could only be a bonus. Oliver had got over his rage at being dumped but still burned with a residual craving for her. Whistling with pleasant anticipation, he locked up the house and backed the Mercedes out of the driveway. It shouldn't take much more than ten minutes to reach Beth's house on a Sunday. With luck, she'd invite him in for a drink.

Beth peered at the crabapple jelly, which seemed to be thickening nicely. Soon she could strain it and then it would be safe to leave it for an hour so they could take their drinks out into the garden. In the meantime, she wanted to hang on in here in the hope that Duncan would call back.

"I don't know what happened," she said, moving to the sink to wash the stickiness off her fingers. "He was about to tell me something frightfully urgent and then the phone went dead."

"Did he hang up?"

"Shouldn't think so. Why would he? No, they've been having electric storms over there which are probably affecting the lines. Never mind."

She wiped her hands on a cloth and turned with a bright smile to welcome Sally properly, but the cast-iron pan caught her squarely on the forehead and felled her with one blow.

Wright's Lane and Campden Hill were a cinch, scarcely any traffic at all, and even the lights were in Oliver's favor as, Wagner blaring on the stereo, he streaked toward Ladbroke Grove. Only when he hit Holland Park Avenue did everything come to a halt and he found himself in a queue of traffic, moving at snail's pace and apparently going nowhere. *What the hell?* He flicked across to Capital Radio and caught the middle of the traffic news.

The Notting Hill Carnival, of course; only one of the major calendar events of the year, stupid of him to forget. With the Valkyrie no longer obliterating extraneous sounds, Oliver became aware of the surrounding reggae beat from a hundred ghetto-blasters turned to full volume, rising all around him like a vast swarm of locusts about to wage war. He groaned. He glanced at the carphone, wondering whether he ought to call Duncan, but decided that was daft. What could Duncan do but worry, and there'd doubtless be a break in the traffic soon. If necessary, he could always walk the last bit but he was wearing a new pair of hand-stitched suede shoes and didn't entirely relish facing that hill in this heat.

You're getting soft, my boy—but it wasn't really a joke. He was certain the vet was overreacting but he'd given his word and wasn't about to let him down; it was now a question of honor. He'd wait another ten minutes or so and then, if it still didn't clear, he'd think again. Ought he to call Beth? He was about to dial her number when good sense prevailed. The sole reason Duncan had involved him in the first place was because of the ill-timed arrival of Sally before he'd had a chance to warn her. Rather than risk alerting Beth and forcing her into a potentially dangerous confrontation, he'd rung off and phoned Oliver instead. What Beth didn't know wouldn't worry her. But it was vital Oliver get there in time to protect her against God knows what.

Oliver didn't know much detail, there simply hadn't been time, but the little he had heard had stunned him. Sally Brown, with her sexy body and pleasing smile, was apparently a psychopath, a convicted murderer who had already killed at least four times—almost certainly more than that—and was capable of doing so again without hesitation once she found her cover had been blown. It seemed incredible but Duncan had assured him the evidence was irrefutable.

Furthermore, she'd been alone with Catherine the night she died and could easily have got to Georgy's house ahead of her and lain in wait, having filched the spare key from the kitchen on an earlier visit. After all, Sally's trademark was that she was everyone's friend, and in both cases it turned out she had also had strong motivation.

Catherine had witnessed the sterilization in Sydney, though Sally was not to know the poor soul had been practically off the wall at the time, distracted by her own personal problems, and had very probably blanked out the whole episode. While Georgy had been fleetingly at the courthouse when Sally was sentenced—but, again, what do you remember when you are only five years old?

But Sally was obviously not one to risk taking chances. She had killed endless times already; another murder or two meant nothing to a certified psychopath. And now she knew that Duncan knew and was likely to warn Beth, so Beth was her next obvious target.

Oliver was suddenly glad that Vivienne was safe in Switzerland; he surprised himself with a warm rush of tenderness for the wife he so badly neglected. But saving Beth was what mattered right now. She might be in actual physical danger while he sat here muttering to himself and wasting valuable seconds. The traffic was beginning to move again, but only slowly, so he abandoned the car at the bottom of Ladbroke Grove and sprinted up the hill.

There was music playing and the windows were all open, while the aroma of something delicate and sweet wafted out on the breeze. A typically tranquil Sunday morning in Beth's quiet enclave. Nostalgia filled Oliver as he slowed down at the wicket gate and wondered whether it had perhaps all been a false alarm. He was going to look one hell of a fool if he rang the bell and found them having lunch. But having come this far he couldn't see a way round it. Instead of going to the front door in the usual way, he walked cautiously round to the side gate, which he knew was never locked, glad of the expensive suede shoes which were as soft and silent as moccasins, and let himself into the garden.

The kitchen door stood open and Barbara Cook was jazzing up "Sweet Georgia Brown." One of Beth's favorite CDs, music to cook by; his too. A feeling of relaxed well-being swept over him at the prospect of seeing her again, with luck alone, with Sally already gone. Maybe this wasn't such a crazy mission after all. He straightened his tie and stepped into the kitchen without knocking.

Sally sat at the table, an open bottle of wine in front of her and her feet, in dirty scuffed sneakers, planted comfortably on the rail of the Aga. Her denim jacket hung like a dead thing from a hook near the fridge. There was no sign of Beth.

"Hi, Oliver," said Sally with pleasure, almost as though she'd been expecting him. "Have you come for lunch?"

She was eating a piece of bread and licking something sticky off her hand.

"It's great stuff," she said, following his gaze. "Not quite set yet but almost there. I sneaked some while Beth's back was turned."

"Where is Beth?" he said suspiciously, looking round.

"Over there," said Sally placidly, nodding toward the Welsh dresser which was partially eclipsed by the table.

And then he saw Beth's feet, sticking out from behind the table, shoeless and frighteningly still. For a second he very nearly blew it as he searched for what next to say, but luckily his public school training came to his support and he managed not to act too precipitately. Oliver was used to thinking on his feet; it was one of the main requisites of his job.

"Drink?" asked Sally, unperturbed, indicating the almost full bottle and inviting him to join her at the table. For the first time he really noticed how inscrutable her eyes were; clear and shallow and totally without feeling.

"Terrific," he said with fake heartiness, at the same time aware of the grim array of professional chef's knives, right at her elbow where she could easily grab one. "Just what I need on a morning like this."

She stretched backward to reach the dresser without getting up, in order to grab him a glass, and he stared at the contours of her generous breasts, outlined beneath the thin cotton of her T-shirt. The T-shirt was even skimpier than usual and rode up to reveal her flat, tanned belly. God, but she was delectable; on any other occasion . . . To his alarmed amazement, Oliver felt a stirring in his groin.

And then he knew exactly what he had to do.

Chapter Fifty-four

Bottoms up!" said Oliver, leaning forward to clink her glass, all the time managing to edge his chair a little closer. Beth's feet had not moved at all; he tried hard not to look at them.

"If I may say so, young lady," he said, loosening his tie, "you are looking particularly fetching this morning in that getup."

Sally, feet now firmly on the ground, gazed back at him speculatively, the clear, emotionless eyes betraying nothing. She swirled the wine around in her glass and licked a few drops from her upper lip with a languorous tongue. Her skin, without a trace of makeup, cried out to be touched. For months Oliver had harbored lascivious thoughts about her; now was hardly the time to be doing something about it but he knew he had no choice. When he glanced down he saw she had kicked off her shoes, which he took as an encouraging sign.

"Mind if I remove my jacket? It's a trifle warm in here," he said. This wasn't his usual style but it had to be done; for all he knew, Beth's life might depend upon it. As it was, he was anguished to be playing out this macabre charade while she lay there on the floor, possibly dying or even dead, but Duncan had impressed on him just how dangerous Sally was and until he could move her out of range of those deadly knives, it was a game he was going to have to follow through. In response, Sally leaned across and silently undid the top two buttons of his shirt, all the while holding his gaze with that strange half-smile he had always found so arousing.

He gulped his wine, reminding himself that he needed to keep a clear head, at the same time anxious not to raise her suspicions. *Softly, softly* . . . He leaned across still farther and kissed her squarely on the mouth, feeling her lips part willingly and her tongue caress his own. She reached inside his open shirt and slid her hand caressingly over his chest. He put down his glass and pulled her urgently onto his lap. He kissed her again, feeling like a traitor and hoping Beth couldn't see.

"Let's go somewhere more comfortable," he murmured into her honeyed hair. Silently Sally took him by the hand and led him out of the kitchen, ignoring Beth's inert body, still lying motionless on the floor. Oliver sneaked a look at her and saw that her eyes were closed and her face was deathly pale, with a great angry swelling on one temple. More than anything he wanted to drop to his knees and cradle that beloved head in his arms, but he resisted. With a supreme effort of will, he averted his eyes and followed Sally from the room.

She was heading toward the sitting room with its voluminous sofa but Oliver needed to get her as far from Beth as possible.

"No," he said, halting her. "Let's go upstairs. On a day like this, why hurry? We've all the time in the world. I've waited this long to get you into the sack, might as well do it in style. But first, let me see to Beth. She looks quite dreadful; I must check that she's all right."

"She'll keep," said Sally, with her strange, luminous smile. "She's not going anywhere, at least for the time being."

"What exactly happened?" Oliver's mouth was so dry he

could scarcely get the words out but it was vital not to betray to this crazy person that he was anything less than cool.

"Oh, she got in the way of a saucepan," said Sally, nonchalantly. "She's not about to disturb us, if that's what's on your mind. I hit her as hard as I could. She'll probably be out for hours."

"So why not finish her off while you were at it?" Thin ice, but he needed to assess the measure of warpedness of this creature's mind.

"Are you crazy?" She turned to look at him, her fine fair eyebrows raised in disbelief. "And miss the best part of all? The whole damned point of it?"

"You've lost me."

She looked at him with scorn.

"The kid," she said. "I'm waiting for the kid to get home. She's already got everything else I ever wanted, smug bitch. Before she dies I need to see her suffer. That's only fair, don't you think, after all I've had to go through? They took away my childhood, now I'm going to do the same for Imogen."

Absolutely loony. Sally smiled at Oliver seraphically, looking so wholesome he could eat her. But this was not the moment to be challenging her. If it weren't for Beth, lying there so helpless, he might try rushing her now, but as it was, the risk was too great. Even though Oliver had done his bit as a soldier years ago, this killer was a professional. He'd heard what she'd done to Georgy and wasn't about to take any chances. He might have greater strength but he couldn't be sure he'd win if he tried to take her now, not sure enough to risk Beth's life. Strategy was what was needed and that took time. Precious time while Beth's life could be slipping away.

Sally ran her sinuous tongue along her succulent upper lip and smiled that beguiling smile which never quite reached her eyes.

"Hang on," she said, slipping past him back to the

kitchen. He willed himself not to follow, tried to look casual—just a slightly pissed, randy man hoping for a quick lay—feeling the sweat gathering on his back and a pulse beating wildly in his neck. A moment's silence, then he heard the gentle thud as she closed the fridge door and she was back, beaming, bearing another bottle in one hand with both their glasses and, for some reason, her denim jacket.

"No sense in stinting ourselves," she said practically, leading the way up to Beth's bedroom.

By the time he had stepped out of his pants, she was naked and spread out on the familiar brass bedstead, legs wide open, inviting him in. Now it really was macabre, a parody of everything he had shared with Beth. Her eyes never left his face as he undid his cuff links and finished the buttons on his shirt, all the while praying for power to perform, scared of what might happen if the horror of the situation robbed him of his usual prowess.

He need not have worried. Her breasts were even more delectable uncovered and he sank his face between them, covering her skin with kisses and kneading his fingers into their silken softness with an ecstasy he tried hard not to feel. Danger made it all that much more piquant. She writhed beneath him and when he moved his fingers to her vulva, he found she was already wet.

Before he went any further, he really needed another drink. This was not a scene he had ever played before and he doubted he could do it absolutely sober. She had left the bottle on the table, on the far side of the bed, and he reached across to grab it, vaguely wondering if it would serve as a weapon. Which was when he spotted the bone handle, stuck down the side of the mattress, close by her hand; Beth's expensive sushi knife, the deadliest of the collection. No wonder she had gone back for her jacket; all the time she had been one jump ahead.

Crafty little bitch. He longed to smack her across the face and finish her off now, yet reason still told him to hold back.

He wasn't out of danger yet; one false move and they'd both be for it. He and Beth reduced to tabloid headlines—just another *crime passionel* between an adulterous man and his faithless mistress—while Sally once again walked free. Downstairs the telephone began to ring but Oliver had more pressing matters on his mind.

"Yes, yes, yes," she whispered urgently, writhing beneath his weight as Oliver kissed her deeply as if he could bite off her tongue and swallow it, driving his knee between her legs in a savage parody of rape. She liked that, he could tell. Her breath came in short, excited gasps and he was aware of the agitated knocking of her heart. So that was her game; that was what she was after. He twisted one nipple roughly between his fingers and felt the involuntary intake of breath as he hurt her and gained control.

"You like that, don't you, you sick little bitch!" he muttered roughly, grabbing her pubic hair in his hand and twisting it hard until she squealed.

"Tell me!" he ordered, almost shouting now. "Tell me you like it and what you want me to do to you."

He bit hard into her breast and jerked once more at her pubic hair. Then, moving his hand to the hair on her head, he swung her roughly from side to side, like a terrier with a rat, and slapped her sharply on either cheek. She screamed.

"I like it! I like it!"

"And what do you want me to do to you?"

"Fuck me, fuck me. Dear God, FUCK ME!"

They could probably hear her in the street by now; just as well the Carnival was in full swing. Oliver kept his eye on that deadly knife, waiting for the right moment to grab it, scared that in their writhings, as his own strength ebbed, she would finally get the upper hand and win. It was like the mating dance of a black widow spider who destroys the male after he has serviced her.

"You know what I'm going to do to you next?" he whispered. Sally's breasts were now a mass of purple bruises and his own shoulders and upper arms had not gone unscarred. Downstairs nothing stirred and his fear for Beth had reached nightmare proportions, but this was a battle he dared not quit, not while there was still strength in her.

"Mm," said Sally dreamily, from beneath her tangle of hair. She lay on her front, with her arms above her head. If he pounced now he could probably overpower her but he needed to be more certain if he was going to save Beth.

He put his lips closer to her ear. "I'm going to beat you," he hissed, feeling a shiver of anticipation run right through her. "And then I'm going to fuck you senseless. But first I'm going to tie you up."

The drawer in which Beth kept her tights was slightly ajar so he edged himself toward it, anxious not to alert her, and selected at random two strong pairs, sufficient to secure her wrists. Running his tongue down the curve of her spine and patting her on the bottom to keep her in the mood, he bound each wrist to the bars of the bedstead while she just lay there and let him, without the ghost of a struggle.

Only then, when he had examined the knots and was certain she could not break free, did he slowly exhale his pent-up breath and head for the door.

"I've just got to go and splash my boots," he said. "And then, my dear, watch out!"

Beth's eyes were closed and the lump on her forehead was now the size of a golf ball and fast turning purple, while the rest of her face remained chalk white, drained of all life. Oliver dropped to his knees beside her and felt frantically for a pulse. He placed his ear close to her mouth to see if she was breathing, then contemplated giving her mouth-to-mouth. He sat on his haunches and gazed at her, the woman who had lit up his life for more than two years, and the thought that he might lose her altogether almost made him crazy. Although the day was warm, the breeze through the open door made the kitchen quite cool so he lifted her gently from the tiles where she was lying and carried her carefully across to the sofa, even though he knew he was probably wrong to move her. He looked around for something to wrap her in and found Imogen's old afghan draped over the edge of the log basket. That would have to do while he called the emergency services and summoned the police and an ambulance to rush her to hospital.

"Beth," he muttered urgently, bending over her inert form, begging her to respond.

"Beth, my darling, please wake up."

He smoothed back her hair, matted with congealed blood from a deep cut caused by the rim of the saucepan, and gently felt the pulse at her throat, fluttering feebly like a baby bird trying hard to survive.

"Beth, my precious. Please don't die. I love you so much!"

He bent to kiss her marble forehead, his eyes full of tears, his throat blocked with a terrible grief—then felt the sudden touch of cold steel in the small of his back.

"Very moving," said Sally, directly behind him, and he turned to confront a naked Venus, smiling broadly and armed with two knives—the deadly sushi knife, with which she was now prodding him, and the smaller, neater vegetable knife she had used to slash through her bindings while he was downstairs, attending to Beth.

"Elementary, my dear Oliver," she said with her radiant smile. "A lady always goes prepared, only you, poor sucker, are far too thick to have thought of that."

Chapter Fifty-five

Comfortable?" asked Sally solicitously as she rummaged in the fridge for another bottle.

Oliver lay spread-eagled on the kitchen table, wrists and ankles tightly bound by neatly severed pairs of tights. He could raise his head just far enough to see Sally's pert backside, still butt-naked, as she moved about in front of him. Beth, behind him, was out of his range of vision entirely. Sally closed the fridge door and moved to the dresser; Oliver heard the pop of a cork. With a bit of luck, she'd get sloshed and pass out but somehow he couldn't quite see that happening. Sally had a strong head and he had never seen her even slightly out of control.

"Drink, Oliver?" She was close beside him now and pouring white wine, in a steady stream, onto his face, making him splutter and choke slightly as he moved his head to avoid it. Sally laughed.

"Had enough, have you? That's often the way with you big macho men."

She stepped up onto a kitchen chair and from there onto the table, to straddle him with her long legs wide apart, grinning down, still swigging wine from the bottle. She certainly had a spectacular body; even in circumstances like this, he could not avoid noticing that.

"Like a bit of rough, do you, Oliver?" The smile he had once found so alluring was daunting now in its purity, teeth white and gleaming, lips soft as petals; the face of an ingenue, an innocent.

"Here, take a closer look." She was standing right over him now, her vagina directly in his line of gaze, and she lowered herself slowly onto her haunches so that he could have licked it had he been in the mood.

"Nice bit of pussy do you, sir?" she mocked, then straightened up again and stood swaying above him, bottle still to her lips, squinting down at him as she drank. Outside the urgent throbbing of the music grew insistently louder, until it was almost deafening; one of the decorated floats must have stopped nearby, steel bands going at full blast. Sally moved her hips to the rhythm in the parody of a go-go dancer, and the solid pine table on which Oliver was pinned vibrated with her movements and the solid beat from the street.

"Kinky, are you?" she persisted. "Or is it just that you like hurting women? Typical Englishman, if you ask me."

She was mocking him and there was not a thing he could do about it. Damn her to hell, she'd been playing him for a sucker all the time. She tossed the bottle across the room and he heard it smash as it hit the floor. Then she stooped to the chair and came up holding the knife again, waving it in time to the music as she continued her macabre dance.

Oliver felt himself sweating. The knots at his wrists and ankles were so tight they were restricting his circulation and no matter how hard he jerked at them, he knew they were not going to budge. This little madam had got him fair and square exactly where she wanted him; he shut his mind to what might happen next and hoped he would have the courage not to disgrace himself when the time came.

She knelt now, her bare knees on either side of his rib cage, her damp, excited vulva pressing down on his scrotum. Her breasts swung above his face as she leaned to lick the wine off his nose and, despite his terror, he felt a reciprocal stirring in his groin. She felt it too.

"Oh there *is* still life in the old dog, is there, Oliver?" This time the seraphic smile did reach her eyes; she was laughing at him. "So let's see what you can do, man."

She sank down onto him in a rocking motion but he knew there was no way he was going to get it up. Not now, not like this. She really had to be crazy if she thought there was even a hope in hell that he could.

Sally moved back so that she could inspect his genitals and slowly caressed his limp penis with the point of the sushi knife.

"You never did have much in the balls department, did you, Oliver?" she said softly, running the point over them now in a circular movement. "Else you'd have long ago dumped that dried-up prune of a wife and gone to where you were already getting it regularly." She jerked her head backward, indicating Beth.

She tickled him again with the cold steel.

"So you're not going to miss them now, are you, old boy?"

The telephone rang and Oliver nearly expired with shock; but at least it served to distract her attention. On and on it rang while Sally squatted there, listening.

"Maybe that's the kid at last," she said hopefully. "Ringing to tell Mama that she's on the way."

She beamed at him, now with genuine pleasure.

"That'll be great, won't it, Oliver? We can both have a go at her in turn, you and me. Do you like fucking schoolgirls, I'll bet you do. Or is rape more your thing?"

He'd got to keep her talking. He swallowed several times, to ease his dry mouth, trying not to show his fear.

"It was probably Duncan," he said. "He knows you're here and that I am too. It was he who alerted me in the first place."

The smile disappeared; for the first time ever he saw her

cross. Her face contorted with hatred and she spat viciously in his face.

"*That's* what I think of Duncan Ross! What a useless bag of shit he turned out to be. All mouth and no trousers, probably a fag. Got something going with him, have you, Oliver? Two pretty boys together? We all know about you English public schoolboys, and he's obviously no better. Why else would he call you from Australia?"

The smile was back but only on her mouth. A thin thread of saliva appeared and dribbled unnoticed down her chin. She moved the point of the knife to his chest and ran it lightly down his breastbone, like someone contemplating carving a turkey. Oliver tensed every muscle and tried to control his trembling.

"Duncan Ross," she muttered inwardly, obviously nursing a grudge. And then she cut him. A straight, hard, no-messing slash the length of his chest from beneath one nipple. It hurt like crazy but he managed not to groan; just lay there and gritted his teeth as he felt the blood beginning to gush.

"Like that, did you, Oliver?" she asked, idly drawing pictures on his skin with his blood, signing her initials—a sprawling SB. "Well, there's more of that to come when you're ready. That's one thing I can promise you."

Sally was stiff, so she got down from the table and paced the kitchen, relishing the breeze from the open door on her skin. Beth was still out of it completely on the sofa, while Oliver seemed to have given up all fight and just lay there, pinioned, bleeding steadily.

Duncan Ross. She still couldn't get him out of her heart, the one man in the world she had ever really wanted but who had spurned her. She glanced across at Beth, eyes closed, face chalk white, still scarcely breathing, and her fury grew.

"What on earth does he see in an old hag like her?" she asked. "Long past her sell-by date? She's practically middle-aged and never much of a looker. What's her secret? You tell me, Oliver. What does Beth have that I don't, eh?"

He was sinking slowly but the viciousness in her voice brought him round. He took a deep breath and gambled for his life. If it worked and it distracted her anger to him, that was all he could ask for.

"She's great in the sack, that's what," he said, and waited for the worst. Sally stopped pacing and pondered this.

"But he doesn't know about me," she said, in the hurt voice of a little girl. "I gave him the chance but he wasn't even interested."

"Then he's a fool," said Oliver, hope filtering back. "Any man worth his oats would choose you. Just give me the chance."

"You're kidding."

"I'm not. Untie me and let me show you. I've fancied you rotten since the day I first saw you."

There was silence. She was out of his range of vision now and the pacing had stopped. He held his breath. Even the reggae music was growing fainter as the afternoon slumbered on, and still help did not arrive. Nor would it. Since all Beth's inner circle were out of town and only Duncan, thousands of miles away, had any intimation of what was going on, and what on earth could he do? He had sent Oliver in to rescue Beth and now look what had happened; he had royally fucked up.

Sally resumed her pacing, muttering now under her breath as if she had forgotten he was there.

"That two-faced cow, that utter bitch," she was saying, "acts like a friend, then steals my bloke. She promised me the man of my dreams, said she was my Fairy Godmother, and I believed her. Then he shows up and what does she do. Miss Goody Two Shoes over there? Swipes him from under my nose, that's what, she who's already got everything else I ever wanted. Well, she won't get away with it, not this time. I'm going to teach her a lesson she won't forget and then I'm going to fix him. I'll teach him to spit in my eye.

Once I've finished with her and the kid, he'll be sorry he ever met her."

She laughed.

"But first, my dear Oliver," she said politely, returning to stand beside him, "you and I have a little unfinished business."

Sally wiped the knife carefully on a tea towel and flexed it over Oliver's face like a fencing foil. She was streaked with his blood like a Bantu warrior but her eyes were clear and brilliant and her smile as luminous as ever. All signs of her gibbering madness had receded; she was as enticing as she ever had been.

Oliver closed his eyes in panic and wondered what she had in store for him now.

"I've often sat here and watched Beth use this knife," she said. "Cuts clean as a whistle, like a wire through butter. You won't feel a thing, I promise you."

She cradled his penis tenderly in one hand and stroked his balls.

"I mean, old chap, with Beth dead what use will you have for this?" she asked quite reasonably—then winced grotesquely and dropped the knife, clutching her chest and staggering across the room as blood cascaded from an eruption in her shoulder. The steak knife had found its target.

"Nice shot, what?" said Beth amiably, as she bent to untie him. "I always knew the Nottingham ladies' darts team would one day stand me in good stead. Old boy."

And then she burst into tears.

Chapter Fifty-six

How exactly *did* you work it out?" asked Beth, as she lay with her head cushioned comfortably in Duncan's lap, still on the sofa in order to conserve her strength.

"It was things that were said and not said," said Duncan, carefully cradling his teacup as he stroked her hair, still trying to fit together the last few pieces. "By her and by the rest of you. You all met in the gynecological ward where all of you were having surgery, yet she was the only one who did not divulge why she was there. Point One. You had fibroids, Viv had a hysterectomy, Georgy was a burst appendix, Catherine an ovarian cyst. All straightforward and aboveboard and all, except in the case of poor Catherine, a total success. So why the mystery? You were the one who picked up on that and it set me thinking."

He took a long sip of lemon tea and focused his mind.

"Then she mentioned a baby in the future from time to time. Almost as if it were a new possibility, something put freshly into her mind. Yet she is thirty-one and has no permanent relationship. Point Two. If she'd been having what the rest of you had, the odds were her chances of conceiving would be lessened, so why—all of a sudden—this interest in babies and conception? Particularly in one so patently unmaternal. Point Three."

He bent to kiss her, careful to avoid the swelling.

"Lastly, there was the thing about her accent. She said she was a New Zealander but she was lying. As she must have lied about so many things. I ought to have picked up on it more than I did but it isn't that easy to tell, even to a native of those parts."

"Why did she lie about that, I wonder? What difference could it make?"

"Just another red herring to keep us off the track. Also, remember that psychopaths are compulsive liars. There are probably loads of other things she told you that just aren't true."

"You clever boy!"

"It wasn't really as clever as all that. If I hadn't had all that time loafing around in Australia, I probably would never have discovered it. Especially not without the help of my mum, who's a smart old bird."

He kissed her again, tightening his grip with passion, but the telephone rang and Imogen came to interrupt.

"It's Vivienne," she said. "Do you want me to take a message?"

Beth snapped her fingers for the phone. The party, said Vivienne, would be on the following Saturday, to welcome Georgy and her parents and to celebrate lots of things, most particularly the closing of the case. She was fresh back from Switzerland, full of excitement, and longing to tell them all about the triumphant success of her trip. Everyone was invited, even Eleanor, and this time around they would definitely make it a party to remember.

On this occasion, Sylvia had come to London too and Georgy glowed with pride as she walked with her two distinguished parents into Vivienne's house, and introduced them to her friends. It was a warm September evening and they were using the conservatory, with access to the garden. Sylvia gazed round with instant appreciation and, watching her, Vivienne knew she had found another friend.

"Care to see the rest of the house?" she asked, already knowing the answer, and the two women slipped away for a wallow in colors and styles and details of interior design. Emmanuel watched them go, and smiled. In his later years it gave him a warm glow when the women he admired were no longer at each other's throats, but learning to co-exist so they could all be friends. Even Myra had lately come up trumps, something he would never have believed possible if he had not been there to witness it for himself. She had deliberately taken a backseat so that Georgy could enjoy her convalescence and return to her friends in London with her father and stepmother at her side. Myra's own time would come later; Georgy was committed to returning to New York for Christmas. Until then she was willing to wait.

Now they were all grouping around him, keen to hear more details of the crime. Yes, he told them, of course he remembered Sally Brown. Except that in those days she went under her real name of O'Leary. How could he ever forget her, the single most dangerous child killer he had ever had the privilege to assess and help bring to justice.

"She hadn't a morsel of remorse or regret," he told them. "Totally without conscience. Your textbook psychopath."

"So why did she change her name?"

"It was her mother's name, Brown. She took it with the home's approval when she finally completed her sentence and they let her go. After all, she'd been in their custody for thirteen years; the least they could do was help to re-constitute her by making it as easy as possible for her to cover her tracks and start again. They also changed her ID number and her Society Security details. Which is how she was able to vanish without a trace."

"What about the rest of her family, her father?" asked one of them.

"Dead. He never really recovered from the original massacre, the loss of his wife, whom he totally adored, and his two small sons, Alec and Ben. He tried to come to terms with Sally's crime but could never forgive her. In the end, he just gave up."

"What happened?" asked Duncan, still fascinated. "He can't have been that old a man."

"Tractor accident," said Emmanuel, checking his notes. He had expected a reception like this and had taken the time to do his homework. They were a decent bunch, his daughter's new friends, and the very least he felt he could do was fill in the gaps for them. With luck, not one of them would ever again encounter real evil like this.

"He died," he told them weightily, "the very same summer that his daughter came out of jail. Sally went to see him for a final farewell but the tractor ran over him while he was fixing the ignition and she never actually got to talk to him. Or so she says."

They were silent, once again stunned by shock. Oh God.

"As it happens," he continued, "it turns out he'd already had one narrow squeak before, when she escaped from the convent and hitched to Wagga Wagga. That's where her father farmed and she was obviously on her way to see him, until she met her sailors and got distracted. So the poor fellow got an extension to his life, without ever knowing it."

"And that's not all," added Duncan. "According to the press reports, a lot of strange accidents have happened over the years to other key people connected with her crimes. There's absolutely nothing they can pin on Sally but an awful lot of people died in violent circumstances— the judge who committed her, the surgeon who sterilized her, the counsel for the prosecution, even one of the nuns. It's like the curse of Tutankhamen . . . death appears to stalk everyone who crosses her path."

"Thanks a lot!" said Gus, with a grin. "I'm sure that makes all of us feel a whole lot better!"

"Come along everyone!" called Vivienne gaily, back from her guided tour. "Upstairs to the studio, if you please. Time for the speeches!"

The room looked exquisite, full of evening sunlight and entirely empty apart from, in the very center, an enormous pile of furs. Vivienne's coats and jackets. What on earth? She stood there, radiant with excitement, more beautiful than anyone had ever seen her, other than Oliver, hovering in the doorway, recognizing for the first time in years the young bride he had loved so much and gone to such extremes to win.

"Glasses, everyone, and let's have a toast. To Georgy and to Beth—and to their continuing good health!"

"Georgy and Beth!" Everyone drank but only Oliver noticed that Vivienne was toasting them in orange juice.

"It's a terrible thing," said Eleanor dramatically, clutching at Duncan's arm. "I still can't believe it's true, all those things they are saying about her. I suppose I'll have to alter my will again, such a nuisance. And she was always so sweet and considerate."

"You can probably write to her," said Duncan. "She'd like that."

"I've got great news," continued Vivienne, triumphantly unfolding a foolscap document and holding it high for them all to see. "The World Wide Fund for Nature—formerly the World Wildlife Fund—are so impressed by Georgy's photographs, they have given us a contract, exclusive for a year, to do all their advertising and publicity pictures, worldwide. And as Georgy already knows, Phoebe has got Cancer Research equally fired up, so it looks as though Georgy's in for a busy winter, as soon as she feels well enough to start working full-time again."

Everyone clapped.

"What about the coats, then?" asked Beth, looking at the luscious mass in the center of the room, where

Ferdinand and Isabella were already asleep, stretched out luxuriously among all the priceless skins.

"Those," said Vivienne portentously, with a fast glance toward her husband to see if he was going to object, "are my hostages to fate. The Fund has finally opened my eyes and made me realize how wrong it is to dress in furs, at the expense of living animals whose lives are more important than the cruel dictates of fashion."

At the back of the group, Georgy groaned and her father squeezed her hand protectively.

"My sable," she whispered.

"It's okay. Keep it until you film in the Antarctic—or Russia. I'm sure that day is not far off. Looks as if you're set to be quite a little globetrotter in future."

"What are you going to do with them?" asked Beth practically. She thought Vivienne was acting brilliantly and she thoroughly approved, but there was a limit.

"That's the problem," said Vivienne. "Dorabella's family have said no to them and even Oxfam won't take them. So I thought we'd have a bonfire. As a symbolic act, to launch our partnership."

Offstage, Oliver groaned. This was going altogether too far. He pushed his way through the onlookers and took Vivienne gently by the arm. She was a great girl and he had to admit he was astonished by what she was achieving, but there was a limit.

"The neighbors," he murmured, "can you imagine what they would say? All that foul smoke, just when they're settling down to cocktails on the terrace? Can we leave this for later and deal with it properly then?"

There was general applause, and everyone drank a large number of toasts, then they all drifted back into the garden to catch the last rays of the dying sun.

Addison arrived late, as seemed to be his habit, flustered and apologetic, held up, he explained, by something last-minute at the hospital. He looked immeasurably better, thought Beth; more relaxed and altogether healthier since Sally had been apprehended and the cases on both Catherine and Georgy officially closed. He greeted his hostess and kissed his wife, then wandered off to join Oliver by the fish pond, savoring the excellent vintage champagne the Nugents had so generously provided.

"Well, old boy," he said, with admiration. "You're quite the hero of the hour."

Oliver smiled, embarrassed, and meekly studied his shoes. They'd talked already, at the hospital while he was being stitched up, but he wasn't particularly proud of the way he had behaved that day. Overall, as commando activities went, all very commendable, but as far as he was concerned, the sooner forgotten, the better. The one good thing was that Sally was inside again and likely to stay there for the rest of her natural life.

"How is the little bitch?" asked Oliver, not without an element of regret.

"Surprisingly perky," said Addison, "though you don't need me to tell you that. I suspect she had the time of her life." His grin was positively lascivious.

"Well, I hope that's the last we hear of her," said Oliver uncomfortably, wishing the subject would drop. One of these days he would have to face Vivienne about all that; he had no idea how it would affect their future but gloomily expected the worst. And as for Beth, well he'd always love her, he knew that now, but he'd just have to learn to do without. At least she was alive. For now that was all that really mattered.

At least, reflected Addison, motoring home with Phoebe, Sally's apprehension had taken the heat off him where Catherine's death was concerned. Having fixed the blame fairly and squarely on Sally, the police had closed their inquiries and Addison was finally, once and for all he hoped, off the hook. The truth was that Sally had administered a lethal dose of morphine sulphate before he ever got there that night and he, seeing that Catherine was already sinking into a coma, had instantly guessed what had happened.

Sally had left and Addison's dilemma had been what to do for the best. The poor creature was mortally sick, in any event, and not likely to live for very much longer. What was the point of dragging her back just for a few more weeks of suffering when it would intensify the risk of his own involvement in her original health botch-up coming to light? He had set his heart on the royal appointment, which was only a whisper away; after all the years he had slaved for such a goal, he couldn't bear to think of losing it because of one small error of judgment half a lifetime ago. Besides, he owed it to Phoebe. He glanced across at her dear face, sleeping now, and knew his decision had been the right one.

Eleanor could have proved a problem but he'd gambled and won where she was concerned too. Beneath the selfish hardness, there did lurk an element of compassion, and that had combined with her own small share of guilt at having wrecked her daughter's happiness by keeping the two of them apart. Who knows what might have happened had she not intervened; that was a whole other story, one that would never be written. But, whatever she suspected about that fatal last night, Eleanor had remained silent—and for that Addison thanked her in his heart. He'd been lucky, he was well aware of that, but he put that down to the luck of the Harveys.

The kitten was making determined forays down the neck of Beth's Victorian nightshirt, but she didn't mind. Neither did Duncan sitting beside her, holding her hand and watching with envy the progress of those tiny scrabbling paws into her cleavage and down between her brown, voluptuous breasts. Her bandages were gone now and only the violet bruise on her forehead, the size of a golf ball, remained to remind them of the trauma she had managed to survive. She would always have a dent there—slightly rakish, Duncan said, like a fencing scar—but the hospital had cleared her and said there would be no permanent damage.

"It's just as well it was only the omelette pan she grabbed," said Beth with a grin. "If she'd had the sense to reach for the twelve-inch fryer, she'd probably have taken my head off."

Duncan squeezed her hand and kissed her. He still felt overwhelmingly emotional whenever she joked like this. To think, he'd very nearly lost her and before he'd been able to tell her how he felt. He leaned across and kissed her again, this time with considerably more feeling.

"Have you got my cat?" asked Imogen accusingly, storming through the door and grabbing hold of the furry intruder. From behind her, in the hall, came the sound of much thumping and swearing as Gus and a couple of stalwarts lugged the new bed up the stairs.

"He's awfully sweet," said Beth, snuggling up, once Imogen and the kitten had removed themselves. "Fancy doing that. Buying me a new bed just because of what happened here?"

"Quite right, too," said Duncan, wishing he'd thought of it first; irritated, as ever, that Gus had the knack of always doing the right thing at the appropriate moment. He could learn to hate him if he wasn't so bloody charming. But the important thing, he told himself severely, was that Beth was safe. He drew her gently closer to him, careful not to hurt her head, treating her like cut glass when all he really wanted to do was ravish her.

Gus came wandering in to tell them the job was done.

"Everything shipshape," he said with a smile. "It's all yours, ma'am, whenever you feel like testing it."

He grinned happily at Duncan and winked as he bent for Beth to kiss him.

"I'll be off now," he said tactfully, glancing at his

watch. "I'm sure you chaps have got a lot of catching up to do."

The new bed looked quite wonderful, with the moonlight streaking across the pale Scandinavian wood through the open, uncurtained window. Beth was still in her white Victorian nightshirt, heavily embroidered and trimmed with Brussels lace, bought at a market stall in the heart of the Dordogne and kept for just such an occasion as this. She looked quite breathtaking, Duncan thought, almost too good to spoil.

They stood, like ingenues, on either side of the pristine whiteness of the bed, and Beth suppressed a giggle as she saw that someone, undoubtedly Imogen, had left a freshly cut rose on each of their pillows. Duncan stood staring at her, in the muted light of the single bedside lamp, and felt like bursting with the weight of his emotion. But instead of speaking, he started to unfasten his shirt, and Beth, watching him closely, followed suit. The thing about these nineteenth-century ecclesiastical garments was all the buttons; she was still fumbling and only half there when she saw Duncan step out of his pants.

"Hang on a minute," she said urgently, crossing the room.

And she firmly closed the bedroom door.

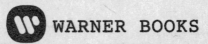